Ruby Slippers, Golden Tears

Fairy Tale Anthologies edited by
ELLEN DATLOW & TERRI WINDLING

Snow White, Blood Red

Black Thorn, White Rose

Ruby Slippers, Golden Tears

Black Swan, White Raven

Silver Birch, Blood Moon

Black Heart, Ivory Bones

More fantasy anthologies from
PRIME BOOKS

Best American Fantasy
edited by Ann & Jeff VanderMeer

Best New Romantic Fantasy
edited by Paula Guran

Fantasy: The Best of the Year
edited by Rich Horton

Ruby Slippers, Golden Tears

edited by

ELLEN DATLOW &
TERRI WINDLING

PRIME BOOKS

RUBY SLIPPERS, GOLDEN TEARS

PRIME BOOKS
www.prime-books.com

ISBN: 978-0-8095-5150-5

Contents

Contents

Ruby Slippers, Golden Tears

Introduction

Terri Windling and Ellen Datlow

WELCOME TO VOLUME THREE IN OUR SERIES OF fairy tales for adults (following *Snow White, Blood Red* and *Black Thorn, White Rose*). It is the aim of this series to encourage the exploration of the literary fairy-tale form, and to make such tales available to connoisseurs of the art.

Literary fairy tales are fictions inspired by the old oral folk tales of many cultures, or reworkings of previous literary fairy tales created by fantasists in centuries past. Although "fairy tale" is the commonly used term for these kinds of stories, "wonder tale" is

1

actually a better description of them. Not all of the tales that fall under the fairy tale heading contain the creatures known as *fairies*; rather, they are about human men and women fallen into a state, or the lands, of enchantment. Nor were these old tales considered children's stories as they commonly are today. The generic name fairy tale comes from the French *conte de fée*, a term coined in the seventeenth century for a literary fashion popular with an aristocratic audience of highly literate adults.

At the heart of the seventeenth century's profusion of literary fairy tales (many of which are still popular today: "Beauty and the Beast," "Rumplestiltskin," "The Sleeping Beauty," "Puss in Boots," "Little Red Riding Hood," "Bluebeard," etc.) you will find the remnants of much older tales. Wonder tales are among the very oldest stories known since the dawn of time; they exist in the oral folk traditions of virtually every culture around the globe. Variants of the "ash girl" motif, for instance, which became "Cinderella" in the hands of the Frenchman Charles Perrault, can be found across Europe, Africa, the Americas, and back into ancient China.

In medieval Europe, the influence of Christianity had threatened to halt the handing down of these old tales, which were associated with paganism, witchcraft, or "the wagging tongues of women" (at a time when silence was considered to be one of the chief womanly virtues). Yet the telling of wonder tales was a practice that proved as impossible to extinguish as women's gossip. The form was revived in Italy in the fifteenth century, popularized by the publication of the adult, rather saucy tales of Giovanni Straparola's *The Delectable Nights* (in which, for instance, Sleeping Beauty is impregnated by her prince as she lies sleeping); as well as by Giambattista Basile's book of fifty fairy tales, *The Story of Stories*. At the same time in

England, Spenser and Shakespeare worked brilliant renditions upon the literary fairy-tale form. Yet it was in France, in the late sixteenth century and in the two centuries that followed, that the literary fairy tale truly flowered.

Folklore historians offer several factors to account for this: In the seventeenth century, the French language was culturally dominant, used at most courts throughout Europe. The growing printing trade fostered literary experimentation beyond the classic Latin works of the academy. And the *salons* of the French aristocracy (where women had considerable presence and influence) proved a fertile ground for literate, fanciful, and (under the innocent magical trappings) rather subversive tales. Although Charles Perrault remains the writer best remembered from the period, many of the most popular fairy-tale spinners of the day were educated bluestocking women. A distinctly feminist subtext is evident in the original fairy tales of such renowned salon habitués as Marie-Jeanne L'Heritier de Villandon (a close cousin of Perrault's), Henriette-Julie de Murat, and Marie-Catherine d'Aulnoy. Yet these elements are largely absent in the versions of their tales that we know today (such as "The White Cat," "Green Snake," or "Beauty and the Beast"), which have come down to us as children's stories, reshaped over the years by the values of male editors in Victorian times, and Walt Disney in our own.

It is worth noting that after mining rich veins of rural folklore to create the *conte de fée*, the works of these Parisian writers, first published for an audience of their fellow aristocrats, were eventually reprinted (in much-abridged form) in a series of inexpensive chapbooks sold to the lower classes throughout Europe. The stories therein were then picked up by oral storytellers, and thus passed *back* into the folk tradition—which is one of the reasons why today we think of so many of these stories as Anonymous ones. It was through the proliferation of these short and simplified chapbooks that fairy tales for children began to become a genre of their own, one that expanded in the eighteenth century, flourished with printing advances in the nineteenth, and one that is still a booming business three hundred years later.

As for the adult tales, in the eighteenth century Charles Mayer collected the most important French fairy tales written during the previous hundred years into a masterwork called the *Cabinet des Fées* (which consisted of *forty-one* volumes.) This in turn influenced the German Romantics at the turn of that century, such as Novalis, Johann Ludwig Tieck, E.T.A. Hoffmann, Johann Wolfgang von Goethe, and the folklore collectors Jacob and Wilhelm Grimm—whose nationalistic German fairy tales have since been discovered to have come, in a number of instances, from French sources.

The German Romantics, in their turn, influenced nineteenth century writers of literary fairy tales such as Denmark's celebrated Hans Christian Andersen (author of "The Little Mermaid," "The Snow Queen," "The Little Matchgirl," "The King's New Clothes") and England's Oscar Wilde (author of "The Selfish Giant," "The Nightingale and the Rose," "The Fisherman and His Soul"). The nineteenth century also saw a greater interest in the collection and preservation of English-language folk tales and ballads extant in the British Isles, as well as in America. The magical motifs of old Scots, Irish, and Welsh tales then found their way into works by Alfred Tennyson, Nathaniel Hawthorne, William Morris, Christina Rossetti, Rudyard Kipling, Laurence Housman, William Butler Yeats, and many other writers of the age.

In the twentieth century, the literary fairy tale has

come into its own in the English language; numerous excellent works have been published in the last ten years alone. Yet a lingering Puritan influence in our culture has created a bias toward strict realism in the arts, particularly in America. Magical works, with their roots deep in ancient myth and oral narrative, are often seen today—as they were in Victorian times—as the province of the uneducated; as fit only for popular culture; as the realm of women and children. As a result, the literary fairy-tale form often bypasses mainstream channels, making a home for itself in fiction published for children, or on the adult genre shelves. Fortunately, other countries in western Europe, Asia, Africa and (particularly) Latin America have retained strong traditions of "magical" adult fiction. The extraordinary works of Magical Realists like Italy's Italo Calvino, Nigeria's Ben Okri, and Brazil's Gabriel García Márquez are slowly helping to break down critical prejudice against such works in England and America. For a suggested reading list of contemporary novels, stories and poems with fairy-tale themes, please see our Recommended Reading section at the back of this volume.

One of the most successful contemporary writers of adult fairy tales is the late Angela Carter, an English writer whose peerless work continues to inspire many of us in the field of fantasy literature. "Ours is a highly individualized culture," Carter stated in her introduction to *The Virago Book of Fairy Tales, Vol. 1*, "with a great faith in the work of art as a unique one-off, and the artists as an original, a godlike and inspired creator of unique one-offs. But fairy tales are not like that, nor are their makers. Who first invented meatballs? In what country? Is there a definitive recipe for potato soup? Think in terms of the domestic arts. 'This is how *I* make potato soup.'"

There is nothing truly unique to be found in the

themes of the stories that follow; for in literary fairy tales, uniqueness and novelty are largely beside the point. The plots herein are deliciously familiar ones, the characters richly archetypal. Like the domestic arts (and other skills associated with women through the ages, as magical storytelling has been), the writing of literary fairy tales is a collective art, not an individual one—for each author in this volume is participating in a dialogue reaching across centuries. Their stories comment upon the older fairy stories that have come before them, and may someday be commented upon in turn by authors in the future.

It is the particular beauty of fairy tales that no one interpretation is the true one, no one version is correct. The ingredients of the tale can be simmered and stirred, flavored and served up in a thousand different ways. Each author begins with common fairy-tale characters, dilemmas, dangers, riddles, and enchantments. Yet with this common straw they make gold, and language is the wheel on which they spin. It is through the language of the tales, and not the plot, that each retelling becomes unique, adding the voices of a new generation of storytellers to the voices of centuries past.

As in the previous two volumes of this anthology series, the stories that follow include bright works of high fantasy, dark works of horror, and numerous other tales that fall somewhere in the shadows between the two realms. Fairy tales that have appeared in the previous two volumes reappear in rather different guise here: "Rumplestiltskin," "Puss in Boots," "The Princess and the Pea," "Snow White," and others form the bones of the stories and poems that follow. Retold tales of China, Japan, Russia, and North America make their first appearance in this volume.

We hope you'll enjoy this third journey into the

Wood. Both curses and enchantments tend to run in threes . . . so we must warn you to be wary as you go.

—Terri Windling, *Arizona & Devon, England*
Ellen Datlow, *New York City*
January 1995

Ruby Slippers

Susan Wade

Susan Wade lives in Austin, Texas, and has had short fiction published in the magazines Amazing Stories, and Fantasy and Science Fiction and in the first two volumes of this fairy-tale series. Her first novel, Walking Rain, a magic realist/thriller hybrid, was recently published by Bantam.

"Ruby Slippers" takes one of North America's most popular contemporary fairy tales, Frank L. Baum's The Wizard of Oz, and entwines it quite effortlessly with Hans Christian Andersen's classic "The Red Shoes." Wade asserts she has always had a fetish for red shoes.

Ruby Slippers

Transcript/Interviewer's Notes—
DG @ Beverly Hills Hotel, 4/16

THE HOUSE? DO WE HAVE TO START WITH THE house? All these interviews are the same. Oh, all right. You have to admit, it was quite an entrance. Not every girl becomes a star her first day in this town, right on touchdown. Lucky break, what can I say?

No—wait! I'm *not* saying it was good luck that my house landed on the old witch! It was an accident, pure and simple, just like the coroner said. [*Ed's note: The coroner's verdict stated that, in the absence of a corpse, no ruling could be made as to the exact cause of death.*]

My nerves were absolutely destroyed by it—ask anybody who was around. The way the siding on the house sliced her feet clean off— ‹Shudders dramatically.› Just thinking about it makes me feel faint.

But you have to understand, seeing the ruby slippers put it all straight out of my head. ‹Lays hand on interviewer's knee.› You see, after my mother died and I went to live with my aunt—well she *did* take me in, I'll give her that. And boy didn't she get some mileage out of it later?

But it wasn't all fresh air and rainbows, the way

9

Auntie makes it sound. She used to make me work in the fields, all the time, and I had to wear these nasty wooden clogs. Clumsy, awful things, and they rubbed my feet absolutely *raw*. The rest of the time, I had to go barefoot, except when we all went to church. For Sunday school, Emma gave me some old black button-shoes from the attic. Way too big for me, and terribly out of style.

So *these* shoes—well just look at the way they sparkle. ‹Poses, displaying slippers.› Paste of course, but the stones really do look like rubies, don't you think? And high-heeled pumps! Jiminy! What girl doesn't yearn for her first pair? So when a lady who looks like a guardian angel appears out of the blue and tells me they're mine—shucks, it didn't take me two shakes to make up my mind.

So she gives the slippers this little tap-tap-tap on the soles with her stick and tells everybody that they'll stay right on my feet, no matter how hard I dance—or something like that, I can't remember exactly. Well, who could resist giving the crowd a little number, after an intro like that? And it went like magic. Almost like the shoes were dancing me, I promise you.

Well, shoot! You don't have to tell *me* all that dancing around after the accident didn't look good—not after the spin the press put on it. But if you'd been there—with Glenn making such a fuss over me, saying what a good deed I'd done by landing on Louella and how this was my big break—well, ‹fiddles with fringe on the divan› to tell the truth, the accident just didn't seem to amount to much. And the old lady's feet shriveled right up, you know. Once I had the shoes on, you couldn't even see there'd been a little mishap.

I'll admit it looked suspicious, me running off that way. Well, shoot, killing people is a hanging offense in Kansas. And I was just a starry-eyed kid, still dreaming on rainbows. So when Glenn said she could send me off to someone really powerful, who could do worlds for my career—it just seemed irresistible. She said Ozzie was omnipotent, and that he could make me a star like snapping his fingers. You know the sort of thing, fame and fortune and all that jazz. All I had to do was follow her guidance and I'd have it made. That Glenn, she's pure hustle. Guess that's what makes her such a hot agent.

"Getting into the studio system is like finding a road paved with gold." That's what she told me. "Just follow the path they lay out for you and you've got it made. And you'll *love* Ozzie—he's a real spiritual type for a producer—and he'll solve all your problems. You won't have to give this little house incident another thought."

How was I to know when she said spiritual, she meant *too* spiritual? Straight off, Ozzie was after me to clean up my image. "Go back to that fresh-faced farm girl routine," he says. Can you imagine? He thought I should lose the shoes—said that red ones made me look *improper*.

‹Gazes wistfully at ruby slippers.›

At least Glenn took my side. She told him, with my looks and these shoes, I was a sure bet. ‹Shrugs helplessly.› What can I say? I was young and naive. I believed everything they told me, let the two of them give me the old tinsel town rush—straight into a studio contract set in cement.

No, there's no truth to that at all. Where do you people come up with these rumors? I never stayed off the set to hold out on the studio. Do I look like the type who'd make trouble for a sweetheart like Ozzie? The man's a perfect saint. We just got our signals crossed for a while, that's all.

Except for his thing about the shoes. Heck, I couldn't give them up, you can see that, can't you?

‹Does a quick tap step, shoes glittering.› Besides, it was that red twinkle that drove Strawman mad for me.

‹Smiles.› Oh, yes. It was special between Strawman and me, right from the very start. Legendary, magical—but I'm not the wordsmith. How would you put it? Yes, that's perfect. Instant harmony. Tip and tap—that was us.

Why, thank you. *I* certainly think we made a great team, no matter what the studio says. It just seemed natural for us to throw in together, and from then on it was one long song and dance, really.

That's right, we added to the act not long afterward. We'd come to terms with the studio by then, and the band was really their idea. They wanted to tone down the couple thing with me and Strawman—said he was bad for my reputation. But it all worked out great. We were lucky that the boys turned out to be such— what's the word?—such *simpatico* partners. The four of us just clicked.

You're absolutely right. ‹Winks.› We *did* have our share of good times. The poppy fields, the boys masquerading as soldiers—but I shouldn't be talking about that. ‹Presses finger to lips and whispers conspiratorially.› The studio people will have a *fit*.

Those really were the best times, you know. When it was me and the boys.

‹Sighs, then looks down, dabbing eyes with hankie.› Excuse me. I do get a little lonely sometimes. Everything was so green and new back then.

Guess it's no secret we went a little overboard with the poppy dust. And then after Lionel got looped that last time—

But you know all this—the papers had a field day. I'll never forget the way he looked that morning, the way he roared off into the forest on one of his little adventures . . .

‹Voice cracks.› Eaten by bears, the centurion said. I was so broken up about it, I simply couldn't face the funeral.

Yes, I did have a kind of breakdown then. Well, my goodness! The papers went nuts with it—all those trashy stories about a crime of passion. And the hatchet job they did on us—claiming that bears couldn't have hacked him up that way and that Strawman was furious with us, all those insinuations that Lion and I had a thing going—

No, the studio did *not* hush it all up! And our deal says you don't even *ask*, for crying out loud! ‹Dabs eyes again, bosom heaving.›

All you need to say is—hang on a sec—‹Checks notes; speaks slowly and distinctly.› It was a very difficult time for all of us.

No, Strawman and I didn't split because of Lion. It was a professional decision, that's all. After Lion's death, Strawman decided to get out of show business altogether. Said he just didn't feel like dancing anymore.

So it was a natural time to break up the act, what with losing Lion and Strawman wanting to quit. Tinman? Why, he agreed entirely with the studio's decision. About calling it quits, I mean. And as for me— ‹Smiles modestly.› Well, going solo has worked out very well.

No, of course the boys don't resent my success. Strawman came to my last show and sent me a bouquet of red poppies beforehand. For old times' sake, he said. And Tinman always says he's very happy for me—he's made quite a name for himself as a guitarist in professional circles.

What do you mean, I seem nervous? Everything's fine.

‹Smiles ruefully.› Well, maybe I am a little jittery, having the whole thing raked up again. After all, I wasn't well at the time—Lion's death hit me pretty hard. But I'm clean and sober now, went cold turkey six months ago and haven't had a snort since. ‹Bats eyelashes.› You'll vouch for that, won't you, you sweet man? What a nice, sober old lady I am now?

‹Brief silence.›

‹DG settles back on divan and crosses legs. Ruby pumps sparkle hypnotically.› Yes, there was some talk about us doing a reunion show last year. But I—that is, *we*—decided it just wouldn't work without Lion. Besides, hanging out with the old gang isn't the same anymore. Strawman's got no bounce, no rhythm. ‹Picks up dog.› And my sweet little To-totum's got arthritis now, don't you, poor baby?

Tinman? ‹Licks lips nervously and lowers voice.› That's the real creeper, you know? The way that new artificial heart of his beat whenever he checked out the ruby slippers. Sounded like a steel drum convention, you could hear it for miles. *Every* time we got together to talk about doing the show. It was a real chiller.

Don't get me wrong, it's nice to know you've still got it. The old twinkle-toes have still got their magic and all that. ‹Mischievous grin.› After all, I'm not getting any younger. But he really does give me a turn, sometimes, the way he's always watching my feet, fingering that axe of his.

Look, it's not like I've got any illusions here. I know I won't be tapping the old ruby sparklers along this golden road forever. Like the studio rep's always saying, red shoes'll bring you to a bad end every time. ‹Edgy laugh.› Just ask old Eastie about that. And her little sister too, when you think about it.

‹Seriously.› My turn's sure to come.

But who cares, doll? The way I see it, anything beats going back to Kansas.

The Beast

Tanith Lee

Tanith Lee lives by the sea in Great Britain with her husband John Kaiine and is a prolific writer of fantasy, science fiction, and horror, including several dark adult stories with fairy-tale themes. Her most recent books include Darkness, I, Vivia, Eva Fairdeath, Reigning Cats and Dogs, Gold Unicorn, *and* Nightshades: a novella and stories. *Her dark fairy tales have been collected in* Red as Blood, *or* Tales From the Sisters Grimmer. *Her stories have won the World Fantasy Award.*

The often romanticized classic "Beauty and the Beast" has come to epitomize the adage that beauty is only skin-deep, usually implying that there is more to a person than physical ugliness. Lee, using her trademark lush language, alters the traditional tale in order to turn its lesson upside down.

The Beast

WHEN HE SAW THE ROSE, HE KNEW THAT ONLY ONE woman in the world could wear it: his daughter. The image and the certainty were so immediate; total. He stood staring.

It was made of amber, rich yellow amber, and the unfolded petals were smooth, translucent, without any of the normal bubbles, or trapped debris. Near the center hung a drop of "dew"—a single warm and creamy pearl. The necklace was a golden briar. It was perfect. And he visualized Isobel, her massy sweep of white-blond hair swung loose from the icy line of its side part. Her pale skin, the mouth just touched with some pale color. The evening dress he had recently bought her in ivory silk. And the rose, on the briar, precisely under her throat.

"He has some fine things, doesn't he? Have you seen the jade horse?"

"Yes, I did." Always polite, and careful, he turned from his scrutiny and regarded the other man. They sipped from their glasses of some flawless champagne that came, not from France, but from the East.

"I've heard he collects anything exquisite. Will go

to great lengths to get it. Even danger. Perhaps your own collection might interest him.''

''Oh, I've nothing to match any of this.'' But he thought, *I have one thing.*

After the brief evening was finished, when they had regained their coats from the golden lobby and gone down the endless length of the glass tower, back into the snow-white city, he was still thinking about it. In fact, if he were honest, the thought had begun at the moment he met their host, the elusive and very private Vessavion, who had permitted them into his home, that mansion perched atop the tower of glass, for reasons of diplomacy. There had only been the six invitations, six men known for their business acumen, their wealth, their good manners. It had been meant to impress them, and because they were, all of them, extremely clever, it had done so.

He wondered, going over what he knew of five personal files in his mind, as his chauffeur drove him home, if any of them had a daughter. But even if they had, it could not be one like his. Like Isobel.

He had always given her the best. She was due only that. And Vessavion—Vessavion also was the very best there might be. Six and a half feet tall, probably about 180, 185 pounds—this was not from any file, there were no accessible files on Vessavion—blond as Isobel, maybe more blond, the hair drawn back and hanging in a thick galvanic tail to his waist. Grey eyes, large, serious. A quiet, definite, and musical voice, actor-trained no doubt. Handsome. Handsome in a way that was uncommon, and satisfying. One liked to look at him, watch his spare elegant movements. A calm smile revealing white teeth, a smile that had nothing to hide and apparently nothing to give, beyond a faultless courtesy amounting, it seemed, to kindness.

The car purred through a city made of snow. Lights

like diamonds glittered on distant cliffs of cement. They came over the river into the gracious lowlands and entered the robot gates of his house. It was a good house. He had always been proud of it. The gardens were exotic. But Vessavion, in the middle of that multitude of rooms, Vessavion had a garden that was like a cathedral, open to sky almost it seemed of space, flashing with stars.

She was in the library, sitting by the fire, an open book on her knee. She might have been waiting. He looked at her. He thought, *Yes.*

"Was it wonderful?" she asked, cool and sweet. There was a lilt to her voice that was irresistible, like the slight tilt to her silvery eyes.

"Very. I hope you'll see it. I left him a note. Something of mine that may interest him ... The African Bible."

"You'd give him that?"

"In exchange—for something else. Perhaps he'll refuse. But he does collect rare and beautiful things."

She was innocent of what he meant. She did not know. He had begun to keep secrets, her father. It had started five weeks before in the doctor's office. Time enough for truth later. Truth was not always beautiful, or desired.

Vessavion's answer came the next day. It was as if Vessavion were somehow linked into his plan, as if this had to be. He invited the owner of the African Bible to a small dinner. The visitor had a daughter, Vessavion had heard. She must come too.

Conceivably, Vessavion had even known of Isobel. The father knew there were files also on him. Had Vessavion perhaps seen some inadequate, breathtaking photograph?

The dinner was set three nights before Christmas. It was well omened, the city in a Saturnalia of lamps and fir trees, wreaths, and ribbons. He said to Isobel, "Will you wear the ivory silk for me?"

She smiled. "Of course."

"And, no jewelry," he said.

She raised her eyebrows. "Do you think he'll hang me with jewels?"

"He may. He might."

"I'm quite nervous," she said. "I've heard about him. Is he really—is he handsome?"

"Tonight," he said, "you'll see for yourself."

The elevator took them up the tower of glass, and at the top the doors opened into the golden lobby, with its French gilt mirrors and burnished floor. A servant came, like all Vessavion's slaves, virtually invisible, and took away their outer garments. They walked into the vast pale room where the log fire was actually real, pine cones sputtering in it on apple wood. On the walls two or three beautiful paintings from other centuries, genuine, obscure, and priceless. Lamps of painted glass. Brocade chairs, *their* unburnt wood carved into pineapples. For the season, a small rounded tree had been placed, dark green, decked with dull sequins of gold, a golden woman on its top holding up a star of crimson mirror. And there were boughs of holly over the mantel of the fire, and tall, yellow-white candles burning. It was charming, childish, almost touching. But then, had it been done only to please Vessavion's guests? Perhaps even to please a woman?

On a silver tray by the fire were three long slender goblets of some topaz wine. Vessavion came in. Immaculately greeted father and daughter. They drank together.

But the father had noted Vessavion's face when he beheld Isobel. There was no subterfuge at all. Vessavion's face changed, utterly, as if a mask had lifted from it. Underneath it was just the same face, handsome, strong, yet now alive. And it was young. The father thought, *He's only two or three years older than she is. I can see it, now.* This delighted him very much.

Isobel had changed a little too. For the first time in a decade, she was blushing, softly, marvelously, like milk crystal filled by sunlight. Her eyes shone. No man who liked women could have resisted her.

They ate the delicious meal—fish from somewhere cold, perhaps Heaven, a soufflé made of clouds—the invisible servants attending to everything, wines floating down yellow-green, red, and clear as rain. There was a blue liqueur.

All the time, he listened to them talking, the girl and the young man, without hesitations. He felt, the father, the pleasure of a musician, whose music plays at his will alone.

He thought, *I must relinquish that. Now they are each other's.* He was glad. He had not wanted to leave things in a muddle. It was not that he felt she could not manage without him, not because she was a woman. No. Women were vital, survivors, even ruthless if they had to be. It was only, he had not wanted to *make* her work at things like *that.* She was meant to soar, not brood among the cobwebs and dusts. And it would be all right. Yes, now it would.

It came time to reveal the African Bible. Vessavion took the huge black book and opened its clasps of platinum with his strong, graceful hands. He read, his lips moving silently. Evidently he understood the esoteric language into which the Bible had been translated. When he glanced up, he said, "I do want it. But how can it be priced?"

The father said, "I would like you to have it as a gift."

Vessavion smiled. He looked at Isobel. His smile for her, already, was feral and possessive, eager and consumed—consuming. Isobel lowered her eyes. Vessavion said, "Then may I give your daughter something? I know what would suit her. Do you remember the amber rose?"

The father felt a pang of agony—it was jealousy, much, much worse than the clawing of the cancer that now, anyway, was kept dumb by drugs. But he was glad, too, of the jealousy. It confirmed he had been right.

They went among Vessavion's collection. It was rumored he had other things, hidden away, but here there was enough to astound. The Han horse, white as ice, the Roumanian chess pieces carved from a mountain, the banner from a war of 1403, the great unfaceted sapphire polished like a ball made out of the summer sea. And more.

Vessavion took the rose from its cabinet, and fastened the briar about Isobel's white neck, lifting away so gently her wave of blond hair. His hands were courteous, they did not linger, but his color too intensified faintly, for a moment. He was a young man.

They sat long into the night, over coffee and wine. Soft music played somewhere, and beyond the conservatory of enormous flowers, that garden, checkered by enormous stars.

Isobel and Vessavion talked on and on. If it was a melody they made, each knew it, where to come in, and where to wait. They might have known each other forever, and been parted for a week. So much to say. How they had missed each other.

Finally, deliberately, he murmured that now they must go away. He relished his cruelty, seeing their eyes clouded, and hearing their voices falling from each other like caressing hands.

Vessavion rose. He named a fabulous production, drama, opera, something for which it was impossible to get tickets. He, of course, had them. Would they accompany him? The father liked, too, this old-fashioned kindness to himself. He declined graciously. He said that Isobel must go. That was all that was needed.

They descended in the elevator, down into the snow world. She was very quiet and still. Self-conscious even. She avoided his eyes.

When they were in the car, she said, shyly, "Is it all right?"

"Yes. Wonderfully all right."

"You're pleased?"

"Can't you tell?"

"You like him?" she said, hopeful as a child.

"Very much."

"But he's so mysterious. No one knows anything about him."

"Perhaps that's part of it."

"Do come to the theater," she said.

He said, laughing, "You'd kill me if I did."

He thought afterward, it was a pity he had said that, although she, too, not knowing, had laughed in turn. It was a pity to accuse her, *her*, even in a joke, of something which was already happening by another means.

He believed she did not sleep that night. Across the court, he saw her light burning on, as he sat through the dark.

Isobel had only been in love in childhood. With characters in books, with the characters that actors portrayed on a screen or a stage. Later, she lost her taste for this sort of love. She was fastidious, and her standards had been permitted to be extremely, impossibly, high. She had, now and then, liked men. But the conquest which her beauty always allowed her to make sometimes brought out in them their worst—

foolishness, bombast, even, occasionally, antagonism. Besides, she did not recognize them.

Seeing Vessavion, she recognized him at once. Not only his personal beauty, which was, if anything, greater than her own. Also his demeanor, and presently his manner, his mood, his mind. When they spoke, of trivial or important elements, they seemed to glide together along the same broad white road. Each found new things there, and sometimes the same things, or things of a fascinating difference which, once shared, were accessible to both.

However, to be realistic, she had fallen in love with him on sight. And in his eyes she presently saw the same had happened for him.

Beyond all this, there was his mystery, and even though, from the first evening of the dinner, he spoke to her of his life, of events in which he had participated, of childhood memories, his air of seclusion remained, sweet and acid at once, luring her on. Could she ever know him? Oh yes—and yet, to be possessed by a handsome stranger that she knew, that she could never know. He did not kiss her until their third meeting. By then she was weak with longing, confused, almost in pain. At the touch of his mouth, his tongue, the pressure of his body, safe tethers of steel gave way in her, she fell all the distance down into the heart of him, and lay there drowning.

She was a romantic who had dismissed her dreams, a young woman with a young woman's libido, who had found no stimulus, until now. She trusted him completely. Yet he was a shadow. It was more wonderful than anything of any sort she had ever had in her life before.

After their eighth meeting, he took her into a vast bedroom that was like a dark blue cave, and here all night, all day, they made love over and over, sometimes drinking champagne, sometimes eating food

that magically arrived without trace of human partic-
ipation.

At first her orgasms were swift and tenuous, flick-
ers, shudders, butterflies of feeling. But he taught her,
with his hands and his mouth, lips and tongue, every
inch of his honed and subtle body, the sword of his
loins, his white hair, his skin, to writhe and to wait,
to simmer and to flame, so that ocean-rushes of pleasure dashed her up and up into a steeple, a vortex,
where she screamed, where she died, and he brought
her slowly back to life, gentle then as the mother that
she did not recall.

After they had lain on that great blue bed, the few
single silver wires of their separate hair, torn out in
frenzy, lay like traceries. Once there was a broken
nail, white as a sickle moon. Or a spot of silken fluid.
Or only the impress of their bodies, one thing.

It was a winter wedding. Her father was there, and
the witnesses, that she did not know and never saw
again. They ate a sumptuous meal in a towering restaurant above an ice blue sea that perhaps was not
real; she did not know or care.

A few days later her father was gone. He vanished,
leaving only a mild and friendly letter, which Vessavion read her as she wept. The house in the lowlands
of the city was now hers, and once she went back to
it, alone, Vessavion's man waiting for her at the outer
door. But the house, where she had always lived since
she could remember, seemed unfamiliar. She saw to
her father's things, what was necessary. It occurred to
her she did not weep enough. She tried to force out
her tears by thinking of his goodness to her. He had
been a dedicated yet not a passionate parent. He had
made her too sure of herself. She found that this section of her life, her years with her father, was over,
and she could fold it away, neatly, and now it did not
matter.

Sometimes she and her husband were apart for an hour or so, or he might be absent for a portion of an evening or an afternoon. She assumed he must attend to his business interests, as her father had done. These separations were tantalizing, nearly enjoyable. Vessavion's mansion had, besides, so many rooms. She was always finding new ones. It was like him. In the winter garden grew winter flowers that burned and seemed to smoke. Rivulets flowed and tiny bells chimed among the hair of vines. Sometimes, too, Vessavion took her away to other places on a private plane. They saw enormous mountains clad in green fur, marble columns, and waterfalls that thundered. But generally they returned quickly from everywhere, back into the blue cave. They made love almost without cease. They made love as if famished.

She said to him one night, in the dark, chained by his hair, locked to him still, "Was there anyone before me? There must have been."

"Why do you want to know?" he said. "Surely you understand."

"Then no," she said, "I'm the first for you as you were the first for me."

"Exactly," he said. "How could there have been anyone? I was waiting for you."

She said, "Will it ever end—this wanting—this electric *tingling*, this *hunger*?"

"If we grow very old," he said, "perhaps."

"Not till then?" she said. "I'm glad."

They made love again and again. She was hoarse from her own crying. She said, "But won't you ever leave me?"

"How can I leave you? You're myself."

She thought, *Supposing the inconceivable took place— if I should leave him instead*? She said, "If someone made me go away from you—"

He said, "I'd die. I'd stop like a clock."

She recollected her father, whom she had left and who had disappeared. She believed Vessavion. She held him fast in her pale arms, wound him with her long pale legs and slender feet. Inside her body she held him. If they died, it must only be together.

In March the snow was still solid and thick upon the city. From Vessavion's high windows, she could see across a polar landscape, all ice and glass, broken only here and there by roadways and obstinate steel turrets.

He returned in darkness, her husband, and as he walked into the tawny chamber that was their drawing room, she saw on his face, so white and calm from the snowscape he had been traveling through, a jewel of scarlet. It was on his cheek, like an ornament. She did not mention it at first, and then it trickled down like a tear.

"You're bleeding." She was concerned but went to him coolly; her frenzies were never for such things.

And he only smiled, and reaching up, wiped the scarlet tear away. "No."

"But it was blood."

"Was it? How strange."

"Did something happen—out there on the street?"

"It must have done. I don't know."

Carefully she led him to a couch and sat down beside him, examining his face that still was not familiar, although recognized from the first.

"Where do you go in the city?"

"All sorts of places."

"Please tell me," she said.

"No," he said, "it would bore you."

Isobel leaned close to him and breathed him in. He was scented by the freezing dark he had come from. And by something else which she had sensed before, but only once or twice outside a certain situation. Animal, the aroma, spicy and intent, not truly human. It was rather like the smell of him in sex. It aroused her and she put her hand on his breast. But when he moved to kiss her she said, "Not that. You have a secret." And she wondered if there could be another one, another woman or a man, someone he went to when he was not with her. But even as she thought this, she knew it was not credible, it was a lie. What then, the reason for this excitement?

"Tell me," she said.

"I tell you everything."

"Not this."

However, he took her to him, and there on the couch he undressed her, unsheathing her body like a flower from silver wrapping. He drew her up onto the blade of his lust, and they danced slowly in the rosy firelight. She stared into his face, remote with pleasure, taut with the agony of holding back.

"Where do you go?" she moaned.

But her blood curdled in fire and her womb spasmed open, shut, open, shut, and arching backward she knew nothing was of any consequence but their life together.

When they were eating dinner, the goblets of blond wine at their fingertips, slivers of vegetable blossom and white meat lying on porcelain, then, he told her.

"I have an interest sometimes," he said, "in people. I watch them a little. Would you believe, I follow them."

"Why?" she said. She was puzzled. People did not really interest her, only he interested her. She had never found people equal to what she was. Only he was that.

He said, thoughtfully, "You see, you're perfect, Isobel. You're like—like the moon. You change, and yet you remain constant. Every line of you, angle of you, the turn of your head, the way you lift your eyes, your voice—all perfect. But most people have nothing of this. And then again," he hesitated, "sometimes there are attractive people who, without any true beauty, are quite marvelous. But, it isn't these that intrigue me. No. Now and then there is someone . . . very ugly, who has one beautiful feature. Their eyes perhaps, or their hair. Their teeth. Their fingers even—Do you understand? The *discrepancy*."

Isobel realized that, all the while she had been with him, she had glowed. Glowed actually like the amber rose, the first thing he had given her. It was like a halo inside her skin. It warmed when she made love with him, soothed and turned darker when they were at rest, talking, or even apart. Yet now, now the glow seeped out of her, and for a moment she seemed to see it shining in the air. And then she was cold.

"You always trust me," she said.

"Of course. Who else should I trust?"

"You shouldn't always trust me."

He paled at that, in the curious way of someone who is already pale. His eyes were somber, heavy. He said, "But why should it affect you, if I talk a little nonsense."

"It isn't nonsense. You meant what you said. That certain people, ugly people, intrigue you because they have one beautiful feature."

"And what does that matter?" he said, lightly.

"It matters to you."

"Isobel," he said, "let's talk of something else."

She smiled and drank her wine, nodding. It was the first falseness she had ever offered him. And he took it from her, without question.

She searched all through March, searched the mansion atop the tower of glass. At the beginning of April the snow held on, an ice age, and she found it. The room. By then it hardly counted. She had been deceiving him all that while, betraying him. Pretending when they made love. Pretending when they talked. He had spoken of visiting some far-off country, and she had pretended to be pleased. It seemed he was fooled by all her pretense, although his eyes had now a shadow in them. After all, probably he wanted her to find the room. He had not quite been able to tell her everything, and the room would do it for him. And it did.

A few days after their marriage, he had shown her the room of his hidden collection, the things he possessed which, until then, he had shown to no one— not from vanity, but more as if to protect his visitors. What he had was so fine, it might wound. But Isobel, his wife, now possessed these treasures, too, it would be safe for her to see. And there were panels from Medieval France, a painting by Leonardo da Vinci not reckoned to exist—a Madonna with seawater skin and lilies in her hands. There were dolls made of emerald and gold, which moved. There were green pearls, and tapestries woven at the time of Christ, a dress of beads constructed for a child in ancient Rome, a shell that had formed in the shape of a castle, a statuette of an angel made from a single ruby. And—more. Much more.

She had liked it, his collection. She had played gently with a few of the items. She had worn the green pearls.

And in March, she searched out the other hidden room, and at length located it, behind a bookshelf which slid. There was a lock and Isobel broke this with an ordinary hammer she had asked one of the invisible servants to bring her. It was quite easy to break, the lock, it did not take much strength. Horribly, sadly, resignedly, she grasped all this was meant to be.

The room was quite small, and tastefully decorated,

although not lavish like so many of the rooms of the mansion. There were no windows, only soft lighting, wisely placed, to point up the objects on display.

As with the other collections, everything was arranged exquisitely. Indeed, it was arranged tactfully. That, of course, was the whole substance of what he had done, what he had intended.

Isobel went about slowly, and thoroughly, an obedient child brought to a museum. She looked at everything. At the lustrous plait of red hair held in claws of gold. At the white teeth scattered, as the pearls had been, over a velvet cloth. At the two eyes gleaming in the crystal of protective fluid. At the small hand under its dome, one finger with a tarnished wedding ring. At the beautiful breasts, seeming to float like sweets. At the ears. The solitary foot. And—more.

When she had seen everything, Isobel went out. She closed the door, leaving the broken lock hanging, and drew back the bookshelf which slid. Then she went to her bathroom and bathed herself, and washed her hair and dried it. She dressed in her dressing room. She packed her bag with the things which were only hers. And on the pillow in her bedroom, which she had never used, she left the amber rose.

She met Vessavion in the tawny drawing room, as the grey wolf dusk filled up the sky, and turned the ice age of the city to iron.

Vessavion looked at her, and she said, "I have seen it."

He bowed his head. He said, "What will you do?"

"I will leave you, obviously."

"Let me explain."

"What can you say?"

"Perfection," he said, very low, stammering. "Until I saw you, I had never come across it in a human thing."

"Even after you had me, you continued."

"Yes."

"Through the snow you hunted them and cut away what was beautiful, and their blood splashed you, and once you were careless, or uncaring, and I saw. But your money and your power protect you. No one will stop you."

"I put what's beautiful into its proper setting. I always have. It must be a mistake—when they have it."

She said, "Good-bye."

"If you leave me," he said, "then—"

She closed the door, and presently she was descending the glass tower in the elevator, down into the iron snow.

There was a week after that like a hundred years. She spent it in her father's house, safe behind the robot gates which would admit no one. She disconnected the telephones. When any mail fell through into the pillar at the gate, someone came and destroyed it.

She did things in that house she had not done for some while. She played the piano, and cooked cordon bleu meals she did not eat, and read books cover to cover, not knowing what they said.

In the evenings she drank wine, too much, but then that did not ever help and so she did not drink wine anymore.

Spring began to come through the overgrown gardens, and small birds appeared, making nests, singing, as if the world existed. There were sunsets and sunrises, too. Laughable.

When the week was over, as she dressed one morning, she saw she had grown thin, had lost perhaps eighteen pounds. And when she combed her hair, some fell in a rain.

She was driven across the city to the tower of glass, and went in, and rose up, and came out into the golden lobby, but it was not gold anymore, the floor opaque, the mirrors misted, shadow in the air.

Isobel entered the mansion of her husband, Vessavion. She walked slowly through long rooms, and L-shaped rooms, and octagonal rooms. The fires were out, there was no light. Cobwebs hung on things. Dust spread over all. The invisible servants had vanished.

She found him in the blue bedroom that was a cave, on the blue bed that they had steeped in flame.

He was naked, lying on his back upon his own hair. His flesh and his hair, like hers now, did not have any luminescence. His light had gone out. She went close and gazed into his face.

Vessavion was quite dead. Quite blank. Empty. Useless. Over.

There was nothing about him to show what he had been. He was thin and worn, and there was already a line of grey in his hair. His face had fallen in. It was old. And it was very ugly, unnaturally so, hideous in fact. Like the face of some nightmare, some beast.

She wished that she could have said something, anything, to alleviate the awareness she had of the attenuated awfulness of pain, like an unfinished sentence caught up on nails in the atmosphere.

But it was no use at all. Nothing more could be said or done. She had loved him, she had betrayed him, she had killed him as no other had the power to do. And here he lay to rot on the bed of love. And he had the face of a beast.

Masterpiece

Garry Kilworth

Garry Kilworth was born into a service family in 1941 and signed up with the RAF for fifteen years, during which period he was stationed in such exotic locations as the Maldives and Singapore. In 1974, his winning the Gollancz/Sunday Times short story competition coincided with his departure from the RAF. He has since published sixteen novels, over eighty short stories, six children's books, and some poetry. His most recent novel is Archangel. He and Robert Holdstock won the World Fantasy award in 1992 for their novella, "The Ragthorn." Kilworth's most recent collection of stories is In the Country of Tattooed Men. He lives in Essex, England.

One of the problems inherent in "Rumplestiltskin" is the underlying feeling that the title character was taken advantage of. Perhaps what the strange little man asks for is despicable but in most versions of the tale, the young girl never even questions the horrible bargain she has agreed to until she is faced with its enforcement. Then, as queen, she refuses to honor it. Rumplestiltskin is obviously a variation on the deal with the devil story, as is Shakespeare's play The Merchant of Venice. In Merchant, Shylock never wins but he does get his day in court, and in some productions he has been portrayed as more noble than those around him, who make deals they have no intention of honoring.

Masterpiece

IT WAS ON ONE OF MY LONG CONTEMPLATIVE WALKS that I met him. I had stopped to rest on a bench below a clump of young oaks. The view over the grasslands leading down to the river, some two miles distant, was soothing. It was a fine spring morning, clear, almost fragile, and the earth looked young and fresh again. If I had not been so troubled, the scenery would have been quite enchanting. As it was, it merely served as a balm for my oppressed spirit.

I saw the man from a long way off. He followed the winding path from the woods in the east, keeping just below the crest of the ridge. I remember thinking he looked strange, a little out of context. He was not dressed for walking: no boots, stick, or hiker's clothes. Instead he wore a dark suit, with a starched white shirt and plain tie. His shoes were black and polished, and on his head was a dark homburg. Reaching the seat, he sat at the far end, and stared out over the same view for a while, before speaking.

"Young woman," he said, turning to me, "you seem a little disturbed?"

I turned to regard his countenance, which was smooth-shaven and rather ordinary. It was one of those bland faces, the complexion pasty and the features unremarkable: a face which you might not remember if you were to meet him again, perhaps in the streets of some distant town. Apart from a slight bulge at the bridge of the nose, and the pale eyes, there was nothing to distinguish it from a million other plain faces.

I was not used to being addressed as "young woman" and I think my expression must have shown this, for he immediately corrected himself, saying, "Perhaps I should have called you Ms. Susan Quarry?"

"You know me? Who are *you*?"

He smiled. "Yes, I know you. You live in that village down by the river. My name is . . . Mr. Black. That will do for now."

That will do for now. The guy was definitely strange and I began to get a little edgy, wondering if I could outrun him if he started anything funny. There was not a soul for miles around and when a man appears out of nowhere and begins a weird conversation the first thing you look for is an avenue of escape——just in case.

He turned to look at the view again.

"Beautiful, isn't it? The river—you can't see the water from here, can you? It's as if the sails of those yachts are moving through the fields. An illusion, eh? The hulls are, of course, hidden by the river's high green dikes."

He turned again. "You're worried about me, aren't you?"

This observation did nothing to alleviate my feelings of alarm.

"Well," he continued, "you should be, but not because you're in any danger. I'm not going to attack you, or anything like that. I've come to make you a proposition."

"Proposition?" I said, falteringly, and then bit my tongue. I had an idea what was coming. I was prepared to be humiliated, perhaps by an offer of money or something. But for the moment I might humor him, until I saw the chance to get away. I felt defenseless and close to tears, the panic welling up inside me. Why did I have to go through this, simply because I was woman and he was a man? I started to loathe him.

I was totally wrong.

"Let me tell you where you're at," said Mr. Black. "You're at the bottom of the ladder. Your father is a successful businessman—a boor, but a rich one. He is what they call 'a self-made man.' And he never stops telling you that he started with just a few coins in his pocket and look where he is today. And you? You can't even marry anyone worth having. Your estranged fiancé is a lowly *plumber*, going nowhere. Anyway, even *he* doesn't want you anymore, now that he knows your daddy isn't going to finance his idle inclinations."

I interrupted here, a little angrily, "How do you know so much about my family?"

He ignored this question. "Your father is highly critical because you've done nothing with the expensive education he bought for you. You don't want to go into business—that's not really you, is it—so it's got to be something academic or artistic. You failed your doctorate, you tried writing a novel, which didn't work, you took up sculpting only to find you were all fingers and thumbs."

I stood up. "What is this?" I said. "You want to sell me something? A book? On how to be successful and influence people?"

"Your latest venture," he continued, unperturbed, "is painting—you think you might be an artist. You've bought the canvases, but your attempts so far have been, shall we say, less than wonderful? You're now in a state of complete collapse and thinking of running away—to India, or Thailand."

His final words astonished me. It was only in the last twenty-four hours that I had been considering the Far East as a means of escape from my father's interminable attacks. I had begun to reason that if I could never impress him, I had to get away from him, out of reach of the telephone. I had certainly not spoken to anyone about my plans.

"You seem to be able to read my mind," I said, sitting down again. "What are you? Did you come up here looking specifically for me?"

"I knew you were here," he said, his pale eyes regarding my reaction. "I've come to help."

He turned and gestured at the world below. "All this could be yours," he said, laughingly.

"I don't want all that," I replied, "but I would like to sell some of my paintings—perhaps get a showing in a gallery."

"That's what I meant. You put these scenes on canvas. I could help with that."

"Wait a minute. You mean you want to help me with the physical act of painting my pictures, not with selling them?"

"Both—that is, I'm not going to stand beside you, telling you what colors to use, showing you what brushstrokes to make—but I shall be helping, just the same. I guarantee that if you accept my offer, you will be selling paintings—*good* paintings—before the year is out. You will be on your way to becoming famous, your pictures commissioned, if that's what you want."

He paused, then added softly, "And eventually—a masterpiece."

"And what do you want in return? Ten percent?"

He laughed again. "No, certainly not. I have no use

for money. However"—he looked at me seriously now—"there is a price. There is always a price. The price for success, my way, is very high. Think of that which you possess and would not part with for the world—*that* is my price—for it is the world I'm offering you, and the world doesn't come cheap.

"What you have to decide is, is the world *worth* your most precious possession? If you decide it is, then success is yours, simply by saying you agree to my terms. In return I will ensure that you get all you desire from your art—wealth, fame, and satisfaction. The critics will love you, and you will sell for huge amounts of money. What do you say?"

At first I began to feel a little disappointed, thinking the guy was probably crazy after all. Yet—yet there felt something indefinably sane about the whole situation. It was somehow not unknown. There was something happening here which had happened before, perhaps many, many times. I had to answer the question. Was I prepared to pay his price? The fact is, we all reach a point in our lives when we would pay anything, *anything*, to achieve our ambition, to realize the success we crave. I had reached that point. I was at the edge of reason, the black pit of failure yawning before me. Since I had nothing, not even hope, why, the price *was* cheap.

I said, "What do we do? Shake hands on it?"

"No need for that. Just give me your agreement now."

I had absolutely nothing to lose. It was pleasant to suspend my disbelief for a few moments, to indulge in pretense and fantasy, and so I told him he had my agreement. He then stood up, wished me good-day, and left me still sitting on the bench. I watched him walk along the path and disappear over the eastern horizon. Once he was out of sight, my fears came crashing back, and I was embarrassed by the whole episode. I had probably been made to look a fool.

Later, I got up and walked back to the cottage, prepared to do some more work before the light fled.

Over the next few months, into the summer and autumn, and out into the beginning of winter, I worked assiduously. I suppose the pace and the energy at which I painted was due in some part to the meeting with the strange Mr. Black. He had, simply by power of suggestion, put some fire back into me. I'm not saying I was *hasty* with my brushes. I'm saying the lethargy had completely gone from my bones and I was full of youthful vigor: able to work quickly and surely. I began to try new color tones, new tints, new brushstrokes and layering, new knife-and-palette approaches. I experimented with fresh perspectives and shapes, changing styles sometimes overnight, until one day I realized I had found a technique which was not only exciting, it felt comfortable, suited to me. I began to feel that I was at last an artist of some worth.

I threw away all the paintings I had done before the autumn. I didn't even paint over the canvases, though I would have saved money that way. I had this fear that sometime in the future someone might look under the top painting and see the worthless effort beneath.

During the winter I continued to work hard, seeing no one but tradesmen and, in the beginning, the odd visitor. I became impatient with the latter and was no great company anyway, being too distracted and eager to get back to my palette and brushes. Soon they stopped coming, all except Daddy. He was at least impressed a little by my dedication, even if he did not understand what I was doing.

"So much energy," he said, "would have got you onto the board of a bank by now."

"Yes, Daddy—if I wanted to be there."

By New Year I was being left alone with my feverish single-mindedness, which some began to call an
obsession. A good friend rang me and asked if I was
ill and advised me to see "someone." She meant a
psychiatrist, of course, and I told her what she could
do with her advice.

By the spring I had twenty-seven new pictures, of
varying sizes. There was a good still life, six land-
scapes, thirteen abstracts, and some life paintings with
a local model, the barmaid of the local pub, who
didn't mind taking her clothes off in front of another
woman. After studying them for two weeks, poring
over them in all lights, I threw away all but the abstracts. I then went up to London and sat outside an
agent's office for three days, before being admitted.

I never had much time for agents before, thinking
them leeches with little taste, but David Rendan had
been recommended by a close friend.

"These are quite good," he murmured, holding one
up to the light. "Not at all bad. Don't think I'm patronizing you, because I'm not. I can't praise them up
and down the street, because they don't deserve ad-
ulation, but I think you've got something—a distinctly different and interesting style—something I
haven't seen for a few years—not since . . ." and he
named an artist who was currently the darling of the
critics.

"I don't think you're patronizing," I said. "I'm glad
you think they're worthy of attention."

"I really like the dominant scarlets and blacks—
you've got a particularly original way of layering the
two, so that they merge. At least, I haven't seen it
before. They're pretty harrowing in a strange sort of
way. I mean, they're abstracts of course, but they have
a startling way of cutting through one's emotional de-
fenses like a saw, leaving one's spirit wounded and
bleeding . . . and raw."

I used to think this kind of meaningless, airy-fairy talk was crap, fit only for the mouths of sycophants. I used to sneer at it, or rather at those who used it, saying it was pretentious rubbish. Now, from David, it seemed to make sense. His too-long, dark, curly hair bobbed on his collar as spoke enthusiastically about my paintings and when he looked up his blue eyes caught mine and took away my breath. It's a magical combination in a man: dark hair and blue eyes.

David agreed to become my agent.

Things moved quite fast after that. We got a showing in a gallery at the end of the season. My pictures started to sell. I painted more. David became my lover and came down to the country every weekend to be with me.

My father began to be impressed, not by my paintings, which he didn't understand at all, but by the interest others took in them. He met and admitted to liking David, who showed Daddy all my reviews. "She's on her way right to the top, sir, you can be sure of that," said David.

"Really?" my father said. "I would never have guessed."

I fell deeply and obsessively in love with David. I never do things by halves. I fell the whole way into the pit. Had he been another man he might have taken advantage of me—used me and still kept his freedom—but he wasn't. He was kind and honorable and though he had his faults, they were minor and of little consequence. He wasn't a drinker, a gambler, or a libertine. He gave me no cause for jealousy and we were good for one another, both emotionally and in business. I painted the pictures and he sold them. He had other artists on his books, of course, but I soon became his main source of income, much of which he spent on me.

Five years we lived and worked together. We had

a baby—Jeremy was born in the early spring—and he was very beautiful. Since I had my work to do one of the village girls looked after him during the day and occasionally kept him overnight. All three of us got together properly at the weekend, when David came home, except of course when I was due at an exhibition myself, though we did occasionally take Jeremy along with us. He was a great crowd-puller, bless him, with his auburn hair and David's soft blue eyes. The three of us got on very well. When my father visited, we hardly got to see any of the baby at all. Grampa was crazy about his grandson.

"This is your greatest creation," Daddy told me, holding him up while he dribbled on his coat collar. "You're a fine painter, so I'm told, but a *brilliant* breeder."

We all laughed at that.

Then, one day in autumn, when the leaves on the trees had exchanged their greens for fiery hues, I began to paint a picture which I thought was just another in a long line of "excellent" works, when suddenly, halfway through it, I knew it was going to be different.

Every stroke just fell into place and I worked as if in a dream, the brush gliding over the canvas with just the right shade of red, just the right depth of blackness. It looked like a tunnel—a long dark tunnel—but a tunnel through the outer being to the human psyche deep inside. It was as raw and bloody as the others, but it had more intensity of feeling, much more pain. It shrieked from an abyss of emotion, saying, this is the agony, this is the terror, this is the torment at the heart of your soul. It had something to say to each individual who was confronted by it—and *confronted* is the right word—about the anguish of spiritual suffering. It was Christ on the cross, it was the heretic on the rack, it was an angel fallen; it was the rejected actor, the abused child, the denied wife; it was the homesick exile, the forgotten lover, the gay unable to come out; it was the loneliness, the poverty, the pestilence of mankind; it was death, it was birth, it was the nothingness of despair. It was all these things and much, much more. Far more than I could put into words, being a painter and not a poet.

When I had finally finished it, in one sitting, I couldn't bear to look at it. I was afraid that if I did it would somehow be different, less wonderful. I sat trembling in front of the inglenook fire, logs burning to ashes, waiting for David to come home. I felt drained but exuberant. There was fear jostling with feelings of triumph in my breast. When David finally arrived, after a long drive from London, I blurted out, "Go up to the studio." He had not even had time to shut the front door.

"What is it? What's wrong, darling? You look terrible . . ."

"Just—go—up to the studio."

There were no more words in me than those I uttered. It must have frightened him badly, because he was dreadfully pale as he crossed the room and climbed the steps to the studio. I think he expected to find a dead body up there.

He was up there a long time, much too long for my nerves, which were screaming at me. I wanted to rush up to him and say, well? well? well? Instead, I put some logs on the fire, and concentrated on getting them to blaze. Finally he came down the steps, very slowly, his face glowing, his eyes alight.

"It's *brilliant*," he said, taking me in his arms.

"Oh, God, are you sure?" I groaned in pleasure.

"Have I ever given you false praise, my darling? Have I ever flattered you? Never. I tell you it's brilliant—and it is. It's a *masterpiece*."

A chill went through me on hearing that word, the

word he emphasized with his deep voice. But the feeling left me almost instantly. It was a foolish notion, that anyone but myself was responsible for my success. A certain Mr. Black had fired my inspiration, and if ever I saw him again I would tell him so, perhaps even dedicate a painting to him, but he was not responsible for my talent. That was mine and mine alone. A gift given to me by God.

David and I made love that evening, right there before a burning log fire, with the front door still wide-open.

I remember seeing the rouged face of the sky through the doorway, as I lay naked with my lover inside me, wondering if someone might catch us there *en flagrante*, and I also remember not caring a jot if they did, because my lover was lean and hard, handsome and small-hipped, with beautiful buttocks, and they could not help but be envious, man or woman.

David took the painting to London as soon as it was dry and I had to wait at home on tenterhooks. David had suggested the title of *Journey into the Soul*, which seemed appropriate. I tried to get on with something else, but I couldn't. It was wonderful that David recognized the worth of my painting, but would anyone else? There were a lot of pseuds in the art world and, unfortunately, some of them had powerful voices. Any one of them could have destroyed my painting with a column in a magazine or newspaper and there was no predicting one of those sharp U- turns of critical favor:

> *Unfortunately, though we have praised Susan Quarry's works in the past, with her* Journey into the Soul *she has revealed the horribly bizarre rather than the interesting unusual with her slashing strokes of crimson and black. The canvas might have been cut directly from the frame of an ambulance*

*stretcher on which a traffic accident victim had bled
his last. One does not quite know whether to recoil
in horror or quietly make one's way to the bathroom.*

These nightmares were not given time to take root,
however, because David called me three evenings
later.

"Well, we've had one or two nice little offers," he
said, and I could detect the suppressed excitement in
his voice.

"Don't tease me," I said, in an agony of suspense.
"Where are you?"

"Guess."

"London? New York? *Birmingham*?"

"No—I'm in Paris."

My heart began to beat faster.

"Paris?" I faltered.

"Yes, darling, Paris," he said gleefully. "The French
want to buy your painting. How would you like to
go into the Louvre?"

"Don't—don't play with me, David, please . . ."

"I'm not playing with you, you dope. You've made
it. They want your painting—they're *desperate* to own
it. There's one stipulation though."

"What's that?" I asked, dreading something that
might prevent my painting from hanging in the most
famous art gallery in the world.

"You have to give an exhibition, here in Paris, September next year. They want to launch you in France
with a lot of publicity, to support the *disgustingly* ex-
travagant amount they've offered me for *Journey into
the Soul*. Think you can make the deadline?"

"Oh David," I said, almost in a whisper.

"Go and sit down, my love, have a whiskey, let it
sink in, then call me on this number . . ."

I wrote down the telephone number on the pad and

then went and did exactly as he had suggested. I was in a daze of delight and fear—terrified that it was all a dream—terrified that something would go wrong before it happened. I didn't know whether to jump up, rush out into the country lanes screaming "I'm famous," or walk quietly down to the river and drown myself while I was at the pinnacle of my career. Instead, I just lay slumped in a chair and sipped a very large whiskey, allowing the feeling of utter joy to soak through me. The whiskey and the heat from the fire did their work and soon I was pleasantly tipsy.

It was while I was in this euphoric state that there was a knock on the cottage door. I jumped up, from my place by the roaring logs, hoping it was one of my friends, with whom I could share my wonderful news.

I opened the door and there on the step stood a woman I vaguely recognized. She was dressed in similar clothes to those *he* had been wearing the last time we met, on the ridge path above the river. Her face was slightly more feminine than his had been, but just as prosaic. I took her for his sister.

"Yes?" I said.

"You remember," she replied. "Can I come in?"

Without thinking any further I stepped aside and she walked into the living room.

"What do you want?" I asked, a little coldly.

"I come to collect payment of course. Congratulations on your success, by the way. Good, isn't it? A very good feeling, success."

I began trembling.

"Who are you?" I asked, falling back on aloofness. "Do I know you?"

"Why are you playing games? You know who I am—you're fully aware you know me. Last time we met I came as a man. This time—this time I thought *woman* would be more appropriate." She smiled. "Ms. Black, I suppose you'd call me."

Fear coursed through me and I wanted to push her out through the doorway and lock the door against her.

"Get out of here," I said, feeling a nerve pinch above my eyes. "I don't want you in my house."

Her pale eyes regarded me with a distinct lack of warmth.

"A bargain is a bargain," she said. "You promised me your most precious possession. We have simply to establish what that is—and then I shall be gone. You don't have to actually hand it over to me physically."

"This is ridiculous." I tried to laugh. "You'll be saying you want my soul next . . ."

"That is a matter of course, depending what you give me," she murmured. "You know what this is, and it's certainly not ridiculous. It may have a touch of the absurd, but that's all."

"Who are you?" I cried, finding her presence in my house revolting.

She laughed. "I have several names. My name, as they say, is *legion*."

"What do you want?" I screamed at her.

She remained infuriatingly calm.

"You tell *me*. What is your most precious possession? Your baby? Your masterpiece? David?"

I swallowed my revulsion, realizing that I could not get rid of her, not without satisfying her. I went to the window and stared out into the early evening. The red and brown leaves of the trees seemed as if they were on fire in the dying rays of the sun. What if I had never met Mr. Black? Would I have been famous, would I have met David, would I have even sold one single painting, had a baby, created a masterpiece? It was impossible to know. I had altered the course of my life that day and my future history, without Mr. Black's intervention, was a blank. It was nothing I could wrestle with—not with any conviction.

"What will you do with the painting, if I say you can have it?" I asked her without turning round.

"Burn it," she answered promptly.

I turned then. *"Burn it?"*

She shrugged. "That's what I do—destroy things. I make the beautiful ugly, the good bad, I kill loved ones. I destroy."

"And I have a choice?"

"A limited one. Sometimes there are several possessions, all as precious as one another."

"And apart from that, I shall burn in hell, if I sacrifice a loved one to my ambition?"

"That, unfortunately for you, is an integral part of the transaction. I told you the world doesn't come cheap."

She smiled a very silky smile which made me want to vomit. This *was* a nightmare. A horrible dream. Yet it was real. I couldn't even tell David, ask his advice, solicit his sympathy, because he was part of the bargain, too. I knew I could never do another painting like *Journey into the Soul*. It wasn't in me. It was one of those singular feats one accomplishes just once, and once only, never to be echoed or emulated again.

I knew of course that any other offer I made would be rejected. She—he—had no use for money or anything I had to give.

At that moment the door opened and Mary, the village girl who looked after Jeremy, stepped into the room. She had Jeremy with her in his carry cot.

Mary flushed. "Oh, I'm sorry. Didn't know you had company or I would've knocked."

"That's all right, Mary," I said quickly. "Could you keep the baby tonight? I—I'm very busy."

Mary's face set into a determined expression I knew well.

"Oh, no—you said it was all right. Tom's taking me out tonight. I can't look after Jeremy. You said it would be all right only this morning."

Mary put the carry cot containing a sleeping Jeremy on the sofa and went to the door.

"I'll be here at eight in the morning," she said. "I'm a bit late now as it is," and then she was gone, closing the door behind her.

Once Mary's footsteps had died away, Ms. Black crossed the room and looked down at the sleeping baby.

"Do you love your child?" she murmured.

I felt myself going very hot.

"Of course I do."

"Not *of course*—how *much* do you love him?"

I remained silent, standing by the fire.

"Do you," murmured Ms. Black, in a voice that sounded like flies buzzing in my head, "do you love him more than your masterpiece? More than David? Which is most important to you?"

I was silent for a very long while, looking down at the carpet, then I lifted my head.

"I don't think I need to answer that."

She stared at me full in the eyes.

"I think you have," she smiled. "I knew anyway. So, there remain only two alternatives—I can't be interested in something that is of lesser importance to you than the painting or your own soul."

"Or my own *what*?" I said, appalled.

"Well, you know it need not worry you for many years."

"Who in hell are you?" I cried, angrily. "Why are you doing this to me?"

"Who in hell am I? One of them in that place—you've guessed that much. But *which* one? Do you know *any* of us at all? We used to have different names, but we lost them," said Ms. Black dreamily. "We all lost our names when we fell. That's sad, isn't it? I'll tell you what—you guess what my old name was—go on, have a try . . . maybe if you get it right, I'll disappear."

"*Lucifer!*" I said, promptly.

She gave out a tinkling laugh. "Oh *no*, I'm not that important. I was very minor."

"I don't know any more names," I cried, the tears springing hotly to my eyes.

"Two more guesses," she said, smiling.

I searched my mind desperately.

"*Astarte*," I murmured, a faint remembrance of something learned in school.

"Wrong," sang Ms. Black.

"I don't know then!"

"How about *Sibma*?" she suggested, craftily. "Try that name."

I screamed, "I don't know, I don't know. I give in. *You* tell me."

"You give in?" she cried.

"Yes, yes, yes, yes . . ."

"It's *Sibma*," she crowed. "Now give me David or the masterpiece. I want one of them. You have to make up your mind—*now*. They're of equal importance to you, so it doesn't matter which one."

"If—if it's David, when—when will you take him? Is it just his soul you want? Will he live on?"

"Tonight," said Ms. Black, harshly. "Before the dawn. I want him tonight. Not just his soul. I want his body first—I want him to burn his loins until he's drained of all energy and desire, until doing it becomes a physical pain, a torture. I want to take your lovely David until he cries for relief, until he wishes he had never heard of the word *sex*. And then I shall fill him with more lust, and more, until he's raw and screaming for mercy, but still he won't be able to stop himself. The passion will be a hot stale breath that will burn his mouth. It'll course through his aching, screaming body, urging him on, to more, and more, and more . . . I want him to bleed—to fuck himself to death. *Then*, and only then, I'll take his soul . . ."

I shuddered, putting my hands over my ears, so that I couldn't hear any more of her ugly tirade. My David—she was talking about my David, the gentle sensitive lover, whose hands had caressed me, stroked away my fears and doubts. David, who *loved* me. I stumbled away from her and went to stare out at the night.

I think I stood by the window, looking into the darkness, for at least two hours. Jeremy thankfully remained asleep and there were no other interruptions. The evening turned to blackness. The telephone rang twice during that time but it was ignored. Two hours may sound a long time, but it was a brief moment to me. My decision involved eternity—my eternity—and two hours was less than no time at all. It needn't have taken two hours however, because I knew what my reply would be, even before I began my vigil.

Ms. Black knew, too, because when I turned, to give her my answer, she had gone.

"David," I said flatly, after picking up the phone and dialing Paris, "thank you."

"What for?" he said, cheerfully.

I felt hollow and wasted. "Oh, for being there at the right time, for helping me become what I am."

"Darling," he murmured, "I'll always be with you—forever and ever . . ."

"Yes, David," I said.

"Sweetheart, are you all right? I tried to ring you a while back, but I guessed you'd gone out for a walk. Look, I'll be home soon, but you know these Parisian art dealers. Darling, you've *made* it. I know it's a bit of a shock after all this time, but you'll get used to being famous," he joked. "I only hope you'll still speak to your lowly partner in life, once they start to lionize you. It'll be great, sweetheart, you'll see."

"I know," I replied, now appalled by my decision, "but the cost . . ."

"Oh, they can afford it, darling," he cried, misunderstanding me. "The French have the stuff coming out of their ears at the moment."

"David, would you—would you have been very disappointed in me, if I had never done a masterpiece?"

"But you *have*. Look, I'll be home soon and we can have all these deep conversations then, can't we?"

I was quiet for a while and he took my silence for assent.

"Listen," he said, "I've got to go—they're throwing this champagne party. I promise to be good. I'll bring a bottle home with me and we can celebrate, in front of the fire—you know, the way we do?"

"Yes, David."

"Good, great. You sure you're all right? It's probably the shock. Post-success blues and all that."

"Yes, David."

"Well, *au revoir* my sweet."

"Good-bye my love," I said, sadly. "I'm so sorry. I did love you, you know . . ."

The phone went dead.

Summer Wind

Nancy Kress

Nancy Kress lives in Brockport, New York, with her sons Kevin and Brian. She is the author of ten books: three fantasy novels, four science fiction novels, two collections of short stories, and a book on writing fiction. Her most recent novel is Beggars and Choosers, *the sequel to* Beggars in Spain, *which was based on her Hugo- and Nebula-winning novella of the same title. Also recently published was her short story collection,* The Aliens of Earth.

Kress's short fiction appears regularly in Omni, Asimov's Science Fiction Magazine, *and other major science fiction publications. In addition to the awards for "Beggars in Spain," she has won the 1985 Nebula Award for best short story. A former elementary school teacher and advertising copywriter, Kress is currently* monthly "fiction" columnist for Writer's Digest Magazine, and frequently teaches seminars in writing science fiction.

"Sleeping Beauty" or "Briar Rose" are variants on the same story. Charles Perrault wrote the "Sleeping Beauty" in seventeenth century France, the Brothers Grimm wrote "Briar Rose." What they all have in common: a princess pricks her finger on a spindle, falls asleep for many years of the curse, is protected by the thorns of roses until the right prince (or the right time) comes to rescue and awaken her with a kiss. Generally, the "sleeping beauty" is powerless and the story is told from the point of view of the young, ambitious prince.

In Kress's version, beauty is not utterly passive and the reader is taken into the world inside those briars to experience the price one pays for wisdom and power.

Summer Wind

SOMETIMES SHE TALKED TO THEM. WHICH OF COURSE was stupid, since they could neither hear nor answer. She talked anyway. It made the illusion of company.

Her favorite to talk to was the stableboy, frozen in the stable yard beside the king's big roan, the grooming brush still in his upraised hand. The roan was frozen too, of course, brown eyes closed, white forelock blowing gently in the summer wind. She used to be a little frightened of the roan, so big it was, but not of the stableboy, who had had merry red lips and wide shoulders and dark curling hair.

He had them still.

Every so often she washed off a few of them: the stableboy, or the cook beside his pots, or the lady-in-waiting sewing in the solarium, or even the man and woman in the north bedchamber, locked in naked embrace on the wide bed. None of them ever sweated or stank, but still, there was the dust—dust didn't sleep—and after years and years the people became coated in fine, gray powder. At first she tried to whisk them clean with a serving maid's feather duster, but it was very hard to dust eyelashes and earlobes. In the end she just threw a pot of water over them. They didn't stir, and their clothes dried eventually, the velvets and silks a little stiff and watermarked, the coarse-woven breeches and skirts of the servants none the worse off. Better, maybe. And it wasn't as if any of them would catch cold.

"There you are," she said to the stableboy. "Now, doesn't that feel better? To be clean?"

Water glistened in his black curls.

"I'm sure it must feel better."

A droplet fell onto his forehead, slid over his smooth brown cheeks, came to rest in the corner of his mouth.

"It was not supposed to happen this way, Corwin."

He didn't answer, of course. She reached out one finger and patted the droplet from his sleeping lips. She put the finger in her own mouth and sucked it.

"How many years was *I* asleep? How many?"

His chest rose and fell gently, regularly.

She wished she could remember the color of his eyes.

A few years later, the first prince came. Or maybe it wasn't even the first. Briar Rose was climbing the steps from the cool, dark chambers under the castle, her spread skirt full of wheat and apples and cheese as fresh as the day they were stored. She passed the open windows of the Long Gallery and heard a tremendous commotion.

Finally! At last!

She dropped her skirts; wheat and apples rolled everywhere. Rose rushed through the Gallery and up the steps to her bedchamber in the highest tower. From her stone window she could just glimpse him beyond the castle wall, the moat, the circle of grass between moat and Hedge. He sat astride a white stallion on the far side of the Hedge, hacking with a long silver sword. Sunlight glinted on his blond hair.

She put her hand to her mouth. The slim white fingers trembled.

The prince was shouting, but wind carried his words away from her. Did that mean the wind would carry hers toward him? She waved her arms and shouted.

"Here! Oh, brave prince, here I am! Briar Rose, princess of all the realm! Fight on, oh good prince!"

He didn't look up. With a tremendous blow, he hacked a limb from the black Hedge, so thick and interwoven it looked like metal, not plant. The branch shuddered and fell. On the backswing, the sword struck smaller branches to the prince's right. They whipped aside and then snapped back, and a thorn-studded twig slapped the prince across the eyes and blinded him. He screamed and dropped his sword. The sharp blade caught the stallion in the right leg. It shied in pain. The blinded prince fell off, directly into the Hedge, and was impaled on thorns as long as a man's hand and hard as iron.

Rose screamed. She rushed down the tower steps, not seeing them, not seeing anything. Over the drawbridge, across the grass. At the Hedge she was forced to stop by the terrible thorns, as thick and sharp on this side as on the other. She couldn't see the prince, but she could hear him. He went on screaming for what seemed an eternity, although of course it wasn't.

Then he stopped.

She sank onto the green grass, sweet with unchanging summer, and buried her face in her apple-smelling skirts. Somewhere, faintly on the wind, she heard a sound like old women weeping.

After that, she avoided all the east-facing windows. It was years before she convinced herself that the prince's body was, must be, gone from the far side of the

Hedge. Even though the carrion birds did not stay for nearly that long.

Somewhere around the thirteenth year of unchanging summer, the second prince came. Rose almost didn't hear him. For months, she had rarely left her tower chamber. Blankets draped the two stone windows, darkening the room almost to blackness. She descended the stone steps only to visit the storage rooms. The rest of the long hours she lay on her bed and drank the wine stored deep in the cool cellars under the castle. Days and nights came and went, and she lifted the gold goblet to her lips and let the red forgetfulness slide down her throat and tried not to remember. Anything.

After the first unmemoried months of this, she caught sight of herself in her mirror. She found another blanket to drape over the treacherous glass.

But still the chamber pot must be emptied occasionally, although not very often. Rose shoved aside the blanket over the south window and leaned far out to dump the reeking pot into the moat far below. Her bleary eyes caught the flash of a sword.

He was redheaded this time, hair the color of warm flame. His horse was black, his sword set with green stones. Emeralds, perhaps. Or jade. Rose watched him, and not a muscle of her face moved.

The prince slashed at the Hedge, rising in his stirrups, swinging his mighty sword with both hands. The air rang with his blows. His bright hair swirled and leaped around his strong shoulders. Then his left leg caught on a thorn and the Hedge dragged him forward. The screaming started.

Rose let the edge of the blanket drop and stood behind it, the unemptied chamber pot splashing over her trembling hands. She thought she heard sobs, the dry juiceless sobs of the very old, but of course the chamber was empty.

*   *   *

She lost a year. Or maybe more than a year; she couldn't be sure. There was only the accumulation of dust to go by, thick on the Gallery floor, thick on the sleeping bodies. A year's worth of drifting dust.

When she came again to herself, she lay outside, on the endlessly green summer grass. Her naked body was covered with scars. She walked, dazed, through the castle. Clothes on the sleepers had been slashed to ribbons. Mutilated doublets, breeches, sleeves, redingotes, kirtles. Blood had oozed from exposed shoulders and thighs where the knife had cut too deep, blood now dried on the sleeping flesh. In the north bedchamber, the long tumbled hair of the woman had been hacked off, her exposed scalp clotted with blood, her lips still smiling as she slept in her lover's arms.

Rose stumbled, hand to her mouth, to the stable yard. Corwin sat beside the big roan, black curls unshorn, tunic unslashed. Beside him, ripped and bloody, lay Rose's own dress, the blue dress with pink forget-me-nots she had worn for the ball on her sixteenth birthday.

She buried it, along with all the other ruined clothing and the bloody rags from washing the clotted wounds, in a deep hole beside the Hedge.

On the wind, old women keened.

Although the spinning wheel was heavy, she dragged it down the tower stairs to the Long Gallery. For a moment she looked curiously at the sharp needle, but for only a moment. The storage rooms held wool and flax, bales of it, quintals of it. There were needles and thread and colored ribbon. There were wooden buttons, and jeweled buttons, and carved buttons of a translucent white said to be the teeth of faraway animals large enough to lay siege to a magic Hedge. Briar Rose knew better, but she took the white buttons and smoothed them between her fingers.

She weaved and sewed and embroidered new clothes for every sleeper in the castle, hundreds of people. Pages and scullery maids and mummers and knights and ladies and the chapel priest and the king's fool, for whom she made a parti-colored doublet embroidered with small sharp thorns. She weaved clothes for the chancellor and the pastry chef and the seneschal and the falconer and the captain of the guards and the king and queen, asleep on their thrones. For herself Rose weaved a simple black dress and wore it every day. Sometimes, tugging a chemise or kirtle or leggings over an unresisting sleeping body, she almost heard voices on the summer breeze. Voices, but no words.

She spun and weaved and embroidered sixteen hours a day, for years. She frowned as she worked, and a line stitched itself across her forehead, perpendicular to the lines in her neck. Her golden hair fell forward and interfered with the spinning and so she bound it into a plait, and saw the gray among the gold, and shoved the plait behind her back.

She had finished an embroidered doublet for a sous-cook and was about to carry it to the kitchen when she heard a great noise without the walls.

Slowly, with great care, Rose laid the sous-cook's doublet neatly on the polished Gallery floor. Slowly, leaning against the stone wall to ease her arthritic left knee, she climbed the circular stairwell to her bed-chamber in the tower.

He attacked the Hedge from the northwest, and he had brought a great retinue. At least two dozen young men hacked and slashed, while squires and pages waited behind. Flags snapped in the wind; horses pawed the ground; a trumpet blared. Rose had no trouble distinguishing the prince. He wore a gold circlet in his glossy dark hair, and the bridle of his golden horse was set with black diamonds. His sword hacked and slashed faster than the others', and even from the high tower, Rose could see that he smiled.

She unfurled the banner she had embroidered, fierce yellow on black, with the two curt words: BE GONE! None of the young men looked up. Rose flapped the banner, and a picture flashed through her mind, quick as the prince's sword: her old nurse, shaking a rug above the moat, freeing it of dust.

The prince and his men continued to hack at the Hedge. Rose called out—after all, she could hear them, should they not be able to hear her? Her voice sounded thin, pale. She hadn't spoken in years. The ghostly words disappeared in the other voices, the wordless ones on the summer wind. No one noticed her.

The prince fell into the Hedge, and the screaming began, and Rose bowed her head and prayed for them, the lost souls, the ones for whom she would never spin doublets or breeches or whispered smiles like the one on the woman with hacked-off hair asleep in her shared bed in the north chamber.

Her other dead.

After years, decades, everyone in the castle was clothed, and dusted, and pillowed on embroidered cushions rich with intricate designs in jewel-colored thread. The pewter in the kitchen gleamed. The wooden floor of the Long Gallery shone. Tapestries hung bright and clean on the walls.

Rose no longer sat at the spinning wheel. Her fingers were knotted and twisted, the flesh between them thin and tough as snakeskin. Her hair, too, had thinned but not toughened, its lustrous silver fine as spun flax. When she brushed it at night, it fell around her sagging breasts like a shower of light.

Something was happening to the voices on the wind. They spun their wordless threads more strongly, more distinctly, especially outside the castle. Rose slept little now, and often she sat in the stable yard through the long unchanging summer afternoon, listening. Corwin slept beside her, his long lashes throwing shadows on his downy cheeks. She watched him, and listened to the spinning wind, and sometimes her lined face turned slowly in a day-long arc, as if following a different sun than the one that never moved.

"Corwin," she said in her quavery voice, "did you hear that?"

The wind hummed over the cobblestones, stirred the forelock of the sleeping roan.

"There are almost words, Corwin. No, better than words."

His chest rose and fell.

"I am old, Corwin. Too old. Princes are much younger men."

Sunlight tangled in his fresh black curls.

"They aren't really supposed to be words. Are they?"

Rose creaked to her feet. She walked to the stable yard well. The oak bucket swung suspended from its windlass, empty. Rose put a hand on the winch, which had become very hard for her twisted hands to turn, and closed her eyes. The wind spun past her, then through her. Her ears roared. The bucket descended of itself, filled with water. Cranked back up. Rose opened her eyes.

"Ah," she said quietly. And then, "So."

The wind blew.

She hobbled through the stable yard gate to the Hedge. One hand she laid on it, and closed her eyes. The wind hummed in her head, barely rustling the summer grass.

When she opened her eyes, nothing about the Hedge had changed.

"So," Rose said, and went back into the bailey, to dust the royal guard.

But each day she sat in the the wordless wind, or the wind whose words were not what mattered, or in her own mind. And listened.

No prince had arrived for decades. A generation, Rose decided; a generation who knew the members of the retinue led by the young royal on the black horse. But that generation must grow older, and marry, and give birth to children, and one day a trumpet sounded and men shouted and banners snapped in the wind.

It took Rose a long time to climb the tower staircase. Often she paused to rest, leaning against the cool stone, hand pressed to her heart. At the top she paused again, to look curiously around her old room, the one place she never cleaned. The bedclothes lay dirty and sodden on the stained floor. Rose picked them up, folded them across the bed, and hobbled to a stone window.

The prince had just begun to hack at the Hedge. He was the handsomest one yet: hair and beard of deep burnished bronze, dark blue doublet strained across strong shoulders, silver fittings on epaulets and sash. Rose's vision had actually improved with age; she could see his eyes. They were the green of stained glass windows in bright sun.

She knew better, now, than to call to him. She stared at his hacking and slashing, at the deadly Hedge, and then closed her eyes. She let the wind roar in her ears, and through her head, and into the places that had not existed when she was young. Not even when she heard him scream did she open her eyes.

But finally, when the screams stopped as quickly as they had come, she leaned through the tower window and scanned the ground far below. The prince lay on the trampled grass, circled by kneeling, shouting men.

Rose watched him wave them away, rise unsteadily, and remount his horse. She saw the horrified gaze he bent upon the Hedge.

Later, after they had all ridden away, she made her way back down the steps, over the drawbridge, across the grass to the Hedge. It loomed as dark, as thick, as impenetrable as ever. The black thorns pointed in all directions, in and out, and nothing she could do with the wind could change them at all.

But then, one day, the Hedge melted.

Rose was very old. Her silver plait had become a bother and she'd cut it, trimming her hair into a neat white cap. There were ten hairs on her chin, which sometimes she remembered to pull out and sometimes she didn't. Her body had gone skinny as a bird's, with thin bird bones, except for a soft rounded belly that fluttered when she snored. The arthritis in her hands had eased and they, too, were skinny, long darting hands, worn and capable as a spinning shuttle. Her sunken blue eyes spun power.

She was sitting on the unchanging grass when she heard the tumult behind the Hedge. Creakily she rose to start for the tower. But there was no need. Before her eyes the black thorns melted, running into the ground like so much dirty water from washing the kitchen floor. And then the rest of the Hedge melted. Beside her a sleeping groom stirred, and beside the drawbridge, another.

The prince rode through the dissolving Hedge as if it had never been. He had brown hair, gold sash, a chestnut horse. As he dismounted, the solid mass of muscle in his thighs shifted above his high polished boots.

"The bedchamber of the princess—where is it?"

Rose pointed at the highest tower.

He strode past her, trailed by his retinue. When the

last squire had crossed the drawbridge, Rose followed.

All was commotion. Guards sprang forward, found themselves dressed in embroidered velvet, and spun around, bewildered, drawn swords in their hand. Ladies bellowed for pages. The falconer dashed from the mews, wearing a doublet of white satin slashed over crimson, the peregrine on his wrist fitted with gold-trimmed jesses with ivory bells.

Rose hobbled to the stable yard. The king's roan pawed and snorted. Men ran to and fro. A serving wench lowered the bucket into the well, on her head a coif sewn with gold lace.

Only Corwin noticed Rose. He stood a whole head taller than she——surely it had only been a half head difference, once? He glanced at her, away, and then back again, puzzlement on his fresh, handsome face. His eyes, she saw, were gray.

"Do I know you, good dame?"

"No," Rose said.

"Did you come, then, with the visitors?"

"No, lad."

He studied her neat black dress, cropped hair, wrinkled face. Her eyes. "I thought I knew everyone who lived in the castle."

She didn't answer. A slow flush started in his smooth brown cheeks. "Where do you live, mistress?"

She said, "I live nowhere you have ever been, lad. Nor could go." His puzzlement only deepened, but she turned and hobbled away. There was no way she could explain.

There was shouting now, in the high tower, drifted down on the warm summer air. Through the open windows of the Long Gallery, Rose saw the queen rush past, her long velvet skirts swept over her arm. A nearly bald woman in a lace nightdress rushed from the north bedchamber, screaming. Soon they would start to search, to ask questions, to close the drawbridge.

She hobbled over it, through the place where the Hedge had been, now a bare circle like a second, drier moat. And they were waiting for her just beyond, half-concealed in a grove of trees, seven of them. Old women like her, power in their glances, voices like the spinning wind.

Rose said, "Is this all there is, then, for the life I have lost? This magic?"

"Yes," one of them said.

"It is no little thing," another said quietly. "You have brought a prince back to life. You have clothed a fiefdom. You have seen, as few do, what and who you are."

Rose thought about that. The woman who had spoken, her spine curved like a bow, gazed steadily back.

The first old woman repeated sharply, "It is no little thing you have gained, sister."

Rose said, "I would rather have had my lost life."

And to that there was no answer. The women shrugged, and linked arms with Rose, and the eight set out into the world that hardly, as yet, recognized how badly it needed them. And perhaps never would.

This Century of Sleep or, Briar Rose Beneath the Sea

Farida S.T. Shapiro

Farida S.T. Shapiro lives in Washington State where she works at a child care center for children of homeless parents. Her poetry has been published in Hysteria, a magazine of feminist humor, and a book of short stories and poems called The Language of Leaves has been published by Pinchpenny Press.

According to Shapiro, "Briar Rose" has always been her favorite fairy tale and "The Sleeping Beauty" was the first ballet she ever saw. Because in most traditional tellings Briar Rose is a passive

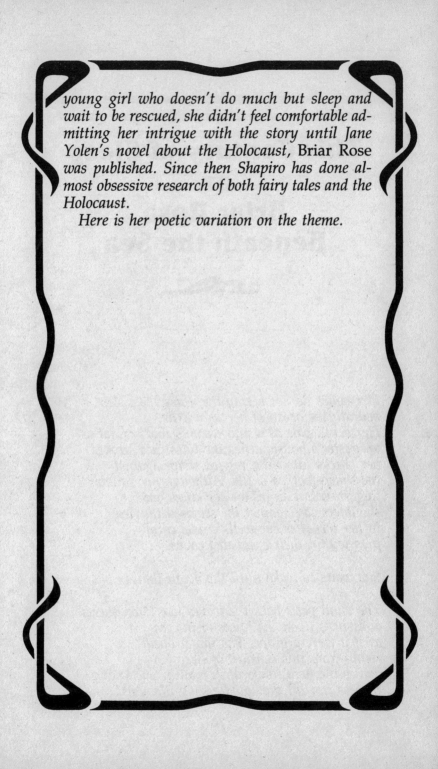

young girl who doesn't do much but sleep and wait to be rescued, she didn't feel comfortable admitting her intrigue with the story until Jane Yolen's novel about the Holocaust, **Briar Rose** was published. Since then Shapiro has done almost obsessive research of both fairy tales and the Holocaust.

Here is her poetic variation on the theme.

This Century of Sleep
or,
Briar Rose
Beneath the Sea

Her bones do not betray the years she's slept
beneath the ocean of her wan exile.
Her skull, pale as a mushroom's root, round as
an oyster's house, defies the tides that stroked
her cheeks into thin, ragged strips against
the sharp-toothed shells. Although her sallow
fingertips tap dirges on her knees, and
shoulders sag against the seaweed tangled
in her toes, her eye-wells cradle coral
fires within their excavated caves.

She waits to wake until the ocean thaws.

The wind peels back the waves like linen sheets
and sucks upon the juices of the sea
as if it were a grape. The raw arousal
rising from this century of sleep
denies the hero's swordfish mouth. She knows
no kiss can lift the spindle's fall, the gall

*within the witch's curse, the sleep that was
not sleep. Her breath hangs stale. The yellowed jaw
gapes loose from famine but her coral eyes
smoke cinders as she burns her satin bed.*

The Crossing

Joyce Carol Oates

Joyce Carol Oates is the author, most recently, of Haunted: Tales of the Grotesque *and the novel* What I Lived For. *She is the 1994 recipient of the Bram Stoker Life Achievement Award in Horror Fiction. Her work has appeared in* Omni, Playboy, The New Yorker, Harper's Magazine, The Atlantic, *as well as in literary magazines.*

Oates is prolific and seems to be able to write fiction on virtually any subject. She occasionally enjoys the challenge of writing for a specific theme.

Another take on sleeping beauty, or Briar Rose.

The Crossing

*M*URMURING HER NAME, HER NAME, HER NAME LIKE *an incantation. Stroking and squeezing her cool, limp fingers. Staring at her face that was papery white and impassive, wimpled like a nun's by tight white bandages that covered most of her head, her shaved and violated skull. It was her bruised eyelids, her injured right eye, at which he stared most intently, leaning as close to her as he could over the bed's high railings. The respirator that breathed for her, the profusion of tubes that sustained her—these he ignored, for they were but temporary, until she recovered consciousness and strength enough to sustain herself. Her eyelids quivered almost continuously, had several times since the emergency craniectomy fluttered open in his presence, the eyes dilated, bloodshot, and terrible to see—her eyes, yet lacking the glisten of consciousness.*

Yet he spoke her name, he kept his vigil at her bedside, he was fired with hope, untiring. He flew into a fury at the mildest suggestion that he should spare himself—the ordeal might be a long one. She was his wife, his wife whom he loved more than his own life, and certainly beyond his own comfort. He was convinced that, in the next minute, or in the next hour, she would open her eyes of her own volition, she would see him and know him: she would break her silence, and speak.

A train whistle faint in the distance—that melancholy sound of yearning. Like her own name being murmured, almost inaudibly. *Martha. Martha. Martha.*

It appeared to be early evening. A wan, soft, sepia cast to the light slanting through tall, distinctively narrow windows. She was alone, yet, a bit uneasily, did not feel alone. As if, beyond, or beneath, or through the surfaces of objects, she were somehow being observed; as if what appeared to her to be solid objects were in fact flat and transparent, like a one-way mirror. On all sides in this spacious room, which she knew to be an upstairs guest room in her aunt Alma Buchanan's grand old house on Prospect Avenue, Chautauqua Falls, Martha felt the presence of others; yet, of course, when she looked about, behind a faded Chinese screen, in the empty cedar closet and the adjoining bathroom, there was no one.

Except herself, so unexpected she gave a little cry: her own reflection in a full-length dressmaker's mirror. Tall, willowy, and tentative in her movements, younger than she would have judged herself, her face blurred with light as in an overexposed photograph.

Why am I here? How long will I stay?

On the high four-poster bed that smelled of lavender sachet and, to Martha's sensitive nostrils, just a bit of dust, her suitcase lay opened atop an ornamental beige lace spread. Odd she'd brought along this old, handsome, but now rather scratched and inconveniently heavy leather suitcase instead of one of her newer, lightweight suitcases. A relic of the early years of her marriage when she and Roger had traveled frequently to Europe, she'd never been able to bring herself to throw it away.

She must call Roger now, she thought. He would

be anxious to know whether she'd arrived in Chautauqua Falls safely, for the journey had been a complicated one—in what ways exactly, Martha could not quite remember.

Damn: no telephone in the room?

How like her elderly aunt, to invite Martha to visit her, and to give her a room lacking a telephone.

This annoyance made Martha's head ache—she was not by nature a patient woman, her intelligence pricked and prodded her into action when, sometimes, action was not possible. Pulses throbbed in her head, in her eyes. And how unpleasantly dry her mouth, as if coated with dust.

Aunt Alma was waiting for her downstairs: it was teatime.

Yet she stood indecisive in the center of the room. (*Was* someone observing her? Surely not through the mirror in which her reflection wavered, for the mirror's bland wooden back was visible.) Her attention was drawn to the peculiar creases, sharp, shadowed, in the lace bedspread, where the heavy suitcase lay. Something terrifying in the *depth, darkness* of those fissures she did not want to consider.

Very likely, Aunt Alma herself had crocheted that spread. It was beautiful, amazingly intricate floral and spiral designs; once snowy white, probably, and now faded to the color of weak tea. A relic of that era when young women of "good" families like the Buchanans had nothing more urgent to do with their time than prepare—what was the word? a French word? antiquated, quaint?—nothing more to do with their time than prepare themselves for marriage.

They were virgins in that era, and they were good girls. Dutiful Protestant-Christian daughters. As if marriage, the very wedding ceremony itself, *husband and wife one flesh*, were both the peak of a woman's life and its death knell.

She would call Roger from downstairs. Too much time had already passed.

Yet the scene outside one of the windows drew her to it, and again she gave a little cry of surprise—the mountains, at the horizon, so vivid! so near! These were peaks of the Chautauqua range, bluish-hazy and crowned with brilliant, if waning sunshine. They were at least fifty miles away, but looked much closer, on the other side of the Chautauqua River that divided the small city into north and south.

The highest peak was Mt. Cataract, twenty-three hundred feet above sea level. Shadowed below, illuminated with sunshine above. The shape of a hand lifted in greeting.

How many years since Martha had seen these mountains? She was not one of the more-dutiful female members of her family; to her shame, she had not visited her aunt since her uncle Dwight's funeral, at least twelve years ago, when her own parents were still alive. These were the first mountains of Martha's life, the mountains of her girlhood more than thirty years ago, when, with her sister, she'd been brought by their parents for leisurely summer visits to this house. The woman she called "Aunt Alma" was in fact her great-aunt, Martha's mother's aunt.

Trousseau was the word she'd tried to think of. Of course.

Martha struggled to open the window, suddenly she was having difficulty breathing, she was desperate for fresh air—forcing the warped lower window partway up, and leaning out, trembling with relief. How fresh, how pungent the air!—how restorative. It smelled of sun-warmed grasses, and the rich dark loamy soil of Aunt Alma's flower beds, an undercurrent of brackish-bitter air borne on the wind from the Chautauqua River a mile or so away.

Now the train whistle was becoming louder, short

distinct percussive cries. A train was approaching
from the east. Already in brisk systolic puffs a locomotive's curling white smoke appeared above a
stretch of trees; in the next moment, the train itself
would come into view, crossing the railroad trestle
above the marsh, a quarter mile to the rear, and down
an incline, from the grand old houses of Prospect
Street. Martha winced at the sound but shaded her
eyes to watch.

As a young girl, how many times she'd awakened
in this house to the sound of just such a train whistle,
and the rhythmic strokes of a train's powerful piston-
driven wheels! How many times awakening in a
strange bed, in a strange pattern of light, her heart
beating with anticipation, not knowing at first where
she was—*What is this place? Who has brought me here?*

As the clattering of the locomotive and its long
string of freight cars CHAUTAUQUA & BUFFALO CHAU-
TAUQUA & BUFFALO CHAUTAUQUA & BUFFALO seemed
to rush into the room and upon her.

*The impact of the collision was such that her right eyeball
had been jolted from its socket. Hanging loose as a jelly on
her cheek like a gigantic tear.*

Teatime with Martha's aunt, in a somewhat airless,
overfurnished corner of the big front parlor. Close by,
a carved mahogany grandfather clock with dully
gleaming numerals and spindly hands so thin Martha
could not see them clearly sonorously chimed the
quarter hour.

"So kind of you to visit your elderly, ailing aunt!
Dear Martha," Aunt Alma said, speaking with exaggerated care, as if to emphasize, by the clarity with
which she uttered the name *Martha*, that she had not
forgotten her great-niece's name. "I know how busy
you are. Your life! You and your—husband—" And

now her voice did drift, for obviously she'd forgotten Roger's name.

Martha spoke quickly to spare her aunt embarrassment. "Oh no, Aunt Alma, I'm happy to be here. I've missed you. And—this house."

The elderly woman was smiling somewhat tensely, leaning forward in her wing-backed chair, poor woman how her back was curved!—such an expression on her face that Martha understood she had not exactly heard. Martha repeated her words in a louder voice, like an actress in a play. "I've missed you, Aunt Alma. I can't think why I haven't visited in so long. I've missed this house, and Chautauqua Falls—it seems to have changed so little since I was here last."

Aunt Alma nodded enthusiastically. "Things have changed so much, haven't they! In all our lives. It *has* been a long time." Her softly creased face puckered, her eyes shone, in a look of affectionate reproach, as if Martha were a child. "I've missed *you*, dear."

Martha laughed, startled and happy. Yes, it was good to be missed.

How rude it would be of her, at this point, Martha thought, swallowing her tea to relieve the parchness of her mouth, if she interrupted her aunt to ask to use a telephone. She simply could not.

So Aunt Alma talked, and Martha half listened. The grandfather clock, tall and stately, a presence in the parlor like another human being, chimed the quarter hour. She was thinking how she'd been so often lonely, in her busy professional life. An educator, married to an even busier and more publicly involved educator. A childless couple, well-known, even renowned, in American academic circles. Countless friends, admiring colleagues. And of course she and Roger loved each other very much—not with the effervescence of first passion, but with the more enduring strength of companionship. Yet, yes, sometimes,

Martha had to admit, she was rather lonely—for what, or whom, she had no idea.

How majestic, how thrilling, the train had been, racing across the trestle above the marsh: Martha had squinted trying to see it more clearly, counting the rumbling freight cars whose corrugated rust red sides had seemed freshly washed, gleaming. CHAUTAUQUA & BUFFALO CHAUTAUQUA & BUFFALO CHAUTAUQUA & BUFFALO. So abruptly familiar to her straining eyes, as if it had been only the day before she'd seen them, and not many years.

Martha recalled how, as a girl, though discouraged from exploring certain areas of Chautauqua Falls unaccompanied, she'd been intrigued by the frequently running trains. The tracks of the Chautauqua & Buffalo Line, the Erie & Oriskany Line, and the New York Central Line, converging at the riverfront, had divided the small city into sectors, like the steep hills and gullies, which perhaps only a restless child, investigating on foot, could quite experience.

That trick of perspective as a train rushes away, if you stand on the tracks behind it to watch: a rapid vanishing as if the train is swallowed by its own speed, the very tracks themselves—rails, ties, interstices of gravel—narrowing and disappearing into a mere point on the horizon.

Where do we go when we go—out?

If we disappear at one point, do we reappear at another?

Martha gratefully swallowed her tea, though it had become tepid. She held a fluted, delicately patterned Wedgwood cup that was a cobweb of near-invisible cracks. The china Aunt Alma used for their tea was beautiful, and fragile; must be a century old, like the elegant, fussy furnishings throughout the house. And the house itself, built 1885; stolid, almost-ugly; but imposing, like all the Victorian houses of Prospect Street. The *frowning house* Martha and her older sister had called it—the juxtaposition of austere, dark brown shingles, steep overhanging roofs, prominent shutters framing oddly narrow, tall windows had inspired them. Martha remembered how, thirty years ago, cascades of English ivy and wisteria vines had shadowed the downstairs rooms; very little seemed to have changed in the interim. The *frowning house* had been old when she'd been a young girl, Martha thought. And now she was no longer a young girl—it was still old. The thought made her smile as if it were an obscure, playful riddle.

These many minutes, Aunt Alma had been chattering warmly; reminiscing, rambling vaguely and happily in the manner of the very old who are grateful for companionship; grown accustomed, not to conversations, but to a simulacrum of conversation, one- sided, wayward, yet invigorating to the speaker, whose fate otherwise would be to sit in silence and solitude, thoughts buzzing round and round in her skull like flies trapped in a glass bulb. At Martha's sudden smile, Aunt Alma smiled too, as if they shared a common memory. For a woman of eighty-six, she did not appear frail so much as tentative; with her watery blue eyes, her finely creased yet still rather beautiful face, her hopeful smile. Her hair, fixed each morning in an elaborate bun, with tendrillike curls on her forehead, was flaxen streaked with silver, resembling the hue of Martha's own hair, which had begun to turn a few years ago; her cheekbones were prominent, and her cheeks just slightly sunken, gaunt; the flesh beneath her chin had gone flaccid, partly hidden, for vanity's sake, by a high lace collar and white silk bow. Aunt Alma was a woman of breeding and means—not really educated, but certainly "cultured"—whose inherited household had always been run by servants; the only one who seemed to remain now was a taciturn housekeeper named Betty, who was well into her sixties. Martha felt the difference between herself and her privileged, yet entrapped great-aunt; how suffocated she would have been, in such a life, stuck in this small town in upstate New York forever! She felt a surge of love for Aunt Alma, tinged with pity. But there was no denying how she and the older woman resembled each other: face, hair, eyes. If they were to appear in public together, any neutral observer could identify them as related.

As if reading Martha's thoughts, Aunt Alma said, sighing, "I've been waiting for you, you know, dear. Of course, your sister"—a sudden blank pause, she'd forgotten Martha's sister's name—"is sweet, to call so often. But I miss *you*, Martha." Her shadowed and slightly sunken eyes blinked rapidly. "But I haven't been impatient—no, not at all. I know how dedicated you are to your life, your teaching career—You and your—husband—"

Martha guessed that Aunt Alma had forgotten what Martha actually did, and where; so quickly she said, "Yes, Aunt Alma, but I'm on sabbatical this spring. I have a grant to finish my new book. So it's a time for research, and contemplation. An ideal time to visit you."

Martha smiled happily. Uttered with such girlish directness, her words had the ring of truth.

The grandfather clock began to chime—not the quarter hour, but the hour. These were strokes of sound pure, melodic, yet somehow piercing, like a blinding ray of light entering one's eye. Martha listened, counting eight chimes—could it be eight o'clock, already?—then nine, ten, eleven—finally, fifteen! Seeing her look of surprise, her aunt laughed, and leaned over to take Martha's hand, gently. She held Martha's hand in her thin, cool, firm fingers, and did not seem to want to let go. Saying, "In Chautauqua Falls, dear girl, you'll find time keeps its own hours."

What *was* the number—?

Martha half sobbed with frustration. Trying to dial her own telephone number, yet, incredibly, fumbling the digits. She blamed the antique rotary phone: on a touch-tone, to which she was accustomed, she would have dialed the ten-digit number swiftly and unerringly, without needing to think.

And damned awkward this was, Martha in an alcove off the downstairs front hall, past which on slippered swollen feet, sighing with arthritic discomfort, the housekeeper Betty plodded, and returned to plod again, and yet again, as if tidying up the parlor after Aunt Alma's and Martha's modest tea was a great task, involving immense effort of which she wanted the visiting niece to be aware.

The strange thing was, Martha's fingers seemed to recall of their own volition a telephone number of more than twenty years ago!—the number of the first house in which she and Roger had lived. Though Martha instructed herself clearly to dial the correct number, some sort of confusion ensued, as she dialed, between her brain's command and her finger's execution. She gave up, and tried again; and again. But when she heard the phone ringing at the other end of the line she panicked, and hung up, quickly, before a stranger could answer.

As Betty the housekeeper plodded past another time. A dour old woman in bedroom slippers and a black rayon dress that fitted her bulky body tightly. *This woman was old when I was a little girl*, Martha thought. *She is the same age, still*. The housekeeper sighed heavily, not so much as glancing at Martha, who stood in the telephone alcove rubbing at her right eye which spilled tears absurdly.

* * *

Extensive damage to the brain stem and cerebellum. Trauma to the body—broken ribs, broken collarbone, shattered right knee, countless lacerations. Eight preliminary hours of neurosurgery to reduce pressure in the brain caused by swelling and internal bleeding—twelve percent of the cerebellum would be removed in all, after subsequent operations. Surgery to repair damage to the right eye was believed to be successful.

She was yet to regain consciousness but he had faith, he would not give up. At her bedside as soon as visiting hours began in the intensive care unit at 8:30 A.M. Reluctant to leave when visiting hours were over at 7:00 P.M. Stroking her fingers, speaking her name. He knew she was, in her deep coma, aware of him—conscious of his presence. Sometimes her fingers twitched in response to his, her eyelids fluttered on the verge of opening, her pale, bruised lips seemed about to shape words. He knew, he knew! He had not realized how much he loved her, and how powerful the bond was between them.

She was standing, breathless, trembling with anticipation. A rivulet of sweat like a tear running down her cheek. Just below the steep grassy railroad embankment at the Seneca Street crossing, in a neighborhood of warehouses, vacant lots, the township water tower on its spindly legs.

Warning   Train Crossing   Stop Look Listen

The X-shaped sign was weatherworn but still forbidding. Beyond Seneca Street was one of Chautauqua Falls' several railroad tunnels cut into a massive hill, for this was a steep and riotous landscape, a mysterious rock-strewn earth where once glaciers the size of the Great Lakes had formed. It was the tunnel that had drawn Martha here, for it was a large craterlike hole in the wooded hill, dark as absolute night; for sunlight, on even the brightest days, could penetrate it only to a degree. A complex tunnel, too, with two sets of railroad tracks running side by side, no more than ten feet separating them; emerging from the tunnel and running over a wooden trestle bridge above the street, and above the marsh, westward into town. Martha had made her way to this no-man's-land of reeds high as her head, spongy ground underfoot, a smell of brackish water, by way of a faint path that led parallel to, though hidden from, the generally well-tended, wall- or hedge-protected back lawns of the grand old houses of Prospect Street. Except for the isolated cries of birds in the marsh, all was silent here.

There was a profound mystery about this tunnel, at which Martha was staring with such intensity her eyes watered. The mouth of the tunnel was framed by a stone portal, of subtle ornamentation, at its crest CHAUTAUQUA FALLS 1913 carved into the surface. Martha understood that, if she was patient, the mystery would be explained to her, with the ease of a sleeve being turned inside out.

And then, it happened: she heard the train whistle, faint but rapidly approaching; she saw the red signal lights begin to flash. But why were there no crossing gates here?—the railroad tracks were exposed, dangerously open to the street. (Fortunately, there was no traffic. For this was early in the morning, just dawn.) Martha waited, barely able to contain her excitement, clenching and unclenching her fists. She felt the ground vibrate just as the gigantic locomotive came rushing out of the tunnel—there was the speed of it, the size, the deafening whistle and clatter of the great spoked wheels turning and the earth now vibrating beneath her feet like a panicked heartbeat. Billowing vaporish smoke was discharged from the locomotive's smokestack, obscuring the sky. As Martha stood, hands pressed to her ears, she saw in the cab a man lifting his gloved hand to her in greeting, and smiling—the locomotive's engineer?—but in the next instant the locomotive was past her, freight cars were hurtling by, only a few yards away, CHAUTAUQUA & BUFFALO CHAUTAUQUA & BUFFALO CHAUTAUQUA & BUFFALO car after car rattling past, amid a choking odor of tar and creosote. Yet she could neither turn away nor hide her eyes. Standing paralyzed, in awe rather than fear, until at last the caboose went by, and rushed westward across the trestle. Martha climbed the embankment to the tracks so that she could watch the train disappear from this perspective: the tracks, too, radically narrowing, coming to a point to vanish.

The engineer, the man in the cab of the locomotive—who was he?

Martha, shaky and out of breath, wiped her sweaty face on a tissue. Like a brash young girl, smiling into the tissue. She had not seen the man clearly, but her excited impression was that he was red-haired, with a redhead's freckled pallor, and he wore a railway cap at a jaunty angle on his head, and his gesture toward her had been high-spirited, flirtatious. His face strong-boned and manly and his eyes intense, direct, boldly fixed upon *her*.

Does he know me? Did he know I'd be here, waiting?

Keeping his vigil. At her bedside. Speaking her name, stroking her arm, squeezing the fingers that sometimes—he swore, he did not imagine this!—squeezed his in turn. And her eyelids fluttered on the verge of opening, and she writhed, twisted her upper body, a deep yearning groan escaped from her, a groan that was his name—he swore, he did not imagine this! Though the doctors were not encouraging but rather neutral, polite. And so the hours following the accident became days, and incredibly the days became sequences of days, and finally weeks, and her deep coma was unchanged, except in those ways that he alone could see.

The respirator had been removed, and she could breathe—in sometimes erratic surges, sometimes quick shallow infantlike and rhythmic breaths. Feeding tubes dripped fluids into the veins of her arms and legs and a catheter bore toxins from her lower body in a continuous stream like the invisible ceaseless motion of atoms. Machines monitored her sometimes-erratic, sometimes-normal heartbeat and the similarly unpredictable activities of her damaged brain. On all sides this powerful humming and vibrating. Life! life! life! *the machines promised.*

In Chautauqua Falls, time keeps its own hours.

And so it was, Martha discovered. For though she was visiting with Aunt Alma for only ten days, each day was endless; and somehow each day was the first day—the first full day, that is, beginning with her waking at dawn to the faint sound of a train whistle, and hurrying out, through the surprisingly over-grown, weedy backyard of her aunt's house, through the dessicated hedge and into the untended, marshy area at the foot of the incline. And so along the der-elict footpath a mile or so in the direction of Seneca Street, the warehouse district, the enormous black crater in the hill into which twinned railroad tracks disappeared beneath the austere stone portal CHAU-TAUQUA FALLS 1913.

Yet, Martha believed, too, that this "first day" had its significant variants, if only she could remember them. For naggingly, as one senses rather than sees an object in the corner of one's eye, she did remem-ber—almost.

For instance: exploring the block-long "downtown" of Chautauqua Falls, strolling in and out of familiar stores, she had several times found herself staring at telephone booths. Wasn't there a call, an urgent call, she should make? But to whom? And why?

What, Martha wondered, could so desperately *matter*?

And another day, idly following a footpath along the river that brought her to the underside of the Federal Street bridge, in a semirural area far from Prospect Street, Martha heard a sound of murmurous voices; and knew, even as her intelligence rejected such a possibility, that she was being observed, closely monitored. She cast her eyes upward to the girdered, grimy underside of the bridge, where mourning doves were nesting. Only doves—cooing doves—of course. Yet: *they are following me! watching me! I am never out of their sight*! Shimmering parabolas of light played against the underside of the bridge, reflected water cast upward. There was beauty here, but also deception. She dared not trust the shimmering surfaces of the world.

She rubbed her eyes roughly, in childish vexation. And—when she opened her eyes again, the underside of the bridge had vanished! Nothing remained, at all. Nor any sky, any substance, beyond. The cause lay not in her vision but in the very structure of the world. Calmly she thought *It's gone. It never has been. I am looking into the emptiness of existence.*

He spoke her name, sometimes so sharply, not knowing what he did, a nurse came to admonish him gently, Please sir, not so loud, you'll disturb our other patients. And he blinked in astonishment and outrage. As if he'd believed himself alone, alone with her—how dare any stranger intervene?

Early each morning, as the locomotive rushed out of the tunnel, as the red-haired engineer saluted Martha with his gloved hand, and mouthed a wordless greeting, Martha could make out the man's features more clearly. His smile was broad, yet rather sly; flirtatious, yet also kindly, protective. And his eyes so keenly fixed upon *her*—she carried the impact of their gaze for hours afterward, like an erotic caress, warming the blood of her entire body.

Of course, Martha did not tell Aunt Alma about the railroad engineer, nor where she went early each morning. Nor did she tell her where, through the long day, and well into the evening, she wandered—the streets, alleys, footpaths, and trails of the small town; the wide cobbled bridge at the town's center that spanned the Chautauqua River, where people drawn to the water as she was, mainly older men, leaned against the railing and gazed down brooding into the churning, frothy water thirty feet below. Because this part of Chautauqua Falls was on a relatively high elevation, you could see, in the distance, a saw-toothed stretch of mountains, on clear days distinctive as cardboard cutouts. Mt. Cataract prominent among them, shimmering, beautiful, crowned with sunshine. The shape of a hand that, teasingly, both beckoned and withdrew in the same gesture.

Strange how, in Chautauqua Falls, Martha never recognized anyone. Nor did anyone recognize her. In fact, they did not seem to see her, or, in any case, with a complacency she might have thought maddening in another context, they looked through her. *As if I am not here. As if I'm invisible.* So long as the red-haired engineer took notice of her, Martha thought, smiling, she really didn't care.

In the eleventh week of her hospitalization, this was noted as a promising sign: her right eye blinked normally as a nurse drew a cotton swab lightly over the cornea.

She was rapidly losing weight, weighing now ninety pounds. And with each day in her comatose state the prognosis was less optimistic. Her intellectual abilities, doctors said, were possibly unimpaired but damage to the brain stem and cerebellum was severe. One chance in one hundred of regaining consciousness.

He, her husband, listened; and heard what he chose to hear. For in such situations we must not hear what we cannot bear to hear; God has not made us strong enough.

This he knew, in his stubborn faith: when he spoke her name, when he leaned over to kiss her cool forehead, occasionally she responded with a fluttering of her eyelids; sometimes her limbs twitched, her upper body became agitated. One morning he was greatly excited: he murmured her name and her eyes flew open, the left eye, the eye that was uninjured, focused upon his face—he was sure! A glisten of recognition that was unmistakable! Her parched lips moved, and a choked, muffled cry issued from her, as from somewhere deep inside her; then she shuddered, and her eyes shut, as the wave of unconsciousness swept over her again, like dark water visibly rising.

But he'd seen! He knew.

She had believed herself utterly safe, protected as a baby in the old-fashioned four-poster bed with the primly hard mattress. But one night Martha dreamt a terrible dream.

She was not herself exactly. Yet the name—*Martha*?—was tauntingly murmured. She had been abducted from her home, trussed up as a specimen in a hellish scientific experiment, like an infant swaddled in restraining sheets; strawlike tubes pierced veins in her arms, legs, and even in her groin; tiny electrodes had been implanted in her skull and chest. She thrashed desperately from side to side to free herself—tried to scream, but could not—one of her captors crouched above her, a cruel melted-moon face, craterous eyes—hideous! *Leave me alone, let me go, don't touch me!* she screamed in silence.

Saving herself, then, as, as a child, she'd saved herself from nightmares, with a convulsive wrenching of her body. She broke free of the constraints holding her, and woke—to her immense, sobbing relief, in the old-fashioned four-poster bed in her aunt's house in Chautauqua Falls.

Thank God, only a dream. It could not pursue her this side of sleep.

Except, next day: in Lyons Pharmacy & Sweet Shoppe where she went to refill a prescription for her aunt, Martha felt a premonition of—she did not know, had no name to give it; she felt that trip of the heart that signals an onset of panic.

She had to—do what? Not the task she'd been sent on, which was perhaps merely a pretext, but—what?

The answer lay somewhere in the store's dingy interior. She had no choice but to go inside. No one appeared to be on duty.

It was remarkable how little had changed in Lyons, in thirty years. The high ceiling of hammered-tin squares, long ago painted a pale sour green; several slow-turning fans that hung from the ceiling; the rows of predictable not-new merchandise—toiletries, medical supplies, cosmetics, greeting cards, candy bars. Immediately to the left of the front entrance was the old soda fountain with its slightly blemished mirror, and the mauve marble counter that was always stickily damp, and the half dozen frayed leather swivel stools. All empty, and no one behind the counter? There were the old glossy poster illustrations of hot fudge sundaes, milk shakes, banana splits; advertisements for Coca-Cola, Pepsi-Cola, Royal Crown Cola, 7-Up. There, the cigarette vending machine forbidden to minors by New York State law. The air, stirred by the slow fans, was stale, cloying-sweet with the odor of syrup.

Martha stood at the counter, smiling nervously—

where was the young man who'd always worked here? Perhaps he was not a young man any longer? But why was he, or someone else, not here, in any case? How badly Martha wanted to order a banana split, just like the one in the picture. Scoops of vanilla, chocolate, and strawberry ice cream, coarsely ground nuts, hot fudge syrup and a dollop of whipped cream and a banana sliced lengthwise—though the banana, Martha recalled, was sometimes too greeny-unripe to have any taste, and sometimes so brown as to be almost rotted.

Martha waited, but no one appeared. "Mr. Lyons?" she called, toward the rear of the store. "Isn't anyone here?"

Even the mirror behind the fountain, laid horizontally to a height of about six feet, was strangely vacant. Where Martha stood, there was blurred light as in an overexposed photograph.

Martha was beginning to be frightened, but Martha was annoyed, too. Boldly she went to the pharmacist's counter at the back of the store, to seek out Mr. Lyons. A sharp medicinal smell, or smells, prevailed here. Behind the first counter was a raised counter, with a frosted glass partition; behind this partition, the gray-haired pharmacist was usually to be found. *And there he is*, Martha thought, *hiding from me*. She believed she could see the man's head, part of his torso, through the frosted glass. "Mr. Lyons? You have a customer," she said. But there was silence, and the figure behind the glass remained unmoving as a cardboard cutout. "I'm here to refill Mrs. Buchanan's prescription," Martha said carefully. "She's my aunt. She's an old, old customer of yours." But still there was no response. The only sound in the store was the slow, vibrating-creaking sound of the ceiling fans as their dust-coated propellers barely turned.

Martha's eyes flooded with tears. She was going to

scream—a sudden shaft of pain pierced her head. *No, no*, she thought. *I will not give in.*

Martha turned to leave the store, but the telephone booth, in a corner near the front, drew her attention. There was something about the telephone booth that was crucial, Martha knew. Hadn't she meant to make a call from it the other day?—she could not quite remember. She remembered the urgency, the excitement, but she could not remember whom she'd wanted to call. Who meant so much to her? She had no living relatives any longer: all were deceased. Except for the elderly aunt whose name, too, for just this moment, she could not quite recall.

Martha stepped into the telephone booth, and eagerly lifted the receiver—this, too, damn!—an old-fashioned rotary phone. She dropped a dime into the mechanism and quickly, before her thoughts could interfere, she dialed the number literally at her fingertips, memorized by her fingertips, a ten-digit number she knew by instinct was the correct number, the number she needed—ah, it was life or death, and life must triumph! She was panting, and her eyes were brimming with tears.

But even as she pressed the receiver so hard against her ear that her entire body trembled, she understood that the telephone, like all of Lyons Pharmacy & Sweet Shoppe, was not in business. There was no dial tone, only dead silence.

Her aunt's name was *Alma*, of course: *Alma Buchanan.*

Though she was not in fact Martha's aunt, but someone else's aunt. Her great love and need for Martha had drawn Martha to her, and so long as that love and need endured, Martha would remain in Chautauqua Falls.

*   *   *

*Feeling sometimes—he swore, he did not imagine this!—
her resistance to the kneading, bending, stretching of her
muscles he'd learned from the physical therapist, a voiceless
tinge of pain.*

*For pain was sensation, and sensation was conscious-
ness, and consciousness was life.*

*For he could not allow it that the most random of acci-
dents should disrupt, ruin utterly the course of two such
lives. A pelting rain, a stalled truck on a suburban road
just beyond a railroad crossing whose warning lights and
automatic safety gates had failed to operate as a train approached. And she, his wife, driving alone—*

Such a set of singularities! He could not accept it.

*Keeping his vigil. Murmuring her name, stroking and
squeezing her cool, limp fingers. And now the exercising
of her stiffening and atrophying muscles that her wasted
body might be deceived into believing itself alive, and normal; and not curl as it seemed to wish to, spine hideously
bending, into a fetal position.*

Returning home at an unexpectedly early hour of the
afternoon. Her first glimpse of the dour housekeeper
Betty standing motionless in the kitchen, oddly motionless but Martha would not think of this until later.
She came to her Aunt Alma who was seated in a cush-
ioned rocker in the sunporch, simply sitting, upright,
her aged, thin hands limp in her lap. "Aunt Alma,
I'm back. I'm afraid I couldn't get your medicine,"
Martha said. The elderly woman seemed not to hear.
Was she asleep? But her eyes were open, a sweet
blank smile on her lips. "Mr. Lyons wouldn't wait on
me! He was there, but he wouldn't so much as—" It
was then that Martha saw, to her surprise, that her
aunt's gaze was fixed upon her, or upon the place
where she stood; but there was no glisten of recognition in the eyes, no more consciousness than in a
pair of marbles.

"Aunt Alma? Is something wrong?" Martha touched her aunt's arm fearfully. The arm was stiff, ungiving. How still the elderly woman sat, like a dressmaker's dummy arranged in a chair. *It's because I have returned too early. They aren't prepared for me.* The softly creased skin of Martha's aunt's face was an intricate lacy skein of wrinkles laid upon a younger face that might have been Martha's own. The opaque eyes were a pale washed blue, like the sky beyond high motionless cirrus clouds. As Martha stared, in horror, she saw something moving in Aunt Alma's elaborately coiffed silvery-flaxen hair—a small, shiny black beetle? Another beetle emerged briskly from her aunt's left ear and, shy of sunlight, darted into the coil of hair at the nape of her aunt's neck, appearing, and disappearing, in virtually the same instant.

Martha lurched backward out of the sunporch, screaming.

She knew: she must leave Chautauqua Falls. Before she became one of the dead.

But she could no longer remember clearly any region that was *not* Chautauqua Falls. Nor any time not eerily distended, watery and concave, as if seen through a prism. In this slow protracted seemingly endless and cyclical time of Chautauqua Falls, how could there be any time *other*?

In the sixteenth week another craniectomy was performed, and tiny blood vessels cauterized, to reduce swelling. Again, to his dismay, she had to be put on a respirator, her left nostril cruelly distended. An aspirator too was hooked into her mouth, making a continuous sucking noise and preventing saliva from accumulating in the back of her mouth and drowning her. To all eyes save his her sleep was deep and profound as an inky sea into which one might fall, and fall, and fall, and never touch bottom. Yet he was stubborn. The long ordeal had, in a way, strengthened his faith. He knew what he knew. And he knew that she knew. Gripping her skeletal fingers in his and occasionally feeling—he swore, he did not imagine this!—their spasmodic pressure against his; that resistance, however fleeting, that signals life, life, life!

Rushing out of the tunnel beneath the stony portal CHAUTAUQUA FALLS 1913, shortly after dawn, was the train. One moment the tunnel was absolute blackness as of a hole gouged violently in the fabric of light itself, the next moment the train blurred with speed. The whistle was deafening, and the clattering iron wheels in their harsh percussive rhythm like some ancient shifting and cracking of the earth's layered rock. Out of the smokestack poured boiling white smoke and vapor, ascending skyward, obscuring the very sun.

She was waiting at the crossing. The locomotive bore down upon her like a great devouring beast but she stood bravely, stubbornly, her head uplifted. She steeled herself for the onrushing clatter to overwhelm her—she was standing only a few feet from the tracks—but instead the train began to slow—in a series of shrieking hisses, the locomotive was braking. The red-haired engineer swung out of the cab to stare at Martha in anger——no, he was smiling—the cap at a jaunty angle on his head, and his eyes shadowed but kindly. Through hissing exhalations of steam he called to her, "Come up, miss! And take care." As Martha trotted breathless alongside the slow-moving locomotive he reached out a gloved hand to her, to grasp; she gave her hand to him, and in a single motion, his other arm securing her, he swung her up into the cab.

And at once the locomotive began to accelerate,

gathering speed as it rushed westward across the trestle bridge.

The call came for him at 7:35 A.M., at home. She'd died within the hour, they'd been unable to resuscitate her. He wept, bitter and aggrieved. He would always so weep, thinking of her, and of this. How, at the end, he'd been nowhere near.

Roach in Loafers

Roberta Lannes

Roberta Lannes lives in Los Angeles, where she works as a teacher, free-lance designer, and graphic artist. Her first published story appeared in Dennis Etchison's 1986 anthology Cutting Edge. *Since then she has had stories published in* Iniquities, Fantasy Tales, Lord John Ten, Splatterpunks, Alien Sex, Pulphouse, Still Dead, Best New Horror, *and* The Year's Best Fantasy and Horror. *She is working on a novel entitled* The Hallowed Bed.

Lannes is best known for her visceral horror so this next story will come as a surprise to many of her fans. It's quirky, and while its titular protagonist may inspire disgust in those biased against certain creepy crawlies, this urbane roach can boast respectable literary ancestry—Don Marquis's archy and mehitabel, *and more recently, Donald Harrington's* The Cockroaches of Stay More. *"Roach in Loafers" is the first of two variations on "The Shoemaker and the Elves."*

Dedicated to William F. Nolan

Roach in Loafers

WHEN ABRAHAM SAPERSTEIN PASSED AWAY, HE left his son Schlomo and his two brothers a tiny Manhattan storefront tailor shop, a half ton of assorted wools, silks, cottons, and polyblends—only half–paid for, and the full debt on two new industrial Pfaff sewing machines. In addition, the legacy included a dwindling clientele and a number of completed custom orders for dead, gone, or unreachable unprepaid customers. Schlomo, the youngest and most naive of the three Saperstein brothers, and the only one with any tailoring experience, took over the shop and its debts. The brothers wished him luck and flew back to their quiet lives out West.

No businessman, it wasn't long before Schlomo was hounded by bill collectors. He found himself penniless and nearly starving. He lost his cramped single walk-up in Brooklyn, and the two sewing machines were about to be repossessed. His sadness over losing his father still consumed him.

One day, he sat staring out the shop's window onto Lexington Avenue, watching the idle rich and the working middle class glide past. He waved his hand at the smell of rusting racks, rotting fabric, machine oil, and dust so thick it shrouded every surface like a constant rolling fog. This was no gift, this inheritance, Schlomo thought, depressed. This was the black hole of debt and doom.

His stomach grumbled in that nagging way he was growing accustomed to. He spotted a huge cockroach scurrying over the cutting table and sighed.

"How am I going to live? Soon I'll be eating out of Dumpsters, showering at the YMCA. Then I'll be talking wildly to myself, not bathing at all, and making a meal of cockroaches."

The cockroach froze. "The hell you will!"

Schlomo blinked, staring at the cockroach. "Say what?"

"I said, the hell you're going to eat *me*." The accent was thick—Bronx and nasal. A lot like Schlomo's Uncle Nate's.

Schlomo wiped his face with his hand. "Cockroaches are a lower form of life that consume anything and reproduce copiously, but, I am certain, they do . . . *not* . . . talk."

The roach pushed his body into a nearly upright position, his antennae waving about over his head. "Look, my unenlightened landlord, we've been here on this planet for many more thousands of years than you humans. You think in all that time we haven't evolved? Haven't learned the lingo? Come *on*."

Schlomo swallowed hard. Starvation was causing hallucinations. "No. No, it's just that I've never heard a cockroach speak before." *That's it Schlomo*, he thought, *patronize the bug*.

"Why should you? What would possess any of my kind to talk with beings whose sole purpose on the planet is to eliminate us?"

Perfectly logical. "Makes sense." Schlomo scratched his head. A cockroach with a point. What a phenomenal delusion.

"Would you converse with beings who went to great lengths to design snappy motels for those of us who travel—cozy little charmers we checked into, but never left alive? And fast-food restaurants that served lethal meals? Meals so good, you always brought home a doggie bag for the family? Turning thoughtful diners into little *murderers*?"

Schlomo frowned. There was a fault in the roach's passionate diatribe. "I must point out here that if you can understand what we are saying, if you listened to our TV commercials, you'd know better than to use those things."

"And so I stand here today, a testament to that data. But what can I say for those of us who don't watch TV? And we have our idiots, daredevils, and psychos, too, you know."

The cockroach dropped back down onto his eight legs and sauntered over to the edge of the table where Schlomo sat chuckling. "If it weren't for your father's generosity, and his refusal to make use of those satanic devices, my huge extended family wouldn't have thrived here for the last fifty years."

"My father saved you? Intentionally?"

"Saved, schmaved. He didn't do anything heroic, if that's what you're getting at. He just never chased us off, never tried to harm us. And he left out so much food overnight, we've got it stockpiled into the next century."

"Poppa . . ." Schlomo began to cry. How he missed his father. Schlomo wished he hadn't made such a mess of what his father had left him. What a failure he was. Now he was sitting in near-darkness making conversation with vermin. The downward spiral of insanity had begun.

"Hey, kid, maybe, for your father's sake, I could help out in some way."

"What could *you* do for me?" He stopped weeping,

and began contemplating the taste of roach chow.

The cockroach scratched its carapace. "Well, first you gotta do something for me. Make me a wardrobe—the finest clothes and shoes—like you would for a prince, or some other kind of important guy. You know, uptown suits, shirts, ties. Some fine loafers. Maybe a pair of oxfords. And a running suit, with cross-trainers, and some casual wear. I know the Saperstein tailoring. You can do it."

"Outfit you?" Schlomo guffawed. "I'm about to lose my sewing machines, can't afford to feed myself, sleep fitfully if at all, and you want me to design clothing for something one-fifth the size of a G.I. Joe doll?"

"Shit, Schlomo, I'm a fucking big bug. Maybe as big as a fist. Now you've done intricate tailoring on cuffs with those fingers. Embroidered initials on pockets. It's a custom job, man. You . . . *can* . . . do it!"

Schlomo chuckled again. Was he beginning to sound maniacal? He wasn't certain. "Look, as I said, things have been very rough for me lately. Why should I spend what time I have left here making itsy-bitsy clothes for an hallucination?"

Exasperated, the cockroach stood itself up on his sleek black backside. "Okay, *don't* do it. Starve to death. Let your father's dream fade into oblivion. Pass up a chance for love, riches, and peace of mind. It's no sweat off my ass, Schlo. But don't come begging me to do you any favors tomorrow. I'll be gone."

Schlomo watched for moving lips. Cockroaches don't have lips. Yessir, he was going bats, coming completely unhinged. So, why not just go with it, he thought? Perhaps death would be gentler this way.

"All right. All right. I'll do it. But what will you do for me? I need food, now. I need business, now."

"Just leave it to me, my friend. Leave it to me."

Forty-five minutes later, Schlomo snapped awake at

the sound of tapping on the front door window. A delivery man was shivering in the autumn night air, his breath issuing from his lips in great clouds.

"Ah, yeah?" Schlomo opened the door.

"Got a dinner order here for a Mr. Saperstein? It's on Mr. Ogrethal's bill. Tip was included." He handed Schlomo three warm bags of Chinese food. "So long."

Schlomo stared after the delivery man, wondering who in the hell Mr. Ogrethal was. His hunger being paramount, he began ripping open bags, drawing the succulent scents in. The name on the bags read "Woo Sing's." The best Chinese on the island. And the most pricey.

Patting his full stomach, Schlomo realized the food delivery had to have been the cockroach's doing. Somehow. He got the message, hallucination or not. Now, it was his turn to do what he'd promised. Make a VIP's wardrobe for a fucking cockroach.

He yawned expansively, deeply contented. "Ah, well, you don't have anything better to do, Schlo."

The cockroach, who called himself Arch, knew the bowels of Manhattan as well as a cabby knew its streets. Well, a cabby who'd been around twenty years. Arch headed uptown to the office of Carter Ogrethal, entrepreneur and crook. He knew Ogrethal was bilking clients out of heaps of dough, doing 900–phone number scams, trading fake jewels for real ones, and selling phony franchises in remote desert resorts. Arch had spent many an evening in the man's office, nibbling on leftover pastrami sandwiches, and listening to Carter bullshit his clients with aplomb. It was Carter's latest cubic zirconium for diamond switch racket that was particularly attractive to Arch.

First, he turned Ogrethal's lightweight cellular phone over and hopped on "Send." Then he went over the menu from Woo Sing Carter always left on his desk, compiled an order for four for dinner, and called the restaurant. He secured a delivery on Ogrethal's bill to Schlomo. Best that boy have the energy for what he was about to do.

Next, he skittered over to the glass case under the cabinet with the real diamonds and wedged himself under the lid and in. Dozens of sparklers glittered in the dim light. Bracelets, rings, earrings, some set with rubies, sapphires. Arch slipped into two rings he liked especially, and struggled out of the case into the office.

Making his way through larger spaces than usual to accommodate the jewelry, he hurried the three blocks over and a quarter mile up undetected. Exhausted by his journey, he found a niche in the particular office he'd traveled all that distance to find, and relaxed. He felt the clean, radiated heat, and fell promptly to sleep.

Late the next afternoon, leaving his cache behind in a planter, he returned to Saperstein's Tailor Shop. There, awaiting him in two cigar boxes, was the finest wardrobe any cockroach could imagine. Slipping into the four pair of loafers, Arch whistled.

"Whew! These babies even have tassels on 'em. And these ties! Schlomo, if roaches could shop, and afford your prices, you'd be a very rich man." Arch began slipping on the clothing.

Schlomo, dipping into his wealth of leftover Chinese food, mumbled something about hoping that he was happy, now.

"Happy? I've been dreaming of wearing this kind of stuff my whole life. You have no idea just how happy I'm gonna make *you*."

"Yeah? You know, I don't even know your name. You roaches have names?"

"How the hell else we gonna differentiate ourselves? Of course. The name's Arch."

"Arch? That short for anything?"

"You bet. When I was born, Ma looked around the shoe store basement for words she might use to name each of us, and there it was on a box. As big as day. 'Arch Supports.' Has a nice ring to it, eh?"

Schlomo snorted. "It's music."

With that, Arch felt their partnership was sealed.

Angela Bright stood before her father and the entire board of Bright, Lietz, and Bhgsyti. Her incisive speech, lyrical delivery, and superb mock-ups for her ad campaign had clearly dazzled them all. As Arch passed through the boardroom, he, too, listened, and was impressed.

Half an hour later, Walter Bright and his daughter swept into her office. Arch sat resplendent on Angela Bright's desk, wearing a three-piece blue serge suit, with tie and matching handkerchief in a strawberry paisley print. The rings flanked him, one on either side.

"Angela, you were great. A little heavy-handed in the self-praise department . . ."

"Dad, the Rorsch account is my single-handed coup, and this presentation brought them in." She backed up until her beautiful bottom slid onto the desk beside Arch.

"Maybe so, but a good campaign earns itself. God!" Walter Bright spotted Arch sitting there, then reached out for his daughter. "Don't look!" He pulled her gently from away from her desk.

"What?" Angela glanced back over her shoulder, detecting Arch.

Arch bowed as well as his rigid body and graceful legs and arms would allow. "Greetings."

"Holy shit!" Angela wriggled away from her father. "Get a load of *this*." She propped a perfectly formed hip back onto her desk.

Her father balked. "Don't touch it!"

Arch went down on all eights. "Hey, man, I'm no ordinary, crawling diseased piece of rabble here, you know. I'm extraordinary."

Walter whined. "Is this the art department's idea of some new campaign? This talking bug thing? You can bet it costs big, too."

Angela laughed. "I don't think so, Dad." She turned to Arch. One of her flawless eyebrows dipped low over her eye. "So then, Mr. Cockroach, what *are* you?"

Arch cleared his throat. "Well, I *am* a cockroach. One shouldn't deny what one is. I'm also an obedient servant, as well. My master, Mr. Stephen Sharp, has sent me here with a small token of his appreciation for you." He pushed the rings toward her.

"My, oh, my. Look at these, Dad." She took the rings and slipped them onto her long manicured fingers. "Absolute fit."

"Angela, you have no idea where those have been. Why do you touch them?" He wrung his hands, impotently.

Arch nodded. "I'd give them a good rinsing before wearing, Ms. Bright. You don't know where I've been."

She smirked, leaving the rings on her fingers. "Who, then, is this Stephen Sharp? And, my creepy, crawly friend, what does he call you?"

"I'm Arch. And Mr. Sharp is an admirer of your work, and especially of you. He hopes to shower you with more gifts and tokens of his heartfelt emotions."

Walter Bright stopped chewing on his lip to bellow, "What kind of idiot would train a cockroach to ferry costume jewelry to a woman he doesn't have the guts to meet face to face? Angela . . . *think*."

Arch chuckled. "My master does not offer costume jewels to a real woman. Only the real thing for Ms.

Bright. You can have the baubles appraised, sir. In fact, Mr. Sharp has something to offer you, as well. He has an inside track in the commodities market, and the advertising world. He knows when deals are going to be made before the companies are certain. He can help put Bright, Lietz, and Bhgsyti back on top."

"Angela, has one of your suitors decided to play games with us?"

"Daddy, if a roach is capable of intelligent speech, I'm going to listen to it, even if it's telling me the Mets will win the pennant this year." She turned from Arch to her father. "Isn't there just a tiny part of you that's interested in these supposedly hot tips?"

Walter Bright fingered his chin, brow furrowed. "I'm only as curious as the insane businessman in me will allow. And right now, that element does seem to be growing."

Arch settled on a notepad. "How about this tidbit then, for starters. Charles Moody, of Pardi, Moody, and Schrew, just pressed General Products for more money to do an additional series of mock-ups on their Kid-Toys. General is on the verge of moving to another firm, your name having been mentioned. Mr. Sharp suggests you move in while they're slipping away from P.M. and S."

Walter snapped closed his gaping mouth. "How the hell . . . ?"

"Mr. Bright, Ms. Bright, I am capable of infiltrating any place on this island, save joints that pump Raid® into their air-circulation systems. Mr. Sharp, who happens to be a clothing designer and manufacturer, allows me to travel in his stead and sometimes . . . I pick up valuable information. You know?"

Angela slid off her desk, the diamonds sparkling on her fingers. "Well, father, I, for one, am *very* curious."

Walter paced. "What if it's some kind of ruse?"

Arch cocked his carapace. "You're awfully suspicious, sir. I wonder how you've gotten this far if you question every offer with such cynicism."

"You'll pardon my skepticism, Mr. Roach, but it's not every day that a bug, dressed in Armani, saunters into our offices and lays a rap on me."

"Granted." Arch wagged his antennae in sympathy.

"And, I can't help wonder what Stephen Sharp wants for all his efforts."

Angela sidled up beside her father stroking her jaw. "Yes, Dad, you have a point there."

"He wants nothing more than to be helpful, appreciative, loving, and inspirational."

Arch then scurried off the desk and down its side to the lush celadon green carpeting, leaving the Brights in stunned silence.

Schlomo listened to Arch's story with a mixture of awe and incredulity. Now that he was eating regularly, and had a room at the Waldorf, he was sure Arch was not an hallucination. After all, the bug had managed to wrangle the best for him, even if it was on the tab of the mysterious Mr. Ogrethal. But to be vicariously romancing the most beautiful and dynamic young woman in advertising today, along with helping her father regain his leverage, by way of a cockroach? Schlomo kept pinching himself.

"Are you saying that Angela Bright is interested in *me*?"

"Well, I've piqued her interest in one Stephen Sharp. But, by sundown Friday, you will *be* Stephen Sharp."

Schlomo slid his chair away from the cutting table. "I'm living off a stranger, I've got crummy clothes, I've got a failed business, and I'm still emaciated from weeks of starvation. How can I be this great guy?"

"Trust me, kid. Your dad was good to me, and I want to be good to you. First, you've got to stop thinking negatively. Look at it this way, you've got a patron, Mr. Ogrethal. And you're not emaciated, you're slim, like a model. So, you're going to be busy designing and constructing a new wardrobe for yourself. Then, in two weeks, business is going to pick up enormously. Lastly, you're just financially challenged. Soon, you'll have everything you need to be Stephen Sharp. Then you'll meet Angela Bright."

"Meet her." Schlomo stood, began pacing the tiny shop's length. "Arch, you seriously underestimate the attractiveness of human beings if you think she'd meet me and find me even the least bit average-looking."

"I know your potential, Schlo. What are you, some whining, depressive, no-talent, jerkowitz loser?"

Schlomo slammed his fist into the cutting table. "I'm not a loser, dammit! Just down on my luck. Don't even insinuate . . ."

"That's my man!" Arch padded in circles cheering. "Yeah."

When he came to rest, Schlomo stared at him. "Okay, okay. I get it. I'm just not prepared for this. I come from meager beginnings."

"You'll adapt. Look, I've got a list of a hundred things for you to do in the next twenty-four hours. Better take this down."

Schlomo wrote. He was overwhelmed. The expectations far exceeded anything he'd ever even considered. "I don't know . . . What if . . . ?"

"What if you could whistle 'Dixie' out your ass while spinning plates on a stick? Just do it. Worry later." Arch hurried across the table.

"Where're you off to?" Schlomo slumped in his chair.

"I've got some graft to prove, a crook to move, and some product to remove." Arch hurried into the night. "Later."

Arch chose a bracelet and pair of earrings for Angela the next night, a necklace the following night, and something new each night after. Listening in at the six other major competing advertising houses, he gathered more tips for Walter Bright. And most fun of all, was learning that Carter Ogrethal was about to take a fall. Arch wouldn't have to continue making calls to the bunco squad, after all. The timing was excellent. Stephen Sharp was going to need a new office, and soon.

Schlomo stood before the shop's three-way mirror. His hair cut and styled, clothing neatly fitted, nerves rattled, he longed for the simplicity of ignorance and poverty. This incredibly slick guy reflected in the mirror was not Schlomo Saperstein.

He even felt like a new man. The recent influx of megawealthy customers who had suddenly found their former tailors inadequate, brought him so much work, he had to hire a new girl just to do hems and minor alterations. The owner of Dunleavy Towers, Malcom Dunleavy, ordered three custom-tailored suits, and news commentator Regina Scott wanted ten jackets to wear on her show. Both were delighted, and sent him new clients. Schlomo felt accomplished. Deeply satisfied. No, Schlomo was ecstatic.

Arch told him he was finally ready to meet Angela. "You *are* Stephen Sharp, now. Look at you. He's really *you*."

Schlomo straightened. He actually looked sort of handsome, and debonair. The new cut he used when he designed his slacks and jacket, worked. He didn't look like a string bean. Svelte. He looked svelte. He turned from the mirror to the table where his gym bag lay. Inside was a new suit, casual shirt, and Gucci loafers Mr. Ogrethal had donated.

"I . . . I'm nervous. I look at myself, what I'm about to do, and I think . . . I'm not a self-made man. I was made by a fucking cockroach. Then I cringe."

"Hey, Stephen . . . *you* did it. I couldn't mold a marble statue out of dog turds." Arch climbed up the side of the gym bag, his feelers gesticulating toward the street. "The limo's here. Let's go."

"Limo? We can walk to the health club from the hotel. It's two blocks!"

"Walk, schmalk. You're Stephen Sharp now. He doesn't walk anywhere. He doesn't have to."

Schlomo shrugged. "Got it."

Sliding into the leather seat out of the rain, a chauffeur shut the door. Inside the limo, he felt different. Sharper. Sharp. Stephen Sharp.

The steam room was nearly empty when Stephen Sharp padded in. Walter Bright sat alone in a corner.

"I hope I'm not bothering you, sir, but aren't you Walter Bright?"

The man sat up, squinting in the steamy air. "I am. And who are you?"

"Stephen Sharp, sir. My apologies for not meeting you in the flesh, sooner." He chuckled, since they were both half-naked.

"Stephen Sharp! I was beginning to think you were a phantom. I have to tell you every tip you've sent over has panned out. We're billing in the millions again. You've been . . . well, how can I thank you?"

"Your joy is thanks enough. I admit, I'm interested in Angela. Perhaps you could speak highly of me, favor me with your praise . . . but only if you find me deserving." Arch had worked with him on that line for hours.

"I think those rocks you keep sending her are going a long way toward speaking for you. And your messenger . . . Arch? How'd you ever get a cockroach to talk?"

He chuckled. "Well, Arch learned English on his own. I just improved his wardrobe and manners."

"Well, regardless, we're grateful. Can you join us for dinner at the penthouse tonight?"

"This evening? I suppose I could. I'm anxious to meet Angela, formally."

"Done. Meet me in the locker room. I'll go phone Angela right now."

Stephen Sharp sucked in the hot air and heaved a glorious sigh. Step one, done.

Once in the locker room, Stephen let Walter come looking for him. Stephen had on the new sporty suit and had his hair combed just right. When he found Stephen, Mr. Bright waxed volumes over the fantastic cut and color of the suit. He wanted a "Stephen Sharp" suit just like it in a steel blue.

"Angela will be impressed. I'm certain."

The praise was delicious. As they slipped into their respective limos, Schlomo Saperstein disappeared for good.

Arch crawled out during the limo ride. "We're all set. Just be your simple wonderful self, Stephen Sharp, and the world is yours."

"I don't know how you did all this, but I owe you far more than I can imagine. How will I repay you?"

"Just keep me around. I have aspirations to be a cockroach of privilege, myself."

Stephen grinned. "I'd shake your hand if I could. You have a deal."

The Brights lived on the top floor of a building facing Central Park. Walter waited for Stephen in the foyer, patting the young man on the back upon his arrival.

"Angela is beside herself. I phoned her from the limo. To be honest with you . . ." They entered the elevator, the operator nodding at Walter Bright. "We were afraid that you were on the disfigured side, or quite unattractive, because you remained out of sight for so long. Angela was pleased to hear you're a rather pleasant-looking fellow."

"Your honesty is well-taken. I would have made a similar assumption. I'm glad I meet with your approval."

"Ah, yes." Walter Bright was fawning. It felt odd.

Angela opened the door, though two maids hurried about behind her. She was smiling.

"Mr. Sharp."

"Ms. Bright. Finally." He took her hand and kissed it. That was how he first noticed she was wearing an abundance of diamond jewelry. She had on eight rings, six bracelets and two necklaces. She stroked the rocks every chance she got, thanking him profusely. It was definite fashion overkill, Stephen noted. When he knew her better, he'd tell her one of each piece would do. They settled in for drinks in the parlor and chatted on amicably.

Dinner was a success. Angela was obviously smitten, and Walter clearly appreciative. Stephen invited Walter over for a fitting in his design office on Monday, and Angela begged to come along. When she heard that Regina Scott wore jackets by Sharp, she wanted Stephen to make up some suits for her, as well. All the way home, Stephen Sharp prayed that Arch had secured the famous office space.

The sound of handcuffs going on Carter Ogrethal's wrists made Arch grin. Thursday night. Right on schedule. The FBI moved almost every stitch of material evidence out of the office, leaving only a desk, the fine art on the walls, and the leather furniture. A huge palm tree was left after an agent sifted through the dirt.

Arch grinned at the simple brushed aluminum nameplate on the door. He hadn't invented Stephen's name out of the blue. Carter had called his organization Sharp Enterprises, Inc. Only he hadn't been sharp enough to fool a cockroach.

Arch got on the cellular phone, also conveniently left behind. Quickly, before Ogrethal's credit cards were frozen, Arch had some serious ordering to do.

Saturday morning, before his date with Angela to go riding at the Bright estate in the Hamptons, Stephen went to survey his new office. Arch had warned him he'd hired some staff sight-unseen, over the phone, and hoped they would work out. They were to be waiting in the office for Stephen's training and approval.

Both of his sales reps were fine. Charming and pushy and in awe of a boss with well-dressed, speaking cockroach. His codesigner was an anorexic, waxen-skinned punker with mahogany red hair. She showed him her work, which was surprisingly conservative. He was impressed. She figured if he could get a cockroach to talk, Stephen Sharp was God. He didn't much care for the secretary, a fleshy matron who dressed too dowdily. Stephen told her Arch would take her shopping. When she realized that meant she'd be going to Bloomingdale's with a roach, she quit. Stephen would have to interview someone Monday morning.

The weekend sailed by, Stephen lolling in the company of the Brights, while Arch enjoyed the local orthoptera. On their way back into Manhattan, Arch told his friend that the eight-legged locals didn't have

the Bronx twang he had. They spoke with the elo-
quence of the butlers and maids they ran from. Arch
observed it was now time to lose his accent.

"We both'll have to adapt, Arch," Stephen told him.

"That's just too bad, eh?" They both fell back laughing.

Angela sat staring into the stylebook offered by one
of the sales reps while Stephen fit Walter for a suit.
Arch made an exception from his nocturnal ways to
join everyone. He sat on the desk munching crumbs
from cookies.

"Daddy, I want one of everything. This stuff is perfect for Wall Street, Madison Avenue, or any corpo-
rate environment, for that matter."

Walter turned away from Stephen. "That sounded
like the ad exec speaking." He grinned at his daughter. "I'm sure he's expensive, so go easy."

Angela batted her eyelashes at Stephen. "If I want
all of these, can we work out a deal?"

Stephen smiled. "I think we can come up with some
equitable arrangement."

Walter leaned close to whisper. "I hope you want
to marry my daughter, Stephen, because I see a beautiful merger here."

Stephen glanced over at Arch, then back to Walter.
"Nothing would please me more."

"Then ask her, man. Ask her."

Stephen set down his chalk and pins, and went to
Angela. Arch slumped, stuffed and weary, against the
cookie plate, listening.

"Angela, if you'll have me, I'd like to give you a
wardrobe for a wedding present. Would you marry
me?"

She leapt up, shrieking, "Oh, Stephen, yes. Yes!
Daddy, can we marry? Oh, Stephen, I *adore* you."

When she stopped hopping madly about, Stephen

held her. He looked into her pale green eyes, and saw forever there. "I love you, Angela."

Arch made his way to the mirrors. As the couple kissed and cooed, he was busy doing business with Walter, asking if he might consider helping Stephen buy up a little tailor's shop on Lexington Avenue. To expand, since he was so damned busy now.

Walter sat down, considering Arch. "You know, that might just be the perfect wedding present. You know the broker?"

Arch crossed his bottom four legs. "Do I know the broker . . . ?"

So began negotiations between the advertising mogul and the roach in fine loafers.

And Angela and Stephen? They lived happily, healthily, and profitably ever after.

Naked Little Men

Michael Cadnum

*Michael Cadnum has published nine novels in-
cluding* Saint Peter's Wolf, Ghostwright, Calling Home, Skyscape, *and* Taking It. *He has
also published several collections of poetry, most
recently* The Cities We Will Never See. *He
lives in northern California.*

*Cadnum's short fiction is generally lighter
than his novels and often wickedly funny. His
story in* Black Thorn, White Rose, *"You Can't
Catch Me"—told from the gingerbread man's
point of view—is fast and furious and utterly
deadpan in its humor. In "Naked Little Men," a
second variation on "The Shoemaker and the
Elves," Cadnum slows down a bit, but his humor
is intact.*

Naked Little Men

MY HUSBAND COMPLAINED.
He came from a country of complainers, tree country; you can find people by following the far-off sounds of complaints drifting through the woods. You get there and feasting is in progress, huge cheeses and jugs of beer, fat, red-cheeked folk, all of them complaining.

Where's the shade? How many do you have—I don't have as many. Why wasn't it this warm last year? Look at her face and then look at mine. Without a pause for breath. I was raised in the city, with its canals and free expressions of courtesy. Among these country people I was always pleasant, and I learned to complain in a modest way. There was always a little skin on the cream or bubbles in the Gouda, something, but you had to be inventive. Things were close to perfect except for the sour expressions of the Complaint-folk.

My husband even sang complaint ballads, songs about how terrible it was in the wind, and in the sun and in the moonlight; how awful everything was. He was a man who wouldn't hang *cobbler* on his eave, it had to be *shoemaker*. He wanted the silk gown trade to walk in and see him sitting there complaining about the light, or the rain, or the way I always answered him so politely that he had trouble making out the words. Out in the middle of field and oak, he wondered where the customers were, pricking his finger every time he looked up to squint at the door.

But while he was complaining he was looking, and when he looked he saw his new wife and his hides on the table, and out the doorway he saw a goose and a puddle and a pasture with three cows. When he looked out the window he saw a puddle and a bucket. And trees. He saw trees, trees everywhere, leaves, branches, moss, bark.

Not one of the trees with a foot needing a sole. He'd rub tallow on the hinges of the shoemaker sign so it didn't creak. He'd complain as loudly as he could how busy he was, so people could hear him in the road. But no one visited the shop. Sometimes a new load of hides arrived, the carter yelling about how far it was all the way out here. It would be triple the price next time, he had no idea, he would say, a city man taking up one of the local habits.

A city woman myself, I've never been good at it. I can't help it. *Good morning* comes out of my mouth quicker than *What are you looking at?*

Shoemaker to the Trees I used to call him and he would make one of his birdlike laughs, because we did have a cozy time or two, me showing him how to wrestle a cutpurse to the ground and hurting his back that time. It's not my fault he's a slip of a man and my mother gave birth to a crop of daughters made to lift and carry.

But we had to move to town, and when we did he wanted a house all eaves, with *shoemaker* hanging off each one of them. It had to be a house down by the market, too, costing half a year's goose-throttling just to pay the landlord to let us have the place until spring (and would he please take the pigs out of the back room—we need to sleep there, the loft full of hides).

So there we were in town. He was complaining just as well as ever, the song about the blue sky so bare it made him empty, and the one about how the bones in his body made him think of bones, and all the other old tree-country songs. I just let him sing, quiet-like, not my only nature, but one of them. City people can open a door and we can shut it, I always say, meaning we can close a mouth when we have to.

But it was a terrible thing, that winter. Not to lift my voice in sorrow or self-pity, but the sparrows froze hard on the slate roofs and the pigeons drifted in the wind, little feet stiff so you could pick them up, squabs flat on one side roasting just as well as the round ones used to.

But soon there weren't any bones in the street, not for dog or man, and the grain we kept in the sacks had sprouted and died already, one year come and gone in the opinion of this particular barley. We had sackcloth bread. We had street-gleaning bread. We had spit-and-cold-air bread, until my husband had traded his last whole hide for a cheese knob and a pot of mustard, the poor fool (too hungry, his judgment gone, I didn't say anything).

We went to bed with a scrap of leather left on the bench, yellow skin fit for one shoe, maybe two if the hand that stitched it stretched as it worked. This was not a country bench, either. It was one of the new city benches, ash and yew, rubbed to a color you'd call pretty if you didn't know it cost the tanned suits of two bullocks just to get it in the door, three to get it pegged together, plus a loaf to the carriers for their pains.

Were we hungry? Not a bit. Hunger had been nine weeks before, when we were eating stick-shaving soup. Hunger had been ten weeks past when we were chewing cat's gristle and calling it sweet.

Hunger would come if we had sat and eaten four days, hour after hour, until we awoke to the beginning of what a normal healthy human being would have started to feel an inkling of. Which would have been hunger.

And cold. Husband like an iron chair in my arms—don't ask about the cold. If it had been cold, we would have been roiling in our sweat. Cold would have had us sunning in our smallclothes. With a fire crackling and all the chinks stopped, heated up for days, we would have ascended to the level we could start to shiver, the shivering long since frozen from our bones.

We slept well that night. There was not a sound.

The next morning when I could open my eyes there he was, a husband driven mad, hunger mad, bleak-winter-sun and empty-future mad, laughing and dancing. All I could think was: where was the priest who was big enough to wrestle a devil out of a man? Was he still living or had he died, too, of the frost?

So I had to pick my husband up myself and give him a little shake. When he woke he was laughing again, saying *shoes*, *shoes*, the poor man, the last word he knew.

When I crept into the shop there was a pair. Lovely, and neat-stitched, not a slip. The sole fine-wrought, Flemish-fit, we call it, the craft most shoemakers skip, mine included, costing too much time. The collar, the tongue, the buckle, all the breath-smooth work you can imagine, and balanced in the hand.

I was a little afraid. I stood there, eyeing the solid bar at the door, the bolted shutters, all of it secure. What happens when the wonderful happens is you think: who did this? And why? I could not meet my husband's eye.

We sold it to the first man in, a silk-capped traveler. A cur had torn his boot. The traveler went from surly to smiles in a trice, slipped them on, and marched away, leaving a palm weighted with gold coin.

Forgive me for sparing the details, the glee, the happy embrace, because we had our joy, this slip of a man and I. We scurried about, bought new hides. And we ate. We lunched on cabbage and eel, and supped on cakes and sow's cheeks. No neighbor could afford such food. It was all so much after fasting so long that sleep was all we hungered for by dark.

The next morning, half-hoping, we were nearly afraid to make our way from the bed. We tiptoed, afraid to speak.

There was a shop full of shoes. There were shoes of every kind: slippers, boots, lady's and lady's maid's and gentleman's guard's shoes and children's first-soles, and all of it matchless. And customers to follow within the hour, a shop full of dazzled, top price–paying folk.

It was my idea.

A city woman, I know what is called for, a thanks to the benefactor, return a smile with smiling. Not for me the country manner, trading a curse for a greeting, a fist for a wave.

"Let's see who does this," I whispered. "Just tonight, hide and look."

The little knot of a man trembled, big-eyed. I implored him, swearing that I knew this was the way to bond good fortune to our future. He finally agreed, shaking his head. And lurking in the feed shelves, hunched up, we saw nothing. Our knees hurt. Our elbows ached. Nothing happened, the watchman bawling the hours in the street.

And then they came.

Some people ask. They want to know. *Oh, tell*, they say. *Oh, say what you saw.*

Naked little men.

There were two. It was a shock, needless to add. It was a sight, the creatures built as men are, town and field, but shameless. You could see their all, but not their fingers, so fast they were a twinkle of needle. They were so quick that in the time a man would take to clear his throat a sole would be attached.

"Tonight we'll thank them," I said when we were alone.

"Thank them!" gasped my little husband, all callous and effort, when he wasn't buoyed by a good round of complaint. This hadn't happened for a while, now; he was not himself, so happy.

Linen is made for my hands. Flax grows looking forward to my needle. What a little naked man can do with thread and leather I can with needle and a cloth, though slow, being human and far from small.

These were breeches and blouses for a king's courtiers, matching, Lincoln green, and caps to fit, the suits for gentlemen, if gentle people came as big as kittens.

My husband the shoemaker said what they needed was a good cursing, a man to say, "Who asked you to sit on my bench?" He said we should act annoyed; they would come back out of spite, just to bother. They did have laughs like blades through kidskin, not music, I can tell you. Or ignore them, he suggested, let them think we tolerate their handicraft, not that we depend on it.

The story goes around that the naked little men put on the clothes, found them delightful, sang a song, danced, and left us to our lives and to ensuing greater happiness.

I am proud, but no more than is required to learn from a night's events. What took place defies faith.

The naked little men seized the clothes and laughed, but it was not the sort of laughter that pleases. Hand to mouth and holding breath, I saw them mock my efforts. They put trousers on their heads, shirtsleeves up one leg. They hopped about, excited in ways I will not describe, except to refer to barnyard matters.

They left us to our winter, which was far from finished.

My husband makes do. His reputation is enough to carry him, although talk is that he has slipped a little in his craft. They say it's the amount of business he does now, with two apprentices and a wife who lets the porridge cool before she calls him.

My husband is happy enough, but he is quiet. My private hope is that my husband will complain again some day. That he will say how terrible it is that walls, and roofs, and land and folk are around at all just to vex him. My hope is that he'll sing the song about the sun, how dull, and the fool, how right, and the beggar should be king for all the sense there is in life.

My hope is he'll complain that nasty little creatures have no business lending hands. My prayer is he'll grumble so loud and so long his voice will carry, through the shutters and the city gates. He will complain so eloquently how fine life is without their tiny needles that they will come again to hear him curse each morning.

And stay.

Brother Bear

Lisa Goldstein

Lisa Goldstein is one of the best of the current generation of fantasists. Her first novel, The Red Magician, *won the Amerian Book Award, and she went on to follow up that early promise with* The Dream Years, A Mask for the General, Tourists, Strange Devices of the Sun and Moon, *and* Summer King, Winter Fool. *Her stories have recently been collected in* Travellers in Magic.*

"Brother Bear" takes off from the English tale about that infamous usurper "Goldilocks," and adds elements from Native American legends and from "animal bridegroom" folk tales that can be found in cultures around the world. The original is usually told in a humorous tone. "Brother Bear" is quite serious, even with its fantasy elements, as it illumines the crucial relationship between bear and human in Native American culture.

Brother Bear

THE TRIBE CAME DOWN FROM THE SCRUBBY HILLS and saw the long tree-covered plains stretching before them. They had not eaten in three days. They were tired from the long trek and burdened with knives, spears, furs, and babies, but they hurried toward the promise of food.

The girl they called Quick ran to one of the trees and pulled down an apple, and the others followed. When they had eaten their fill they rested among the trees and looked around them. It was late in the season; the leaves had started to turn gold and red and the wind carried the sweetish smell of apples starting to rot. Despite the wind, though, it was hot. Flies buzzed around the bruised fallen apples.

The elders looked back toward the hill they had come down and saw ledges and overhangs, enough to shelter them when the heavy rains came. "Home," one said, and waited to see if anyone would argue. No one did. The strongest men and women in the tribe carried the knives and sleeping furs to the foot of the hillside.

They slept there that night. In the morning some of the men went hunting, and the women and children and old men gathered up apples and roots near the hillside. In the evening the hunters returned with kill, a small deer and two rabbits.

After they had eaten, some of the hunters stood and danced, showing how they had stalked across the plain, how the deer had bounded from them, how their spears had brought it down. The tribe laughed and applauded, moved to joy by their good luck. "Apples, roots, deer," someone sang. "Fur and meat," another sang. "Fur and meat."

One of the dancers rounded his shoulders and shambled back and forth across the sleeping place. The tribe grew quiet. The hunters had found bears. They had seen bears before, but always from a distance, and always the bear had been too quick and strong for them to bring down. A bear would give meat for a long time, and fur to keep out the cold that pierced like spears.

Some of the people cried out and sang—"Fur and meat, fur and meat!"—but the elders shook their heads. Bears were canny, chancy.

The night grew cold. Stars shone in the darkness, the strange night world they had never reached no matter how far and long they traveled. They huddled close together among the deer furs and slept.

The next day was the same. Quick went out with the tribe to pull roots from the earth, stopping every so often to sit and eat what she had found. A beetle scurried up a tree trunk and she snatched for it, brought her dirt-covered hand to her mouth.

When she turned she saw that she was alone. A little frightened, she glanced around for the rest of the tribe. Far off in the distance she could see some of the women bending and pulling roots, their yellow hair shining in the sun. She laughed, comforted. She looked up to the blue sky, to the sun coming through the branches of the trees, and she laughed again.

Her happiness reminded her of the tribe the night before, and she began to sing: "Fur and meat. Fur and meat." She walked farther along the foot of the hill.

The sun went down. The shadows of the trees grew longer, tangled with each other on the ground. Birds called, and from somewhere she heard the snarl of a large cat.

Her fear was still there, but it had been joined by curiosity. What was around the next bend? And the next? She felt called, pulled by something outside herself. She had had her first blood, and her initiation, and since then she had felt many new things, thrilling and strange.

And look—here was a deep overhanging ledge, better than the one her tribe had found, almost a cave. And scattered berries, and places to sleep that were sheltered from the wind.

She realized she was hungry. She ate several handfuls of berries before she found some that weren't either rotten or sour. These were wonderful, plump and sweet and full of juice.

When she finished she licked the sticky juice from her chin. The stars were out again, the small lights of the far land. She yawned. The tribe would worry about her, hit her, probably, if she came home after dark. But it was too late to return. She would go back in the morning, show them the cave she had found. Maybe if they liked it, they would not be angry with her.

She tried two or three sleeping places before she found one that was warm and comfortable. She stretched out in the dark and slept.

She awoke to a noise. A voice, low and rumbling. It was not one of the tribe and she sat up, suddenly afraid.

"Berries gone," the voice said.

"Who?" said another voice.

"Who?" said a third.

"Berries gone," the first voice said again.

"Look," said the second.

"Here," said the third.

In the dim light of the stars the girl saw three bears ranged around her. They smelled sharp and wild and frightening, like the sweat of the men when they came home from a good hunt, but also like the smell of the animal they brought back. Her heart pounded.

"Who?" one said.

"Quick," she said, giving them her tribe's name for her. "Who?" she asked.

The third bear growled. "Swift salmon catcher in cool streams in morning," he said. A moment later she understood it was his name.

"Mine," the third bear said. His huge paw pushed her against the cave wall; then he dropped to the ground next to her and curled up to sleep.

She saw that she had taken his sleeping place. She moved closer to the wall and made herself as small as possible. She slept fitfully, thinking of his huge claws, his muscled hide. Once he snorted and rolled over and she stood quickly, terrified that he would crush her.

She woke to feel a rough hand on her back and she turned to face him. Not a hand, paw. The bear had been stroking her yellow hair.

"Quick," he said. He continued to stroke her, her small breasts, her belly, her golden fur below that. He growled low in his throat.

She shrank away from him. His paw returned to her hair, twining the strands in his claws. In the morning light she could see his brown, matted fur against the bright hair that she shared with all her tribe. She understood that he was trying to be gentle, but he pulled at her hair and hurt her. "Oh!" she said.

The bear growled again, soothingly. It sounded like

crooning, like the deep singing of the tribe. His great paws moved to her skin, and he caressed her more softly than before. She felt herself opening to him, the way she had opened to a boy in the tribe after her first blood came.

She ran her hands over his warm fur, dug her fingers deeply into it. He smelled comforting now, stronger and more powerful than the scent of the tribe.

He entered her with great tenderness. His growling became louder; he sounded fierce, even angry. She clung to him, terrified and exhilarated at the same time.

He gave one final cry and rolled away. She felt cold after his protective warmth, and burrowed into the fur of his back.

She slept. When she woke her bear was no longer next to her but with the others at their morning meal. He motioned to her to eat. She felt a great tenderness toward him; perhaps this was what others in her tribe had called love.

She did not go back to her tribe that day, or the next. Her love for the bear grew, and was returned. She understood that she had married him, the way men and women in her tribe sometimes married. "Brother Bear," she called him now, whispering to him late at night. "Brother Bear."

Her life with the bears was not very different from what she had known. During the days she gathered roots and berries. At night she ate with the bears and listened while they told their stories, strange murmuring tales of wind and rain and running water, of long sleeps and small creatures who hunted and were hunted in their turn. The stories would continue from night to night, one great dreamy tale with no beginning and no ending.

The blood that visited her every moon had stopped,

and she wondered if she were turning into a bear-woman. She studied her arms and legs for fur, ran her fingers over her teeth for sharpness, but nothing seemed changed.

The days became colder, and the bears' fur grew thicker and heavier. One day when she woke she saw that they still slept. She poked and prodded each one in turn but could not rouse them. She burrowed into the warmth of Brother Bear and went back to sleep.

She slept for a long time, waking only to eat some of the food the bears had stored for winter. It was a strange, confused time; she dreamed vast dreams like the tales the bears had told, and when she woke she could not tell what was true and what was not. Sometimes she was back with the tribe, singing and dancing, sometimes with her new family. Several times she saw a small bear, a cub, running toward the entrance to the cave.

When she awoke fully it was warm outside. The apple trees had put forth small leaves and the air smelled fresh, new. She blinked, delighted by the warmth and light.

She started to roll over but was stopped by something in the way. She looked down and saw that her stomach had rounded out, grown huge. Then she knew what she had been aware of in a dreamy way all winter: she would soon give birth to a bear cub.

The birth pains started a few weeks later. Her bear stroked her stomach while she screamed and panted, and when the cub emerged in a gush of blood he bit the cord that connected them. He gave her the cub and she held it, but then he growled and took it away. One of the other bears, a female, came and licked the fur clean.

When the cub had been washed they saw that it was a male, and that the fur was golden, like her hair.

She reached for him, lifted him to her breast. He bit once, hard, before he began to suck.

The seasons passed. She and her bear had another child, a daughter, golden like the first one. She foraged with the tribe, slept huddled with them during the cold winter months. The cubs grew quickly. She had named them Sweet and Beauty, though she had noticed that the bears had much longer names for each other.

One day the long evening tale changed. "Men," one of the bears said. "Small men with rocks."

Their interest quickened. "Men where?" another said.

The first stood and walked upright a few steps in imitation. The bears growled low in anticipation.

"Hurt," Quick's bear said. "Rocks hurt."

"Blood," another bear said. "Blood and hurt."

The bears lifted their muzzles in a keen.

The next day while she was out gathering roots she saw a small shape beyond the trees. It looked strange, like a badly formed cub. Then she remembered the bears' story the night before, and she realized that it was a person, like her. She had nearly forgotten people in her years with the bears.

Over the next few days they all saw the man, or another like him. She wondered if her old tribe had returned, but she felt no curiosity or desire to visit them. Her place was here, with Brother Bear and their children.

The people grew bolder. Every day they came closer to the bears' cave, and every evening the bears told the same story, danced the same man-dance.

One day while searching for roots she heard someone shout. She turned quickly. "Quick!" a man said. "Quick?"

The man looked familiar. Older now, and taller, but still—yes. One of the tribe, a man who had been a boy when she had left. "Wolf," she said. They had named him that for his skill at the hunt.

"Quick!" Wolf said again. He came closer. "Quick not dead! Quick not dead!"

She backed away. "Quick dead," she said. She meant that the person Wolf and the tribe had known had gone beyond returning. Wolf looked puzzled. "Quick gone."

He stepped toward her again. "Quick here," he said. "Bear here. Bear, fur and meat." Other men from the tribe joined him. They sniffed the air and raised their spears and throwing knives.

"No," Quick said.

"Yes," Wolf said. "Smell bear. Fur and meat."

"No."

He moved closer, stopped. He scented the air again, and Quick knew that she was the bear he smelled. She had lived with the bears for so long that she had taken on their odor.

"Quick bear?" he asked unwillingly.

"Yes. Quick bear."

"No. Quick person."

"No. Bear brother. Bear tribe."

"No." He raised his spear again and turned quickly. She followed. Brother Bear had come out of the cave and was heading toward them.

"No!" she said. Too late, her bear saw what was happening and tried to back toward the cave. Wolf and several of the others threw their spears. Two hit the bear in the chest and one in the shoulders, and he dropped heavily.

"Fur and meat!" Wolf said, exultant. "Fur and meat!"

More bears came from the cave, growling. One reached out with his paw and swiped at a hunter who had come too close. The hunter fell.

Quick's eyes filled with tears. She heard screams

and growls, and keening from both groups of hunters. Someone shouted a command. Someone else—she could not see if it was bear or man—lifted her and carried her away. She closed her eyes.

She opened them a long time later. She was in a cave; Wolf and a few of the others were leaning over her. Many hands caressed her, and someone gave her water to drink. She saw that one of the hunters, the one who had come too close to the bears, was not there; perhaps he had been killed. She did not know how to think about that.

"Quick?" Wolf asked. "Why cry?"

She shook her head and closed her eyes again. She wished she could sleep for the next few moons, sleep as if it were winter.

She woke to the smell of meat. She looked around; the tribe had removed the bear's skin with knives and was carving the flesh. She shuddered, sickened.

Someone was speaking, one of the elders. "Brother Bear," she said. "Our tribe and your tribe now one tribe, our flesh now one flesh. We thank Brother Bear for his fur and meat, as he thanks us for ours." She cut a piece of meat and held it to Quick. "We thank Quick. We thank Brother Bear. We thank our tribes."

Quick understood. Because she had bound herself to the bear for life, because she had had his children, her tribe and the bear tribe were tied together forever. Hunter and hunted, eater and eaten, they would be one flesh for the lives of their children, and their children's children, without end. Each would eat of the other; their abundance toward each other would never fail.

She had seen to it that the tribe would never starve. She could not eat of the flesh of her husband, but she had made a bargain that would outlast eternity.

The Emperor Who Had Never Seen a Dragon

John Brunner

John Brunner is a British science fiction writer best known for his prescient novels Stand on Zanzibar, The Sheep Look Up, Shockwave Rider, *and the fantasy cycle* The Compleat Traveler in Black. *This prolific author has also published thrillers, mainstream novels, and volumes of poetry. He has won the Hugo Award, the British Science Fiction Award, and the French Prix Apollo.*

In recent years, Brunner has written several fine fantasy stories, some of which have appeared in The Year's Best Fantasy and Horror.

About "The Emperor Who Had Never Seen a Dragon," he says, "As I have learned from my beloved wife LiYi, many Chinese tales concern the overthrow of unjust rulers. Especially popular are those whose moral is that common people need not slave forever under an imperial yoke, but rather seek a chance to liberate themselves. Here's an example. One with dragons in it . . . ."

The Emperor Who Had Never Seen a Dragon

"BUT I," SNARLED THE EMPEROR INTO SUDDEN SI-lence, "have never seen a dragon."

Time hesitated, then stumbled backward in the guise of memory. Before those words:

Alert to a change in their master's mood, brought on perhaps by his latest draught of red sorghum wine—alert because those who attended him must be preternaturally so or risk waking in the morning shorter by a head—General Chou Li-yen signaled their unwilling host, the abbot of this temple, to interrupt what passed for entertainment to accompany their communal meal. It consisted of an old monk from the attached monastery reading aloud stories about legendary nobles from the ancient scrolls that formed the temple's chief treasure. Not that he could, in fact, be reading very much by the dim light of the stinking butter-fed torches that were necessary in this almost-windowless hall, although outside it was only late afternoon, and his filmed and bloodshot eyes made it still more likely that he was reciting from memory.

Though he mocked it as looking like piss with blood in, the emperor was not stinting himself of the wine here. He raised his empty cup without even glancing round. Over his shoulder the one of his four personal attendants whose turn it was today to taste his food and drink poured more. The emperor drained the replenished cup at a gulp, hurled it across the table so that it scattered dishes and goblets like a ball striking skittles, and stormed out of the hall, his escort at his heels. There was a long pause, and, finally, a sigh of relief.

"Why this sudden outburst about dragons?" the abbot whispered.

"How should I know?" Chou retorted. "I'm not in his confidence. I only serve him because I must." Then, realizing he had made a potentially damaging admission, he hastened to cover it with a pleasantry. "Maybe your wall paintings proved too much for him."

Many of them depicted dragons, that was true. Religiously (and that was a precise term in the context) maintained by dedicated priests who renewed every damaged part by turns, though they were said to be a thousand years old, they looked as fresh as yesterday. The fact had elicited coarse comments from the emperor. But once or twice a draft making shadows waver had startled even the hard-headed Chou.

The abbot, though he smiled, did not let amusement reach his eyes. He went on waiting for a substantial answer. The general summoned his depleted reserves of politeness.

"Oh! Because, though the stories we have been listening to are in an archaic style, your interpreters have made it clear through their admirably comprehensible summaries that most of them concern the power which righteous rulers wielded in the distant past thanks to the favor of such beings, not to mention tortoises and phoenixes."

The abbot nodded, but still looked expectant. Chou, who had been strict with himself thus far, decided that after drinking so much the emperor was unlikely to reappear before tomorrow, possessed himself of a half-full wine cup, and emptied it before continuing. The contents turned out to be powerful stuff. His assumption about the emperor seemed more probable than ever.

"Because, moreover," he resumed, "he hates being under a stone roof. He belongs to a people who regard buildings like this as little better than caves, the lairs of wolves and bats. To them, a shelter is what you make yourself and carry with you."

The abbot, who was a very brown, very short man with deep wrinkles around his eyes, gave a wise nod. "A plainsman," he said. "Why does he come to these mountains where he feels so miserable?"

"The same reason he got angry about dragons."

"I suspect I know what you mean," the abbot murmured. "But I wish to clarify." He gave a near-imperceptible signal and Chou found his cup brimming anew.

Well, the wine was surprisingly good, considering what a backwater they were in. Not a city, not even a town in the strict sense—just a hill with this largish temple perched on it, and a surrounding settlement of peasants turned tradesmen who earned enough to support a remarkable number of smaller temples. He had seen while the army was undertaking its symbolic sack of the place. The authorities (which basically meant the abbot) had cheated the troops of most of their fun by offering no resistance.

So he muttered thanks and drank again. And said, feeling the warmth of the liquor perfuse his body,

"Oh, you know as well as I do, abbot! Why, he as much as admitted it!"

"He is"—delicately—"aware of being a usurper, and cannot bear to rule less than his predecessor did legitimately. That is what you are implying?"

Chou permitted himself a vulgarism.

"And—"

"And the drunker he grew the more he was able to convince himself that you were mocking him for not being a proper emperor." Chou spat out bitter dregs found at the bottom of his goblet, but waved away an eager novice offering replenishment. "These plains-dwelling barbarians are remarkably unsophisticated, you know. If they're told that real emperors meet and talk with dragons, that's what they're apt to insist on."

There ensued a gloomy pause. At length Chou hauled himself to his feet.

"My lord and master is going to have one hell of a head when he wakes up. I'd better be prepared for—Why! Your Highness!" He improvised a sketch for a kowtow, which the abbot and his acolytes made haste to imitate.

Leaning on a door pillar, glaring like a dragon himself, the emperor roared, "Who paints your dragons?"

"Ah—Forgive me, but . . ." the abbot stumble-tongued.

"You heard me! *Who paints your dragons?*"

"Well, these in the temple are centuries old, and we only make them good when—"

"I know that!" thundered the emperor. "But while you were showing me around your squalid streets I saw new ones, hear me? New!"

"Ah . . ." The abbot swallowed hard. "Ah. I believe I know what you are referring to."

"You'd better!"

"I think you may mean the work of an old man they call Ling Long."

"Is that his name? 'One who gets to meet dragons!' It's unbearable!"

"Forgive me, but I don't quite—"

The abbot's words were cut short.

"Don't try and fool me!" The emperor took a pace forward, hand falling to his waist in search of the sword he normally wore. But his attendants had prudently removed it.

"In what way do you feel—?"

"In every way!" The emperor stamped his foot. "To think that dragons, the symbol and prerogative of imperial power, come at the beck and call of a painter in a village slum, yet refuse to show themselves to me! Me who am emperor by right of conquest!"

Panting, he set his feet wide astride. For fear he might lose his already-precarious balance, one of his permanent attendants took station on each side of him.

"But, Highness," whimpered the abbot, "painters of dragons do not work from life, from reality!"

"You're trying to tell me these—these artisans are so superior to emperors, they can *invent* images like these on your walls without ever seeing the original?"

"Ah . . . Yes, Highness! Yes!"

"Then you're a sniveling besotted liar, and if you persist in singing the same tune, you'll wind up singing from the top of a sharpened pole! Where is this painter who makes such wild boasts?"

"You mean Ling Long?"

"Yes, the man who by his very name insults his emperor!"

"It isn't really his name, Highness. It's just a nickname bestowed on him because—"

"By acquiescing, he claims acquaintance with dragons! If that's true, he must be able to show one to me!"

"Highness, I—"

"Shut up! Chou! This fool doesn't know that I mean what I say. You do. Don't you?"

The general had cause to remember evidence to that effect, especially how before a certain obstinate city a pyramid of its defenders' skulls had been heaped up, taller at last than had been its crumbling walls. He made a sour obeisance, the more willingly because those never-resting escorts menacingly stroked the hilts of their weapons.

"Find him. Tell him to show me a dragon, or die! And you as well! Bring him here before first light!"

"Highness!" The abbot attempted one last valiant delaying action. "Outside a storm is gathering! It is expected to break before nightfall!"

"What does nightfall mean to me, here in this worthless land of rocks and rubble? What does it mean to you and your monks, who by this time ought to know the way around your alleys by the smells alone? And as for storms—why, rain is called for to cleanse away such muck! Do as you're told!"

He staggered away, pausing after three unsteady steps to hurl an afterthought over his shoulder.

"Failing which, I'll loose my soldiers on the town. The men would relish that, Chou, wouldn't they? Especially access to the women. Not that monks would care about such matters! Rather get up one another's arses, wouldn't you? Well, shit knows where it belongs!"

Crowing with self-satisfied laughter, he finally departed. When the last echo of his drunken cachinnation had faded, the abbot said, "It would appear that the reputation which preceded our new overlord has gained little or nothing in being passed from mouth to mouth. Would he truly give the army license to . . . ?"

"Yes."

"And you, General? Would you?"

"No."

"Why not?"

"I don't believe you can cow people into loyalty. Subservience, maybe. But then you must always trust the retainer who guards your back."

"As he does."

"But they are his men, not mine."

"I think you would make the better emperor."

"I have no such ambitions," grunted Chou. "It was my honest hope to serve well and truly the emperor prescribed for us by heaven."

"And—?" The abbot sounded genuinely interested.

"Was it my fault, or the fault of the diviners who swore it was a favorable day, that on the very field of battle against the barbarian invader pestilence laid low our rightful lord without a warning? That we were left to choose between cooperating with enemies for the moment at a loss thanks to the scale of an unlooked-for victory won by disease, not force of arms, and certain massacre as soon as they reverted to their customary arrogance?"

The abbot pondered a while. He suggested at length, "Contact with the Middle Kingdom has done little to civilize this child of the cityless plains."

"Only insofar as now he calls himself an emperor and demands to meet a dragon....Who is this painter whose name boasts he does so?"

"Ling Long? A poor ragged fool. Lives alone but for a daughter who should have been married years ago. There are many who would cheerfully lodge and feed a father-in-law with his talent."

"And earning power?"

"He could have plenty, were it managed by someone more worldly than his daughter. But she has absorbed his principles. She wouldn't dream of trying to stop him from trading even his finest paintings for barely what the two require for food and shelter. When he receives a windfall he gives alms to beggars, or the priests and monks at one of our temples. He looks like a nobody. Yet . . ."

"Yes?" the general prompted. The abbot spread his hands.

"Yet were you both to walk the streets around his home, you in your general's finery and he in his usual rags, the people would more likely bow to him than you. Sometimes they describe him as an *arhat*." He meant a Buddhist saint.

"And you?"

"Oh, no. Such a term has never been applied to me."

"That wasn't quite what I meant. . . . Never mind. I'd better muster a squad and go looking for him. And pray the rain holds off for a while at least."

"I'll assign one of our novices as a guide. Tian-wu will suit; he's a local boy. I'll tell him to bring umbrellas." The abbot hesitated. "By the way, Ling Long and your emperor have something in common."

"Their preoccupation with dragons?"

"Apart from that."

"Well?"

"An astonishing capacity for sorghum wine."

The sky was darker even than the approach of sunset implied. In principle householders were supposed to set out flambeaux for the benefit of passengers; however, on an evening like this few were inclined to risk them being doused in the downpour that threatened. The abbot had advised Chou's party to carry torches, and they were glad they'd done so. Some of the alleys Tian-wu threaded his way along were so narrow, and so nearly did balconies on either side meet overhead, that they must remain midnight-murky at a summer noon.

As well as the weather, the presence of imperial troops had already cast a general mood of gloom over the populace. The few who were out and about at the moment, late to finish work or trudging home to supper with provisions from a bean curd–seller or a noodle-cook's, shrank aside on seeing armed men approach, while folk who spotted them from windows made haste to close their shutters, announcing in tones meant to be overheard that they were acting thus solely because of the impending storm.

At a crossway irrigated by puddles that, charitably, might have been there since the last rain, or more credibly (being yellowish and foul-smelling) stemmed from an overflowing necessary in one of the adjacent houses, Tian-wu checked in the fastidious act of seeking the shallowest route and breathed, "There goes his daughter!"

"The artist's?" Chou snapped.

"Yes!"

"Arrest her! Make her lead us to him!"

The young monk gave him a puzzled frown. After a moment he said, "But, General, with all respect, she's not a criminal. Is she?"

"Well—uh . . ."

"And her father isn't on the run? He won't be hiding from you?"

"I suppose not." Chou was beginning to feel embarrassed.

"So can't we just ask her to guide us to their home?"

"I suspect," the general said heavily, after a measured pause, "I've spent too long in the company of our new emperor. Carry on."

And indeed as soon as the girl—rather more than a girl, as it turned out: perhaps twenty-six or -eight—learned that the emperor had seen Ling Long's work and wanted to meet him, as Chou tactfully put it, she was downright eager to introduce them. There was no room for all the visitors in the cramped room she shared with her father, she explained, so only Chou and Tian-wu followed her up the rickety stair. Above, they learned the truth of the abbot's charge. The artist was in the very act of filling from a straw-wrapped pottery jar, and not for the first time, a chipped rice-ware bowl. Suspicious on the instant, fearing he might be obliged by courtesy to offer his liquor to these intruders, the old man—who was not in truth very old, just ill clad, dirty, and scrawny, as much of a mess as the room around him—showed barely a hint of relaxation when told that he was summoned by the emperor.

"All very flattering, I suppose," he granted at last. "But I haven't had my supper yet. Girl, where is it? And you needn't think we're going to share with you lot!"—suddenly sharp—"I do that with the poor and the honestly religious. But not fine gentry like you! Not that you'd fancy fare like ours, is my suspicion. And you're not splitting the wine, neither. By the look of you, you can afford your own. I don't mean you, monk . . . Say, your face looks familiar. Do I know you?"

Tian-wu bobbed his head.

"I come to this quarter now and then to visit my honorable grandparents. They worship in the White Jade temple that you embellished with so many splendid images."

Which, if true, Chou reflected, was nearly as surprising in reality as the emperor held it to be in a fit of drunken bad temper. Nothing about this room suggested its tenant was an artist. There were no brushes, no scrolls, no jars of pigment to be seen. Of course, his work must mainly be done on the spot, at the temples whose priests hired him. Even so one would have expected at least rough drafts and sketches . . . .

"And I don't like what I hear about this new emperor," Ling Long pursued. "Can't imagine someone like that as a patron of the arts, let alone a devout follower of Sakyamuni. Still, a commission is a commission. I'll come along in the morning."

The matter being in his view settled, he gulped half the contents of his bowl and growled at his daughter another demand for supper.

Raindrops started to patter on the roof. Those nearby shutters that were still open slammed with an irregular succession of bangs. Chou cleared his throat.

"I'm afraid that won't do," he said with an attempt at politeness.

Ling Long blinked.

"You come now," the general amplified. "One doesn't keep emperors waiting."

Tian-wu made as though to speak. Chou plunged on.

"There's plenty of wine at the monastery. Food as well, I have no doubt. Please come now."

" 'One doesn't keep emperors waiting!' " the painter repeated in a high mocking voice. "And what's so urgent, in his opinion?" He supped his wine again.

"He's jealous because you can see dragons," Tian-wu declared before Chou could scowl him into silence.

"See dragons?" Ling Long was so astonished, he nearly dropped his bowl. Luckily he had more or less emptied it. "The only dragons I ever saw were painted ones! And half of them I'd painted myself!"

How in the world did I let myself in for this kind of farce?

Wearily Chou said, "You leave me no alternative." He strode to the window. The girl had not got around to closing its shutter and the densening rain splashed his face so hard he had to shut and wipe his eyes.

Then, shouting, he summoned two of his men, and between them they dragged Ling Long downstairs and out into the rain, their straw sandals slipping madly in the mud as he jerked and tugged. He was surprisingly strong despite his pipestem thinness. His daughter proved equally recalcitrant until one of the soldiers slapped her hard enough to make her lurch against the wall, head giddily in hands.

Wrists lashed behind his back, howling at the top of his lungs, the painter had no choice but to obey. But, aware of eyes staring at him from behind shutters on all sides, aware of the expression on the young monk's face, between puzzlement and contempt, Chou found this successful execution of his mission one of the most distasteful experiences of his life.

It was full dark when the party regained the temple. The rain was still comparatively gentle, although the peaks of the mountains to the south were being fitfully illuminated by lightning and occasionally the veering wind carried a rumble of thunder, scarcely louder than a child's feet grinding gravel. Waiting for them were the abbot and one of the emperor's bodyguards.

"You found the fellow?" the latter demanded. By this time Ling Long had shouted enough to make his throat sore and was having to content himself with curses in a near-whisper. "Is that him?"

"Yes."

"Bring him this way, then."

"Is the emperor still awake?" countered Chou, who had been hoping the opposite.

"And in no sweeter temper," the abbot confirmed, before a warning glare from the guard silenced him. In a straggling line they followed to the quarters, poor though they were, that had been assigned to the important visitor for lack of anything more luxurious.

Not, Chou thought sourly, that the emperor much appreciated comfort.

He was sitting on a mat, scowling by the light of a single smoky lamp. "That's him?" he rasped without waiting for the due ceremonies. "The man who boasts about his knowledge of dragons?"

"I never—" the artist burst out indignantly. One of the guards cut short the words with a cuff to the back of the neck.

"With respect, Highness," the abbot exclaimed, indignant at this display of violence on premises dedicated to the Buddha, "he did not ask to be given his nickname."

"No more did he refuse it," was the sullen retort. "You, fellow! You've been told why I brought you here?"

Ling Long's wine-fuddled brain had been a little cleared by his unwilling trudge through the rain. He hazarded, "You want me to paint you a dragon?"

"No! I want you to show me one!"

"Then you must be a fool even though you call yourself an emperor—"

"No, please, no more violence!" blurted the abbot as the guards made to strike the painter again. The emperor glowered, but waved his men aside.

"You have until dawn to show me a living dragon," he said in a drink-slurred growl. "Take him away."

"Hey! What about my supper?" cried Ling Long. "I was promised supper, and more wine!"

"Show me a dragon and you may have all the food and wine you want. *Take him away!*"

And they did so, paying no further heed to his protests, just as the storm finally advanced over the town.

Nowhere in the temple and adjacent monastery was to any marked degree waterproof, and the cell where they confined Ling Long was emphatically the reverse, for it consisted of an open gallery partly cut into, partly strutted directly against the mountainside, with a sheer drop above and below. The only access was from within the monastery. Once the artist had been rudely pushed through the door and it had been slammed and barred behind him, all he could do was squat on the floor and rehearse anew his vocabulary of imprecations.

By the time he had exhausted the lot, to the accompaniment of thunder and lightning and the continual trickling noise as rain dripped from the thatched roof and leaked away under the crude though strong wooden half walls not designed to keep the weather out, only the occupant from leaving, the fumes of alcohol had evaporated from his brain, though lack of supper meant they endured longer than usual. It was, he guessed, nearly midnight, for the last lights had winked out in the town below and its roofs were illuminated only as the mountains had been earlier, by flashes of lightning. Then at last he felt the chill of sober reality stab him through and through, like crystals of ice forming in his heart, his liver, his lungs.

He said aloud, "If I don't show a dragon to this crazy man who calls himself an emperor, at dawn he's going to kill me. And I can't imagine anyone who might stop him. Down in the slums where I live and work people will probably be sorry if I'm not around anymore to decorate the walls of their temples. There isn't much color in the lives of my people—hasn't been much in mine either, or my daughter's, or my wife's before she died of fever trying to bear me a son. Well, what I could, I did. There's some color, some brightness, in those narrow muddy streets that wouldn't have been there without me. And I've never overcharged them. They're poor. They can't afford much. Yet they've always fed me, let me have a lodging, kept my jar full of wine... Well, not always. Mostly.

"What about this loathsome bully, though? He's an emperor! Surely emperors can have all the fun and color anyone could want, and just by asking! Musicians, jugglers, acrobats, dancing girls! But here he is threatening to kill me—and he will! The look on his evil face...

"Wish I had a swig of wine to wash away the memory of that image."

A particularly brilliant bolt of lightning struck, so close that the thunder followed in a single heartbeat. Knowing it was absurd, knowing his throat was too sore from earlier shouting for him to be heard more than a few paces away, he nonetheless filled his lungs and husked:

"Are there really dragons? Do even emperors get to see them? I think not. Certainly not an emperor like the new one! But we want them, we need them, because they are nobler than the real world allows. Some people say the idea came from lightning! Pure fire, unalloyed with the crudity of common flesh like mine....

"Well, there's plenty of lightning out there... Hey! Listen! If that's what you dragons really are, save me! I've spent my life painting you and bringing you honor. How about a favor in return? How about it?"

The last word turned into a jaw-stretching yawn. His head lapsed sideways, his eyelids drooped, and in the fraction of a second before he fell totally asleep he heard and felt himself snore.

And, it seemed, in no time at all became alert again, at least in the sense of being able to perceive, albeit not to move or speak. On the mean wooden platform that extended this gallery out from the side of the cliff there were unexpectedly present certain personages, very bright in red and gold, far more so than he could ever have achieved with even the most expensive pigments, vastly graceful, and (though he could not tell how he knew this) strong. Strong in the way not of a man or animal, but of a river, or a rock, or a storm. He could discern neither their features, nor their attire, nor—though he was certain they were engaged in debate—their voices. Nonetheless he was convinced of one thing.

If these were not dragons, then they must be emperors fit to see and speak with dragons.

After a while he was asleep again.

And then, as abruptly as though he had fallen from a height, he was completely awake, and the first object his eyes reported to him was the highest mountain in the range that reared up to the south, clearly visible in the light known as the false dawn. As though it were being spoken over and over in his mind, by a voice like the tolling of a great bronze bell, he heard its name—not the name by which scholars formally referred to it, but the one children used, that he had not heard since leaving school.

Children said, "Dragon's Snout."

Also he detected tension in the air, as when blood returns to a limb from which it has been cut off, a tingling and a stinging, a sensation like pain in a mirror. The storm had calmed, but there were still thick clouds, and the steady march of raindrops tramped the roofs like the rear guard of an army, and sometimes there was muffled thunder.

What was most amazing, though . . .

My skin is itching as though I had been beaten with nettles. On the backs of my hands, on my forearms, on my shins, the hairs are standing up, coarse and black. My robe is old and ragged but it is good silk, gift of a patron years ago, and I can feel it trying to lift away from my body.

"*The presence of a dragon can be inferred . . .*"

Scraps of half-forgotten memory flashed across

Ling Long's mind. A shiver crawled down his spine. But it was born less of fear, more of knowledge, and not at all of cold. He was on his feet before he knew it, thumping at the door with both fists.

"Rouse your emperor! Take us to the highest tower! He wants to see a dragon before dawn, and if he hurries, so he shall!"

Blear-eyed, stumbling as much from the aftereffects of last night's wine as from having his sleep interrupted, the emperor followed the messenger who had dared to rouse him—as it happened, the novice Tian-wu. At every step he uttered threats against whoever might cheat or defraud him.

However, there was something about Ling Long's intensity of manner, the fierceness of his half-inaudible words, that swept him along, and the growing entourage that assembled in his wake. By the time the party reached the foot of the steps that led to the tallest tower of the temple even General Chou had joined them, though he was an elderly man and needed his rest.

To all queries and demands the artist returned the same answer.

"I don't want to die! So I spent all night praying to the dragons of the mountains, and they have sent me a sign! Hurry, there isn't long until dawn!"

Indeed, when they emerged on the gallery that overlooked the southern mountains, the sky in the east was turning red. It was still, however, the underside of storm clouds that reflected the impending sunrise; rain still sifted down; and the air still seemed on the verge of crackling, like pork rind thrust into boiling oil. Perceiving this, even the emperor ceased his tirade and looked about him nervously.

"This is where I am to see a dragon?" he demanded after a worried pause.

"Yes, Highness! Any second now!" Ling Long pointed to the mountain known to children as the Dragon's Snout. "Look there, look there!"

But with his other hand he was covering his eyes.

"You don't want to see this dragon you have promised will appear?" demanded the emperor.

"It's not for ordinary mortals! Only an emperor, only a trueborn ruler, can endure the sight!"

That was the abbot, wheezing as he breasted the stair top.

"He's right!" the painter shouted. "And are you one of them? The way you treated me and my daughter—"

"Shut up! Of course I am the rightful emperor, and I'll kill anyone who denies it!"

"Highness, don't waste your breath on squabbling!"

"You're very solicitous for me all of a sudden!"

"You swore that if you don't see this dragon, you'll kill me! Your general confirmed you keep your word! So I'm trying to keep mine in order to save my life! Look yonder!"

Even the sleepy, wine-sodden emperor now registered how the world confirmed the insistence of the sleepy, wine-sodden artist. The very air smelled of embryonic lightnings. Blue light dripped from cornices; the wind wheezed back and forth like breath in the throat of a beast . . . of a dragon?

"Ah, he's unfit," Ling Long said scornfully. "He's afraid to—"

"I'll cut you down where you stand!"

"Rather than look at a dragon?" countered General Chou. Sluggishly, but just in time, he had caught on to what the artist had in mind.

Glaring and breathing hard, the emperor squared his shoulders and turned to gaze toward the Dragon's Snout. There was a pause. Just as he was filling his lungs to shout that he had been betrayed—

He saw the dragon.

It was more gold than gold, more red than red, more white than white. Its claws rasped the tops of mountains. Its tail raked between the clouds. Its mouth snapped air with such force it made the bite sound solid. It lasted just long enough to be seen.

Just long enough for the emperor to see it.

Just long enough for its image to be branded on his eyes, the vast inevitable tracery spanning the welkin from horizon to horizon, the gaunt and graceful web of lines that could only show not where a dragon was but merely where it had been.

The sole, unique, and dreadful picture that the emperor would see for the rest of his life, and nothing else.

"I'm blind!" he screamed.

To which, with contempt:

"You were blind already, save to greed and power."

And even as the words vibrated in the air, the temple shook with thunder like the beating of every gong on Earth at once.

His bodyguards dragged the moaning emperor back to their army's camp. After a while the troops departed. General Chou was not among them. He was leading a party in search of Ling Long, to offer him a post at the capital when the legal dynasty was restored.

But his daughter barred access to the room, saying her father had enjoyed a decent breakfast and a bowl of wine, and now wanted only to be left alone and dream of dragons.

Billy Fearless

Nancy A. Collins

Nancy A. Collins is a native of Arkansas who lived in New York City for several years with her performance artist/filmmaker husband, Joe Christ. They have recently moved to Denver. Her vampire novel, Sunglasses After Dark, won the 1989 Bram Stoker Award for first novel. She has also won the British Fantasy Award. Her three subsequent novels are Tempter, In the Blood, and Wild Blood. Her short fiction was recently collected in Nameless Sins.

Collins, like Lannes, is best known for her horror fiction. She has a unique voice in which she has written several superb regional stories such as "The Two-Headed Man," "Freaktent," and "The Sunday-Go-To-Meeting-Jaw." "Billy Fearless" is based on the Brothers Grimm's "A Tale About a Boy Who Went Forth to Learn What Fear Was." Collins gives it a Southern flavor.

Billy Fearless

LESTER MCKRAKEN WAS A MILLER WHO LIVED IN THE town of Monkey's Elbow, Kentucky, which is somewheres near Possum Trot, which is a hundred miles north of Paducah, more or less. Now Lester had himself two sons he had to raise on his own when his wife fell to her death after the neighbor kids moved the McKraken outhouse back ten feet one moonless night. The older of the two boys was a fine young figure of a man, with a good head on his shoulders and a strong back and the gumption to make something of himself. The younger boy was—well, let's just say he was Billy.

Now, there weren't nothing seriously wrong with Billy upstairs. He wasn't feeble-minded, not like the washerwomans' young 'un. It's just that Billy, well, Billy tended to take things at face value, regardless of the face. I guess you could say he lacked imagination, more than anything else. Old Lester saw it as a case of being mule-stupid. And maybe he was right. But one of the strange side effects of Billy's thick headedness was that the boy was immune to fear.

From the day he learned to crawl, Billy was always getting himself into some fix or another, like the time

155

he came home leading a dog on a leash thinking it was in need of a shave because of the foam on its jaws. It wasn't long before his schoolmates were coming up with all kinds of outlandish tasks to try out on him, which Billy would dutifully perform. By the time he was nine years old he'd gotten the nickname of "Billy Fearless," which most folks called him more than his rightful name of McKraken. Much to Old Man McKraken's relief.

Billy's father had tried his best to school the boy in common sense. When Billy was no bigger than a grasshopper he told him that there were things he should never do, for fear of his life.

"How will I know when I should be scared, Daddy?"

"You'll know you're scared of something if it gives you a shudder."

Unfortunately, Billy didn't know what a shudder was. He was under the impression it was something not very nice, but he wasn't sure. He was afraid to ask his father for fear of the old man's temper, so he never did find out.

When Billy turned sixteen he was put out of school, like most boys his age. Billy figured he'd end up working at the mill, just like his elder brother had before him. But Old Man McKraken, while he loved his son as a father should, had pretty much worn out his worrying bone on Billy. He figured it would be better if his younger son found himself employment somewheres beside the mill. So Billy went knocking door to door, looking for work. When no one wanted to hire him in Monkey's Elbow, he walked the ten miles to Possum Trot and knocked on doors there.

One door he knocked on belonged to the town gravedigger, a fellow by the name of Shanks. Shanks looked Billy over and saw that he was young and strong and eager to work. But he also knew that even

strong men often turned weak when it came to digging graves in a lonely cemetery late at night.

"You seem to be a right enough sort," Shanks said.
"But I have to ask you one thing before I can hire
you—are you skeered of ghosts?"

Billy blinked and thought and blinked again. "Ain't
never seen a ghost, I reckon."

"Would you be scared if you *did* see one?"

Billy shrugged. "I don't know."

Shanks wasn't sure if Billy was putting on being
brave or was out-and-out lying to him, so he decided
he would test the boy to discover the truth. Later that
afternoon he handed Billy a shovel, a pick, and a Cole-
man lantern and pointed to the most remote section
of the cemetery, where the grave markers were old
and leaned at strange angles.

"Billy, I just got word from Reverend McPherson
that there's to be a funeral the day after tomorrow. I
need you to dig me a grave six long and six deep over
yonder, near the weepy willow. I have to go to town
to see to some business and I might not be back 'till
the morning. I want you to work on that grave until
midnight, understand?"

"Yes, sir, Mr. Shanks," replied Billy. And without
any word or complaint, the boy took up his tools and
set off to do as he was told.

Shanks went into town and sat in the local bar,
drinking with a couple of his friends until it got dark.
Then he sneaked back to the cemetery, where he
dressed himself in a cast-off shroud and whitened his
face, hair, and hands with flour. Then he sneaked out
to where he could see the light from Billy's lantern.

It was very dark and the night air crisp with the
coming autumn as the gravedigger darted from
gravestone to gravestone. The cemetery smelled of
dead leaves and lichen, with the ever-present odor of
rot lurking just under the surface. Somewhere up in

the weeping willow an old hoot owl cried out. Shanks had to bite back a drunken laugh as he thought of how frightened the new boy was going to be when he laid eyes on him, white and ghostly, standing on the edge of the freshly dug grave.

As he reached the plot where Billy was working, he could see that the grave was almost finished. Indeed, Billy—smeared with dirt and sweat—was in the act of boosting himself out of the hole. Shanks waited until the boy was reaching in his pocket for a bandanna to wipe the sweat from his face, then stepped out from his hiding place, moaning like a lost soul.

"Ooooohhhhhh!"

Billy looked up from his labors and frowned at the white-faced stranger who stood on the opposite side of the grave he had just dug. "Who's there?" he called out.

"Whooooo!" Shanks replied, waving his arms a little to give his performance a most-ghostly effect.

"You better answer me proper or you better git," Billy said, getting to his feet with the aid of his shovel. "You got no business here at this hour, mister."

Shanks wasn't sure whether to be pleased or irked. He'd been expecting the boy to turn white and wet his pants with fear or, at the very least, flee, as any sensible person might do when confronted by a ghost. Still, the boy's bravado might not be as strong as it looked, so he decided to continue his little masquerade.

"Oooouahhh!" Shanks moaned again, shaking imaginary chains at the boy.

"What do you want here?" Billy demanded, this time starting to sound angry. "Speak if you're a honest man, or I'll whup you upside the head!"

Shanks was convinced that Billy's threat was mere bluster, so he stood his ground, waving his arms and moaning and groaning to beat the band. So Billy hefted his shovel and struck him upside the head with the flat of the spade, knocking him into the grave. Billy then packed his tools and headed for the gravedigger's shack to await his employer's return from town so he could show him the nice new grave he'd dug and tell him about the strange fellow who'd pestered him.

The next day there was a knock on Old Man McKraken's door. When he answered it he found Shanks standing on his front porch with a plaster on his head and two black eyes. Sitting in the back of the gravedigger's mule cart was Billy.

"What in tarnation is going on here?" he demanded.

"I'll have you know, McKraken, that boy of your ain't nothing but bad luck on two legs!" Shanks snarled, wincing as he spoke. "He whopped me on the head with a shovel and left me to lie in an open grave all night long! I'll be lucky if I don't get the rheumatism from the damp!"

Aghast, Old Man McKraken promptly grabbed Billy by the ear and yanked him from the back of the mule cart. "What kind of mischief are you up to boy? The devil must be in you, child, to play such unholy pranks!"

"It weren't my fault, Daddy!" explained Billy, fighting back the tears as his father gave his ear another twist. "He stood there in the night, all covered in flour, and wouldn't talk when I asked him to. I thought he was some rascal, out to do me harm—"

Old Man McKraken might have had his doubts about his son's mental strengths, but he knew the boy was incapable of lying. So he gave Shanks five dollars for his trouble and brought the boy back into the house. After a couple of days he called his son to him and sat him down in front of the fire.

"Billy, I'll be blunt, son—while I love you as the

flesh of my flesh, I can't take any pride in you. It's time that you went out into the world. I'm giving you fifty dollars cash, a cart and horse, a turning lathe, and a carving bench so you can go forth and master yourself a trade. But tell no one where you come from or who your father is, for I am ashamed of you."

Billy didn't seem to take his father's words badly. He simply shrugged and said, "If that's all you want out of me, Daddy, I reckon I can do that."

So that very same day Billy, dressed in overalls and a red flannel shirt, wearing his only pair of brogans, took the fifty dollars, the cart and horse, the turning lathe, and the carving bench his father had promised him and rode out of Monkey's Elbow, never to be seen again.

During his sixteen years Billy had never gone any farther than Possum Trot. Although he knew there were other towns and villages outside the valley of his birth, he'd never once visited them. He'd also heard tell of other states besides Kentucky, although he had a hard time picturing them. But now, true to his father's wishes, he found himself heading into the world.

By dusk Billy was two valleys away from his home, passing through scenery that was both strange and familiar to him. He came to a crossroads with a huge oak tree in the middle. As he was tired and his horse weary, Billy decided this was as good a place as any to stop for the night.

Billy made himself a small fire at the base of the tree and set about making himself comfortable for the night. As he ate his simple meal of cheese and bread, he heard a creaking sound coming from the branches over his head. Looking up, he saw a man hanging from his neck by a rope.

"Howdy!" Billy called up to the hanged man.

The hanged man didn't say howdy back.

"It looks to be a chilly night," Billy observed. "Aren't you gonna get cold up there?"

The dead man didn't say anything, but a gust of wind blew him to and fro, making the rope creak all the more.

"Lordy! Look at how you're shaking and shivering!" Billy said. And because he had a good heart, he shinnied up the tree and used his knife to cut the hanged man down and lower the body to the ground, so it could share his fire.

Billy had hoped he would have some company to while away the hours before he fell asleep, but the hanged man didn't seem very appreciative—or talkative. In fact, all he did was stare at Billy with his tongue sticking out black and bloated. He also smelled a tad high and was missing an eye, which looked to have been pecked out by a bird.

"You don't seem to have a lot to say," Billy sighed, poking the fire with a stick.

As if in answer, the one-eyed corpse fell headlong into the fire, setting its hair ablaze.

"Watch out!" Billy cried. When the dead man made no move to pull his head out of the fire, Billy quickly leapt to his feet and yanked the body clear, stomping out the burning hair.

Billy clucked his tongue in reproof, much the same way his father used to do. "Tch! If you can't do no better'n that, friend, I'll put you back up in the tree."

The hanged man just lay there and smoldered, looking the worse for wear after Billy had stomped out the fire. Disgusted, Billy went to sleep.

The next morning the dead man still hadn't moved. Billy had been thinking of offering the stranger a ride to the next town, but decided not to, seeing how unfriendly the fellow had turned out to be. So he hitched his horse back up to its cart and headed on his way.

After traveling most of the day, Billy finally came

upon a little town on the edge of a big lake. In the middle of the lake was an island dominated by a huge mansion made of gray stone. It was getting on to late afternoon and Billy was hungry and thirsty and didn't cotton to the idea of spending another night under the chilly stars, so he decided to stop at the inn near the lake.

The sign over the door said The Ghost Lake Tavern. When he entered everyone turned as one to stare at him, their faces showing a mixture of curiosity and dread. When they saw it was just Billy, they let out a collective sigh and returned to their drinking and tid-dlywinks.

Billy eased himself into a seat and signaled to the barkeep that he wanted a drink. In the wink of an eye a pretty young girl with hair the color of a new penny set a tankard of ale in front of him.

"You're new to town," she smiled.

Billy nodded, his cheeks coloring. He couldn't help but notice how pale and fine the barmaid's skin was and how her hair shimmered in the lamplight. She was the most beautiful thing he'd ever laid eyes on in his short life.

"What brings you to our village, stranger?"

"I've just left my home and I'm out to seek my fortune."

The barmaid nodded sagely. "A fortune is a good thing to have if a man wants to find himself a wife. Youth and good looks play their parts, as well—but a fortune is the most important of the three."

"Do you have a room for the night?" Billy all but blurted, his face now so red it felt as if he was hiding live coals in his mouth.

"You'll have to ask my father," she said, gesturing to the heavyset man behind the bar.

Billy cleared his throat, hoping his voice would not crack. "Do you have a room to let, innkeeper?"

"Sorry, lad. I'm full up."

Billy glanced out the window at the island in the middle of the lake with its huge house.

"What about that place?" he asked, pointing in the direction of the lake. The entire tavern had fallen quiet as a church, drinks and conversations forgotten.

The innkeeper looked up from rinsing out the tankard, frowning at Billy. "What place?"

"The big house on the island. Do they have any rooms?"

"Aye, they have rooms enough, I suppose," the innkeeper replied slowly. "For those foolish to stay there."

"Is there something wrong with it?"

The innkeeper looked at Billy as if his head was made of mattress ticking. "Son, haven't you ever heard of the house on Ghost Lake?"

"I'm from Monkey's Elbow," Billy replied, as if this explained everything. Perhaps it did.

"There once was a man named McGonagil who sold his soul to the devil for the riches of Croesus. Once he got his wealth, he started worrying about people stealing it, so he bought himself that island and built himself a mansion, so's he wouldn't be bothered by thieves. When Old Scratch finally came for him, he refused to go unless the devil promised to protect his gold for all eternity. So the devil granted his dying wish and dragged the old bastard to hell.

"McGonagil's treasure is still somewhere in that house. The story goes that anyone who can spend three nights in the house shall claim the gold for his own. But the house is haunted by all manner of ghosts and goblins and of the dozens of fortune hunters who have braved the island, none have survived the first night!"

Billy listened to what the innkeeper said and looked back at the empty house standing on the island. He then looked at the barmaid, who was smiling at him. "Would you marry me if I had a fortune?"

"I might do it even if you did not," she replied, a twinkle in her eye.

Billy looked back out the window at the island, then stood up and announced, "I really don't like sleeping in the open this time of year. It don't agree with my bones. I'd be more than happy to pay someone to ferry me and my belongings to the island yonder."

There was a rumbling of excited voices and a broad-shouldered man stood up. "I'll ferry you over and back, lad, for three dollars. But it's got to be cash on the barrelhead, as I don't cotton to taking money outta dead folk's pockets."

"Fair enough," replied Billy, handing over three silver dollars. He turned to the innkeeper and said, "Can I keep my horse and cart stabled here? I'll pay you for their keep—"

The innkeeper shook his head. "I won't take your money, son. If you live to the third day, *then* you may pay me. If not, I'll keep them for my own. Before you go—tell me your name, so I can send word to your family of your death."

"I swore I'd never tell my true name, but I've been called Billy Fearless."

The innkeeper did not seem terribly impressed. "Have it your way," he grunted.

As Billy followed the ferryman out of the tavern, the barmaid hurried to him and threw her arms around his neck.

"Be safe, my brave Billy!" she whispered, planting a kiss on his cheek.

Billy blushed even deeper than before, muttered thank you, and hurried away, leaving the barmaid to watch after him, a tear glimmering in her eye.

* * *

Billy had the ferryman load his carving bench and turning lathe into his launch, along with enough food and drink for three days. By the time they reached the island it was near dark, and the ferryman was loath to do more than unload Billy and his things at the old wharf.

The front door of the old house was unlocked and Billy placed his carving bench and turning lathe in a large room on the first floor that had a fireplace at one end and an old canopied bed in the corner. While the house was very dusty and smelled of mouse shit and mildew, it didn't seem to be in such bad shape. So Billy set about building a fire in the old chimney, found himself a stool, and prepared a simple dinner of black bread and sausage.

As he sat in front of the fire, chewing on the last of his bread, there came a sound like a tormented soul.

"Tch! Such a noisy wind," Billy said, shaking his head.

Just then the fire in the grate blazed incredibly high, filling the room with exaggerated shadows, then fell to a tiny flicker. Billy jumped up and grabbed the bellows and began fanning the flame.

"Tch! Such a drafty room!"

There was a noise in the far corner like that of someone crackling paper and a strange, high-pitched voice cried out, "Meow! How horribly cold are we!"

Billy, who had returned the fire to its former strength, turned in the direction of the voice and squinted into the darkness. "If'n you're cold, come sit with me by the fire."

Out of the dark corner paraded not one, but two, coal black cats, walking on their hind legs as nice as you please. The cats had huge yellow eyes and little red boots on their feet. They sat themselves down on the stool next to Billy and warmed themselves by the fire.

After a while one of the cats turned to Billy and said, "It looks to be a long night, friend. How about a nice game of cards?"

This didn't take Billy aback none. He reckoned if a cat could walk on its hind legs and wear boots, not to mention talk, why shouldn't it want to play cards?

"Why not?" he replied. "But first, let me see your nails."

The cats exchanged looks, shrugged, and stretched out their claws.

"Boy-howdy, y'all sure got long nails!" Billy exclaimed, grabbing them by the scruffs of their necks. "Here, let me shorten 'em up a tad before we commence to playin'!" With that he placed them on his carving bench and screwed down their paws very firmly.

The cats began hissing and spitting and cursing him in cat-talk, which isn't very pleasant to the ears. Billy picked up one of his carving knives and with four clean strokes, severed the cats' front legs. Instead of blood, a substance that looked and smelled like tar boiled forth from the wounds and the cats vanished in a cloud of foul-smelling brimstone.

Billy looked about and scratched his head. Finally he shrugged his shoulders and said, "Tch! Well, I didn't really want to play cards with them, anyways!"

As Billy returned his attention to the fire, there was a horrible commotion—as if the gates of hell had been thrown wide-open and all the attendant demons sent forth. Suddenly the room was filled with huge black dogs with eyes the color of fresh blood. The hounds launched themselves at the fire, digging at the burning logs with their great paws and snatching burning embers between their massive jaws and worrying them like rats. Billy stood and watched the dogs, not sure what to make of what was going on. Then, one of the hounds started digging at the hearth, sending hot embers and soot flying. One of the cinders got into Billy's eye, making it water and burn.

"That's enough! Now you've gone beyond a joke!" Billy said, and seizing the poker from the fire, cracked one of the dogs across the head, killing it instantly.

The rest of the pack came to a dead halt and stared at their fallen companion, whose crushed skull oozed the same foul-smelling tar as the cats. Then, as one, they raised their heads and fixed their bloodred eyes on Billy.

"*Git*, you mangy critters!" Billy yelled, raising his arms and waving the poker at the hellhounds. "You heard me—go on and git!" With that he took a swing at the nearest hound, who yelped and promptly turned tail and fled the room. The other dogs followed suit, leaping out windows and even climbing up the chimney in order to get away from Billy and his slashing poker.

After the last dog had disappeared, Billy carefully picked up the pieces of his scattered fire and put them back in the fireplace. He then caught himself yawning and decided it was time to go to bed. He kicked off his shoes and climbed, fully dressed, into the four-poster bed in the corner. The bed was made out of solid wood, with little clawed feet clutching carved balls, and although the bedclothes were a tad musty, he was quite comfortable.

As he drifted off to sleep he fell into a dream that he was riding a horse. At first the horse would only go slow, clip-clop, but soon it was going faster, clippity-clop, then even faster still, clippity-clip. Billy opened his eyes and was surprised to find the walls and ceiling of the mansion speeding past him. Sitting up in bed, Billy discovered it wasn't the house that was moving—it was him. The bed's legs were moving as fast as they could, hurrying him from room to room, up stairs and down, over thresholds and around corners as if it were drawn by six strong horses.

Billy clung to the mattress the best he could as the bed shot down the long, dark corridors, sheets flapping behind them like pursuing ghosts. Finally, with a great bound, the bed flipped over on itself with a great crash, landing atop Billy. He struggled out from under the tangle of blankets and pillows, rubbing his bruised rump and shaking his head. The bed's feet were still pedaling at the air, like a turtle trying to right itself. Billy laughed and patted the bed appreciatively.

"Thanky kindly, old thing! That was the damnedest ride I've had since I rode the Flyin' Jenny at the country fair last year!"

And, with that, he gathered up his pillow and blankets and made his way back to the room on the first floor, where he curled up in front of the fire and fell sound asleep.

Early the next day the innkeeper, at the prodding of his daughter, paid the ferryman to take him to the island to check up on this so-called Billy Fearless. In the thirty years since old McGonagil was given his just reward, he'd seen the house take its share of victims; most of them young fools like the boy, all of them with dreams of treasure. Each and every one of them had been removed from the old house feet-first, stiff as boards and whiter than milled flour, the very life scared out of them. He figured the same would prove true of the latest boy. It was too bad his daughter had taken such a shine to this one. It was going to break her heart. . . .

The innkeeper entered the mansion and opened the nearest door off the great hall and saw Billy sprawled before the fireplace. He shook his head sadly. "What a pity!"

"What is?" Billy yawned, sitting up.

The innkeeper was so surprised to see Billy move he clutched at his chest. "Lord A'mighty, boy! I never thought I'd see you alive again!"

"Why shouldn't I be? Granted, I had some bother with cats and dogs and my bed disagreein' with me, but I had a nice enough night."

The innkeeper could only shake his head in disbelief. Maybe there was something to this Billy Fearless, after all.

The second night began uneventfully enough for Billy. He set up his fire and fixed himself a simple meal from the sausage and cheese the innkeeper had been kind enough to leave for him, believing it to be his last meal. It was nearing midnight, and Billy was settling down to a pipe of tobacco before going to sleep, when, with a horrible, bloodcurdling scream, half a man from the waist down fell from the chimney and landed on the hearth at his feet.

Billy craned his neck to look up the chimney and yelled; "Hey, up there! There's another half wanted down here—that's not enough!"

Presently there was a second, even more hideous scream, and the top half of the man dropped from the chimney.

"There, that's better," Billy said. "Here, let me stir up the fire for you." So he got off his stool to prod the fire. When he turned back around, the two halves had somehow joined into a whole man with an ugly face. Actually, ugly was being kind. The stranger's skin was the color and texture of a mushroom, the nose whittled down to nothing and the lips withered and black. One of his ears was missing and the other was hanging by a flap of skin. But to make matters worse, the ugly man was sitting on Billy's stool.

"Here now! You're sitting in my spot!" said Billy.

"Get up and find your own place to sit!"

The ugly man growled something in a low, liquid voice that sounded like his chest was full of honey, and shoved Billy away.

"There's no point in being rude," Billy admonished. "And I am the soul of human kindness, taught to turn the other cheek as the Good Book says. But I was also raised to defend what's mine and stand up for myself." And with that he grabbed the stool and yanked it out from under the ugly man, sending him sprawling.

The ugly man got to his feet, rubbing at his rear end and looking at Billy as if he'd just jumped over the moon.

Billy, having reclaimed his seat, settled back down to smoking his pipe. But before he had time to take a decent puff, another man dropped down the chimney. And another. And another. Within a couple of minutes there were six men, each uglier than the last, sitting in front of the fire. One of them got up and opened a closet door and produced nine skeleton legs and a human skull and began setting them up like ninepins.

Billy watched with great interest as the six ugly men rolled the skulls at the leg bones. While he did not hold with their manners or their looks, he did have a fondness for ninepins. After a couple of sets he asked the ugly men if he could play.

The ugly men looked at one another then one of them smiled, displaying rotting teeth and blackened gums. "You can play if you have money."

"I've got money enough." Billy pulled a wad of bills out of his pocket and showed it to the ugly men, who muttered amongst themselves.

"Very well. You first," the leader said, and handed Billy the skull. The others stood aside and tittered amongst themselves, waiting to see what Billy's reaction would be.

Billy hefted the skull and frowned. "Tch! Your ball isn't very round. I think I can fix that, though." He went to his turning lathe and worked the skull until it was completely smooth. "There!" he said, holding it up to admire his handiwork. "Now it'll roll much better."

So Billy played ninepins with the six ugly men until the break of dawn, losing a dollar or two along the way. When the cock crowed morning the ugly men seemed genuinely startled, as if they had lost track of time, and rushed about the room in a panic. Then, as the first light of morning broke through the window, they set up a racket like a gaggle of frightened geese and disappeared in a foul-smelling gust of wind.

Billy, glad his strange visitors had finally left him alone, yawned and curled up by the fire. As he drifted off to sleep, he wondered what he might expect in the way of guests for his third and final night in the house.

His third day at the old house had proved uneventful. The innkeeper had stopped by again and was even more amazed than before to find Billy in the land of the living. This time he left behind a roasted chicken and some wine for his dinner. As night fell, Billy sat by the fire and whittled a toy whistle to bide the time. He had almost finished putting the final touches on his whistle when he heard what sounded like footsteps in the hall outside his door. He looked up from the fireplace to see the door swing slowly open on squeaky hinges and six skeletons dressed in the top hats and black crepe of pallbearers, march into the room carrying a coffin. The skeletons carefully lowered their burden to the floor, then, without a word, turned around and filed back out of the room.

Billy, curious to see what the skeletons had brought him, got up and opened the coffin. Inside was a man his father's age, dressed in his best Sunday suit, his hands folded atop his chest, his mouth stitched shut with black thread and his eyes covered by gold coins. Billy touched the body and quickly drew his hand back.

"Tch! You're colder than stone, friend! Come, let me warm you by my fire."

Billy reached into the coffin and lifted the dead man by his armpits, dragging him free. As he did so, the coins fell from the dead man's eyes, causing the lids to fly open like window shades. Billy paused in his labors long enough to scoop up the coins and stick them in the pocket of his overalls. "Tch! That's a funny place to keep your money, cousin. Here, I'll keep track of it for you until you're feeling better."

After some considerable grunting and groaning, Billy managed to wrestle the dead man over to the fire. He laid the corpse on the hearth, thinking the warmth would unfreeze its joints and put the color back into the stranger's cheeks. Satisfied he'd done the best he could, Billy resumed his whittling.

An hour passed and the dead man was still as cold and stiff as when Billy first touched him. Billy frowned and thought on what he should do. He recalled how his daddy had once said how two people laying in bed together could make enough heat to spark a fire, so he decided to put the stranger in his makeshift bed and warm him with his body.

Billy took the body and placed it on the pallet he'd made for himself after the bed had run away, lay down beside it, and drew the covers over the both of them. Presently, he felt the body beside him grow less and less stiff and begin to move. At first Billy didn't think much about it, but then he felt the dead man's hands creeping about below the covers, feeling up his thigh.

"Here now!" Billy cried, sitting up. "I'll have none of that! I stopped that foolishness when I was twelve!"

The dead man cast aside the covers, his eyes staring wide and sightless. "Give me back my gold!" the corpse wailed, tearing loose the stitches that held his mouth shut. "Give me back my gold!"

"Are you accusing me of being a thief? Is that all the thanks I get after trying so hard to make you warm and comfortable? Then you can have your old gold—and you can go back to where you came from!" With that Billy grabbed the dead man by the hair, forced open his mouth, shoved the gold pieces under his tongue, and threw him back inside the coffin.

As suddenly as they had first arrived, the six skeletal pallbearers reappeared, marching two abreast, picked up the coffin, and left the room. Billy watched them leave and scratched his head. People sure acted different outside of Monkey's Elbow.

Just as he was ready to shrug it off and go back to bed, a cold wind came rushing down the chimney, extinguishing the fire. Billy dug around in his pockets and found a book of matches, which he used to kindle another, smaller fire in its place. As the light from the fire grew stronger, Billy saw that he was no longer alone in the room.

Standing in the corner was an ogre. He was taller than Billy even though his back was hunched, and he had a hooked nose with a wart on it and horrible crooked teeth that stuck out of his mouth like the tusks on a boar. His arms were so long they almost touched the floor and his legs were bowed and ended with feet as broad and callused as a bear's. The ogre glowered at Billy with an expression of the utmost hate.

"Howdy, stranger," Billy said. "Who might you be?"

"I am the haint in charge of scaring folks away from this place. You are a troublesome man-child," the ogre said in a voice that sounded like two rocks being rubbed together. "You've given me more problems than all the others of your kind put together. What is your name, human?"

"I'm called Billy Fearless."

"Billy Too-Damn-Stupid-To-Know-When-To-Be-Scared is more like it, if you ask me."

"You sound like you been talking to my daddy. You ever been to Monkey's Elbow, mister?"

The ogre shook his head in disgust. "Old Scratch put me in command of the ghosts and ghouls that haunt this house more than thirty years ago. Up until now there ain't been a soul that survived the first night! Why, if the hellhounds didn't do 'em in, the bed finished 'em off! But you—you! You kilt my cats, skeered my dogs and wore out my bed! If Old Scratch hears of this, he'll have me back in Hell muckin' out the harpy nests! I worked hard to get myself a nice, cushy job haunting the upper world—I ain't about to let some no-count hayseed such as yourself ruin it for me! Say your prayers, boy, because I'm going to choke the life outta you!"

The ogre straightened up as best he could, lifted his arms, and advanced on Billy, grimacing and growling like a beast. And, to his surprise, Billy commenced to laugh. This nonplussed the ogre something awful.

"What in tarnation are you laughing about, boy? Can't you see I'm going to kill you?"

"That's a good 'un!" chortled Billy, wiping a tear from his eye. "A wretched old thing such as yourself thinking he can kill the likes of me."

"I can kill you three times over, boy!" bellowed the ogre.

"I wouldn't be so sure of that," Billy warned. "I'm stronger than you might think. So don't go boastin' you can kill me."

"Oh, is that so? Well, we'll soon see if'n you're stronger than me or not. I'll show *you* a thing or two, you pesky turnip seed!" Grabbing Billy by the straps of his overalls, the ogre dragged him through the house to the stable around back, which had once—judging from the stone-cold forge and the anvils lying about—boasted its own blacksmith.

"See that anvil lying yonder?" the ogre asked, pointing at a particularly large specimen. "Watch this, boy." Spitting in his palms, the ogre grabbed up a nearby ax and, with one mighty swing, split the anvil in two as cleanly as a hot knife through butter.

"That's nothing!" Billy snorted. "I can do better than that!"

"Can not."

"Can too."

"Can not."

"Just hand me an ax and you'll find out."

Chuckling to himself in anticipation of rending the smart aleck country boy from limb to limb, the ogre handed his victim an ax. "So what are you gonna do, boy?" he sneered.

"Gonna do the best I can," Billy replied, and promptly brought the ax blade down on the ogre's head with all his strength.

The ogre fell like a poleaxed steer, brains leaking from the huge split in the middle of his head. The foul, tarry material that had oozed from the dogs and cats in place of blood now bubbled out of his ears, nose, and mouth.

"Maybe now a fellow can get some decent shut-eye," sighed Billy, dusting off his hands as he returned to the house.

* * *

The next morning Billy woke up to find a huge chest of gold at the foot of his humble bed. He took the chest, along with his carving bench and turning lathe, and carried them out to the dock, to await his passage to the mainland. He was sitting on the treasure chest, smoking his pipe, when the ferryman arrived at noon. When he saw Billy waiting for him on the dock his jaw dropped clean to his chest.

"You did it! You survived the three nights!" exclaimed the ferryman.

"Aye, that I did."

"What about the treasure?" the ferryman asked quickly. "Did you find the treasure?"

"Aye, that I did."

The ferryman scratched his chin and eyed the chest Billy was sitting on. There was no one here to see what would become of a nameless young man, or to discover the truth of what had happened to the miser's treasure. But what thoughts he might have had concerning disposing of Billy and shanghaiing his gold quickly disappeared. Any man—no matter how young—who could spend three nights in the company of ghosts and hobgoblins and come out of it with both his wits and life intact was not a man to tangle with, no matter what the reward.

So Billy Fearless returned to the Ghost Lake Tavern and showed the barmaid his chest full of gold coins and asked her father, the innkeeper, for permission to marry her. Of course he said yes. They put on a real big do and the whole valley was invited to dance at the wedding.

Billy had a nice big house built for his wife and the family that was soon to follow. His father-in-law, now one of the richest men in Ghost Lake, bought the old haunted mansion and, after some renovating, turned it into a big fancy hotel that attracted visitors from far and wide on the strength of its being a "real, live haunted house." Ghost Lake became a fat and happy little resort town, with everyone ending up with electric lights and indoor flush toilets. And they all had Billy Fearless to thank for their newfound prosperity.

Still, Billy was still Billy, no matter how rich and famous he might be. And although his wife was a patient soul, she was only human. One day, after he'd brought home yet another wolf as a pet, she asked him, as they lay in bed, how it was he didn't know enough to recognize danger when he saw it.

"Well, I was told by my daddy—the Lord keep him—that I'd know when to be scared of something because it'd give me a shudder. And to this day I have yet to shudder—or even know what such a thing as a shudder is."

"Is that all?" Billy's wife kicked back the covers, slipped on her shoes, grabbed up a coal scuttle and trotted down to the creek that ran behind their house. Once back in the house, she crept up on her husband as he lay in bed and dumped a scuttle full of minnows down the flap in his long johns. "Now, Billy, do you know what a shudder is?"

"If that's the case, then I'll be damned if I weren't scared the whole time!"

After that Billy Fearless was renowned throughout the valley as the soul of prudence and common sense. And if his wife knew better, well—she lived happily ever after anyway.

The Death of Koshchei the Deathless

(a tale of old Russia)

Gene Wolfe

Gene Wolfe lives in Barrington, Illinois. He is one of the most gifted and respected writers in the field owing to such extraordinary works as The Book of the New Sun, The Urth of the New Sun, The Fifth Head of Cerberus, Soldier of the Mist, The Island of Doctor Death and Other Stories and Other Stories, *and many other books of fantasy and science fiction. His most recent novel is* Calde of the Long Sun. *He has won the World Fantasy Award, the John W. Campbell Memorial Award, and the Nebula Award.* "Koshchei the Deathless" *is a Russian fairy tale. In reading the original, Wolfe was struck by the things left out or implied, presumably to protect young ears. He decided to fill in the blanks for adults.*

The Death of Koshchei
the Deathless
(a tale of old Russia)

MY NAME IS PRINCE IVAN THE SIMPLE, AND I AM THE son of Prince Ivan the Bold. But should having two Prince Ivans confuse you, you need not concern yourself about the matter. For the truth is that I am very like my late father in every respect. There's his portrait on the wall. You took it for a picture of me? I thought so!

We are—I will speak of him in present tense now, though he perished soon after I was born—both tall and fair, as you see. Our honest blue eyes are our most pleasing feature, perhaps. Large noses, full lips, and yellow hair that will never lie flat. My governess called me weedy and gawky, and I do not doubt that my father's described him in similar terms; I'm told his mother referred to him in private as "the stork."

Like him, I am honest to a fault, disposed to be easygoing and forgiving, and touched by the misfortunes of animals and the poor. I feel the ties of birth and family more deeply than most men, I think—more deeply than even most noblemen. And I am quite incapable of deception. As for those stories of sagacity and wizardry, don't believe a word of them—nothing could be further from the truth. The peasants hereabout wish to impress you travelers, and to entertain you. They make up such stuff all winter, sitting around the stoves drinking tea and cracking nuts and scaring one another silly; and because our winters are very long—well, you see. They'll have me flying off upon a wooden horse next, the sort of thing they tell about the Shah, poor old fellow! Peasants are savages, really. Take away Holy Mother Church and they'd be dancing around fires and cutting their children's throats on the knees of idols inside a week.

But let us return to Prince Ivan, my father. He was his father's only son, just as I am; but unlike myself— I am an only child—he was blessed with three sisters younger than himself. The family face, which looks so foolish over a sword guard—

That's very kind of you, but my mirror presents stronger arguments. I was about to say, though, that a face like mine doesn't look so ill upon a woman. The prince's maiden sisters, my aunts, were all quite good-looking, tall with blue eyes and great masses of golden hair. Their features were everywhere said to combine great regularity and sensitivity with the very soul of aristocratic delicacy. They were just like mine, in other words. Yes, that's one of them over the sideboard, my mother.

When my grandfather died, he charged my poor father very strictly to make the best marriages he could for his sisters. And my father, having wits no better than mine, decided that the best marriage any girl could make would be that which she made for herself; so he resolved to let his sisters marry whom they pleased. He adored all three, and could never bear to deny them anything, anyway.

It was only a month or two, I believe, before a peasant—I've told you about them, so you know what to expect—dashed into the palace shrieking, "A falcon, a falcon! A falcon has come to take Princess Marya!" My poor father ran outside and was still wondering what in the world was really happening, when the Graf von Falkonstein came galloping up with a falcon on his shield and another on his helm, and a couple of hundred of the most villainous men-at-arms the land has ever seen at his heels. I never met the graf, but I know the type and I'm sure you do, too. A Prussian, bred to kill Lithuanians exactly as terriers are to kill rats, the kind of man who whistles for his grooms when he wants his wife beaten.

This lean, scarred, and arrogant party sprang from his charger, landed at my poor father's feet like a thunderbolt, and shouted, "Hail, Prince Ivan! Before I came as a guest. Now I return as a wooer! I propose for your sister, Princess Marya!"

My poor father—who would have scampered away like a rabbit, I'm sure, if he hadn't feared a crossbow bolt between his shoulder blades—could only mutter, "If you find favor in the eyes of my sister, I won't interfere with her wishes. Let her marry you and go, in God's name."

A feast, an announcement, a ball, and they were off. My poor father ordered the wall doubled in thickness and trebled in height, cleaned out the moat and filled it, buried two dead footmen, sent twoscore ravished maids back to their parents, and thanked St. Michael on his knees that things had gone no worse.

The work on the wall had scarcely begun when a peasant—the same one, I suspect, eager to be the center of attention again—dashed in shouting, "An eagle, an eagle! An eagle has come for Princess Olga!" It was the King of Poland, as soon developed, and of course he had the Polish eagle on his shield and so on, and a thousand uhlans trailing after him like an army of wolves. It's an elective monarchy and not worth a bent brass kopeck, but my father could only gasp out the phrases he had used before. "If you find favor in the eyes of my sister, I will not interfere with her wishes. Let her marry you and go, in God's name!" His steward had got a bit of practice with the Prussians, and the Poles were on the road home in ten days, with my unfortunate Aunt Olga slung, figuratively at least, over the king's saddlebow.

A raven from Hungary got my Aunt Anna. I won't bore you with the details, which were so similar to Olga's that I have always suspected the graf coached his brothers-in-law. The whole thing threw my poor father, Prince Ivan, in a blue funk that lasted for a couple of years. He was, exactly as I am, a man exceedingly fond of his family; and between the last snow and the first his parents had died and all three of his sisters had been carried off to the ends of the earth. He forgave my late grandmother a thousand times over for having called him a stork, and he wept regularly on his own father's grave, begging forgiveness for having let the three birds make off with his daughters—though I imagine it must have occurred to him more than once that if only his father hadn't had them up to hunt and drink with him, those three sorry episodes would never have occurred. There's my grandfather's portrait in the corner: the surly old donkey with the beard.

A couple of years passed, as I said. Most men would have picked up a wife and half a dozen mistresses in that time, but my poor father—

His heart, you see, was like mine, the heart of a true Russian. How well I understand him! He wasn't looking for eyes like two pools, cheeks like apricots, and all the rest of it. No! He longed for the faces and voices he had known since childhood, and nothing else would do.

So when the third summer rolled around, away he galloped, utterly alone except for his valet, a cook, and so on, swearing by Our Lady of Tikhvin that he would embrace his sisters again or perish. He was like the Spanish knight errant. Do you know the one I mean?

Yes, Don Quixote, although the old Spaniard had more sense than my father and I put together, if you ask me. If it hadn't been for his sisters, my father would have tried to locate the World of the Dead, like as not, without a single honey cake for Cerberus, and fetch home his parents. He was that sort of Russian, just as I am.

He had been wandering the roads for weeks and was utterly, frightfully, irretrievably lost, when he stumbled upon a battlefield. There were corpses everywhere, with crows pecking out their eyes and terrible old women with clubs murdering the wounded for their rings. You've seen the sort of thing, I'm sure. He found one man who wasn't quite dead yet, and by bribing him with water managed to get him to talk a little.

My father was no linguist, you understand. French, what we call kitchen Russian—stop that, hurry up, and get out—a smattering of Latin, and as much Greek as you could write on a child's slate. But he managed to find out that the man was a Lettish pagan, and that he and his friends had been defeated by some sort of fighting Prussian countess whom he called the Goddess of Battle.

That was all he knew, so my father let the old women have him and called his servants together, recounted everything he had learned, and impressed on them that they would be beaten half to death and robbed of all he had if they came across the soldiers of this warrior countess's army.

I needn't tell you what happened next, I suppose.

You know me, so you know my poor father, Prince
Ivan. They were captured by the victorious army
within the hour, despoiled, bound hand and foot, and
flung down in the sun to writhe and curse their patron saints and try to pretend nothing had ever happened and they were back home about to wake up to
a good breakfast, like yourself.

The sun had set and the stars come out before one
of their captors, a trifle kinder than the rest, conde-
scended to tell my poor father that the countess
wanted to see him but was busy at the moment shar-
ing out booty and plotting the sack of Rome and
whatnot. My poor father replied as politely as he
could that he would await the countess's pleasure, but
he really ought to wash and change into something
more suitable first; he was just getting around to sug-
gesting vodka and a bite to eat when the man went
away, leaving him no better off than before.

The moon rose, and a nightingale began to sing.

That's the way I've always pictured it, at any rate,
and quite possibly the countess had an Italian
somewhere who could play the guitar; somebody cut
the ropes that had bound my poor father's ankles,
stood him on his feet, and trotted him off to the countess's tent.

It was an exceedingly dark tent, or so I've been
given to understand. Perhaps there was a single silver
lamp suspended from the centerpole. Perhaps there
wasn't. In any event, the countess was as kind as my
poor father could have wished—as kind as a woman
can be—and he received a strong impression of enchanting and almost otherworldly loveliness. My late
mother, the Countess von Falkonstein, was never as
positive about the lamp as one might expect, but upon
that point she was rock-solid. Every account that she
ever gave me of that night insisted on it. Shortly before midnight I was conceived.

Imagine my unhappy parents' discomfiture when the level rays of the morning sun awoke them both! My defiled mother—that is to say, my Aunt Marya—wept inconsolably all morning when she was not giving orders to her troops about breaking camp and the like, and my poor father kicked his cook until she would have fled, had she not been bound still.

None of which did the least good, to be sure. My father and the countess—that is to say, my mother, Aunt Marya—were hopelessly in love; moreover, as each explained to the other at length, each now felt that marriage to anyone else was out of the question, because the unsuspecting bride or bridegroom would have to have the whole matter explained in advance lest it be discovered later. And since each felt very strongly that death would be preferable to such an explanation, their only recourse was to marry each other. Fortunately, the Graf von Falkonstein had succumbed to a stomach disorder not long after his honeymoon.

Thus it was done. My father was introduced to my mother's troops as an immensely wealthy Russian nobleman closely linked to the Tsar by ties of blood, all of which was true enough for Germans. A grand wedding at Castle Falkonstein was followed by a whirlwind tour of Europe—I was born in Paris before its close.

Our return to Falkonstein was precipitated by restlessness among the Balts. Within a month of our arrival, my mother set out on a fresh expedition, intending to capture, despoil, and burn Memel, Libau, and Mitau; my poor father remained behind, a martyr to indigestion and diarrhea.

Here I must return, if only briefly, to the night before their wedding. On that night, my mother had treated my poor father to a tour of Castle Falkonstein, and during the course of that tour had cautioned him concerning a certain door in its dungeons. To this door (or so she had informed him) no key existed; it opened upon a bottomless pit communicating with the nether reaches of Hell. I need scarcely add that her army was hardly lost to sight when my father searched her apartments, discovered the key, and opened the door. You would have been wiser, I feel sure; but I know that I would have done the same thing myself. Legend declares that at the christening of our family's founder a somewhat deaf fairy who had been asked to render him and his descendants mettlesome, made us meddlesome instead.

Conceive of his surprise when the single, flickering taper he carried revealed no pit, but a chained man of great stature, horribly emaciated, with skin the color of iron. My father, who had expected to discover the graf, was thunderstruck. "I am Koshchei the Deathless, Prince Ivan," gasped this forbidding prisoner.

Now tell me, if I were to say here that Koshchei thundered forth dire threats against my Aunt Marya as soon as my father freed him, and vanished in a cloud of sulphurous smoke, would you believe me?

I thought not. You and I are educated people, after all, not superstitious peasants. Yet that is what our peasants will tell you. My Aunt Marya used to recount the story to visitors, you see, and as was only to be expected, she was overheard—most imperfectly and with very little comprehension—by the servants. The whole matter had become what is called common knowledge, eh? You know as well as I how terribly common such knowledge is.

He did nothing of the sort, to be sure; but explained to my father that he was a Lettish king captured by the countess, who had condemned him to perish of hunger and thirst. My poor father fetched him several buckets of water—a bucket being the only container

he could find—and explained in turn that he himself
was a Russian prince—

Oh, the iron-colored skin? It was tattooing. Those
pagan Balts tattoo boys throughout their adolescence,
and the higher a boy's rank, the more tattooing he
gets. Koshchei was of very high rank indeed, and his
boyhood must have been a continual torment.

Where was I? Well, it doesn't matter. Let it suffice
that my father freed and fed him, and installed him
in a guest room near his own. Neither of them cared
for Prussians, and that formed a bond between them.
By the time that my father's digestive complaint had
cleared up, they had agreed on terms of peace; and
together they rode away to convey this happy news
to my mother.

Alas, it was not to be. Koshchei, beholding her for
the first time without her armor and a sentence of
death in her mouth and so forth, fell helplessly in love
with her. She had picked up several hundred pris-
oners by then, and he contrived to free them and steal
some horses. Away went he and they and she, she
quite literally slung across the successful suitor's saddlebow.

As for my father, he returned to Falkonstein with a
broken heart. There in a year or two, he received a
letter from the Holy Roman Emperor inquiring about
the countess, his wife, and stating very firmly that if
she was dead the castle must revert to the von Falkonstein family, in this instance embodied by a most-
objectionable Prussian Junker, a cousin-german of my
late uncle the graf, who delivered it.

I need hardly say that this would not do. My poor
father sent Koshchei an urgent message reminding
him of the kindness shown him, blessing his union
with my mother (for my father had by then discovered that his digestion was vastly improved in her
absence) and imploring him to permit her to write to

the Emperor declaring that she was yet among the living.

Koshchei responded in the friendliest possible fashion, urging that my poor father visit him in Riga, bringing some high official of the church who could subsequently affirm my mother's continued life and good health. As it happened, the Bishop of Rheims was in the vicinity, and my father persuaded him to make the trip.

At first everything went swimmingly. There were feasts, fetes, tournaments, and so on, with some very decent hunting and hawking thrown in; but it was not to last. The Prussian knights my father had brought considered my Aunt Marya—that is to say, the Countess von Falkonstein, my mother—the true object of their loyalty; and she, detesting both Koshchei and Riga, declared herself homesick for Falkonstein and never for a moment permitted the bishop to forget that she was united by the bonds of Christian marriage to her brother. Ill feeling grew, harsh words were exchanged, and not to put too fine a point on it, my poor father, Aunt Marya, and the bishop and his retainers left Riga in flames. It was on this occasion that my father was awarded his sobriquet of "Bold," though in fact he was not, as I have tried to show.

Koshchei then inquired whether they might be overtaken, to which his horse—actually his Master of Horse, presumably—is supposed to have replied, "It is possible to sow wheat, wait till it grows up, to reap it and thresh it, to grind it into flour, to make five pies of it, to eat those pies, and then to start in pursuit—and even then to be in time."

In short, my suffering parents' pack mules were so heavily laden that they could scarcely be induced to move faster than a walk. Not surprisingly, they were overtaken by Koshchei's army at the crossing of the Vendava, where a slam-bang fight ensued. My father, as I've told you, was by no means a warlike man; but faced with the possibility that he might never return to these, our family estates, he surprised himself by displaying the sort of desperate resolution sometimes seen in the mildest at their last resource. Taking his stand before the baggage train, with sword and mace he beat off charge after charge. Koshchei and his Balts had recaptured my mother, however, and returned with her in triumph to what remained of Riga.

As for my poor father, he retreated to Falkonstein with his wounded and his dead, and was able to build a little dacha on the Black Sea. It's still in the family, and a charming place, though one is apt to become lost until one masters the arrangement of the rooms; I winter there occasionally.

You would have thought he'd have the wit to leave Koshchei alone after that. And he did have the wit, although he was a foolish-enough fellow, as I am myself. What he did not have was the heart. He was forever thinking of his sister, and the games they'd played as children, and how Riga had no proper samovars; after a year or so, somewhat strengthened by a couple of thousand Cossacks and some Swiss, he marched north again, firmly resolved to make amends for the earlier unpleasantness and resume what he by then considered his old friendship with Koshchei the Deathless.

Truth, it is said, makes her home at the bottom of a well. Her sister Peace, is still less hospitable, flying fastest from those who pursue her with the greatest ardor. My poor father was captured, held in Riga for nearly a year, and released only when he reminded Koshchei the Deathless—

Oh, that? It means nothing, really. All of the kings of that line were named Koshchei, and there was a pagan pretense that they were all the same ruler. You know the sort of thing, I feel certain.

As I was saying, my poor father reminded Koshchei
of his kindness to him in the dungeon—kindness that
he very much regretted by then, I feel sure—and
Koshchei agreed to let him go. My Aunt Marya, who
was at least as anxious to put the whole Baltic coast
behind her as he was, contrived to borrow armor and
accompanied him in the guise of a knight banneret of
Pomerania. My father ought never have permitted it;
but you, conversant with our character as you are by
this time, will have anticipated that he did.

Again—this according to the legend you understand—Koshchei questioned his Master of Horse,
who assured him, "It is possible to sow barley, to wait
till it grows up, to reap it and thresh it, to brew beer,
to drink ourselves drunk on it, to sleep our fill, and
then to set off in pursuit—and yet be in time."

He was correct upon this occasion as well, unfortunately. My Aunt Marya, as I was forced to call her
here in Russia, and my poor father were apprehended
and returned to Riga in chains, where Koshchei explained to my father that even the most deeply felt
gratitude has limits. My father replied graciously that
he was in full agreement, and that if Koshchei freed
him again he would deed him full and uncontested
right to my Aunt Marya, and endeavor to secure her
sisters for him in addition.

Koshchei declined.

My father inquired, as between friends, whether
Koshchei intended to put him to death, and Koshchei
frankly and openly conceded that such was his intention. My father then made bold to request a final favor; he asked that his body be returned to his
family—instancing Aunt Olga and Aunt Anna—from
whom he might receive a proper burial. Koshchei assured him that he would do far better: he would provide his rescuer—that is to say, my poor father—with
the largest tomb the world had seen; and he would,

moreover, take care that his body should be preserved until the end of time. So saying, he chopped my poor father to pieces, threw the pieces into a barrel, and had the barrel filled with boiling pitch, sealed, and cast into the Baltic. Here my father's story ends, and my own begins.

I was brought up here by servants, packed off occasionally to that little place on the Black Sea I told you about, and now and then sent to the court of Poland, to Aunt Anna in Hungary, or to Falkonstein, which I came to detest. As was inevitable, there was gossip as it became increasingly noticeable that I resembled my late father in every respect, down to the smallest details. On my twenty-first birthday, the blow fell. Either I must turn the castle over to the von Falkonsteins, or I must bring the Countess von Falkonstein to court, where she would be examined regarding my parentage. After pondering the letter for a fortnight, I set out alone for Riga, earning my sobriquet of "the Simple."

Thank you, you are extremely kind. But it wasn't courage, really; rather it was the realization that I am quite unfitted for military command, and that my estates could not bear the cost of another expedition, even if I desired one. I did not go straight there, however, as I should explain, though I had planned to. Like my poor father before me, I was utterly lost within a day—it's a wonder I did not end up in your London. Do you know of Baba Yaga?

No, no! Not the witch they talk of to frighten children. All that is purest superstition, though we call it now by the polite name of folklore. By "Baba Yaga" I intend the Grand Duchess, that terrible old woman. We never call her Baba Yaga to her face, to be sure. And yet . . .

Well, never mind. I ended up on one of her estates after a great deal of wandering, and wondering how long the Emperor would wait, and sleeping in flea-ridden country inns; and as it happened she was there. She welcomed me with old-fashioned boyar courtesy—turning out her serfs to cheer, and the rest of it—and told me, as people had been telling me all my life, that I was spit and image of Ivan the Bold. After a day or two, I worked up the courage to explain my plight, and she advised me and got me tattooed.

Right here. Wait, I'll push up my sleeves. See the black lines? I've a lot more of them, too. Around my neck and knees and ankles and so forth, marking all the places where Koshchei had chopped up my father's body. That was part of her advice, and as it happened there was an old man on the estate who could do it, although every tattoo made me ill for days on end and hurt dreadfully.

She lectured me about women, too. I think that was really much more important; and so must she have, because she kept me there for months, getting tattooed and getting sick from it and recovering, while she recounted long stories from her past and asked, when she had finished each of them, how the woman at the center of it would act. What her decision would be and whether she'd stick to it. Often they don't—but no doubt you knew that.

When I was better—recovered from one tattoo, but not quite ready for the next—we took long rides over the steppe. Meadows or moors or uplands you call them in England, but I won't use any of those terms, which would be like calling the sea a basin of water. You do that, you know, speaking of the Mediterranean basin and so forth; it's nonsense and the worst and most poisonous sort of nonsense, too. You and I spoke last night of your great moors, and you told me about your walking tour, in which you crossed one such great moor in three days. Well mounted, Baba

Yaga and I couldn't even have reached the Dnieper in three days, and there the steppe has scarcely begun. If you were to try to ride it from one end to the other on the best horse in the world, that horse would die long before you had reached your goal, and you with it.

But I was going to say that we'd ride out from Baba Yaga's villa (which you would call a palace) in the morning, and never halt until the story was finished. On the ride back, I'd tell her how I thought the woman in it would have acted at the end, and why. If I was wrong (and at first I was in every case), she would show me where I had gone astray in my reasoning. No one, I think, has ever looked deeper into the human heart—into women's hearts, particularly, for men's are simple things by comparison—than old Baba Yaga. Once we came across a ryabchik and her brood, the chicks just big enough to eat. I had my bow, and I told Baba Yaga I'd kill a pair for us. The servants could pluck and roast them, and we'd have them with our luncheon. She shook her head and told me that the ryabchik was a woman, too, and we wouldn't start home until I had made friends with her. I learned a great deal during that long afternoon, riding slowly after those seven birds and sitting cross-legged on the yellowing grass. Baba Yaga taught me how to charm wild bees, too—and how to leave their honey behind when I'd done it. Last of all the wolf, who is not the monster that we think her, but God's dog, half-mad with hunger and the memory of His hands upon her head.

Yes, we Russians are all sentimentalists, as you say; and I'm not called Ivan the Simple for nothing.

At the first snow I rode for Riga, taking Kinzhal and her half-grown cubs. We surprised the Balts, you may be sure, but I dismissed my wolves at Izborsk out of fear that someone would harm them. It didn't matter—their reputation rode faster than I. By the time I got to Riga, they had become a pack of hundreds, so that I felt like my own uncle, the Polish king.

Thanks to them, Koshchei heard of my coming long before I arrived and was eager to see me. I let him glimpse the marks I showed you without ever mentioning where I'd acquired them, and when he wanted to know how it was that I was alive once more, I explained that my sisters had married an eagle and a raven; and the eagle—whose eyes were sharper than Saint Michael's—had seen my barrel and towed it to shore. My sisters, I said, had restored my limbs to their proper positions, except that they had exchanged my right hand with my left. See here?

Yes, of course it's conjuring. But I won't tell you how it's done. We conjurors never do, and it's the only trick I know.

Then, I said, the raven had flown to the Fountain of Life and fetched back a bottle of water. My sisters had sprinkled me with it—and, well, he could see the result for himself. He didn't believe my story any more than you would have; but he didn't know what to think, and he was eager to keep me around until he had plumbed my secret. That was all I wanted, really, so I was quite content.

As for Aunt Marya, she'd adapted to life among the pagans as well as a woman could, queening it over her subjects worse than Baba Yaga, taking part in their ceremonies with Koshchei—perfectly revolting ceremonies, some of them, which I dare say was how they got Koshchei as a king to begin with—and wearing a round ton of red gold and amber, with a handful of sapphires and rubies thrown in for good measure. I've always thought she must have guessed who I was; but she never betrayed it by a word, just told me I'd better stay out of her bed as long as Koshchei was alive. Thinking has never come easily to me; I

scratched my head over the matter and after an hour
or two decided that if she were to bear me a child it
would be my son or daughter—and my half brother
or half sister, too, as the child of my mother by a different father—and my cousin-german as the child of
my father's sister. I'd already seen far too much of
cousins-german, and so I decided not to do it, though
Aunt Marya was a remarkably attractive woman,
even after all she'd been through.

Not to try to put too fair a face on things, I avoided
her whenever I could. For one thing I'd grown up
without seeing my mother, except for the portrait over
there; and I had formed my own picture of her, one
that the Lettish Queen fit badly. For another, she was
forever dropping things for me to pick up, and calling
me over to hear whispered secrets—anything that she
could think of, and a lot of it excessively silly—or
calling me into her private apartments and contriving
to reveal one breast when she adjusted her gown.

For a third, I had a great deal to tell the Lettish
women at court that I couldn't say in her presence:
the things Baba Yaga and I had worked out about
foreign queens and the like, and how the rest of Europe looked at it and them; I sympathized with the
men's discontents, too, of course, and I soon got their
wives to help me with it.

Baba Yaga and I had estimated that it would be a
year or more before the revolt, but they surprised us.
It hadn't been quite six months when the smell of
smoke woke me. There was a lot of fighting—about
half Koshchei's bodyguard had remained loyal—but
I took as little part in it as possible; my task was to
saddle two fast horses and get Aunt Marya out alive.
I had reminded myself of that, and where the horses
were stabled, and how I could break into the tack
room and all the rest of it, every night before I slept.

Baba Yaga and I had not foreseen that Koshchei

would flee with Aunt Marya and me, but he did. Perhaps he truly loved her; he declared repeatedly that he did. Perhaps he merely counted her as his chief treasure, the Goddess of Battle, or his last.

Certainly he seemed to feel that we had a better chance of escaping alive with his help, and in that I believe he was quite correct. He knew the country that had been his very well, and shrewdly assessed the loyalty of his former subjects in every village and hamlet we passed through, though he made a most-unpleasant companion.

No, he's dead now. We had hardly returned home, that is to say we had hardly reached this Russian estate of mine, when he happened to walk behind an unruly horse and was kicked so severely he died. I'd like to show you the room he occupied, but as it happens I've lost the key. If you'll look out here, however, you ought to be able to make out his window in the moonlight. That small round one high in the tower. See it? The wind howls in it at times, I'm sorry to say. North winds and east winds especially.

Before Koshchei died, the three of us had been living at the Emperor's court in Aachen. My Aunt Marya did not long survive her second husband; she was struck down by the family stomach complaint within the year. I would have had to yield Falkonstein to the von Falkonsteins if Koshchei hadn't declared the Baltic kingdoms—he pretended to rule them all, as did several others—a part of the Empire, and himself a vassal of the Emperor. The very trifling price he asked was that Falkonstein be declared to have passed to him by marriage, in perpetuity—his property and his wife's, to descend to their heirs, several or joint. I detest the old place, as I've said; but there's a certain income attached to it, and it's useful at times to be a German nobleman as well as a Russian one.

Now we'd better be off to bed. If you need more

blankets, or would like a bite to eat or some such, call for Tasha. If the wind howls, shout for Dmitri. He'll climb the tower stairs for you and pound on the door until the wind stops.

Sleep? Oh, you won't sleep. Don't worry about that. Or rather, you already are. Mine was the Russia that never was, you see; and because it has never existed, it cannot fade away like your country, which is vanishing as we speak. It's a pity you can visit us only in dreams, eh?

Still, dreams are better than nothing. Tomorrow night I'll introduce you to Baba Yaga and the firebird, or they'll introduce you to me—it doesn't matter.

Yes, I hear it. *Dmitri!*

Good night, my friend. Just keep your own window shut, and put your head beneath the covers. I'm going to have that window walled up one of these days, I swear.

Dmitri, spishytye! Zadirzhytye yivo!

(The preceding story is based upon "The Death of Koshchei the Deathless" as found in Andrew Lang's *The Red Fairy Book*, first published in 1890.)

The Real Princess

Susan Palwick

Susan Palwick's first novel, Flying in Place, *won the International Association for the Fantastic in the Arts' Crawford Award and has been optioned by Columbia Pictures. Her short fiction has appeared in* Asimov's Science Fiction Magazine, Amazing Stories, Pulphouse, Best of Pulphouse, *and the anthologies* Spirits of Christmas, Ghosttide, *and* Xanadu 3, *as well as in a number of* Year's Best *anthologies.*

Palwick recently completed her doctorate in English Literature at Yale University. She is currently working on her second novel, Shelter.

The tale of the princess and the pea is usually told and retold humorously; even the musical version, Once Upon a Mattress, *treats the theme as a joke. Yet the premise: a powerful man searching for a woman so delicate that she bruises from the tiniest pea at the bottom of dozens of down mattresses hints of sinister motives. Palwick's version delves into those motives.*

The Real Princess

EVERY MORNING, IN THE DARK KITCHEN WHERE THE servant slept on the flagstone hearth, vengeance his only pillow, the King came to him with a dagger. "Kiss it, kitchen boy, and remember your tongue." Every morning the King said this, although the servant had not been a boy for many years, and although both of them knew he would never forget. Some days, if bad weather prevented hunting, if the roast had been burned, if there was no woman to amuse and distract the King—especially then—the servant had to kiss the dagger more than once. If the King was very bored, there would be other rites. The King's ceremonies became more inventive the longer he had been without a woman.

There had been no women all winter. It was spring now, a season of perpetual rain and wind, of a moist warmth in which everything rotted. There was no woman, and for a week the King had been unable to hunt. The weather was very bad, and his favorite hound had died. The first day after the hound's death, the King raged, howling; the second day, he sulked. The third, he brought the hound's collar to the kitchen and said, "Wear this, kitchen boy," and presented the dagger to be kissed, and used it to prod his servant, on all fours now, up the steep, narrow stone stairs to the King's bedroom.

My name is Malcolm, the servant thought as he struggled up the stairs. My name is Malcolm. I am not a beast and I am not a boy and he serves me; more than I have ever done his bidding he does mine, and he does not even know it, this rank-proud King. The stairs stank of mildew; the collar was too tight, and the King's hard boots dug into his backside. My name is Malcolm.

"You aren't moving quickly enough," the King said, almost kindly. "I can do whatever I want to you, because you're mine. Sometimes I think you forget that. Never forget, kitchen boy. Remember, and move faster."

The servant, already moving faster, closed his eyes and remembered.

Once upon a time a beautiful woman married a terrible man. Every day he beat her, and every day she crept, weeping and covered with bruises, to his servant for consolation. When the King went out hunting the woman sat with the servant beside the hearth while he sang ballads about noble kitchen boys who saved beautiful women from cruel husbands. "I will take you away from here," he told her, "and we will be married, because I love you." That was what happened in all the songs he sang; the women, out of gratitude, married the servants who had saved them.

"Yes," she always answered, "please, please, take me away from here." And so he did. They escaped one dark winter night, and he took her back to her father's shabby house with its small stony field and barren garden, its leaking roof and leaning chimney; and there they found the King waiting for them with his sharpest sword and his finest dagger and his three fiercest hounds, and there the servant discovered the limits of gratitude.

"They belong to me," the King said. "I want both of them back. Did any of you think I wouldn't know where to look?"

The dogs growled, and Celia's father shook his head. "I didn't know they were coming here, Sire, I promise you I didn't. Celia, child, you're his wife now. He gave me six goats and a cow for you, and they're gone now, Celia, eaten, I can't give them back. You have to stay with him."

"I can't," she said, and began to cry. "He'll kill me. He never stops, it doesn't matter if I do what he says or not, he beats me anyway. Send the servant back, throw him to the dogs, I don't care what happens to him, but let me stay."

Malcolm, weary with worry and travel, blinked, certain he hadn't heard her properly. "Celia? You said you'd protect me. You said your father—"

"Father," she said, sobbing, "send him back, I don't care about him, but let me stay with you, let me stay here, you have to let me stay. I'll die if I go back."

The King grunted. "True enough. You would. I thought you'd last longer. No stamina at all: a waste of six goats and a cow, that's what you are."

Her father coughed, and the dogs growled again. "Sire—"

"Quiet, all of you. Let me think a minute." The King thought, ignoring them, while Celia pleaded with her father and Malcolm pleaded with Celia and the dogs slavered, straining at their leads. After several minutes he spoke again. "Yes, all right, it's better this way. If she comes back and she dies, she's of no further use to me, and if she dies this wretch will have his revenge for her betrayal. Whereas"—the King smiled—"if I let her stay here and take him back with me, he'll always know that she betrayed him, and that she's still alive.

You'll torment yourself imagining her with other men, won't you, noble kitchen churl? Giving them what she never gave you, what she told you she was too modest to give to any man not her husband? You'll always know she didn't truly love you, and you'll always wonder if she's in the hayloft with some priest or sneaking into the barn to fuck the stallions—"

"Sire," Celia's father said tightly, "stop this. You go too far."

The King scowled at him. "No one gives me orders, old man. I am your King, and you are nothing. I can go as far as I like."

"Celia," the servant said, begging, "don't let him do this. You can't let him do this. I love you. He'll kill me."

"Yes," she said, her eyes averted, "he probably will."

"No, I won't. Not yet, anyway. Not until his suffering grows tedious, and he's quite a bit stronger than you are. I think he'll last a good while. And he does cook a fine stew, for all he talks too much." The King nodded to himself, and began to tether his grumbling hounds to a stunted tree. "Why, now that I think of it, I'll let you have a tender memento, sweet girl. Since you claimed to love his wagging tongue, you may keep it for your own stew; in fact, I think you should have the honor of cutting it off."

"Me?" she said. "Do something like that?"

"Yes, you. After what you've already done to him, this should seem like nothing. In any event, beloved bride, either you do this for me or you come back home."

"I can't," she said.

"Can't what, my love? Cut him, or come home? You have to do one or the other."

She shook her head. "His tongue—"

"You'll find it easy, once you start," the King said

briskly. "Your father and I will hold him down. You'll need a very sharp dagger—here, take mine—and a very hot poker. I think his tongue would go beautifully with some liver and onions, myself, but that's up to you. You'll send me your recipe, won't you? Yes, of course you will, because I'm your King."

An hour later the King rode away with his servant, nearly unconscious from shock and loss of blood, trussed and lashed to the saddle. Where his tongue had once been there was now only a cauterized stump. The recipe never arrived, but other women did. The kingdom was appallingly poor, rich only in fathers desperate for their daughters to be married, daughters who came knocking at the King's door and slept on the pile of twenty featherbeds and dutifully pinched themselves black and blue, that part of the story having become general knowledge; and when, after the inevitable weddings, they came bloody and weeping to Malcolm, offering him gold or jewels or their battered bodies, he ignored them. All women were liars. He knew that now. And these were fools: what had they expected, from a man whose only requirement in a bride was tender skin?

Four women had died, after Celia, or maybe five; Malcolm had done everything he could to lose count, to forget their names, their faces, their screams. As the King had predicted, he had never forgotten Celia.

I will kill him, Malcolm had promised himself, every day for months after he lost his tongue. I will kill him and I will be a man again. Every day he had promised himself that he would kill the King, and every day he did nothing. After the third woman died, or maybe the fourth, he began to understand why. He hated the King's wives; he wanted them to die. Because one woman had hurt him, he hated all women, and hated himself for hating, and hated women even more for making him hate. Whenever one of the King's wives screamed, Malcolm had the comfort of knowing that the King was the murderer, and that he was not. Perhaps he was not wholly innocent—since he loved so much now to hear them scream, since he did nothing to save them, since he always pictured Celia dying in their stead—but at least he fought his own desires. He stopped his ears with wax to block out the sound he lusted for; he prayed most fervently, dawn and evening, for his own soul and the King's damnation.

He wept the night he realized this. He tossed and turned on the hard flagstone hearth, and wept, and hated himself and women and the King. Only at dawn did he realize at last, in wonder, that he already had his revenge.

He serves me; he who prides himself on taking orders from no one takes them from me whenever he bloodies his women, for it is my wishes he carries out, all unknowing. He is the wicked one, and I am unstained. As long as he lives, this wicked wicked man, I need kill no one. He is my slave and my salvation.

There was a rat in the King's bedroom. It was missing patches of fur. It ran ceaselessly against one wall, back and forth, back and forth, seeking an exit. "You know what I want you to do," the King said. "My good gray Wolfgar would have caught and killed this vermin for me; my good gray Wolfgar is dead, and so the task falls to you."

It took him an hour; the King would not allow him to use his hands, and as hard as he tried he could not pretend that the rat was a woman. That would have been some joy, to have imagined killing Celia or one of the others, to have the taste of blood in his mouth, and all the time to know that really he killed only a beast. But it was not possible, because the rat squeaked and squealed but never screamed.

Afterward, bleeding where the rat had bitten him, he wept and vomited, and the King, his eyes very bright, said, "Wolfgar would have had this little prize for his supper. Would you like it?"

He vomited again, and the King's breath quickened. "Wolfgar would have eaten that, too—"

He was interrupted by a pounding on the kitchen door downstairs, blows raining on the heavy wood. "Ignore that," the King said sharply; but after a heartbeat, it came again, more insistently, accompanied by a thin wail. "Whining beggars. Let them whine!"

Another whine, and words this time, traveling impossibly through the thick, weathered door and up the stone stairway. "In! Let me in! In!"

"Is that a woman?" the King asked, his breath catching. "Wolfgar—"

My name is Malcolm, he thought, and got up and bolted out of the room, on two legs again at last. He nearly fell, going down the stairs. His knees kept buckling, and his hands shook; it seemed to take an age to raise the heavy iron latch, even with that howling whine from outside goading him.

Someone small shoved past him the minute he opened the door. "In! Let me in, out of this water!" When Malcolm turned around he found himself confronted with a young girl, bundled in layers, who tore off her dripping cloak and threw it into the far corner of the kitchen.

"Rain! Nothing but rain, for three days! Does the sun never shine in this wretched kingdom?"

Malcolm shook his head, and she glared at him, shivering. Her eyes were bright green, her chin sharply pointed, her hair black as midnight. In her thin damp smock, she looked even younger than she had at first, but she was too angular to be beautiful. She returned Malcolm's frank gaze and sniffed, her eyes narrowing as if in pain. "I smell something dead.

What died here, and why are you bleeding?''

Many things have died here, lady. But he would not have told her that, even had he been able to. Instead he opened his mouth grotesquely wide and shook his head, pointing to the stump of his tongue, pantomiming a sawing blade. "Oh," she said, and grimaced, or smiled; Malcolm could not have said which. Her teeth, he saw, were as pointed as her chin. She reminded him of the rat. "How exceedingly unpleasant. Where's the King? You aren't the King, are you?''

She sounded almost hopeful. He shook his head, and she sighed. "Just a servant. Well then, servant, I need things you can give me without talking. Rest and shelter and meat. Especially meat.''

Meat, Malcolm thought, the rat's blood liquid metal in his mouth. He felt laughter bubbling up in him like a scream. Yes, lady, we have meat for you. Fresh meat, newly killed; and if you stay here you'll become meat, mincemeat for the King, who is my slave. He smiled at her, baring his teeth, the rat's blood dripping down his chin. Any other woman would have squealed the way the rat itself had, but this one only tapped her foot impatiently.

The King entered the kitchen then, and saw the girl, and smiled. "Welcome, fair maid! You must excuse my half-wit servant Wolfgar. He had an unfortunate accident some years ago—''

"So I see," said the girl, dryly.

"He was making love to another man's wife—he couldn't be blamed, poor thing, it was her fault really, playing on his lust and his addled wits, and so the enraged husband arranged for his tongue to be—''

"No more," she said, and shuddered again.

"No more," the King agreed, "yes, that's exactly right. No more tongue. But ever since then, he's fancied the taste of blood. It excites him. His lust and his punishment became entangled in his poor confused mind . . . Wolfgar, go clean yourself. This is no way to greet visitors."

Knowing that the King would find some way to hurt him if he resisted, he went to the water bucket and began rinsing his face. Malcolm, he told himself, Malcolm, Malcolm. And you are my slave, however it may look. You do more terrible things for me than ever you have done to me.

Behind him, the King had begun his courtship. "So, lady. Are you a princess?"

"Aye," she said, "and have traveled far on my quest, and perhaps this be its end."

"I hope it is," the King said smoothly.

"I hope so too," she said, and yawned. "Kind lord, I am weary after my travels. You have, I believe, a quantity of featherbeds?"

"Indeed," said the King, and they left the kitchen together and Malcolm, done cleaning the vile taste of the rat's blood from his mouth, put the rest of the water on to boil. The King would want his morning tea and the girl, when she awoke, would want to bathe. They always did after the first sleep, claiming to be stiff and sore from the lumpy mattresses. This one, who had not even waited until nightfall to demonstrate how easily she bruised, was dispensing quickly with the preliminaries.

She came downstairs at noon, limping and scowling; the King hovered around her in conspicuous concern, his eyes gleaming in the firelight. It was still raining. "Meat," the girl said, with something like a snarl, and the King looked inquiringly at Malcolm, who shook his head. There was no meat in the house except the rat, and a rat was hardly suitable fare for a King and his guest, even had this one been large enough to feed two. The cupboard held only bread, which sprouted ornate patterns of mold, and tough, stunted vegetables.

"You shall have meat," the King said with a smile. "I will hunt for your supper, fair lady."

"In the rain?" the child asked with a shudder.

"Anything for you," the King said lightly. "My best hound has just died, but I shall take the others and go hunting through the forest. I will bring back venison, or maybe a bear. Will you accompany me?"

"Not in the rain," she said. A gleam of disdain came over the sharp features. "Happy hunting, my lord."

The King bowed, sweeping himself out of the kitchen into the dripping, gusty wet. When the door was safely shut behind him, the girl made a face. "I'm too hungry to wait, kitchen boy. Take me to the creature you killed."

Malcolm squinted at her, his stomach rebelling, and shook his head. Stupid girl! Did she think it was a pretty rabbit he'd killed, a doe, some dainty morsel? He could not take her to the rat, no, not that hideous mangled thing. If once she saw it, surely she would flee, and the King would lose his true game and Malcolm his heart's desire.

"You refuse me?" she said. "You dare question the appetites of your future Queen?" She laughed. "Oh, yes, he's asked me already, never fear. He wishes me to feel honored that he stoops to wed a penniless, starving orphan, but I know desperation when I see it. Desperation and lies, kitchen boy. He can't even tell the truth about his food. All the deer have been hunted off this land, and the bears are too smart for him. He traded all his livestock for women long ago, and now he eats whatever he can find. If I hadn't arrived, he'd have dined on the thing upstairs, wouldn't he? Since I'm here, he'll do his best to bring back something more appealing. I can't wait that long. I'm sick of roots and berries, kitchen boy. Take me to the meat."

Stupid girl, Malcolm thought, chilled and uneasy and trying to be scornful. Stupid, stupid girl. If you know so much about the King, why did you come here? Why did you tell him you were an orphan? An orphan princess would be a queen, stupid girl, even I know that much. If you have neither father nor money to protect you, the King needs no wedding: he can begin to beat you whenever he wishes.

Let her eat the cursed rat, if it would make her happy. She had worse than that awaiting her. He bowed, mockingly, and led her upstairs. Surely she would scream, when she saw that mangled and bloody carcass. Even if she fled afterward, he would have the joy of hearing her scream, and all because he had done exactly as she asked. But when he opened the door to the King's bedchamber the girl darted forward with a cry of joy and scooped up the rat's limp body with both hands. As Malcolm watched, his hand still on the iron latch of the door, she began to devour the corpse, tearing it with her teeth.

He turned and fled, reflexively crossing himself, too stunned even to be ill. The fiercest of the King's fierce hounds had never eaten as desperately as she. Surely she wasn't human: no woman would eat like that. She must be something else, something evil, a punishment sent upon the household for its sins. I must leave here to save myself, Malcolm thought, but where can I go? Wherever I run this thing will travel with me. I will become the evil if I leave, with no slave to do my bidding for me.

Cold sweat bathed his neck; his hands shook as helplessly as they had when he killed the rat. I am afraid, he thought, more afraid even than when I saw Celia standing over me with the dagger. His fear filled him with rage.

No, he told himself, fear not; have faith. Whatever she is, she cannot be as evil as he is. He will destroy her just as he destroyed all those who came before her, and we will be safe again.

The King brought home two rabbits, a squirrel, and a pheasant, more game than he'd caught in weeks. "The bear got away," he said, "although I chased it for miles after wounding it; it might have turned on me at any moment, the great brown beast. I tracked it half the day, but I didn't want to leave you alone any longer—"

"You've been tracking it for years, in your dreams," the girl said mildly. She had spent the afternoon napping, curled contentedly near the kitchen fire like the cat her meal had made her resemble. While she slept, Malcolm had cleaned the King's bedroom, disposing of the polished bones and bits of fur she had left behind. "Your kingdom isn't hours wide, my lord. But you enjoyed killing the rabbits, didn't you?"

The King smiled, a tight grimace that showed the tips of his teeth. "Rabbits, pfaugh. Minor game. The dogs did that."

"Nay," she said quietly. "I can see their legs well enough, the bite of the traps. Minor game is all you have left, and you don't want the dogs to get to it before you do, because you can't feed them enough and they'd eat your supper if they could, poor brutes . . . so you set traps for rabbits and squirrels and such. You're as hungry as any common poacher, for all you call yourself a king. Were these still alive when you found them?"

The King cleared his throat; Malcolm could see him trembling. "You take liberties, Princess. I have never been a commoner, and anyone who calls me common will be felled to lie in the common dust—even you, for all your beauty. Hear me, and listen well: you will never speak such an insult again." He gestured haughtily for the girl to remove his drenched cloak; she hung back instead, wrinkling her nose at the muddy wool. Malcolm, coaxing a memory of heat from the carefully banked embers of the hearth, wondered in amazement how she could speak to the King this way, and how dirty clothing could possibly disgust her after raw rat.

"I will speak truth," she said, "and you will return the favor. How many rabbits were still alive?"

"One," the King said, hatred seething in his voice. Again he gestured for her help with the cloak, and again she refused; Malcolm stepped forward instead, and the King let him. No doubt the King expected her airs to vanish quickly enough. A few hours earlier, Malcolm would have thought so too. "One of the rabbits lay kicking in the trap, Princess. I broke its neck, its soft thin spine, and it writhed and struggled in my hands but to no avail, because I twisted its head until—"

"Until it died," she said sharply. "Thank you. That will be enough."

"Perhaps it won't be enough," the King said, his eyes gleaming, and flexed his hands. He must at last have sensed a difference in this one too; usually he refrained from actual blows until after the wedding. But maybe there would be no wedding after all, since she had admitted she was an orphan. "Perhaps I'll have to show you exactly how I killed the rabbit. Do you think you'd enjoy that?"

"If I thought I'd enjoy it, I'd have hunted rabbits with you," she said.

"Oh," he said scornfully, "but you're squeamish, aren't you, a weak woman who can't bear to see anything suffer, a real princess." The loathing in his voice made Malcolm's skin crawl. If she were what she seemed, a small weak girl with passing sense, surely she would bolt from the house this very moment.

"A real princess," she agreed, and smiled. "The question is, have I found a real king?" Most strangely then, she looked at Malcolm.

Malcolm had been right. There was no wedding: the girl spent that night, not on the twenty featherbeds, but in the King's chamber, without blessing of clergy. She hadn't missed much. The King's weddings were shabby affairs, attended only by the priest who had performed every other wedding, and who always left the house with a shining share of the King's meager store of gold, the hard wealth he hoarded for just such occasions. Gold bought God's silence.

No need to buy anyone's silence about this strange waif. Malcolm went to bed earlier than usual that night, and plugged his ears with tallow to block out the screaming he knew would follow as inevitably as evening follows noon. He took too much pleasure in the screaming; his pleasure blurred the line between himself and the King, the thin thin line he must maintain for his soul's sake, the line between the servant and the served, between innocence and sin. Tonight he would be deeply asleep by the time the screaming started.

And so he was, but the screaming woke him anyway. All the tallow in the world couldn't have shut out that keening wail, so different from the abrupt, ugly shriekings of the others. This sound was like mourning, like death, like all the grief anyone had ever felt in the world, all rolled into one endless moan, rising and falling, punctuated with blows that grow ever louder, more insistent, more rhythmic.

No screaming had ever lasted this long. The noise went on and on, howling, filling the house, making the walls hum and the windows whine. How could someone so small create so much sound? Malcolm, terrified, thought of banshees and damned souls, but when he tried to pray to the Blessed Virgin he kept seeing Celia instead, as she had looked in the instant before she began to cut away his tongue, the last moment in which he had been able to hope.

At last, near dawn, the blows stopped, and the keening with them. Malcolm slept, and dreamed that he was back in the King's bedroom, hunting the rat. In his dream the animal kept running toward him, squeaking and squealing. "Run away," he told it, discovering that in the dream he could speak. "If you will not run away, how can I take pride in hunting you?" He flapped his arms and clapped his hands at it, trying to make it flee, but it insisted on following him. "What do you want?" he asked, despairing. "What do you want? Go away. Why do you not try to save yourself?"

"You must save me," the rat said. Its voice was Celia's. "You must save me if you wish to save yourself."

"I did save you," he cried. "I did, and you betrayed me, and now I will kill you."

"Then you will never taste my pleasures, my sweet sweet flesh," said the rat, and as it spoke it changed into a woman, a woman with tangled hair and soft breasts and warm full buttocks, who spread her legs to receive Malcolm into a warmth that rocked to the rhythm of the sea.

He awoke in a cold sweat, into the reawakened ache of his missing tongue and the chill of the dying fire, to discover that he had spent himself on the stone floor of the kitchen and that the girl was sitting next to him, mottled with bruises, her nose bleeding and her lips puffy. She regarded him calmly, and said in a low voice, "Do you want me? I can make you a king, my good man, yes indeed, and give you a tongue again too, but only if you protect me from that other one, your demon, your dark twin. If you do that

I shall truly make him your slave. Do you want me like this, raw and bloody, or would you rather have me whole, all yours forever?"

I want you dead, he thought, shaking with rage and loathing. Had Celia sent her? Was she some trick of the King's, to see if he could once more be beguiled into dangerous desire?

The girl shook her head. "Fear not; I risk more than you do. I could never hurt you, not with a dagger or anything else, not if my very life depended on it, and I cannot leave this house without your help. I can't so much as open the door, because the latch is iron."

Neither princess nor orphan, then, but a witch. Witches feared iron. Everyone knew that. But if she were a witch, why didn't she save herself? She didn't need to lift the latch: she could fly out the window, if she were a witch. She could conjure all the meat she desired out of stale bread and wet wool. She could turn the King into a rat.

"I could free you from this place forever," the girl said gently, as she sat bleeding beside him, "if only you will free yourself from your master. You can rule him only by being stronger than he is."

I already rule him, Malcolm thought, his fists clenched. He is my slave.

"If you would rule him, or rule yourself, you must challenge him," she said. "Your fear puts you in thrall to him, even as his first wife was in thrall. He told me that story, to frighten me, but even in his telling I could tell that she betrayed you because she feared him, and was ashamed. Even if, in the end, she'd been content to marry a kitchen boy, she never could have lived with someone who'd seen her bruised and bleeding. I have no such qualms. I require no rank in my husband but courage, and so you must redeem yourself and fight him for me."

And become the monster, forever, all hope of redemption lost. He stared at her, stonily, and shook his head. It was all a trick. Whether she was woman or devil or both, he knew better than to make deals with her.

"What are you talking about?" the King said, entering the kitchen. He was angry. His voice hissed with hatred, and Malcolm's own anger turned to the queasy fear of which the girl had accused him. The King was never angry after the beatings; he loved his marked brides, loved their cringing terror of him. Angry—and he was angrier now than Malcolm had ever seen him—he would lash out at anything.

"I was talking about marriage," the girl said.

"To him, lady impudence? I made my first wife cut off his tongue: I'll make you cut off his manhood if you sneak away from my bed to dally with him." He struck her across the mouth, knocking her to the ground; she did nothing to resist, but only looked up at Malcolm.

"Aren't you going to beg him for help?" the King said. "Your hero, your savior? Look at him cringing there, like a whipped dog. Beg him, my sweet."

She yawned. "I have, my lord, and he refused."

"He refused because he's afraid of me," said the King. "He refused because he isn't a man at all. Do you know, in all these years, he's never once tried to kill me? He could have done it easily enough, any number of times: crept up on me as I slept, smashed my head in with the poker or stabbed me with my own dagger, the bright blade he kisses each time he wakes. But he never even tried, because he's a coward."

I could have done it whenever I chose, Malcolm thought in fury. I never did it because I needed you to rid the world of women. If I once killed a person, and not a rat, I would be damned as surely as you are.

"And yet you were unable to cut out his tongue yourself," the girl said pleasantly. "You made a trembling woman do it instead. I think you're the true coward in this house, Sire."

"Strumpet," the King said, his voice very low. "Whore. Bitch. You call *me* a coward?" He picked up the iron poker and struck her with it, and she screamed.

Her earlier wailing, terrible as it had been, seemed like the sweetest of music compared to this. This scream shattered pottery on the kitchen shelves and sent small insects running in maddened circles over the floor. Outside, the King's hounds began to howl, crazed by the noise. Malcolm's eyeballs ached; his bones rang with the screaming, and he thought his skull would burst. Only the King seemed impervious, kicking her as she screamed, raising the poker to strike her again, although the very iron vibrated with her agony.

Iron. A witch couldn't fight iron, but Malcolm could. She was right: the king was a coward, and he would not have a coward for his slave. *I will free you from this place forever*, she had said, and now he understood. He would prove his manhood by killing the King, and then he would kill her with the poker, as he truly wished to do, and then—for he knew he would be sickened by the work, however much he relished it—why, then he would kill himself and save God the trouble. He was already irrevocably damned, for having seen so much: he knew that now. He was tired unto death of this place, of the hard hearth and the meager meat and the King's gruesome games. He wanted to be rid of his life, and the King richly deserved to be rid of his own, and surely even the girl wished to have hers taken from her, or she would not lie there on the floor so meekly. *You must fight him for me*, she had said, and now he knew she meant not for her favors but for the merciful task of releasing her. He leapt for the King's neck, his hands outstretched.

The King turned and saw Malcolm, and raised the poker to strike. "You die first," he said, but suddenly the room was filled with a cold blue light and the King stopped, frozen, as the girl got up, her blood blowing away in a sprinkle of golden dust, her wounds closing as easily as eyes shutting for sleep. Malcolm discovered that he could not move.

"Ah," she said, "ah, my lovelies, I have indeed reached the end of my quest. I am no witch, no mortal woman, but the Queen of Elfland's daughter: changeling child, princess and orphan both. The human parents who raised me are dead, but my other mother lives, and awaits my return to her realm. And now I have a prince and a kitchen boy to bring with me." She laughed, a merry rill. "I have found my heart's desire: a husband who would kill for me but will never contradict me, a husband who is as handsome as any storybook prince but as willing to forfeit his soul as any heartless villain, a husband who can teach the cook to make a good stew."

She reached up to caress Malcolm's cheek and then stood on tiptoe to kiss him, fire flooding his brain and his groin at the same time. When she had taken away the wet warmth of her mouth, she said, "You see, my love, you shall not miss your tongue when we are married, because each night I shall give you mine. And you need no longer fear death: in the lands I rule, the lands where you will someday reign as King, you shall live forever. Your hatred will make you a fearsome foe to my enemies, and your wish to watch others destroy them will make you a brilliant commander in chief."

She laughed again, exulting, and the fire in Malcolm's brain became ice. "And you," she said, turning to the other man, "are an even rarer find. We love meat, I and my people; we devour it whenever we find it, but we cannot kill the creatures who produce it. No one of my kind can kill so much as an ant, because we who can feel the pain of anything alive cannot bear the pain of death. But you, you who revel in it, you who are only spurred on to fiercer blows by the most piercing shrieks—ah, my lord, you will make a priceless kitchen boy.''

The Huntsman's Story

Milbre Burch

A nationally known storyteller, writer, and re-cording artist, Milbre Burch has performed from Maui to Martha's Vineyard. She has produced five cassette tapes, and her monologues and sto-ries have been published in various magazines, in the anthology Xanadu 2, *and in* Best-Loved Stories Told at the National Storytelling Fes-tival. *She lives with her husband and daughter in Pasadena, California.*

She wrote "The Huntsman's Story" in re-sponse to the discovery of Polly Klass's body two months after the twelve-year-old's kidnapping.

The Huntsman's Story

THE HUNTSMAN DID TOO GOOD A JOB THIS TIME, AR-riving unbidden at the castle. The child—a budding beauty it's true—had stirred no fires of jealousy in her mother's sleeping breast. No wicked stepmother with a golden circlet and a magic mirror called him forth from a forest deep as hell. No one said, "Take her into the woods and kill her there. Bring me her heart and lungs to prove you did it." He found his way unbidden.

Was it a ghoulish bit player's revenge? Never any character development, always too few lines. Many people find the huntsman's part in the old story forgettable. The castle keepers felt complacent, never wondered if those unaccounted-for years on his résumé were spent in their own dungeons. They'll be sorry now that they never checked his references, or inquired of his motivation. He rehearsed this one on his own, offstage, twice before.

The girls were surprised to see him in their sleeping chamber. Like the huntsman of old, he had a knife. She followed him mutely, not out of literary convention, but because he bound her mouth with duct tape. They did not walk together; he carried her away into the woods. And there, his eyes, two mirrors without magic, reflected the last moments of her life. He cannot say for sure what happened. He does not remember clearly anything except the spot where he left her. Alone.

No seven small men to befriend her. When it's time, there will be six pallbearers, and perhaps a seventh— her father—to weep at the head or foot of a closed casket. A crystal coffin would be out of the question; it was two months between death and discovery, after all. Instead her beauty's been preserved on milk cartons and posters in pet stores the length of the nation. No further encounters with the witch-queen, not even time for another "Good-night, Mommy, I love you." No prince's sweet kiss and whisper can awaken her, nor can the bone-piercing shriek of a mother who's outlived her child.

The huntsman came unbidden this time. He came through the sleepy countryside on a task of his own imagining. He says even he's sorry now, for taking the story into his own hands. We all are. Years from now both their ghosts will continue to stalk the landscape of our dreams. She, luminescent, bright-eyed, smiling still. He, bearded, returning, always returning to the castle door, with heart and lungs in hand, asking "Where's the one that ordered me to kill Snow White?" In the moment before we awaken screaming, we'll always hear our own voices saying, "We did."

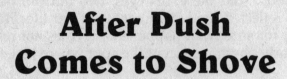

After Push Comes to Shove

Milbre Burch

Burch wrote "After Push Comes to Shove" during the 1993 Los Angeles fires.

After Push
Comes to Shove

I am curled in a fetal position
in the darkness and the heat,
surrounded on all sides by my red-hot iron tomb.
My limbs tied
in a careless knot of falling inward,
sacrificed because my own naïveté
outweighed that of a little girl.
My hair frizzles in a flash,
my eyes melt, my tongue bakes,
my flesh splits and oozes,
my grease spatters the sides of the oven.
In a way, it is a relief;
a diet of children is very rich
both in calories and karma.
And now, by their actions,
they are become what I once was.
She tricked me, the little hussy,
egged on by my poor eyesight
and bad judgment.
Pretending to passivity no more,

she's saved that worthless brother of hers,
all meat and ill-begun ideas.
They'll take my treasure
the same way they gnawed my house
as if it were their due.
They'll share their ill-gotten gains
with their foolish father.
He, meanwhile, for sentimental reasons
will have discarded the clever second wife.
He no longer needs her thrift;
his future's certain now.
They'll, all of them, grow soft and mean.
The father putting aside his trade as a woodcutter
and going to brothels till
his advancing age and worthlessness
cause his beloved children
to rid themselves of him.
If there's any justice in the cosmos,
they'll desert the old man
in the woods on a winter's night.
He will have long since forgotten the way
and freeze to death before hunger gets him.
Hansel and Grethel will fight
over the inheritance, and end
by poisoning one another
with a glass of lemonade
and a dish of gingerbread.
I take some comfort in this
as my organs become ash and
I am burned away to what's at my core:
a child alone in the woods.

Hansel and Grettel

Gahan Wilson

Gahan Wilson is descended from such authentic American folk heroes as circus and freak king, P.T. Barnum, and silver-voiced orator, William Jennings Bryan. He was officially declared born dead by the attending physician in Evanston, Illinois, but, rescued by another medico who dipped him alternately in bowls of hot and cold water, he survived to become the first student in the Art Institute of Chicago to actually admit he was going there to learn how to become a cartoonist.

His work has appeared in periodicals as diverse as Playboy, The New Yorker, Weird Tales, Gourmet, Punch, *and* Paris Match *and the cover of* Newsweek. *Selections from this accumulation have appeared in over fifteen cartoon collections, most recently in* Still Weird. *Wilson has also written children's books and has had*

many spooky stories for grown-ups published in
Playboy, Omni, Fantasy and Science Fiction,
and numerous anthologies. He has authored two
mystery novels, Eddy Deco's Last Caper *and*
Everybody's Favorite Duck. *He has done*
graphic novels on Poe and Ambrose Bierce; and
has completed his first animated movie, a grue-
some cartoon short called Gahan Wilson's
Diner. *A ROM disk interactive game called Ga-*
han Wilson's The Ultimate Haunted House
is out and another is in the works.

Hansel and Grettel are usually seen as poor,
helpless innocents (except for devouring a tasty
house that doesn't belong to them)—Wilson in
his inimitable way, does a little twist.

Hansel and Grettel

ONCE UPON A TIME THERE WAS A SIMPLY ADORABLE brother and sister who were so lovely that it is almost impossible to describe to you how really lovely they were, but I shall try, my dears, I shall do my very best.

The one you noticed first would always be the sister, whose name was Grettel, my sweets. She was so very beautiful that when she entered a room all heads would turn in her direction—absolutely all of them without exception—and their eyes would follow her as she made her way to the very best table in the restaurant or the finest seat in the theater, and the men would do their best to try and hide it from the women they were with how furious they were to be with those women instead of being with Grettel. And the women would try to hide it from the men they were with that they knew their men felt that way and would wish deep down in the darkest depths of their hearts—oh my God how they would wish it!—that they were as beautiful as Grettel and that the men they were with were dead and buried and out of the way so that they could enter a room as *she* did and have all the new, the fresh men, gaze at them with that much yearning and desire.

But then the women would notice Hansel.

My darlings, it was a quiet thing that Hansel did, getting this second notice, but oh what a noticing it was, for when they saw Hansel the women forgot all about Grettel and the men they were with and all that was in their pretty little heads were dreams of themselves running far away with Hansel, to Hawaii, perhaps, or to any place where the men they were with would be distant, forgotten creatures, someplace where they and Hansel could and would spend twenty-four hours a day, day after day, making love to one another.

And the men they were with would shift in their chairs and glance sidewise with squinting eyes at their women from behind their menus or their theater programs and when they saw the rapt expression on their faces as they gazed, dreaming, at Hansel, they would glare unseeing at their menus or theater programs while they plotted how to kill the women they were with very slowly so that they would suffer excruciating agonies before they finally died.

But the sad thing about it was, you know, the real pity was that Hansel and Grettel never did a thing about it. All those hopeful, yearning men and women, and they never did a thing about a single one of them. Not ever. Not once.

They seemed totally unaware of all those yearning looks, did handsome Hansel and lovely Grettel, as they entered those rooms or restaurants or theaters. They smiled and glowed and shone and sparkled and flowed gracefully before all those adoring gazes without appearing to notice a single aching glance nor hear a solitary heartfelt sigh.

But of course they did notice, my dears, they noticed every one. They lapped them up. They would have died without them.

Still one must have sympathy for Hansel and Grettel as their story was rather tragic, rather sad. Their parents had cast them out, you see. Not once, but twice. The first time is still quite a well-kept secret, my dears, a *very* well-kept secret. No one who knows about the first time speaks of it, and of course you darlings won't say a word about it, now, will you? Of course you won't because you know that would make your Aunt Meryl very sad and very angry. Very angry. And you wouldn't want me angry at you, would you my dears? No, of course you wouldn't.

There, there, did I frighten you? Now don't fret so or I won't go on with the story. That's better. That's my good little darlings, my bitsy snookums.

Well, anyhow, when they were very young, just as young as you are, there was a great financial depression going on and all those funny people you see when you're out in the streets were losing their jobs in amazing numbers and looking more ragged and dirty by the day. Of course that was nothing near so bad as what was happening to people like ourselves, darlings, people who had *real* money to lose.

Hansel and Grettel's parents were starting to notice that there wasn't quite as much to spend as there used to be and less all the time and it dawned on them they'd have to do something very serious about it if they wanted to avoid dipping into their capital, so, just like that, they decided to kill their children.

Now, now, don't look at me that way, my dears. It's only that sometimes grown-ups have to do things they'd really rather not. It's just the way it is, so stop fretting.

As it happened their plan didn't work out and the children lived because Hansel was very clever and left a little trail of stones which led them back to safety, you see. Grettel was most impressed, and of course their parents were fit to be tied.

There was quite a to-do about it at the time—headlines in the tabloids and things like that—but Hansel and Grettel's mother and father still did have quite a bit of money in spite of the depression, *and* considerable influence, and after the family spent a year or two in Europe the whole thing had blown over and their lawyers told them they could come back home.

But the truth is the whole business *did* something to Hansel and Grettel. For one thing, it seriously affected their attitude toward their parents, and, for another, it rather embittered them toward the world in general.

Things never really did work out emotionally in the family after the episode, and it was finally arranged that when Hansel and Grettel finished with their education they would receive an enormous amount of money—for you see, darlings, that nasty depression thing had run its course and everyone was rich again—and go off on their own and nobody would ever again mention the unfortunate business about the attempted murder.

So Hansel and Grettel permanently left their parents and just traveled and traveled and traveled to their hearts' content, my darlings, and bought everything they wanted, and at first they rented things, *châteaux* in Switzerland and *mas* in the south of France and golden palaces in Thailand and so on and so on, but then they settled on the grand hotels, darlings, because it seemed so much simpler that way. No permanent servants, you see, no fussing about with gardens and all that, and it was such a delightful game finding the very best suites and getting more service and attention from the management than anyone else in the place.

Of course the hoteliers loved them, simply adored them, couldn't get enough of them. They knew their season was made if Hansel and Grettel decided to spend it with them and they were very careful to see to it that they did have the best accommodations since they were of course aware that Hansel and Grettel always knew at once if they *didn't* have the very best accommodations, and they tried to anticipate their every wish, giving them all the little treats and extras they could possibly desire, and to dream up and arrange a few delightful surprises if it was at all possible.

But as time went by Hansel and Grettel began to realize they were staying at the same places again and again because, my darlings, the awful truth is there simply aren't that many really good grand hotels, some of them are not even all that grand if the truth be told, so eventually they very understandably began to fret at the lack of novelty.

They were brooding about it in the salon of the very best suite in the very best grand hotel in all of Belgium when Grettel suddenly brightened, gave the most exquisite little cry of joy, and sat up in her chaise longue.

"I know what," she cried happily, turning to her brother. "Let's discover little places no one tells anyone else about because they want to keep them for themselves—People will be ever so deliciously *furious* when they've found out that we've found them!"

"Oh, what fun!" said Hansel, gazing dreamily into space and imagining all those hilariously angry people as he neatly popped a new Astrakhan cigarette into his holder.

So they started a whole new game and what a perfectly delightful one it turned out to be, darlings, what a marvelous time they had tracking down lovely, tucked-away resorts which people had spent fortunes trying to keep hidden and ferreting out exquisite auberges whose very existences had been jealously kept secret by their wealthy clientele for generations.

And what a highly satisfactory sensation was always reliably caused when the regulars of these establishments arrived at their previously exclusive hideaways and not only discovered Hansel and Grettel there before them, but occupying the very best suites or cabins in the whole place! Oh, they *were* furious, my darlings, you can be sure of that. Wildly, uncontrollably furious. Though, of course, they did their very best not to show it.

Naturally locating these marvelous spots wasn't at all easy because, of course, considerable ingenuity had gone into keeping them secret, but Hansel and Grettel were both not only very clever, they were also, as I've told you, very beautiful and charming and they knew how to use these things to worm secrets out of positively anyone. And it goes without saying they had the money and the common sense to hire a number of highly efficient agents to help them in their continuing quest.

Well, it did turn out to be absolutely marvelous fun, my dears, just as Hansel had guessed it might—uncovering the most fabulous places and spoiling them for everybody else; finding more and more deeply concealed retreats as they and their agents grew increasingly skillful at sniffing them out, but never, not in their greediest, gaudiest dreams, did they imagine what a strange and magical place all of this would eventually lead them to!

They first learned of it while staying at a tiny spa attractively blended into a Rumanian hill village, in full possession of a sumptuous but amusingly peasanty cottage which had up to then always been occupied during the season by an industrialist and his fat wife who were presently sulking in a definitely inferior sort of hut down the glen.

Hansel and Grettel's cottage had its very own mineral bath built into the rock grotto of its terrace and the two of them were gaily splashing about in it, enjoying a little soak, when the steward came by with a particularly interesting report which had been wired to them by one of their very best agents, a wealthy young American woman, Bobsie, who had taken the job as a kind of hobby. You can imagine their excitement, darlings, when they read that Bobsie had managed to track down a spectacularly thrilling new find and the more they read, the more their excitement grew.

Her first clue came, Bobsie told them, when she remembered hearing marvelous rumors as a little rich girl in Philadelphia about a wonderful secret castle somewhere in Europe to which only the very, very wealthy could go on account of its being so expensive, you see, and because none but the absolutely best people were allowed.

Once she recalled this charming childhood tale she couldn't resist looking into it to see if there might be some truth to the story. At first she could find absolutely no hard information to back it up and she began to suspect that the whole thing might only have been a girlish fantasy her little friends had made up to amuse themselves on rainy afternoons, but then she started coming across tiny bits of really solid, *grown-up* gossip about it here and there, and in the end her persistence and her connections won out—she was, after all, the daughter of a prominent senator and the heiress to several large newspapers from her mother's previous marriage—and the truth finally tumbled into her lap.

The place was located deep within the Black Forest and was without doubt the oldest and most distinguished retreat any of Hansel and Grettel's agents had come across so far. No one knew when it had actually been built—the report by no means dispelled the charming air of mystery which enshrouded all of the establishment's history—but its tall towers with their

conical roofs and its surrounding moat appeared to
mark it as medieval, and since its general grandiosity
left no doubt that some unknown regal hand had been
involved in its construction, it had come to be known
as King's Retreat, only in German of course, my darlings.

Royals of various nations were always associated
with the place, the Hapsburgs primarily, but Bobsie
had discovered that it was a favorite hideaway of
many foreign blue bloods such as Queen Victoria's
duke of Clarence when he felt like being especially
naughty on the Continent, and scads and scads of
other sorts of famous people went there, darlings,
whom you may learn about when you get a little
older and interested in such things. Zelda and Scott
Fitzgerald just loved the wine list, for example, and
Hermann Goering simply adored the hunting.

Of course you can see that nothing would do but that
Hansel and Grettel must go to King's Retreat as soon as
possible, so Bobsie—and an *awful* lot of money—saw to
it that the absolute best suite in the whole place
would be ready and waiting for them the very next day.
Off they went, darlings, leaving the rich industrialist
and his fat wife to take over the Rumanian cottage
which, of course, would never again give them anywhere near as much pleasure as it had before.

Grettel fell in love with King's Retreat at her first
sighting of it from their Rolls' window. It was perched
proudly atop a mountain with bright white, bannered
turrets and spotless, gracefully curving walls which
had an interestingly irregular glitter of gold running
along the rims of their high upper edges. It seemed
in every way to be just like a castle in a fairy story,
darlings, which of course is why I'm telling you about
it now at bedtime. Naturally Grettel was thrown into
a perfect transport of delight.

"It's so sparkly and bright," she cried happily,

tightly grasping one of her little pink hands with the other. "It looks like a candy castle!"

"Why so it does!" said Hansel, pouring them both another glass of champagne without spilling so much as one single solitary drop.

It shows you both what a grand job Bobsie had done and what an impressive reputation Hansel and Grettel had gotten among hoteliers when I tell you that when their Rolls pulled up to the graceful bank of steps leading to the main entrance of King's Retreat, they observed not only the majordomo himself in all his regalia awaiting them, but, to the total astonishment of them both, they saw, standing regally by his side, none other than the formidable, the nothing short of spectacular person of Opal Driscoll, herself: the legendary and years-missing queen of all the society hostesses of Washington, New York, and Palm Beach.

Flashing her famously toothy smile, she reached out one diamond-ringed hand each to Hansel and Grettel as they emerged from their Rolls, frankly gaping up at her.

"Now you have the answer to the first question everyone's been asking since I left them flat," she said in her grand, full voice, leading them up the steps like two children. "I am here."

She paused at the entrance as its huge, golden doors were swung gently open by minions and her smile grew even broader.

"The answer to the second question?" she asked, giving both their hands an affectionate little squeeze. "The answer is that once I found King's Retreat I simply could not *stand* the thought of hanging around those silly people in those silly places, desperately trying to force a little sparkle into their dreary parties. I knew from the day of my arrival here that my final fulfillment was to be its hostess. King's Retreat is my Shangri-la."

And then she studied Hansel and Grettel with such a long and thoughtful look that they both grew just a little intimidated, which was very unusual for them, my dears.

"I think you two will fit in very well," she said finally, giving them both a little nod and a pat each on their rosy cheeks. "As a matter of fact, I think you're *made* for the place."

And the more Hansel and Grettel saw of King's Retreat, the more they began to suspect that what Opal Driscoll had said was true as true could be, darlings. Everything was just right for them, every last little detail was absolutely perfect. Grettel rather summed it up for both of them one morning while they were having breakfast on the spacious balcony which curved along the wall outside her bedroom.

"I just love this balcony," she said. "I love this table and this chair. I love the way the egg has been cooked for exactly three minutes, and I love that it's been brought to me while it's still nice and hot. I love the air, I love the view, I love absolutely everything I can see and feel and taste and smell and hear."

"It is really grand, isn't it?" said Hansel, adding just enough cream to his coffee to make it perfect.

There was one aspect to the castle, however, which stuck out from its unobtrusive, universal perfection in a way that both Hansel and Grettel had to admit was distinctly odd. It was not in the slightest way irritating, actually it was quite lovely, actually it would be fair to say that it was even extraordinarily beautiful, but it *was* undeniably odd.

I told you that when they first drove up to King's Retreat Hansel and Grettel had noticed a golden glittering along its upper ramparts. A day or so later, after they had both got themselves comfortably settled in, the majordomo—every one called him Herr Oskar—took them on a delightfully complete tour of the castle starting from its deepest basements and dungeons and bringing them all the way up to its tallest roofs and spires.

As a climax to this tour, after going around and around and higher and higher on the almost comically interminable spiraling of a stone staircase, Oskar led them out into the brisk, fresh breeze blowing onto a high rampart's walkway and proudly spread both his arms wide with a great sweep like some gold-buttoned eagle. Following the pointings of his fingertips, Hansel and Grettel looked first one way, then the other, and they discovered that the glittering they had seen came from seemingly endless rows of golden statues which stood upon those ramparts.

Standing almost elbow to elbow, the statues gazed up at the sky, or peered far off toward the blue alps lining the distant horizon, or stared with varyingly thoughtful expressions down the great drop into the green and peaceful valley far below. They were exactly life-size, all dressed in the costumes of Imperial Rome, and their togas and sandals and occasional spears and shields put the cultured viewer—you will be sent to schools and become cultured in time I am sure, my dears—in mind of the figures painted on antique vases or carved into friezes running round the tops of ancient temples.

"It was begun, they tell me, as a whim of our original royal founder," Herr Oskar told them in his deep, carrying voice, and then he raised a large, white-gloved hand and pointed its forefinger to a tall golden figure standing where the highest end of the topmost rampart connected smoothly with the tallest tower.

"That statue was the first, and is the oldest," he informed them, indicating a dignified figure wearing the costume and regalia of a Caesar. "But you will see that every leaf on his laurel crown shines as bright as new. They never need polishing nor any kind of maintenance, these marvelous likenesses. They are pure gold, all of them, and every bit as perfect as when first they were made.''

Then Oskar told them a most-interesting fact about the statues—it seemed that every one of them, without exception, looked exactly like an honored guest who had stayed at the King's Retreat at some point in its long and interesting history.

They followed the majordomo on a tour of the castle's high and windy walks, halting behind him as he now and then paused before a particular golden image, and listened with increasing interest as he proudly spoke the name of the famous or infamous person which it so perfectly resembled. Occasionally he would smile and tell a little story concerning why some guest had been chosen for so notable an honor. Sometimes the stories were solemn and sometimes they were quite amusing, but he told them all with the utmost dignity and respect.

It is not easy to visibly impress people like Hansel and Grettel—you will find that out as you grow older, darlings—but the statues and Oskar's stories concerning them managed to do the job quite nicely. Their eyes grew wider and wider as they heard of the great statesmen and scientists and artists and captains of industry who had spent every moment they could possibly spare from their busy and highly important lives at King's Retreat and who, at the end, had eagerly accepted, had sometimes even fought over, the great distinction of having their exact likeness added to the long, gleaming, golden line which wound its way along the crenellated heights of their beloved hideaway.

Inwardly delighted at how thoroughly his little tour was impressing his guests, and seeing how each further revelation increased the effect, Oskar became, perhaps, just a trifle too pleased with himself, just a little too eager to bedazzle his charges.

"There *is* another group of them, you know," he said in a portentous tone, ignoring a cautionary voice which had begun to whisper warnings with mounting alarm deep down inside him. "A *secret* group. A much more important group than even *these!*"

The sudden, sharp interest which flared in the faces of both Hansel and Grettel, the abrupt increase somehow in the *shine* of them, both these things abruptly warned Oskar that he had gone too far and said too much. He stood with one gloved hand barely touching the burly golden arm of a statue perfectly resembling Germany's greatest writer of operas and warily observed his guests edging ever closer to him like a couple of foxes closing in on a cornered hen.

"Indeed?" said Hansel, smiling up at Oskar with an intense attention which gleamed brighter by the second in his already-bright blue eyes. "And who, pray, is in this so very special group, Oskar?"

"Yes, Oskar," chimed in Grettel. "And where are they hidden?"

"We must definitely see them," said Hansel, employing a tone of quiet firmness Oskar had learned to recognize, respect, and dread in his most important guests. "We must hear all about them."

"You must take us to them at once," finished Grettel.

They stood silently while the poor fellow studied their raised brows, their cold little smiles, and their unwaveringly steady gazes. It is greatly to his credit that he weathered all this for almost a full minute before he buckled and—without another word——turned and led them where they'd asked to go.

He took them on a complicated and devious route which traversed territories in the castle completely unexplored by their previous tour. It involved secret panels and hidden staircases and cobwebby hallways and dark chambers which were made hideous by the flappings and billowings of dusty, ragged tapestries tossed by mysterious and clammy drafts.

Eventually they passed through an opening provided by the smooth sliding aside of an enormous oil portrait of a family whose faces had all been macabrely distorted by centuries of smudgy soot and found themselves stepping into what seemed to be the transept of an enormous cathedral whose high arches could only be dimly made out in the darkness far above them.

Grimly, the Major Domo led them past the choir toward the cathedral's sanctuary and a dim gleaming ahead slowly resolved itself into a bright, curving row of golden statues standing on a large raised platform made of oak blackened by the passing of centuries. The statues surrounded and stared at a sort of hollow altar which stood in the center of the platform and was made of the same somber wood. Oskar bowed slightly and indicated the figures glittering before them in the surrounding gloom with a dignified sweep of one gloved hand.

"Here, before you in this holy place," he intoned with the greatest possible solemnity. "Commencing with no less than His Original Majesty, stand all the past hosts of King's Retreat!"

Hansel and Grettel studied the golden statues carefully and in silence, beginning with the King—who was, indeed, crowned and who bore a royal scepter and wore an ermine-edged cape—and going on through at least two dozen statues until they'd reached the last one, a distinguished-looking man in modern evening dress who sported a monocle.

It was immediately clear to both brother and sister that there was something about these statues, something disturbing, something sinister, which set them entirely apart from those which stood so proudly in the clean, fresh air and sunlight so high above this dim, dark place, but full minutes passed before Grettel managed to put that difference into words.

"They're afraid," she breathed. "They're all simply terrified!"

The majordomo cleared his throat, looked at her nervously, then cast a hesitant glance over his shoulder at the statues ranged somehow ominously behind him.

"I have noticed that seeming effect, myself, Miss," he began, "But I have always put it down to—"

"*OSKAR!!!*"

The majordomo's lips snapped shut and his head cringed as far back down as it could into his high collar as that terrific, terrible shout rung and echoed all about them, then mingled with the sound of determined footsteps marching up the transept.

"What have you *done*, you foolish man?" cried Opal Driscoll as she neared her unfortunate flunky. "What *foolishness* have you been up to?"

Only then did Hansel and Grettel notice another figure lagging somewhat behind their hostess. It was none other than General Brigham S. Parker, a fellow guest at King's Retreat, the hero of the battle of Bestokia, and lately the Supreme High Commander of the Allied European Forces, looking more than a little uncomfortable and perhaps even a tiny touch ridiculous in the leather kilt and feathered helmet of a Roman soldier.

Opal Driscoll noticed the direction of their gaze and immediately tempered her mood—albeit with a shudder which shook her from head to foot—from total fury to a kind of philosophical annoyance.

"Ah, well, ah, well," she said, glaring at Oskar, but then smiling on Hansel and Grettel and upon General

Parker as he managed to catch up with her in spite of his cumbersome sandals.

"I suppose it can't be helped," she said with a sigh and a shrug. "I suppose it's the sort of thing that's simply bound to happen, now and then."

And then she graciously explained that she had brought the General to this secret place to pose for a sculptor who was to model a statue of him as a Roman soldier which would then be cast in gold and set up on the ramparts.

"Of course you must not tell anyone any of this," she said, smiling at Hansel and Grettel benignly. "Nor about this place, which is the very heart of King's Retreat."

She paused and looked at them with great significance.

"You understand that if Oskar had committed this breach of security with ordinary guests we would have had a very serious problem," she said. "But since he committed his indiscretion with you most especial people, the situation is manageable since . . ."

She paused again, then reached out and put her hands on Hansel and Grettel's shoulders with the air of a high priestess conferring initiation.

"Since it has already been decided that both of you, in time, will be chosen to pose for statues of gold."

Of course, darlings, you can see that Hansel and Grettel were initially delighted to learn that they were to receive this remarkable honor, but as Oskar began to lead them away from the hidden cathedral, leaving Opal Driscoll and General Brigham S. Parker to await the arrival of the sculptor, a thoughtful look began to grow upon Hansel's face.

The trip back from the cathedral was, if anything, even more arcane than the approach had been. It was almost as if Oskar was carefully selecting the most involved and confusing pathways he could devise, and it even seemed that sometimes he was carefully improvising additional complications as he led them along. Secret panels opened upon trapdoors which exposed twisting stairways leading to hidden tunnels which wormed unexpectedly up to perilously high catwalks that blended into mysterious labyrinths occasionally interrupted by underground waterways which had to be negotiated by means of gondolas and led to bat-infested caves requiring smoking torches for traversement.

In the end they found themselves exiting into a lovely salon with which they were perfectly familiar and there Oskar left them after much bowing and scraping and multitudes of apologies for any inconveniences his lack of judgment might have caused.

Only when the majordomo's footsteps had faded entirely away did Hansel grin slyly at his sister, wink, and hold up a small appointment book which he always kept on his person. He opened it and slowly turned its pages to show her that only three or four of them remained.

"I just *knew* you were doing that!" she said proudly, smiling and patting him affectionately on his arm, for what Hansel had done, darlings, was a variation on what he had done before to thwart the murderous plans his father and mother had set in motion against himself and his sister when they were helpless little children such as yourselves—he had left a trail so that they could retrace their steps, only this time he had used little bits of torn paper instead of stones.

Wasn't that extremely clever of him, darlings?

Without a moment's hesitation on either one of their parts they both smartly turned around and—going from one bit of torn paper to the next—easily retraced the complicated route Oskar had created in order to confuse them. In almost no time at all the two of them had once more made their way through

the involved innards of King's Retreat and were tip-
toeing as quietly as they could back into its hidden
cathedral.

Opal Driscoll was standing before the dark platform and staring thoughtfully at General Brigham S.
Parker, who was looking rather lost in the center of
the hollow altar as he held a wide Roman sword out
awkwardly before him. There was no sign at all of
any sculptor.

"Grip the sword as if you were about to kill
someone with it, General dear," said Opal Driscoll
firmly. "And please do try to look a little fiercer."

The General attempted both of these things, and
when she saw he was not being particularly successful with either one of them she sighed and shrugged.

"Well, I suppose it will have to do," she said. "But
you must promise not to move!"

The General nodded obediently.

And then, darlings, Opal Driscoll carried out the
most extraordinary, the most absolutely peculiar actions you could possibly imagine, one right after the
other.

First she stuck both her arms straight up into the
air and began to revolve them round and round with
her fingers spread out like the ribs in bats' wings, and
somehow this made nasty little sparks leap out from
the sides of the altar to attack the General like a horde
of glowing wasps whose massive stingings instantly
and firmly paralyzed the poor fellow into his heroic
posture; though, if you looked very closely, you could
see his eyes were bulging slightly from their sockets.

Then she stamped her left foot and then her right
foot as hard and flat as she could on what Hansel and
Grettel now perceived to be strange cabalistic patterns
worked into the marble floor, and this made the altar
glow with a throbbing yellow light that began to
spread insidiously forward into the body of the Gen-

eral, who now began a muffled screaming, which was made considerably more horrible by the soldierly calm—save for its bulging eyes—into which his face had been frozen.

Then she opened her large, toothy mouth very, very wide and howled out a series of perfectly ghastly words, darlings, which I absolutely will not repeat to you at this time—even though I *do* know them, every one of them—because they are terribly dangerous and I don't want any harm to come to my darlings, no I don't, because I love them, because they do everything I say.

Anyhow, the General's screaming chopped right off at the sound of the very first ghastly word and the yellow light began to crawl in funny, twisty ways through his stiffened body like so many glowing worms, and the next thing you knew he had turned into solid gold and Opal Driscoll was laughing and laughing like a crazy mad thing, fit to beat the band.

After a while she calmed down a bit and when she'd got her breath back she began to study the General and it was obvious she was highly pleased with the overall effect. She stepped onto the platform and paused before the altar to get a closer look at what she'd done.

It was at that point that Grettel noticed that Hansel was very carefully studying something she had seen him copying down on the pages remaining in his notebook just a moment or so ago.

Then Opal Driscoll stepped forward and the moment Hansel saw for sure that she was standing *inside* the hollow in the dark altar, next to her brand-new golden statue, he stuck both his arms straight up into the air and began to revolve them round and round with his fingers spread like the ribs in bats' wings, and he kept on going through all the magical steps exactly as he had seen Opal Driscoll do them, stamp-

ing on the floor and howling the ghastly words—
which I'm sure you've guessed, darlings, is what he
had copied into his notebook—and Opal Driscoll
went through all the eye popping and screaming and
turning into solid gold the General had suffered, but
she did it much more visibly and gruesomely because
she knew what was happening to her, having done it
so many times to others, so that by the time she was
transformed entirely into a statue she was crouched
low with her fingers clawed out viciously before her
snarling face, looking for all the world like a rat
trapped by a farmer about to smash it flat with his
hoe.

Following Hansel and Grettel's instructions, the
majordomo installed Opal Driscoll at the end of the
line of statues curving round the altar, and then he
stood the General up on the ramparts so that the old
soldier might forever hold his sword menacingly before him as though he was about to kill someone with
it, and even now his somewhat bulging eyes still glare
fiercely into the void from that high perch. Once I saw
an eagle land on his golden shoulder, darlings, and I
confess the effect was really quite magnificent.

Of course Hansel and Grettel then became the host
and hostess—for that is the ancient tradition—and
they are to this day, and it's not likely anyone will
come along who'll know how to find their way into
the secret cathedral and say the ghastly words and
turn *them* into golden statues and thus take their place
as the *new* host and hostess of King's Retreat.

Not unless they're as well informed as *you*, my darlings!

Match Girl

Anne Bishop

Anne Bishop lives in upstate New York and enjoys gardening, a variety of arts and crafts, and music, especially playing Celtic folk music on the hammered dulcimer. Her stories have appeared in small press magazines including 2AM, Figment, and The Tome, as well as in the anthology Imaginary Friends. "Match Girl" is her first professional sale.

Hans Christian Andersen's "Little Match Girl" is a story that seems heartless, cruel, and tragic. Bishop's version adds brutality and terror and a pinch of magic to the tale. She says, "To those who find the story frightening, I can say only this: while I embellished or modified details to fit the fictional place, I didn't make up the instruments of torture. They all exist."

Match Girl

I STUMBLED BEHIND THE WAGON AS IT STARTED ACROSS the bridge to Brimstone Spere. Even with rags wrapped around my torn boots, my feet were frozen past feeling, and I kept falling farther and farther behind. I'd been walking since sunup because Da said the horse couldn't pull the extra weight. Da always drove the wagon, Moll insisted she was too old to walk, and William, their grown son, was too delicate to brave the cold.

That left me.

No point thinking about that. As Moll always said, a stray picked up by the side of the road could earn her keep or stay by the side of the road. I'd seen too many girls lying in roadside ditches, frozen and crow-picked, not to know that, no matter how bad living with Da, Moll, and William made me feel, it could be worse.

Besides, there was no place to go, no promise of something better. Oh, travelers said there was a place of fire and magic on the other side of the mountains, a place full of dream-spinners and spell-weavers, but that was just camp talk. No one had ever found a road leading to the mountains, and no one had ever found a way over them.

Still, to have warmth and kindness, to have a roof and walls, to stay in one place and watch the seasons fade one into another until the cycle started again, to cup a handful of sun-warmed earth as if it were holy . . . what would I be willing to do to find such a place?

While I longed for that wishful flutter of warmth, my numb feet slipped in a rut and I fell, turning my ankle as I hit the frozen ground.

The wagon continued across the bridge.

Blinking back tears and biting my lip, I staggered to the bridge and clung to the railing. No point crying out. They'd never look back to see if I was all right. They wouldn't help if I wasn't. If I fell by the roadside, they'd pick up the next likely stray and the cycle would start over.

Half-blind from fatigue and the waning light, I kept my stiff hands on the railing and shuffled over the bridge's badly mended planks.

Once we made camp, there'd be a chance to rest. Once I fetched the water and firewood, I'd be able to pull off my wet boots and, hopefully, rub some feeling back into my feet.

The thought of fire pushed me into a limping run as I followed the fading wagon over the bridge and down the narrow road.

Despite my best efforts, the horse was already unhitched by the time I reached camp, and Moll was waiting for me. Her lips were a sharp line, and her eyes held that bright, brittle look that always meant pain.

"Dawdling again, you lazy slut?" Moll swung her arm.

The heavy hand slammed my shoulder into the

wagon. I cried out, loud enough to satisfy Moll, muffled enough so Da and William could ignore it.

Moll looked me over. "You're a worthless piece of trash."

"Yes, ma'am," I whispered. My shoulder throbbed, but I didn't dare rub it.

Moll stepped closer. "Don't go speaking under your breath at me, girly."

"Yes, ma'am," I said louder.

"Yes, ma'am what?"

My ribs squeezed my heart. "I'm a worthless piece of trash."

Moll's eyes glittered with satisfaction. "Don't forget it again." She sniffed and pulled her shawls closed. "The cold's brought out the ache in Da's back, and William's chest is rumbling again so you'd best get the fire started before filling the buckets at the well. It's just a bit of a ways down that path." With a last sniff, she left to assure Da and William that their needs would be met shortly.

I stayed behind for a minute, furiously blinking away tears. "My name's Phoenix," I whispered, swallowing the sobs that would earn me a strapping. "Phoenix, not girly. And I am not trash. No matter what they say, I am not trash."

It was full dark before the chores were done and the precious ham bone simmered in the pot. Da and William sat by the fire on two of the three wooden crates we used for chairs. Moll fussed by the wagon. Sighing, I stretched my hands toward the fire.

Three pairs of eyes stared at me.

Moll pulled a drawstring purse from the wagon and thrust it into my hands. "A penny apiece. Bring back bread for the supper and a jug of wine for Da and William."

Confused, I opened the purse and stared at the matches. "Where do I sell them?"

Da hawked and spat. "Stupid as well as shiftless."

Moll shoved me away from the fire. "Town's on the other side of the trees. If you weren't always dreaming, you'd have seen the fires when you went to the well."

I turned away, not daring to glance at the fire or the pot that hung above it. I was just out of the fire's light when Moll grabbed my arm and pinched hard.

"I don't want any selfish, whining excuses outta you," Moll hissed. "You get that bread and jug of wine if it takes all night, you hear?"

"Yes, ma'am."

"I've left better than you in the ditches, girly. Just remember that."

I closed my eyes. The frozen, crow-picked girls didn't go away. "Yes, ma'am."

She let me go with a shove to help me on my way.

The path curved past the well and widened as I reached the town. The moon was the only light in the soot black sky, but it looked smeared, as if a hand had tried to clean it but had left a layer of dirt. I wished it brighter because I'd already tripped twice, and my hands and knees were raw from landing on the hard ground. When I saw the town, I wished the moon gone.

Brimstone Spere was a burned-out soul captured in a rotting shell. On both sides of the wide main street, crumbling buildings leaned over dark, narrow alleys which, despite the biting cold, stank from excrement and rot. Piles of garbage supported broken stairs. Shattered windows were covered with oiled paper that didn't keep out the cold. No smoke rose from the chimney stumps.

The town's residents seemed to live around the small bonfires in the center of the main street. At least the men did. They sat on wooden crates that circled the fires, passing around jugs of whiskey, laughing, and gambling, filling the night with harsh words and dark intentions. Between the bonfires, merchant carts sold everything from bread and withered vegetables and whiskey and wine to remade clothes and boots to things made of brass and leather I was glad I couldn't name.

I thought I was too cold to be scared, but Brimstone Spere produced a shiver deep inside me. I wasn't sure if I was afraid of the danger I could see or the danger I could only feel.

I crept from building to building, staying in the shadows, hoping the men wouldn't notice me. I had to sell the matches, but only a fool would approach wine-flushed men who had that hard, hungry look in their eyes. Were there any women around the bonfires farther up the street or were they all huddled inside the crumbling buildings? I'd already passed the wine-seller and the bread cart. Neither had much left to sell. If I didn't hurry, I wouldn't get the supplies, and if Da and William became angry because they didn't get their wine, Moll would tie me to the wagon wheel and strap me again. Besides, there was a bowl of ham soup waiting for me.

With the threat of the strap and the promise of a bowl of hot soup spinning in my mind, I flitted past two more bonfires before pausing near an alley half-hidden by garbage. I pulled a fistful of matches from the drawstring purse I'd tied to my belt.

A hand grabbed my shoulder and spun me around.

He was a big, raggedly dressed man with a dark, greasy beard. His breath smelled of garlic and whiskey. The rest of him just stank.

Greasy-beard grinned at me in a way that loosened my guts. "You're a bit skinny, tart."

I took shallow breaths through my mouth. "I'm not a tart, sir," I said politely, hoping politeness wouldn't get me hurt. "I'm a match girl."

Greasy-beard's eyes glittered. "Well, match girl, I've got a candle that needs to be lit. How much?"

My hand shook as I wiggled one match out of my frozen fist. "A penny, sir." I held up the match.

He laughed. "A fair enough price." His fingers dug into my shoulder as he shoved me to my knees and fumbled with his clothes.

I flailed wildly, hitting his thighs and trying to break his grip because I knew what he was going to do and his fingers hurt the shoulder that was already bruised.

He yelped in surprise and let go, but before I could scramble away, he pulled me up by my hair and slapped me twice. "Hit me again and I'll break your hands," he snarled. He yanked back on my hair, forcing my mouth open.

I choked and gagged while he used me. When he finished, he pushed my face against his groin and grunted with pleasure. "That's the only way a woman should use her mouth."

Finally he pushed me away and slapped me again when I turned to spit. The blow sent me flying into the pile of garbage. I threw my hands out to protect my face, the matches scattering on the wet cobblestones in front of me. I felt a tickling shiver as a broken bottle sliced through the meaty part of my left hand. A moment later my body recovered from the shock, and the tickle became a throb of pain. I sat there, numb, staring at the blood pouring onto the cobblestones from the deep, jagged cut.

Laughing, Greasy-beard dropped a penny in my lap and returned to the bonfire.

I don't know how long I sat there, whimpering and watching the blood run, before I regained enough sense to pull the rags off my boots and wrap them around my hand. My skirt was soaked with slush and blood, and my legs ached from sitting on the wet cobblestones. I needed warmth and a place to hide.

Light-headed, I giggled. I could hide in the alley, and I had all those nice little matches to keep me warm. Not all of them, no. Just one. Just for a little warmth. First I had to pick up all the ones I'd dropped. They were wet and probably useless, but I'd never be able to explain losing that many and Moll would think I'd used them and strap me.

Cradling my left hand against my belly, I got to my knees and reached for the dropped matches.

They were wet and red, floating in a pool of moonlight. As I stared at them, the wooden sticks changed to soot black and the match heads became tiny moons.

I picked one up. My fingers tingled as if they could already feel the warmth.

I gathered the matches and crawled into the alley, ignoring the smell and the rustling and squeaks. Dropping the white-headed matches into my lap, I held one up and stared at it.

It flared and burned.

Within that white halo was part of a clean, simple, cozy room. In the back corner, an iron stove stuffed with firewood sent out waves of heat. A large loom filled the front corner, positioned to catch the light from the side and front windows. Below the windows were shelves stuffed with woven baskets holding skeins of wool neatly sorted by color. There was a large throw rug in front of the stove and a rocking chair, still moving as if someone had just left.

I longed to sit at the loom, to hold those skeins of wool, to pick out colors in the winter light and create something beautiful as well as useful. I longed for that as much as I longed for the stove and the rocking chair. I imagined I was the one who'd left the chair rocking and would return in a minute. Drawn by the warmth from the stove, I leaned forward and . . .

the match went out.

I quickly lit another white-headed match and waited impatiently for the room to reappear. Instead, there was only the smeared moon and an ancient, ageless voice.

There's the fire that burns from without and the fire that burns from within. One consumes, the other cleanses.

I stared at the burned-out match, puzzled by how a voice I'd never heard before could sound so familiar.

The cold burned my legs. I ignored it as I fumbled with the drawstrings and made sure the purse had an inside pocket. After placing the white-headed matches into the pocket, I staggered into the street.

Other men approached me, but I ran from them, afraid they wanted more than matches.

I found the women at the far end of the street. Gray in color, gray in spirit, they shuffled silently around their pitiful fires.

As I approached, an old woman, sitting alone, looked up and beckoned.

"Come, child," she said, smiling. "Come and warm yourself."

I hesitated, frightened by the twisted body wrapped in black rags. One of the crone's eyes was half-hidden by a scar-thickened lid, but there was intelligence in the other hazel eye and kindness in the wrinkled, scarred face.

"Thank you, ma'am." I sat on a wooden crate and held my hands toward the fire.

"Name's Nix. Tch! What happened to your hand, child?"

"I cut it."

"Let me see." Nix unwrapped the dirty rags and shook her head. "Tch. Has to be cleaned or it'll never heal. See?" She held up her left hand. There was a thick, jagged scar on the meaty part of her palm. "Thumb's not good for much because of that." She pulled a cloth sack into her lap, fumbling and muttering, finally pulling out a large bottle. "Hold still."

I bit my lip and cried silently while the liquid from the bottle burned and bubbled in the cut.

"Hurts fierce," Nix said, wrapping my hand in clean rags, "but it'll heal now if you take care." She fumbled in the bag once more, pulling out pinches of herbs and dropping them into a tea ball, which she lowered into a pot. "A medicinal tea. My own recipe. It'll help the healing."

"Thank you, ma'am." I closed my eyes and tucked my left hand against my belly. It hurt, but it was a clean hurt.

Nix poured the tea into two tin cups. "Why are you here, child?" she asked gently, handing me a cup.

I sipped the tea, pleasantly surprised by its taste. "Da and Moll wanted to come to Brimstone Spere to rest before going back out on the road so I had to come, too."

"Why?"

The scuffled footsteps of the other women seemed far away. If I closed my eyes, I could almost imagine the warmth from the fire coming from an iron stove. I shook my head. That place didn't exist. No point in dreaming. "I've got no choice."

Nix snorted. "There's always a choice, if you've courage enough to make it."

Unable to think of a reply, I looked away straight into the misery-filled eyes of a woman standing near another fire, wearing an iron cage around her head.

"Scold's bridle," Nix said quietly. "Her man slapped her because he didn't like the food on his plate, and she spoke sharply to him. That's her punishment. It was a first offense, so her tongue's spooned instead of spiked."

Horrified, I couldn't look away. "I don't understand."

"I hope by all that's sacred you never do, child."

The woman in the scold's bridle moaned.

Ashamed of staring at someone else's pain, I turned toward the fire. "I have to go." I set the empty cup on the ground. "Thank you for the tea, ma'am."

Nix studied the fire. "Tell me, child. Do you really believe you're selling matches in Brimstone Spere?"

I wondered uneasily if she could tell somehow what Greasy-beard had done. "What else would I be selling?"

The haunted understanding in Nix's eye chilled me. "Perhaps little bits of your soul? Small sparks that, dribbled away, mean nothing but together could create a glorious blaze?"

I studied Nix's scarred face. "Do I know you?" I asked hesitantly. "Your face seems familiar, but . . ."

Nix's soft laugh was full of gentle bitterness. "Does it now? Dreams seen in the fire can become real, you know, if you've courage enough to embrace the fire."

I glanced at the bonfire.

Nix shook her head. "There's more than one kind of fire, child."

I shivered. How could Nix know about the room in the white-headed match or what the voice had said? "Who are you?"

Nix pulled a few coins from her sack and pressed them into my good hand. "Here. That should be enough."

"I can't," I protested. "You'll need them for yourself."

"Will I?" she asked softly.

Mumbling my thanks, I hurried down the street.

Nix's voice followed me. "Remember, Phoenix. There are two kinds of fire. Which are you going to sell?"

I whirled around.

There was no one, and nothing, there.

The soup was gone by the time I returned to camp,

but Moll grudgingly gave me a piece of fried bread and a cup of water while Da and William passed the wine jug between them.

Moll cuffed me for not being able to clean the dishes properly, but no one asked about my bandaged hand. When the dishes were finally put away, Moll said tightly, "Turn in."

There was only one reason I was allowed to turn in this early. I wasn't sure I could stand William shoving his thing inside me tonight. "I-I haven't finished the chores."

Moll's voice was flat and hard. "Turn in."

Not daring to argue, I climbed into the wagon, un-rolled the two thin mattresses, and spread the blankets. I'd just managed to pull off my wet boots when William stumbled up the wagon's steps and fell heavily beside me. I tried to set the boots in a corner so the blankets and mattress wouldn't get wet, but William was already pushing me down, pulling at my clothes.

"Not tonight, William," I pleaded, pushing at his shoulders, hoping, just once, he might listen.

He tossed the boots aside and rammed his knee between my legs.

"Please, William, please. Not tonight."

He stared at me through narrowed eyes. "Why?" he asked, his voice slurred. He grabbed a fistful of my hair and pulled. "You been giving it out tonight? That why you don't want to do your duty?"

Tears leaked from my eyes. "No."

Grunting, William thrust into me. I whimpered.

"Tell me." There was a queer note in his voice. "Tell me what you did." His hand clamped on my breast and squeezed.

I told him what I'd been forced to do.

He rode me hard but finished quickly. When he

rolled off me, he said, "Maybe we've got you selling the wrong thing."

I left the wagon before sunup, got the fire started, and had fetched one bucket of water from the well before Moll climbed down from the wagon. William had used me again last night and had roused Da from his wine-soaked sleep enough to demand woman's duty from Moll. Now she watched with bitter eyes as I tried to pour the water into the holding barrel.

"Slut," Moll hissed, yanking the bucket out of my hand. "Can't control yourself enough to let a decent woman get some rest."

No point telling her I wanted William's attentions even less than she wanted Da's.

She grabbed my bandaged hand and squeezed. I floated on the pain.

"If you're too delicate to earn your keep here, you can earn it in the alleys." Moll sniffed and closed her shawls. "Should've known something like you wouldn't try to do respectable work. Now git." She shoved me against the water barrel. "We need a slab of bacon and some bread for breakfast."

I cradled my bleeding hand. "I-I don't think there's enough coins left."

Moll's lips tightened. "I expect you'll find a way to earn them."

The sun was well up by the time I reached Brimstone Spere. The town looked worse in daylight. Except for a few starving mongrels nosing around the garbage piles, the wide main street was empty. Still, the merchant carts had to be somewhere, so I trudged up the street, slush seeping into my torn boots and freezing feet that still hurt from yesterday. My hand throbbed. I pressed it against my belly, savoring the fever heat.

It took most of the morning to find the hog man

and buy his last bit of bacon. It was mostly fat with
a sliver of meat in the middle, but it was all he had
and all I could afford. The bread cart had fresh bread
already dusted with soot.

I sold a few matches to the women scurrying from
cart to cart before scurrying back into the buildings.
The rats were bolder than the women in Brimstone
Spere. Since I had enough coins, I bought a half jug
of wine for Da and William, hoping Moll would be
pleased.

Moll wasn't pleased. She sported a fresh bruise on
her cheek, Da's reaction to waking with a wicked
head and a sore back and finding no food waiting for
him. Moll said nothing as she took the supplies from
me, but her eyes promised that the punishment would
be worse because it was delayed.

No point asking if I'd get any of the food.

As soon as Moll started preparing the meal, I bolted
for the trees, hoping I wouldn't stumble over Da or
William. Moll wouldn't yell and call attention to herself today, and she wouldn't come after me if I got far
enough away fast enough. It would give me a few
hours before having to face the pain. A few hours of
being wet, cold, and hungry.

The second time I tripped over a root, I gave up
and crawled behind a tree, hoping it would shield me
from anyone coming down the path. With my back
pressed against the trunk, I pulled out a white-headed
match and stared at it.

The match burned.

A different room, but part of the same place. Another iron stove, much larger than the first one. A
well-scrubbed pine table sprinkled with woven mats
of woodland browns and greens. Two places were set.
Two thick slices of fresh bread lay on a cutting board
with the rest of the loaf, waiting for the creamy butter.
In the center of the table steamed a pot filled with

thick chunks of meat, potatoes, carrots, and onions. Beside each plate was a mug of fresh milk.

I leaned forward and breathed deeply, my mouth watering. I couldn't imagine why there were two places set or why I'd want anyone living in my house, but I imagined it was my table, my plates, my food. I reached to pull out a chair and sit down.

The match went out.

I cried out in disappointment, hurriedly dug out another white-headed match, and then hesitated. Last time, the picture didn't come back. Last time, there'd been that ageless, ancient voice.

I licked my lips and stared at the match.

There's more than one kind of hunger.

I dropped the match and slowly got to my feet. There might be more than one kind of hunger, but if I didn't get some food and warmth soon, the other kinds wouldn't matter.

I spent the rest of the day on the edge of Brimstone Spere, my mind as numb as my body. When night fell, I once again crept along the wide main street.

The bonfires promised warmth to my sluggish body. The men circling the fires promised something else. A few of them bought matches from me, satisfied with a quick grope before letting me go. A couple thought I owed them more than a match for the penny price, but something made them nervous enough to step away after a few obscene gestures and suggestions.

Shivering and exhausted, I stepped into an alley, leaned against the wall, and raised my right hand to my face. It was the only way I could tell if I was still holding the matches.

So cold. I stared at the bonfires. If I threw myself on top of one, would there be a moment of warmth and comfort before the pain? If I sold my body to those men, would they let me stay by the fire? Would they give me something to eat?

I pushed away from the wall.

"There's more than one kind of hunger, child." Nix's voice floated from the alley's depths. "There's more than one kind of cold. You can warm the body and still freeze to death."

"Doesn't matter," I said through chattering teeth.

"You think not?" A twisted hand pointed past my shoulder.

I looked where the finger pointed. A woman lurched down the street, her lower legs encased in wood.

"Leg presses," Nix said softly. "The screws are tightened every few hours. The bones are crushed by now. The wood's the only thing keeping her up."

"Why's she trying to walk then?" I whispered, feeling sick.

"Punishment. She tried to run away, tried to get out of Brimstone Spere. Now she has to walk from one end of the street to the other. When her master finally removes the presses, she won't be able to run from anyone or anything. More than bone is crushed in that wood, child."

I turned. "How do you know—"

I stared at the empty alley. Cold, exhaustion, hunger. I knew they were real because they hurt. But Nix? Maybe Nix was nothing more than a dream dressed in hunger and cold, no more real than the place that existed in the white-headed matches.

At least that dream place held a measure of peace.

I fumbled with the purse's strings, trying to open it without dropping the matches already clutched in my hand. My left hand was almost useless, but it was so numbed by the cold it no longer hurt. I was concentrating on the purse so hard I didn't hear the approaching footsteps or realize anyone was there until two hands pressed me against the wall.

"I've been looking for you, match girl," the man said.

He was the first man I'd seen in Brimstone Spere who had clean, unpatched clothes and didn't stink. Because of that, he scared me more than the rest of them put together.

"You want to buy a match, sir?" I raised my hand timidly.

The man's soft laugh held a cruel note. Gripping my chin, he turned my head from side to side. "You'd be passably pretty if you were clean and fed." He pulled aside my ragged shirt, cupped my breasts, and smiled, satisfied, as my nipples stiffened beneath his thumbs.

I shivered. No point saying my body was reacting to the cold and not his touch.

He continued to cup one breast and tease the nipple while he reached beneath my skirt and thrust his rough fingers into me.

He released my breast to muffle my scream, pressing my head against the wall while I twitched and jerked like a puppet. Then he pulled out his fingers and thrust his thing into me, scraping my back and buttocks against the stone wall.

When he was done, he squeezed my shoulders and smiled. "You're tight enough, but too dry to give much pleasure." He laughed and ground his hips against me. "That's no problem. I've got medicines that can change that quick enough. You'll like being one of my women, match girl. You won't have to sell little fire sticks when you've got something hotter to sell." His fingers dug into my shoulders. "I take good care of my women as long as they treat me right." He stepped away from me and arranged his clothes. "I'm sure your master and I can reach an agreement."

I waited until his footsteps faded before peering around the corner.

The street looked different. The bonfires weren't in the same place. A woman wearing a wool cape over a velvet dress wearily climbed the steps of the building I leaned against. She looked feverish and drunk in a strange kind of way and, despite the warm clothes, I could tell she was frozen.

"Phoebe!" The man who'd just left the alley strode up the street, his teeth bared and his hands clenched.

The woman turned toward him. "Master Colton," she said in a dead voice.

Colton reached the stairs and gripped the rail. "Damn you, Phoebe! Stop acting like a dried-up bitch and get your ass in there."

Phoebe's lifeless hazel eyes stared at him a moment before she climbed the rest of the stairs and went into the building.

Shaken, I stepped farther into the alley. William didn't own me, but he'd sell me fast enough for the price of a few jugs of wine. Moll would complain bitterly about having to do all the work, but they'd pick up another bewildered, starving child once they started traveling again. That was the world, the only world I'd ever known except for that place in the dreamscape.

I pulled out a white-headed match.

It was late spring, maybe early summer. A soft ivory shawl slipped off my shoulders as I followed the sun-dappled path up a gentle slope, brushing aside low-hanging branches with an easy hand. Birds flitted through the trees around me. Out of sight but nearby, water sang over stone. I was in no hurry, simply walking to enjoy the afternoon warmth and the smell of rich earth.

As I neared the top of the slope, I reached for a handhold to help me up the last few feet.

A man's hand reached down.

Startled, I jerked back, almost losing my balance. The hand remained still, silently offering its strength. There was kindness and understanding in the man's face, and his eyes held respect as well as desire.

I smiled shyly and reached for his hand.

The match went out.

I held up another white-headed match.

If you have the courage.

I stared at the match for a long time. The courage to do what?

I knew. Just as I knew that the place in the matches was real, or could be. Just as I knew that the stories about dream-spinners and spell-weavers living on the other side of the mountains were more than camp talk. I knew . . . but I didn't have the courage.

I drifted through the next day, stumbling from one chore to the next. The wind had picked up, and I froze despite my exertions. I couldn't feel my legs below my knees, and my fingers were too stiff to bend. It didn't matter. Soon I'd be nothing more than a burned-out soul captured in a rotting shell.

I was too numb to wonder why William tensed every time I left camp for water or firewood, or why, as the afternoon waned, he watched me so anxiously. I was too numb to remember there was a reason to be afraid.

Night fell early that last day. Da had already gone into Brimstone Spere for the cockfights, so it was just the three of us gathered around the fire. Bitterly silent, Moll filled tin cups with soup. William pressed a cup into my hands, smiling queerly. The hot tin burned my hands. I didn't feel it.

I was half-finished when William took the cup from me and pulled me to my feet. "Time to go," he said, still smiling. He grabbed a blanket from the wagon and threw it over his shoulders before gripping my arm and heading up the path to Brimstone Spere.

"We've got a big night ahead of us. Don't want you to fall and hurt yourself," he said cheerfully, tugging me along, never noticing that I couldn't keep up with his longer stride.

Colton waited for us by the largest bonfire, his smile cruel and knowing.

That's when I remembered the danger. Something inside me snapped.

I jerked out of William's grasp, struggling to keep my balance. Scowling, William grabbed for me. I knocked his hand away.

"Don't give me any trouble, you selfish bitch," William snarled.

A spark of anger burned in my belly. I spat the words like venom. "You spineless, grubby little prick. You don't own me. Nobody owns me. I won't be sold so you can fill your belly with wine."

"Bitch!" William lunged at me, screaming.

I dodged him and tried to run, but suddenly there were men all around me, grabbing my arms and legs while I bit, kicked, scratched, screamed, did everything I could think of to get free. Pinned, I watched William's fist come toward my face, but Colton grabbed him.

"If she's damaged, the deal's off," Colton snapped.

William hesitated, then stepped back, pouting. "Bitch."

Colton smiled and clapped William's shoulder. "A couple of hours bridled and saddled will take the fight out of her."

I kicked and screamed as the men dragged me toward an unlit bonfire. While one man started the fire, others dragged a piece of canvas off a wooden device. The front of it looked like the stocks I'd seen in other towns, but low to the ground. The rest was a terrifying triangle of wood and leather straps.

Greasy-beard came up the street carrying two head cages. "Spooned or spiked?" he asked Colton respectfully.

"Spooned," Colton replied. "I don't want her mouth damaged permanently."

Greasy-beard dropped one cage, opened the other, and held it over my face. The spoon was a piece of nubbed metal shaped like William's thing. "Open wide," he said with a leering grin. "You know how to do that."

I clamped my teeth together.

Undisturbed by my small rebellion, Colton pulled my shirt open and pinched my nipple until I screamed. Laughing, Greasy-beard thrust the spoon into my mouth. The nubs scoured my tongue. Once the metal cage was locked around my head, Colton released my nipple after a final squeeze.

I moaned. I couldn't help it. The nubs scraped my raw tongue, and the cage forced my mouth closed so that the metal cut my lips.

Greasy-beard locked my head and hands into the stocks while William and Colton forced my legs apart and strapped them to the saddle. When they were done, Colton threw my skirt over my back and thrust his rough fingers into me. I squealed and struggled, but the straps held me tight.

Colton laughed and gave my ass a hard slap. "Who wants to ride the fidgets out of my new mare?"

Men laughed. Coins clinked as they changed hands. Then hands squeezed my breasts as the first rider mounted.

After the third man, William squatted in front of me and smiled. "Tell me you're sorry, and I'll let you go."

I tried desperately, but I couldn't form words.

William shook his head. "Not ready yet? Just as well." He patted the front of the cage. The spoon scraped my tongue until it bled.

I screamed while William drank and Colton laughed and man after man rode me hard. When I couldn't scream anymore, they let me go.

I sat on the wet cobblestones until Colton hauled me to my feet. I stared dumbly at him as he removed the scold's bridle. Blood dribbled from my mouth.

Colton smiled. "After this, you'll appreciate having something softer in your mouth, even if it's just as hard."

Men slapped their thighs and laughed. William staggered by, grinning obscenely.

"Don't try to run away, match girl," Colton said with soft menace. He pointed to a woman crawling toward a bonfire, dragging what was left of her legs, and shook his head. "A damned shame she tried to run away. She was a good tart. Made a decent profit for me."

Colton sauntered to the largest bonfire, whistling confidently as he swung the scold's bridle from his fingers.

My mind started working again. Run? Oh, I was going to run. Even if my body never left this place, I was going to run farther than he'd ever imagine. Better to freeze in the warmth of a dream than live another day in Brimstone Spere.

But I was still scared.

Struggling to stay upright, I turned away from the men and hobbled up the street. I looked back once. Colton watched me, smiling, sure I couldn't escape. Keeping to the shadows, I passed the last bonfire crowded with bent, gray women and slipped into the alley.

I braced my back against the wall. I didn't dare sit down because I wasn't sure I could get up again. It took both hands and my teeth to open the drawstring purse. I pulled out a white-headed match.

I ran through the large garden behind the cottage, searching desperately. I rushed past vegetable beds that would have held me spellbound a few hours ago. I ignored the magical pull of the herbs. I was blind to the glorious flowers. I cried as I ran, sure the match would go out before I saw her.

When I finally found her, she was kneeling beside a flower bed, cupping a handful of sun-warmed earth as if it were holy. There were moon silver streaks in her shining black hair, and her hazel eyes were shadowed with old pain and shining with hard-earned wisdom.

"Choose, Phoenix," she said in a voice that was ancient, ageless and familiar as my own.

I dropped the burned-out match and pulled three more from the purse. Bracing my arm against the wall, I faced the front of the alley and held the matches up to the full moon.

Nix studied me from the white fire of the first match. Phoebe stared at me from the second. Phoenix watched with haunted understanding from the third.

New life rises from the ashes of the old, child, Nix whispered.

The match burned out and she vanished.

Phoebe flinched, said nothing, and vanished.

You know what to do, Phoenix urged as she began to fade.

"Will it hurt?" I asked, knowing it was a child's question but too scared to care.

Of course. But you already knew that.

Yes, I did. I pulled out the last white-headed match.

"Phoenix!"

Startled, I dropped the match. William blocked the exit.

"What are you doing in here? Colton wants you." He stepped into the alley.

I grabbed the match and scrambled backward. "No," I whispered, wondering if I was too late, wondering if he could stop what would happen once it began. "No."

"Don't give me any sass," he snarled, pushing me farther and farther back.

One more step and I'd lose the moon.

Shaking, I held up the match.

William raised his fist.

The match flared bloodred before turning a cold, burning white. I tipped my head back and dropped the match down my throat.

My soul caught fire and shattered my life. I burst into flames.

William screamed and ran.

Pain blazed through me as nerves sizzled, flesh melted, bone charred, skin crackled and split. My hair stood on end as fire leaped from my skull. The last thing I saw before my eyes exploded was the moon riding full and clean in the soot black sky.

I opened my new eyes. They were hazel, the color of the woodland.

I took a deep breath. The sweet, steady Fire burning inside me tingled. I studied the thin, clean scar on my moon white hand and smiled as I brushed shining black hair from my shoulders. My gown was a soft, midnight rainbow. When I raised my arms, the sleeves lifted like wings.

I was Dream-spinner, Spell-weaver, Woman.

The people of Brimstone Spere would call me other things. It didn't matter. Beyond the mountains were other women like me and men with the strength and courage to embrace a woman of fire.

I left the alley and glided down the street.

I passed Colton. He made a sign against evil and fled. As I passed Greasy-beard, he picked up a chunk of wood. Fire spat from my fingertips. The wood burst into flames, and he screamed.

Da and William stared openmouthed for a moment before stumbling after me, calling to me, telling me to remember everything they'd done for me.

I passed the well and followed the path to the camp.

Moll stared at me with bitter eyes. "I could have been like you." Her expression softened and she reached out. "Stay, girl. Stay and help Moll."

I shook my head. She didn't want to embrace the Fire, she only wanted to use mine, and Fire is too sacred to be given away to those who will not cherish it.

Moll cursed me when I turned away and followed the narrow road to the bridge. As I crossed the gray, rotting wood, curls of smoke rose from my footsteps. A path opened before me. Never looking back, I walked toward the mountains and the life beyond while the bridge to Brimstone Spere burned to ash.

Waking the Prince

Kathe Koja

Kathe Koja lives in a suburb of Detroit with her husband, the artist and photographer Rick Lieder, and her son, Aaron. She is the author of the novels The Cipher, Bad Brains, Skin, Strange Angels, *and* Kink. The Cipher *won the Bram Stoker Award for Superior Achievement in a First Novel. Her short stories have been published in magazines such as* Omni, The Magazine of Fantasy and Science Fiction, Asimov's Science Fiction Magazine, *and in various anthologies, including* The Year's Best Science Fiction, Best New Horror, *and* The Year's Best Fantasy and Horror.

    Koja is one of the master stylists of the horror and fantasy fields. In this version of "Sleeping Beauty," she mirrors historical and contemporary perspectives adding a nod to changing gender roles and a dollop of sexual politics.

Waking the Prince

IN HIS BEAUTY SO PALE, THE PALLOR OF FALSE DAWN beneath glass smooth and cold as his skin, ceremonial glass on which one sees the imprint of many kisses, fingertips, palmprints pressed to warm what cannot be warmed, evidence of balked desire for what lies so deceptively near. White and rapt and naked past that barrier unseen, long limbs, knees and elbows slightly bent, hair the color of cinnamon on his chest and legs, nestled wiry about his manhood which sleeps as well. There is it seems in the air above the case the faintest odor: as of sachet, or dried cosmetics, or sweets crushed dry and secret in a drawer; not everyone can smell it, but for those who can its scent is maddening, a delicious corruption, the body unrisen decomposed to candied light.

The case, or casket, lies beneath a heavy canopy, gilt and royal purple, flags and tassels and shiny bunting; he is a king's son after all, will be, yes, king himself should his father die, his father who in a mounting rictus of dry despair can bear to spend no time within the same walls that house his son, has moved both hearth and seat of government to a manor house some leagues away, where he eats,

sleeps, keeps a mistress—but like a curse fulfilled,
some wicked habit irresistible still returns to stand in
that hall, before that case and on his face gall-bitter
the chase and crawl of his thoughts: *How much hours,
how much of life lost already, young life lost and gone* and
bent crooning like a nursemaid, crooning curses like
a soul damned to hell and "This is hell," His Grace's
mutter, "*this* is hell," to his son's slack sleeping face,
shaped both of beauty and death; perhaps it is that
irony as much as her husband's slow decampment
which has driven the queen his mother mad.

See her: as around the barbican she creeps, up and
down the twilight halls in red gown and clattering
boots, hair loose down her back as if she were a girl,
a maiden unwed and *Who has stolen it?* she says, to
the walls, to herself, her voice the voice of fever and
disease, of the sore that grows like hunger in the
spread feast of the flesh, insisting in her mania that
her son is jailed, locked inside the case: glass case
which bears no seals, no seams, no indication of man-
ufacture as if it had always been there, had formed
cold and strong as a carapace about the sleeping body
of the beautiful prince. *Who has stolen the key?* for she
insists there is a key, one true key the presence of
which will bring to light the lock unseen, will turn
that lock, will free her boy from his silence and his
pallor, her naked son in the glass cask of that womb.
She hears no other voices, will listen to no one—the
vizier or maidservants, ladies-in-waiting or her husband the king who, when confronted by fresh evidence of her madness limits his answer to a shrug:
"What will you?" to that vizier, those maidservants
weeping into their cupped palms as if kept tears will
solve the matter. "Scamper like a rat, crawl like a
snake, what matter? She is broke, inside; let her be."

The queen in torment; the king in hiding; the kingdom captive beneath the lids of the sleeping prince.

Outside the palace the gardeners tend the gravel paths, the massed banks of flowers: lily, aster, kiss-me-quick; inside the wine steward checks the vintage for the evening meal.

"So what's he like?" Tanisha's question to Cissy sitting on the floor: beer sucked through a straw, gold bubbles, gold earrings to swing and dangle, make motion in the motionless air. "This guy, he's an actor, you said?"

"He's in commercials." More beer sucked through that smile; she felt as if she had been smiling ever since they met. "He did that one for Edie's IceDream, you know the one with the guys on the lake? And they all fall in the water? Well he's the third guy, the one in the bandanna. The perfect one."

Inner squint of memory: "They're all perfect."

"Well, he's *perfect*-perfect." Dark hair, dark eyes and that heavy underlip like a child's, pouting child too sweet to be called spoiled. Picked out like pure gold in a box of fakes, kick of instinct there in the thrash bar angled up against the rail; *finders keepers*, Cissy's smile and moving closer, watching him watch her walk. Glass in hand, gin and grapefruit juice cloudy and sour and he had let her taste it, one swirling sip and "You like it?" with half a smile. "Like how it tastes?"

"Sure," and his arm around her, casual across her shoulder, above her beating heart. "It's, it's different," and he had laughed, bright laugh as if what she had said was a joke and "He's different," she said now to Tanisha, "he's not like anybody else."

"One of a kind, huh?" Nodding to the empty can: "You want another one of these?"

"No.—Yeah, I'll split one with you but then I gotta go, I gotta get ready." For tonight, another night and again the reminiscent smile: sour grapefruit aftertaste, head to one side and at first she had tried to be cool, not wanting to smile too much, get too close too soon but oh he was so beautiful, perfect like a magazine model, like on TV and naked even better, her own mouth sucking sweet on that underlip, biting like ripe fruit and afterward lying on his belly in her bed, pink sheets and his skin the color of caramel, of honey in the comb. Like a wish you make, genie in the lamp, what's your pleasure? and "—body home? He*llo?*" and Tanisha was handing her the beer can, pushing it cold and smooth into her hand. "So you going out with him again tonight?"

"Dancing," she said. "We're going dancing." Her suggestion: said into silence, *you like to dance?* and he had shrugged and smiled, lying present-wrapped, pink-swaddled in the sheets, lids low and lower, closing as if draped at last by dream: had he answered, yes or no? Yes. No.

Consultations have been made, of course; priests and witches and necromancers, scores of them, lines of them to advise Their Majesties: spells tried, prayers and incantations, the burned flesh of beasts on altars but all without effect and these efforts then devolving to applications of more temporal force: iron and fire, saws and cunning tools made to cut rock, six strong men with leaden bars to batter like thunder against the glass, the queen in the room's far corner weeping alternately from hope and terror, *oh have a care, have a care!*—but the sweat flew to no effect, the tools lay blunted, the bars themselves left bent and shattered in a corner of the room.

In the arched doorway the queen cries out once, as a woman in labor cries out in the tunnel of birth: and then is gone, off on her endless rounds, stubborn as the prince himself: more opinions sought and solicited, ears cracked for any whisper no matter how unpleasant or bizarre and finally anyone with a plan is allowed to enter and speak, in these last mad days before the king's decampment, before the queen is swallowed whole by her grief: mountebanks and beggars, the deranged, the ones said to be gifted by the second sight, the ones with extra fingers or missing legs and through the halls they move, pilfering, loitering, stealing food from the kitchens, their sticks and bloody bones playing that tune peculiar to the halt, the ones not whole and across the glass sarcophagus they clamber, slack and shivering limbs in an insect's communion, the feeder and the fed: but even those grotesqueries mean nothing, nothing changes, and in the halls still the weeping queen, the king enraged, the prince sealed and sleeping in his transparent tomb as if he will sleep forever, as if not even death can wake him now.

Well then, not *perfect* after all: her sweet actor turned out to be a lousy dancer, pure wood which was somehow endearing, his one fault but how could she care when everything else was so right? And anyway who needed to go dancing, the important thing was to spend time together, be with him every minute she could and she did what she could, late to work and leaving early, spare clothes in her totebag so she didn't have to go home first, could head straight to his place, be there waiting when he got back: from the studio, from a shoot, this week it was work boots for some outdoor-fashion magazine and to see him coming toward her, coming up the street made Cissy feel as if she had won the lotto, luck's blessing like a magic wand and *his* magic wand, oh yeah, blessings of another kind and they spent hours in bed, her hands learning the landscape of that body, what he liked, what he needed—the little tweaks and touches, the way he liked her to whisper what he wanted her to say—and afterward he always slept, little catnaps and she would lie beside him and look, just look, just watch him doze and think to herself *this is it:* past definition to surety, her head beside his on the pillow, pillowed on a sweetness she had not imagined: nothing like this had ever happened to her before, and nothing she did or could do would be too much: to keep it all happening, to keep him here.

And Tanisha on the phone, other friends, girlfriends asking with a mixture of envy and delight *So how's it goin'? Still good?* and "Great," she told them, told Tanisha over coffee, too hot and gulped too fast but she was in a hurry, she was meeting him for dinner: "At Pumpernickel's," shucking shoes under the table, tired feet slipping into cool pumps carried careful in her bag all day. "We're celebrating, it's six months today." Six months of good times, well almost all but it all took a lot of work, a lot of planning and traveling around, but it was nothing to complain about, not really because she was so lucky to have him and now Tanisha, stirring coffee, and "You talked any more about moving in?" Gritty sugar spill, wind chime sound of the spoon. "Remember you said you were going to?"

"Yeah, I—yeah, we did." Changing earrings, gold studs for flashy gold hoops and they *had* talked about it, she had talked plenty but to everything she said that shrug, sweet smile and it ended like it always did, everything in the end down to pink sheets and catnap yawns. So "We decided to wait awhile," another gulp of coffee, burning her mouth, her throat going down. "I mean he really likes his place, you know, and I like mine, so we'll just wait."

Tanisha's gaze, calm and dry and something else and "What?" Cissy said, a little too sharp. "What's that look for?"

"Nothing," said Tanisha. "Just, you look kind of,

you know, tired. You getting enough sleep?"

"Long day," with her own gaze level and cool, "just a long day," which by the time she hit the restaurant was longer; his job to make the reservations but he had forgotten: again: and she had to wait for a table, sit there drinking water and wondering, wondering but finally here he came: and that lift inside, dependable as physics to see him cross the room, hands in his pockets and leaning like ballet to kiss her, careless kiss on half her mouth and "You're late," she said, surprising them both, it was not what she meant to say at all and he lifted his eyebrows, leaned back and smiled.

"Traffic," he said. "I had to come across town," and then busy with the menu, busy with his drink when it came, *happy anniversary*, and she decided to bring it up again, moving in: six months was a long time after all. "You know I've been thinking," she said. "About what we said, you know, about us moving in together," and step by step her careful logic, money saved, less travel time meant more time together, so on and so forth and it really sounded good, no it sounded *right*, *she* was right and turning now in the slippery leather booth, wedging sideways to look into his eyes—

to see him looking past her, peaceable over her shoulder; one hand loose around the wineglass, the other warm around hers and he could have been sleeping, he could have been on the moon or a million miles away and some sound made, some noise because "What?" his head swiveling toward her, smile like a distracted child's. "What is it, babe?" and then the waitress with their dinner, flat red plates, burned smell and *Nothing*, she said; had she said it aloud? "Nothing," more firmly but now he was joking with the waitress, he was not listening, he had not been listening at all.

*   *   *

It has been rumored that His Grace is considering some action, *one* last plan which would bring to the situation if not peace then resolution of a sort, yet when it comes the announcement is its own surprise: All of them, court and kind, lords and maidservants are to be removed to the former hunting lodge, now officially the royal residence; this castle is to be, if not strictly abandoned, then certainly shuttered, manned by a staff of no more than five to keep the building free of tramps or vandals; the rest will accompany the king and court to what His Grace calls, with a cynic's hope, the kingdom's new home.

No one says it aloud, no one asks in words but *What of the prince?* to one another, said with their gazes, their lowered lids and "What of Her Grace?" asks the vizier, voice free of opinion, alone with the king in what had once been the privy chamber. "Does she approve of this action?"

"It is not her function," says the king, voice heavy and cold, "to approve. Or disapprove."

"Then she will be—leaving, as well?"

"And why should she not, my lord vizier?" the king close and closer, breath warm as an animal's, thick with wine against the vizier's cheek. "What holds her here?" and the vizier knows that now the prince is to be understood as dead by all but those five unfortunates, that wretched staff left behind like curs in a kennel to tend what asks no tending, to watch what none would steal: "Nothing," says the vizier, gaze calm upon the king. "Forgive my lack of understanding."

And now past the locked doors they hear it, the sound of passage: ragged gown and boots gone heelless, the queen stumbling down the hall and the vizier says nothing, sits inspecting his fingers, the tips of his boots, politely, as one avoids noticing another's pov-

erty, another's idiot child. It is murmured that in her
spiraling torment Her Grace has passed through
darker gates, places no Christian should go; some
claim they have seen men moving about the palace at
night, when all but Her Grace are in slumber, men in
dark cloaks who wear—are they?—masks like the
heads of goats, men who make no sound as they pass
but hear her now, rush and stagger and the king rising, pushing at the table, and in this light it is impossible even for the vizier not to mark how he has aged,
His Grace, aged badly past pity or help and "I will
speak to the chamberlain," says the vizier, moving
now toward the door in the wake of the king, who
moves as if to his own death, a slow and tired motion
grotesque in a man of his years. "There is much to be
done."

At the doorway the king turns, one hand poised on
the jamb: "See the place is emptied in a fortnight,"
and now the open door, the hall: to the left the dying
sounds of the queen's passage, to the right the branch-
ing turn which leads to the room with the glass case,
the shadows and the silence and with great delicacy,
the vizier, looking neither right nor left: "Her Grace
has been—informed?"

No sound at all, there in the early darkness.

"I will tell her now," says the king.

"Remember I told you," Cissy still smiling; like lifting
weights, but still a smile. "March twenty-fourth. It's
Jenny's wedding, and it's going to be black tie, so you
need to rent your tux pretty soon. Okay?"

"Mmm," rolling over, eyes closed and she said it
again, "March twenty-fourth, don't forget," and
"Who's Jenny?" he asked. Sirens outside, clipping
past and "You know who she is," trying not to sound
angry, trying to sound like nothing at all. "My sister's
girl. My niece." Stepniece, stepdaughter, so what;

family was family and she wanted to show him off,
black tie and "Don't forget," she said, "okay? This is
important, write it down or something," which was
ridiculous, he never wrote anything down: *I keep it all
up here*, he would say, sweet curve of that smiling
mouth—and then the wasted theater tickets, the broken dates and missed dinners, *weren't you listening?*
and his kiss, his shrug, he was always sorry, he always said he was sorry.

"Please," she said: black-and-white quilt like a
checkerboard drawn up over his chin; like a kid, a
little kid and "So he's going?" Tanisha at lunch, kiosk
sandwiches in the snowflake drift, Cissy's ungloved
fingers red and stiff and "Sure," she said, "sure he's
going," not looking at Tanisha because Tanisha had
heard this particular refrain before but this time, "This
time," she said, "is different. Because he knows, all
right? He knows how important it is."

"Well sure," Tanisha said. Coffee gone cold in the
Styrofoam cups; her careful smile. "It's an important
day."

Don't remind him: like a mantra, *don't remind him
anymore* and she said nothing, only circled the date,
big red circle and a big red J on the supermodel cal-
endar he kept in the kitchen and "So are we finally
going to meet this guy?" her sister in the store, they
had picked out their dresses: mother-of-the-bride in
tasteful ecru, Cissy in strapless black and "Mom's dying to see him," her sister said. "Listen, is he really
that gorgeous? Mom said you said he was perfect."

Half-closed eyes, black and white; yes and no.
"Yes," she said, "he really is," and that night she
showed him the dress, tried it on: strapless black, tight
across her breasts, and "Oh wow," that lazy smile as
she turned on her heel, self-conscious pivot like a
model, supermodel, and "Gorgeous, gorgeous," he

said, rising up on one elbow. "So what's the occasion?"

See, then, the caravan: Her Grace in last hoarse protest, bundled dry into the carriage with her maids and ladies, her chaplain and his staff: the last to leave is, of course, the king: already mounted, looking down at the five who have chosen to stay and "You have all my gratitude," says His Grace. The horse's steaming breath, the heavy air to threaten snow and then he is gone, joined at a distance by his equerries, their sound the only sound in the landscape made of grey: the dying year hung with grey branches, the dying castle in which all the wings but one have been permanently closed, to save fuel, to allow the dead to bury their dead.

No one visits the room with the glass case.

Before the spring, all of the five have gone.

"You look terrific," her sister said; ladies' room tissues, offering her lipstick again; someone tried to open the door but her palm kept it shut. "But you have to stop crying, OK? Cause I have to get out there, I'm paying for all this."

Her smile dry and unhappy, mother-of-the-bride and "You go on," Cissy said, "go on, I'll be out in a minute. I just want to fix myself a little, wash my face—"

"Are you sure?" one hand still on the door but Cissy waved her away, *go, go,* and alone now, water in the basin, borrowed lipstick, and *You promised me,* not screaming, she had kept her voice reasonable, shaking voice and trembling hands, strapless black, and *You promised me!* to his sad shrug: he had not meant to make her angry, had just forgotten, it was hard to remember everything and "Listen," rising to reach for her, take her arm, "listen I can get washed up, you know, in a minute, I can put on a suit or something—"

"No you can't," she had said, with the first of the tears, "it's *black tie*, black tie, you son of a bitch," and moving then, out the door and down the stairs and he might have been looking, there at the window, might have watched her drive away but she did not look, did not turn her head to see if he was there. Frost on the windshield, the heater on high; the new dress tight across her breasts, her shoulders smooth and cold as glass, as if no one had ever touched them, as if she had never been touched before. Halfway there she realized that she had left her purse on the counter, but kept on going; she was not going back, not there, not tonight.

Glossed cold with dust the castle floors, the shattered glaze of the windows; inside is only silence, the empty nestle of owls, stray leaves and feathers, the detritus of solitude and light.

Now and then, if anyone were there to see it, the prince in his case is known to smile. Whether or not he dreams, no one can say.

The Fox Wife

Ellen Steiber

Ellen Steiber lives in Tucson, Arizona. She has published many books for children and three of her adult pieces on fairy tales appear in the recent anthology, The Armless Maiden. She is currently at work on her first novel for adults.

Steiber says, "The traditional folklore of Japan contains a wealth of stories about kitsuné, the fox. Kitsuné is, among other things, a shape-shifter and a trickster who creates illusions to bewitch unsuspecting humans. According to Kiyoshi Nozaki's book Kitsuné: Japan's Fox of Mystery, Romance & Humor, accounts of the magic of kitsuné date back to the year 711. Kitsuné is also known for the ability to possess humans. For centuries, many of the conditions we now describe as mental illness were attributed to fox possession. This story was inspired by the medical records of a Japanese doctor who treated a number of these cases in the Shimane Prefecture in the year 1892."

The Fox Wife

"**H**E'S HAD TWO WIVES BEFORE ME, AND BOTH OF them are dead."

This is what Haruko tells me after her father has summoned her to the veranda.

I watched them, standing there in the winter wind: he speaking, she listening. I've watched them both since she was a child. He likes it when the one listening is cold or tired or has been kneeling for hours. Koyata is a merchant, and yet he approaches every exchange as if it were a battle. He prefers it when the other is uncomfortable. She's grown up learning never to show discomfort. And yet to me she's always spoken her heart.

I make her sit beside me and let me stroke her hair. "You are your father's only child," I remind her. "You do him great honor by marrying into a samurai family."

"They're both dead," she repeats, her voice hollow with fear.

It's my duty to help her accept the marriage. "The first wife was sickly," I assure her. "And the second, a tiny thing who died in childbirth, no bigger than a child herself. You have nothing to fear. You will bear Lord Ikeda fine, strong sons."

She pulls away and looks at me, her eyes gone curiously pale. Her eyes are unusual among our people: light brown with a hint of gold. Her mother took sick shortly after she was born. When she could no longer care for her child, I was summoned to be the infant's maid. The baby was in my arms when her mother died. It was a hot summer afternoon, the air thick and still. Haruko had been crying for hours. I fed her, changed her, held her. Finally, I took her outside, so as not to disturb the sick. I walked her around the house, rocking her in my arms. When I passed the room where her mother lay, the woman's voice broke with a last aching cry. Then I heard Koyata frantically calling his wife's name, and I knew she was gone. I remember making soothing sounds, hushing the child, telling her there was nothing to fear. Haruko stopped crying, as if agreeing to what I'd asked, and for the first time the gold came into her eyes. Her father has often worried that she's a quick one, too clever for her own good. But it's more than that. From the day her mother died, Haruko has seen into what is meant to be concealed.

Now her eyes darken with anger. "You knew," she says in accusing tones. "You knew he was going to marry me to that stinking old man. How could my own maid know and not say a word?"

She turns from me and flees into the garden. Her father has only planted it three autumns past. The cherry trees are still saplings, bare and thin, their bark slick with ice. Her scarlet robe is like a flame between them, her slim form shaking with sobs.

It is the first time I've betrayed her.

*   *   *

Spring has come and with it, the matrimonial gifts.
Her father has sent Lord Ikeda a bronze bell in the
shape of a dragon, green Kutani porcelain, a Buddha
carved of jade, and his finest mare.

Lord Ikeda has sent two of his retainers. They bring
Koyata lacquered screens, silk quilts, and a bowl of
beaten gold. They bring Haruko ivory hair combs and
the black kimono she will wear as a married woman.
She wants none of it. She has told me to return it all,
knowing I can do no such thing. Once the gifts have
been exchanged, there is no turning back.

Lord Ikeda's retainers do not return to him but remain here, awaiting his arrival. Koyata is flustered,
for though he is far from poor, there are no extra
rooms in his house. He has no place to put the two
retainers. To hide his embarrassment, he snaps at the
servants and gives constant unnecessary orders. Finally, he tells me that we cannot ask samurai to sleep
in the barn. I will make a bed there for myself and
the girl. The retainers will have her room.

She catches me at it, in the loft, laying quilts on the
straw. She climbs the ladder, quick as a young boy.
Below us the horses nicker softly.

"O-Shima," she says, "what are you doing?"

Hesitantly, I tell her this will be our room until her
marriage. Though her father has never seen it, she has
a temper like a cat, calm one minute, furious the next.

But she laughs when I explain. "So we sleep with
the horses," she says. "Better than sleeping with Lord
Ikeda."

"You must not speak that way of the man you will
marry," I warn.

"Why?" she asks. "Will he melt? Change into a
moth? Perhaps he will choose another to marry. That
would not be so bad."

She is seventeen, nearly a bride, too old to be
scolded and yet I can't stop myself. "You're acting

like a child," I tell her. "You must act as an honorable wife. And you're old enough to know that an honorable wife does not speak disrespectfully of her husband."

She sits in the straw without care for her fine silk robes or my scolding. "O-Shima-san," she chides me, "what have you done?"

I reply for the second time that I am setting out the quilts so that we might sleep.

"That's not what I meant," she says. "I'll tell you what you've done. You've raised me to be obedient and honorable. And that honor makes me lie with every breath."

I've been betraying her from the start.

Lord Ikeda is to arrive tomorrow for the wedding. Usually it is the bride who goes to her husband's house for the ceremony. But Ikeda and his household are making their annual journey from Tokyo to his summer home. He has sent notice that Koyata will hold the wedding feast.

Lord Ikeda's mother and half a dozen servants are already here. Lady Tama now sleeps in Haruko's room. She is a wrinkled little woman with a bitter mouth and clawlike fingers. Lord Ikeda's servants and the retainers have set up a tent for themselves in the garden, but during the days they all hover around the house, making sure the lord's mother is content.

For the last week our entire household has done nothing but prepare for the wedding. Everything has been cleaned and blessed. A scroll has been painted with the gods Izanagi and Izanami, the first to marry in our land. The gardener has cut pine and plum and bamboo branches to wish Haruko and her husband long life. The cook has made soups and rice dishes and bean curd cakes. Tomorrow at dawn she will go to the fish market and buy enough fish to feed the entire wedding party. And I have packed my belongings and Haruko's. Except for the dresses from the English shop. Lord Ikeda gave special orders that anything Western was to be left behind.

This morning the final gift from Lord Ikeda arrives: Haruko's wedding robes. She stands silently as I open the box and lift out heavy white brocade—a pattern of birds, flowers, and branches, a weaving more intricate than anything except the forest itself. White is the color of mourning in our land. A bride wears it to symbolize that she has died to her own family, and that she will never leave her husband's household except as a corpse. Beneath the brocade kimono is an obi of crimson and gold tapestry, and beneath that three layers of silk undergarments and the *tsuno-kakushi*, the "horn concealer," a silk veil meant to cover the bride's horns of jealousy.

Koyata rubs the brocade between his fingers. "The obi alone is worth the price of a stallion," he says. "Your husband has honored you, Haruko. White brocade of this quality is reserved for the samurai, and yet Lord Ikeda gives it to a merchant's daughter."

"I am most fortunate," Haruko says.

Koyata grunts his agreement. It never occurs to him that what his daughter says is often the opposite of what she means.

Haruko waits until he leaves the room. "I wonder if his other wives wore these robes," she says quietly. I begin to reassure her, but I see the glint of gold in her eyes and stop. She nods, as if to say, "Yes, of course, these are the same robes they wore," and then changes the topic. "I spoke with Lord Ikeda's mother this morning," she tells me in a conversational tone. "Lady Tama doesn't like me at all. She doesn't think her son should marry beneath him. I agree with her."

"That's just an old woman jealous of your youth," I say. "You're good enough for any man."

"I have heard," Haruko says slowly, "that in the West, women choose their own husbands."

She'd undoubtedly heard this from Furuya-san, an associate of her father's who sells silk. Furuya-san often travels into Tokyo and deals with the English and the Americans. He brings back one outrageous story after another. I've always suspected that less than half of them are true.

"What women do across an ocean does not matter here," I tell Haruko. "Especially since you are marrying a man who keeps the traditions of his ancestors."

"Keeps the traditions?" she echoes. "He strides around as if he's going to restore feudal Japan."

"Give him a chance, Haruko. After all, he's been very generous."

"Has he?" she asks. "The cost of all of these presents is nothing to him. He's the last surviving heir of one of the oldest samurai families. We both know why he wants a young wife. Why couldn't he take one of his own class? Maybe the other samurai don't trust him with their daughters. He—"

We've had this conversation before, and it's senseless. I cannot count the number of times I've lost patience with her this week. "Your father worked very hard to find you such a husband," I remind her.

"I know." She slides open the shoji screen and steps out onto the porch, leaving me holding her wedding robes. "I think they would look much better on you," she says, and walks toward the garden.

She often wanders in the garden; her father has forbidden her to go beyond its walls. Although I suspect she goes much farther, I've never followed her. It's the one thing she would never forgive.

Now darkness has fallen, and I wait for her in the barn. Tomorrow will be a long day. We should both be asleep. But the hour grows late, and there is only myself in the loft and the horses down below.

It is after midnight when two of Lord Ikeda's retainers escort Haruko to the barn. "On the night before her wedding we found her running," one of them says sternly. He gives me the sly look of a man who does not trust women. "Running away perhaps?"

"My lady would never do such a thing," I tell them.

Haruko stands with her eyes downcast. "Forgive me," she murmurs. "It was my cat. He slipped out of the garden. He's never gone over the wall before. I wanted to catch him before he got lost."

She does not have a cat.

"It's the night before her wedding," I remind the men. "The child is excited. Please forgive her foolishness."

"See that she does not cause trouble," the shorter man says.

Haruko bows low and again begs their pardon.

She waits until they leave the barn and then climbs to the loft. "If it wasn't for Ikeda's guards," she tells me, "I would have gotten away."

We wake at dawn on the day of the wedding. A bath has already been prepared for Haruko. One of Lord Ikeda's maids takes her from me. I stand for a moment in the garden. The bright green of early spring is gone from the leaves. The heat of summer has begun, and already the air is humming with flies. The morning skies are grey, dark with the promise of rain. Haruko has never liked rain. Thunder terrifies her. I know she will take this weather as a bad omen.

I am to ready the wedding robes. A corner of the main room has been screened off with Lord Ikeda's lacquer screens so that she may dress. I wonder if in Lord Ikeda's house I will still dress her. I understand that I'm being brought along as a courtesy, a way of helping Haruko keep face. It is to seem as if she were a woman with many servants, a member of Ikeda's own class. Of course, no one will actually be fooled by this. No matter, she will be the most exquisite bride ever to enter Lord Ikeda's house.

It's wrong of me to be prideful, but in a crowd of one hundred beautiful women, Haruko is the one people would remember. By the time she was fourteen, she was spoken of as the most beautiful woman in Kyoto. It is her beauty, of course, that made a samurai lord willing to marry a merchant's daughter. She has that rare comeliness that they say can only be a gift from the gods. Her hair falls to her waist, thick, black, and gleaming. She has long, delicate bones—a graceful neck, slender hands, and a narrow waist. She is not perfect. It's not fashionable for a woman to have eyes so light. And yet it is her eyes that make her so striking, and something inside her—a quickness of spirit—that makes her more than the others. She has no vanity. "How could I take pride in my looks?" she once asked. "I had nothing to do with them. Were it up to me, I'd have been born a boy." She has always seen her beauty for what it is: her father's most valuable bargaining chip.

The rain starts midmorning, the wedding in the afternoon. The priest begins the ceremony, and his prayers rise above the sound of the rain on the tile roof.

The purification is complete, the wedding vows spoken, the cups of *saké* exchanged. Haruko's face is composed. She looks at her husband, then beyond him to the open door. I see a hint of a smile and I look, too. Rain still falls in sheets, but through the rain the sun is shining. Much later, Haruko squeezes my hand. "Maybe it won't be so bad," she whispers. "After all, the sun shone for us during the ceremony."

Something nags at me, a superstition about weddings and sun in the midst of rain, but I can't remember what it is, and so I say nothing except, "Long life, Haruko. Long life to you and all your kin!"

Before evening falls we are part of Lord Ikeda's retinue, riding to his summerhouse in the mountains. We start through the city streets. Haruko rides near the head of the procession in a covered palanquin. Lord Ikeda's mother is in the first palanquin, and Ikeda and his retainers ride horses. I walk behind with the other servants. We pass through the winding streets of Kyoto, a maze of low wooden buildings—familiar shops and houses and shrines. We pass the street where I grew up, the cemetery where I buried my parents. I have lived here all my life, and now that is changing.

We cross a stone bridge over a dry streambed, and the streets become narrower. We are leaving the city now. The farther we go from the city, the narrower the streets become. Dusk colors the sky charcoal grey, and paper lanterns light the shops. Soon the lanterns are spaced farther and farther apart. The road beneath us is damp from the rains, and the air smells of cedar and pine. We are traveling a country footpath that will take us into the mountains.

At the head of the procession, Lord Ikeda calls a halt. His servants rush to light pine torches. I approach Haruko's palanquin. She's been so quiet that I want to make sure she's all right.

"Haruko?" I call softly as I stand beside the litter.

The curtains part, and Haruko looks out at me. "What?"

"We've left Kyoto," I tell her. "And the rain has let up. Aren't you curious to see what lies beyond the city?"

Obliging me, she peers into the darkness. I see her eyes widen.

"What is it?" I ask.

She points. In the darkness near the base of a cypress tree two eyes watch us, glowing like topaz in the reflection of the torch fires.

"It's just an animal," I tell her. "Nothing to be frightened of."

"That's not what frightens me," she replies, and vanishes behind the curtains again.

It's nearly midnight when we stop at the inn. Lord Ikeda's household is obviously used to travel. For though we are all exhausted, it is only minutes before the horses and palanquins are in the stable, and all of us and the baggage are inside the inn.

Food is ordered for everyone, then Lord Ikeda barks an order at another servant to lead Haruko to one of the guest rooms. Her eyes meet mine. It is the first time since she was an infant that she and I have slept apart. Tonight she sleeps with her lord and her eyes are wild with terror.

It's enough to make me do the unthinkable. "My lord," I call out.

Ikeda turns and stares at me. Even though he's seen me many times, it's clear that this is the first time he's truly taken notice of me. "What is it?" he demands.

"A thousand pardons," I begin, "but my lady, Haruko, has not been well these last few days. I've been nursing her back from a stomach illness. Might I stay by her side tonight?"

He shows no anger but something hard and implacable enters his eyes. "My wife sleeps with me," he answers. "I will see to her stomach if there's a problem." He glances at Haruko. "Are you sick?" She shakes her head and stares at the floor.

"There is no problem," he says, as if his pronouncement makes it the truth.

I watch Haruko being led away, and then I am led into a room with the other women servants.

"Tell me," I say to the older woman on the pallet beside me. "What did his other wives die of?"

She laughs. "Not of bedding the lord. Don't fear. Your chick will be alive in the morning."

I do not sleep all that night. In the morning I am the first one up. It seems hours before breakfast is served, and Lord Ikeda and his wife emerge from their room.

Haruko is indeed alive. She greets her mother-in-law with a bow, me with a nod. She wears the expression I have seen her wear so often after a talk with her father. She is as composed as the Buddha himself, the embodiment of her name, which means "the Tranquil." But for Haruko the appearance of serenity is always bought at great cost. When her eyes are calm as a windless dawn, it's certain that she's hiding just how badly she's been hurt.

We travel for the better part of the day before reaching Lord Ikeda's summerhouse. Now the journey is all steep, winding mountain paths that cross each other, as though part of a web. Lord Ikeda's retainers ride with a mysterious knowledge of when to turn and when to continue, when to leave the path entirely and cross a stream—for there are no markers or signs from which to gauge direction. I wonder where the trails lead and find it hard to imagine that they go anywhere but deeper into the forest. Haruko and I are being taken a very long way from the life we knew. It is clear to me now that we will never find our way back.

Lord Ikeda has ordered me to walk beside Haruko's palanquin today. Perhaps he senses that she needs comfort. But she asks for none. Again the curtains remain closed, as if her litter were empty. And so I spend the day watching my new lord.

Haruko called him "a stinking old man," but no

one else would describe him that way. Rather, he is a man in his mid-fifties, thick bodied, with heavily muscled forearms. His hair is greying at the temples, and deep creases line the sides of his mouth. His eyes give away very little; I think that he and Haruko may be well matched in that. In many ways he is similar to other men. He's used to giving commands and being obeyed. Though he does not seem to anger easily, something about his presence makes it known that to defy him is to invite disaster. Like his ancestors, he has trained with the sword and bow since he was a boy. You can see it in the way he walks, the way he sits a horse, the way he holds himself. He has the meticulous, assured manner of a master swordsman. He smells of pine soap.

We all knew of Lord Kenjiro Ikeda long before he saw Haruko's picture and sent word to Koyata that his daughter would make him a fitting wife. He is the descendant of a Tokugawa shogun, noted for both his cruelty and his nearly successful attempt to seize half the country. It has been years now since the samurai ruled Japan and the clans warred against each other. Ikeda does not wage war. Instead he has become a close friend to the Emperor, a trusted adviser. But I suspect that isn't enough. For beneath his calm there's the restlessness of a man born too late for his destiny. Kenjiro Ikeda was raised to rule the Japan of his ancestors. Nothing less will really do.

It is nearly dusk when we cross a mountain ridge and see a large village in the valley below. After traveling so many hours without encountering a single dwelling, it's good to see so many signs of life: houses and rice and bean fields, children playing by a stream, chickens, horses, dogs. Near the center of the village is a row of narrow shops, their rectangular paper signs swaying in the wind.

"That's Nanshu," a woman servant named O-Yuki tells me. "It's a very prosperous village."

I look for a house that seems grand enough to belong to Lord Ikeda and see only the usual small houses, barns, and shops. There is one that is somewhat larger than the others. "And Lord Ikeda lives there?" I ask.

O-Yuki laughs at me. "That's a hospital," she says.

"A hospital?"

"That's how you can tell it's a prosperous village. They even have a doctor from Tokyo who's studied Western medicine. Actually, he's the son of the head of the village. He returned just last year."

We do not go down into the village, but continue along the ridge until the retainers follow yet another path up into the mountains. Soon the village is lost behind the trees. We travel alongside a stream whose banks are lined with wild iris. It is as though here in the forest it is still spring. The sound of rushing water fills the woods, and we come to a waterfall whose white mist soaks us. All this time Haruko has not looked out of the litter, even once.

It's not far beyond the waterfall that we reach a high stone wall edged with plum trees. Two guards wearing Lord Ikeda's crest stand by a gatehouse.

"Now, this is the summerhouse," O-Yuki says proudly. "It was built by the lord's great-great-grand-father."

We enter the gate, cross a moat, and then pass through an inner gate. You cannot even see the roof of the house from here. It's well hidden beyond the guardhouse, stables, a dog compound, servants' quarters, and a series of gardens. We cross a footbridge that spans a stream and pass through a cherry garden, a rock garden, a garden that is heavy with the scents of jasmine and wisteria. We pass a teahouse set on the bank of the stream, and then finally we approach the house.

Perhaps "house" is the wrong word, for it is far more than a house though not nearly as grand as Kyoto's Imperial Palace. A low stone wall sets it off from the rest of the grounds. It has a Chinese pagoda-style roof made of jade green tiles. O-Yuki informs me that it has fourteen rooms.

Lord Ikeda dismounts and gives his horse to a servant. The palanquins are set down. Lady Tama gets out of hers, complaining that the ride was not smooth enough. Haruko emerges from behind her curtains. She stands, a little stiff from the ride, then turns. I expect to see a look of amazement on her face for we are in one of the most beautiful places I have ever seen. Her eyes register nothing.

Even Ikeda notices this. "What do you think of your new home?" he asks.

Haruko does not meet his eyes. "I am sure I will be content here" is her reply.

Haruko has been married for three weeks. Although I now sleep in the servants' quarters, I am still her maid whose duty it is to dress her and see to her needs. We've had very little chance to speak. When Haruko does not need my services, I am sent to help the cook or the gardener.

For me life in Lord Ikeda's household is not so bad. The worst of it is that I do not spend much time with Haruko. But I get along with the other servants, and I am still amazed to wake up every morning in such a splendid place. I sleep beneath a silk comforter now, and my kimono are made of silk. Like all who are part of the household, I eat the finest food. There is even a small shrine in the garden just for the servants. And I have never seen so many colors as I see in Lord

Ikeda's gardens. I will never tire of them; I cannot imagine tiring of this place.

The only time I'm uneasy here is at night. That's when I'm reminded of how far we are from anyone outside the walls. At night, even when the screens are closed, you can hear the low tones of owls calling and the high ones of foxes barking to their mates. Once I even heard deer drinking at a stream. I still don't understand how; they couldn't have been inside the compound—the walls are too high for them to leap. It is possible that the deer were nowhere near the house. At night the winds sweep down off the mountain, and the scents and the sounds of the woods fill Ikeda's halls and chambers. At night, it's as if these stone walls which make us feel so safe have dissolved.

I don't know if the nights bother Haruko. Lady Tama commands most of her time. Lady Tama has servants of her own, and yet it is Haruko whom she orders to fetch her hairbrush or put away her bedding or take her for a walk in the gardens. Nothing Haruko does is good enough. She is a stupid girl, a careless girl, a clumsy girl, a girl who has no talent for the koto or arranging flowers.

Yesterday, Lady Tama marched Haruko out to the teahouse and ordered her to perform the tea ceremony. Moreover, she ordered several of us to attend them. The other servants looked as surprised as I; attending tea ceremonies is not one of our usual duties. I took it as an honor, a privilege sometimes granted to those living in Lord Ikeda's household.

Haruko had barely begun the preparation before Lady Tama told her that she'd been brought up with the manners of a peasant. She wasn't rinsing the whisk correctly. She was using too much tea powder. Is that how she handled a tea bowl that had been passed down through four generations? Couldn't she do anything properly?

Haruko didn't acknowledge her mother-in-law, but continued the ceremony. It is, after all, a meditation. Still, she knew by then that Lady Tama can't stand to be ignored. The old woman began to tremble with rage, all the while heaping more insults on her. My eyes met O-Yuki's; it was clear to both of us why we'd been summoned. This humiliation had been planned.

Haruko went on with the ceremony as if the lord's mother didn't exist. Finally, Lady Tama could bear no more. She reached up and slapped Haruko hard. I can still hear that sound and picture Haruko as she set down the tea bowl and brought her hand to her face. Her eyes went gold then, and I feared for what she might do in return. But Lord Ikeda had seen it all.

"You may not do that again," he told his mother. "If my wife is disobedient, you will tell me and I will punish her. Continue what you were doing," he instructed his wife.

Without looking at either her husband or her mother-in-law, Haruko completed the ceremony.

I cannot tell if Lord Ikeda is a cruel husband or kind. In our three weeks here, though we're far from the cities, he has entertained a number of visitors, most of them emissaries from Tokyo. He receives them in the upper hall, or serves elaborate dinners in the great hall, or has moon-viewing parties in the garden. At these times he keeps Haruko by his side. It is her one reprieve from Lady Tama.

There was a day last week when Lady Tama was not feeling well. After making Haruko read to her for hours, the old woman finally fell asleep.

The noon meal had just been served. The other servants were already preparing the great hall for that night's dinner. I was alone in the kitchen, cleaning up, when Haruko found me.

"O-Shima," she said. "I miss our talks."

"And I. But Haruko, this is foolish. If someone tells

your husband that you snuck into the kitchen to see your maid . . . you shouldn't be here."

"I shouldn't be in this house at all," Haruko agreed. "I hate it."

"How can you say that?" I asked. "How could anyone not find the upper hall beautiful?" In the upper hall the screens are painted with scenes of the sea—an island rises out of the ocean, a lone ship floats on moonlit waves, mist clings to trees that edge a curving shoreline. To enter that room is to look into other lands.

"How you can bear the upper hall?" Haruko replied. "The paintings make me feel as if I'm about to be swallowed by fog."

"Well, what about the main hall?" The main hall has plain white shoji screens that are usually open to the verandas and the gardens. To be in the main hall in the summer is to be surrounded by greenery.

"It's bearable when the screens are open," Haruko conceded. "But I don't like the narrow hallway that leads there."

I put away the last of the rice bowls. "You sound like a woman determined to find fault. What could be wrong with a hallway?"

"The floorboards squeak," she answered quite seriously.

"Lady Tama has been a bad influence on you," I teased. "You are getting every bit as fussy—"

"No," Haruko cut me off. "Those floors were specially built to make noise when you step on them. That way no one can move through the house without my husband knowing. And haven't you noticed the wooden panels in the ceilings? They conceal hiding places for his guards. And the chamber where Ikeda and I—sleep . . ."

"What is it?" I asked, worried. "You've told me nothing of your husband."

"There are wooden panels that can be pulled down over the shoji screens," she went on in a flat voice, "so that no one can hear what goes on inside." She glanced toward the bedchamber and shuddered. "I would think that this house would tell you a great deal about my husband."

Still, I did not want to believe the worst. "I only know that he honors you by having you at his side before distinguished guests."

"I am a showpiece," Haruko said. "He also takes his guests to the stables to see his stallion, and to the lower hall to see his collection of porcelain. My husband likes displaying fine things."

So I asked the question whose answer I had not wanted to hear. "Does he hurt you?"

"He—" she hesitated. "He asks me to do things I would not choose to do. And he will not allow me to refuse."

At the end of that month more envoys from Tokyo arrive. One is a man who has been here before, Baron Hiroshi Nakamura. Nakamura is a young, handsome man who clearly likes Lord Ikeda's pretty wife. He tells her of Tokyo, of telegrams and electricity and railroads, of Japanese women who now dress only in English gowns with their small waists and full skirts. Haruko's eyes grow wide with delight but beside her, her husband stirs restlessly, making it clear that he does not approve of such talk. This is when Baron Nakamura brings out the gifts he has brought: leather saddles for the horses, calligraphy paper, brushes, and inks for Lord Ikeda, and the finest kimono for Ikeda, his mother, and his wife. The colors of the silks are so delicate that even Haruko reaches out to touch them.

Nakamura smiles at her as she reaches for the fabric. "For you, lady, I have a special gift." He hands her a black lacquer box no larger than a teapot.

Haruko removes the lid from the box and lifts out a smooth white egg-shaped stone.

"A rock, Hiro?" For once Ikeda sounds amused.

Nakamura shrugs. "I found it when I was hunting in the mountains this spring. It's worth no more than any stone you might find in the woods, but I thought your wife might like it."

"It's beautiful," Haruko says, "so white and perfect." She holds the stone between her hands, as though it were a precious jewel. "I thank you for your gift, Baron Nakamura."

"Put it back in the box now," Lord Ikeda instructs her, and she does.

That night at dinner Haruko becomes flushed with fever. Ikeda, seeing this, tells her she may go to bed. I follow her to her chamber to undress her and lay out the bedding.

As I begin to untie the obi Haruko stays me with her hand. "I'll do it," she says. "Please see to the bedding, O-Shima. I need to lie down."

I do as she asks, laying out the futons and the quilts. "Everything's ready," I say. "Come and rest."

"In a moment," she tells me. She's standing beside the shoji screen, holding the black lacquer box. She lifts the lid and a glow lights her face. "Look," she says, her voice filled with awe.

In its black box the white stone is glowing as if it were the moon itself.

"Touch it, O-Shima. It gives light yet it doesn't burn."

"Close the box and get rid of it!" I say at once.

"Why? It's beautiful." With fevered movements she removes a candle from one of the paper lanterns and places the rock inside it in its stead. "See?" she says. "It lights the whole room."

"Do you want your husband to see that?"

She sighs, removes the stone from the lantern, and replaces the candle. But she kneels by the screen, holding the glowing stone in her lap and touching it as if it were a child.

"Haruko," I say, "you've got a fever. You should be in bed."

It's as if she doesn't hear me. Everything in her is focused on the stone. Furuya-san, the silk merchant, once showed us a piece of Austrian crystal he'd gotten from an English trader. It was a piece of clear glass cut with facets. In the sunlight it held all the other colors. The stone is like that, too. Bright, white light, but when you look carefully you can see bits of pink and green, red and purple, yellow and blue. Though it holds the shape of the stone, its light, like that of true fire, is never still. Something inside it is spinning.

"Haruko, listen to me now. Ordinary stones don't shed light. You're holding some sort of witchery. Let me take it. I'll throw it in the stream, and it will never bother you again."

Haruko looks at me with eyes that are nearly amber. "I'll put it back in its box now," she says quite reasonably. "But if you touch it or try to take it from me, I will have Lord Ikeda return you to my father's house."

I stand there, unable to speak, unable to believe she's threatened me.

She sets the glowing white stone in the black lacquer box and replaces the lid. "Go now," she says. "I need to sleep."

Haruko's fever is no better the next day. Her cheeks are flushed, her lips parched, and her body feels like it's on fire. Lord Ikeda orders his wife to stay in bed, and orders me to feed her broth and stay by her side. She sleeps most of the day and eats very little. O-Yuki tells me that two demons have appeared in the village, cholera and typhoid. But Haruko shows no signs of disease other than the fever. Late in the afternoon, she wakes and asks to the see the black lacquer box.

"No," I tell her. "That stone is dangerous. It may well be what's making you sick."

"I think it's what will make me well," she says. "Bring it to me, O-Shima."

I bring her the lacquer box. This time when she opens it, the stone does not glow; once again it's an ordinary white rock. This makes no difference to Haruko. She lifts it carefully from the box and cradles it in her arms. "You don't belong in this house," she tells the rock. "You are far too beautiful for such an awful place. Don't worry, little one, I will return you to a place that is worthy of you."

"The fever is causing delusions, and you are talking like a madwoman!" I say. I take the rock from her and shut it securely in its box. "Haruko, you're frightening me. Do you want me to ask your husband to send for a doctor?"

"A doctor can't help me," she replies. "No one can."

"I won't listen to such nonsense," I tell her. "I'm going to soak cloths in cold water and put them on your forehead. That will bring the fever down."

She sits among the quilts, her pale silver robe falling in folds around her, her eyes nearly as pale as the robe. "It's not necessary, O-Shima. The fever will be gone soon. You'll see."

"And what about that stone?"

"Let it be, O-Shima. I promise you, it will do me no harm."

Darkness falls. The night is dense and black and heavy with midsummer heat. I light lamps in each corner of the bedchamber. I cannot help looking at the black lacquer box. If inside it the stone glows like the moon, there is no sign. The room is silent except for the sound of Haruko's breathing. She's still feverish, sleeping restlessly beneath the quilts. In the upper hall, her husband confers with the envoys from Tokyo. For a while I'll stay with her.

And then it happens again. The scent of sweet damp earth fills the house, and an owl calls so close I turn to make sure it's not in the room with us. I can hear the sound of a stream running, of light, rapid footfalls on the forest floor. Once again, a presence belonging to the mountains has slipped over the walls and through the screens. Something of the wild comes in, glides along the floors, sinks into the quilts, and makes itself at ease like a guest among us.

It wakes Haruko. She sits up and throws off the covers. The bedding is drenched with sweat.

"Are you strong enough to get up?" I ask her.

"I think so," she says, but her eyes are disoriented, as if she's returned from a great distance. "I've had such strange dreams, O-Shima."

"It's just the fever. Let me change the quilts before your husband comes in and sends me back to my own bed."

She stands slowly and sways. I reach out to steady her, but she pushes me away. "I've been sleeping all day," she says. "I don't want to sleep anymore. Bring me my *geta*, O-Shima. I want to walk in the gardens."

"You know Lord Ikeda won't permit it when you're ill," I tell her. "Perhaps if your fever breaks tonight, tomorrow he will let you walk in the gardens."

"It is to be hoped for," she says gravely. "If Lady Tama does not have other plans for me, if my husband is in an indulgent mood, and if the planets rearrange themselves, then perhaps I will be so lucky."

"Hush," I say, and strip off her robe. Though the night is hot, she's shivering. In just over a day the fever has eaten at her. Her body is thinner, her breasts as small as they were when she was a girl of fourteen. I dip a facecloth in a basin of cool water and rinse the sweat from her body. Then I clothe her in a robe of coral silk, and brush out the long ebony hair.

She lets me bathe and dress her without protest, her eyes fixed on something beyond the screens. "O-Shima," she says, "do you think it's possible for a person to change his karma?"

"If the planets rearrange themselves," I tease, but I see her stiffen, as if I've hurt her, and so I answer her seriously. "I don't know. From what I've seen, we all live the lives we were born to."

"I was born to be a merchant's wife."

"No," I tell her. "Your beauty destined you for much more. You could not have been a merchant's wife."

"Nor can I be a samurai's," she murmurs. She glances toward the screens again. "It's new moon tonight," she says. "I think it is no moon. I think once a month the moon gets bored and leaves the sky and leaves us all in darkness. I wish I could go where it goes."

"Lie down again," I say. "You need rest."

She sits among the quilts, and pulls them up around her shoulders. She is still shivering. "Listen," she says.

Somewhere just outside the house a vixen is howling, her call high and lone and urgent.

"She's searching for it," Haruko says softly.

"For what?"

"Don't you know?"

I do, of course, but I have not wanted to name it. For if I did, I would have to go to Lord Ikeda and tell him just what sort of gift Baron Nakamura brought his wife.

"She's very close," Haruko says.

The dogs begin a round of crazed barking only to be quickly silenced by their keepers.

"Too close," I agree. "How does a fox get over a stone wall taller than a man?"

"Walls have never kept out foxes," Haruko answers. "Especially when we've got something that belongs to them."

Still, I'm hoping I'm wrong, that I'm only a silly maid who has listened to too many stories. "What do we have that a fox would want? The cook's chickens?"

Haruko makes a slight gesture with her head, tilting it toward the black lacquer box. Around the rim of its lid I see a hair-thin perfect rectangle of bright white light.

"*Kitsuné-bi*," she says. *Fox fire.*

I am a weak woman, a coward. When Lord Ikeda comes to the bedchamber that night, I do not tell him what is in the lacquer box, which, of course, has stopped glowing. I bow and leave quickly.

I know I should speak up. I should tell him that it is fox fire, that it may have caused her fever, that we must get rid of it at once.

I wonder about Baron Nakamura, who departed for Tokyo late last night. Did he know what it was he brought? Or did he really think he was making a gift of a simple white stone? Either way, it would disgrace him for me to inform Ikeda of its true nature.

And what of Haruko? I cannot tell what passes between her and her husband. I know I cannot risk his being displeased with her, for he is her only protection. And mine. Haruko named my fear correctly. From the day I left Koyata's house, I have been afraid that Lord Ikeda would send me back.

So I do not tell Ikeda any of this. For all I know, I could have him open the lacquer box and find only a smooth white stone. It would be very like a fox to play such a trick. It is possible that it is nothing more than a stone, and Haruko and I are the ones deceived. For where there are foxes, there is illusion.

What it really means to have a ball of fox fire find its way into your home is this: that you have begun a journey into a place where no one will ever again be quite sure of what is real.

I lie awake worrying until the dense black sky starts to lighten. Just before dawn I fall asleep, and then suddenly I'm kicked awake. I open my eyes to see muscular bare feet at eye level with my pallet.

Lord Ikeda stands over me, his hands on his hips. "Where is she?" he demands. "Where is your mistress?"

Somehow I get from the pallet to my knees and kneel until my head touches the floor. "I don't know, my lord. When I left the room tonight—when you came in—she was there, sitting among the quilts."

"She is not there any longer," he says quite distinctly. "Where did she go?"

I have an idea, but I know he will not like it. "I don't know," I murmur, which is close enough to the truth.

"Get up," he says. "You will find her."

I'm given no chance to get up. Two of his retainers pull me up by the arms and drag me from the servants' quarters through the gardens to the main house and then to the sleeping chamber where I am dropped on my knees.

"She's not here," he says.

Indeed, there is no sign of Haruko.

"Where is she?" he repeats in clipped tones. It's the first time I've seen him let the anger show, and the reason for it is clear. She did not disappear when her maidservant was caring for her, but while her samurai husband slept by her side.

And there is something else, something he muttered to one of his men as I was being dragged through the halls. "She's stopped bleeding. She must be found." Though I've seen no sign of it, Haruko is carrying the lord's child.

"I don't know where she is," I answer. "Last night she said she wanted to walk in the gardens, but I told her you would not permit it."

Ikeda barks an order at his retainers and they go to search the gardens. But they won't find her there, I'd stake my life on it. Because one thing more is missing from the bedchamber: the black lacquer box.

All that morning there is confusion. The cook is missing his salted salmon. A mare has foaled well before her time. Six of Ikeda's men cannot find their shoes, and none has the courage to explain this to Ikeda. They settle for disgruntled whispering and are reprimanded by Lady Tama, whose mood is even fouler than usual. Today she claims that her favorite mirror is gone. The mirror is later found inside one of her cabinets but until it is, every servant in the house must search. In fact, some of us are called away from the search for Haruko to find the mirror. Were I not frightened for Haruko, it would be funny.

Haruko reappears just after noon. She still wears the robe of coral silk, but the fever is gone from her eyes. She finds me polishing the inside of a brass incense burner, another task that Lady Tama has set me.

"That's a waste of your time," Haruko says. "It will only blacken again the next time incense is burned."

"Don't talk to me of incense burners! Where have you been?"

"You know," she answers. "I followed the fox fire. It will lead you if you let it."

I shut my eyes. "You cannot do such things."

"I had to return the *kitsuné-bi* to the vixen," she explains. "I told you it was too beautiful to stay in this house. It would have sickened here."

"My lady, you are the one who has sickened. How could you just leave in the middle of the night? Your husband was not pleased to find you gone."

"O-Shima, have you ever been in the forest?" she asks me. "Not with Lord Ikeda's retinue. On your own. Do you know what it's like to be among the trees? I—" She hesitates, as if deciding whether or not to continue. Her voice drops to a whisper, "They shelter you and teach you secrets. The leaves know things about the wind that even the birds haven't learned. And there are places the forest guards, places where the scent of the earth is rich and wet and where with one breath you can tell if a badger has just gone past or a squirrel has birthed her young or if a deer drank from the stream—"

"Stop!" I press my hand against her mouth. "Haruko, these things you're telling me have no place in this house. What you need to think about is what you're going to tell your husband when he asks you where you've been. Think. What will you say?"

She tells me about the moss on trees, how it differs from the moss on stones. I begin to wonder if she and I are having the same conversation or even speaking the same language. Perhaps I say one thing and she hears another. "Haruko," I try again, "you are the lord's wife."

"The lord's wife," she repeats slowly. "O-Shima, do you know Tadashi?"

"The old gardener with one hand? What does he—"

"He once stole a salmon from my husband's table. My husband took his hand in return."

No sooner does she say this than Ikeda enters the

hall, his face a mask of calm. "Haruko."

"My husband," she says. "I was just asking O-Shima where I might find you."

"Come with me," he says. He strides toward the bedchamber, not looking back. There is no question that she will follow. Haruko bows her head and walks a few steps behind him. She does not hesitate but something in her shoulders stiffens, as if she's bracing herself. I trail behind her, see the door to the bedchamber slide shut. Lord Ikeda begins to speak in a low voice; I can't make out his words. And then I hear a sound that I've never heard before and yet there is no mistaking it: The wooden doors are being lowered so that no one may hear what goes on inside.

The next morning Lord Ikeda is still in the bedchamber when I go to dress Haruko. "See that you do not lose your lady again," he tells me. He leaves me alone with her then. She has already put on the first inner robe of her kimono.

"What are you doing?" I chide her. "Let me help you."

"I'm tired of being helped," she says, and puts on the second robe.

"They're not lying properly," I tell her, adjusting the robes. It's the first time she's ever dressed herself. "Haruko, why didn't you wait for me to dress you?"

"Because I'm sick of needing someone to do it for me. I want clothes that I can put on myself. I want Western dresses."

"Western dresses have hooks and eyes and buttons all down the back," I remind her. "They're no simpler than kimono. Haruko"—I don't know how to phrase it—"perhaps you are covering something?"

Her eyes go bright with anger. "Bruises?" she asks. "Are you curious to know whether my husband punished me?"

"I—"

"I'll show you," she offers.

With one move she drops both of the robes to the floor and stands before me naked. There isn't a mark on her.

"Forgive me," I say, unable to conceal my relief. "I didn't mean to pry. There's something else—are you—the lord said you'd stopped bleeding."

She looks at me with contempt. "Do you really think I'd bear his child?"

I dress her then without incident. But when the obi is finally tied she is wearing the calm gaze that has begun to frighten me. "O-Shima," she says, "there are two things you must understand about my husband. He's a man who values subtlety. And he's a man who's spent years mastering arts whose purpose is to destroy. For him to leave a bruise would be crude."

She does not eat all that day except to take a spoonful of rice and beans, and that is mostly to stop me from nagging. She patiently attends her mother-in-law, as she has since she came to this house. That afternoon when the old woman begins to snore Haruko slips out of her room and heads for the garden.

"Where are you going, my lady?" I ask.

"For a walk. Will you come with me?"

I follow her but she makes it difficult to keep up. She moves swiftly, cutting across the grounds without heed for the paths. White peony and pink azalea petals fall in her wake. Her kimono catches on a wild rose. She pulls it loose, never noticing the tear in the silk or the one pale flower whose stem breaks from the plant and clings to her.

"My lady!" I call out.

If she hears me, she doesn't slow or turn.

We've just passed the teahouse when Ogawa steps out from behind an oak tree. Ogawa, a thin wiry man with bowlegs and eyes like a serpent, is Ikeda's most trusted retainer. "I will accompany you," he says.

"We don't need your company," Haruko tells him.

"I will accompany you," he repeats.

Haruko keeps walking, ignoring us both. She follows a path through the willows and jasmine and wisteria. She crosses the garden of stones and then strides toward the first of the footbridges. She stops at the stream and turns to Ogawa. "Do you know how to swim?" she asks him.

"Yes."

"I should like to see that," she says. "Please take off your clothes and swim."

Ogawa, whose emotional range consists of registering various states of obedience, stares at Haruko as if her skin had just turned bright purple.

"Swim!"

What can I do but distract her? Whatever is said to Ogawa is certain to be repeated to her husband.

"Haruko, look at the carp!" My voice is overly bright, idiotic, as though I'm talking to a three-year-old, but it's the only thing I can think of to say.

To my amazement she looks at the carp, bright red-gold against the moss-covered rocks. She looks at them with interest, her body perfectly still, her eyes following the longest one.

Ogawa watches her as intently as she watches the fish.

I know what is going to happen the instant before it does, and so I stumble, my ankle hooked behind his, knocking him down. We fall together, and I make sure that my hand flies up and my sleeve covers his eyes. So he cannot see the moment when Haruko's hand darts into the water and darts back out. He cannot see that she takes the carp from the water as easily as I might take a floating branch. She holds the fish in one hand, unmoved by its frantic struggles. Its scales shine like new metal by firelight.

I'm still struggling in Ogawa's grip, ignoring his curses, making a deliberate tangle of my robes, when she puts the head of the fish into her mouth and bites straight through the wriggling red-gold body.

The next day Haruko doesn't eat at all and announces at the midday meal that when and if she does eat, she will take food only from my hand. Her husband listens to this, nods as if it were expected, then sends her to their chamber to await him.

In the early evening, just as dusk has dropped down from the mountaintop, he tells me to see if his wife will eat something. I decide to bring her a bowl filled with ripe plums from the garden. The house has been chilly all day, and with darkness the forest has again slipped inside. The low murmur of a dove comes from the end of the hallway, and the smell of wet black earth rises from the polished wood floors. In the corridor outside the bedchamber, I glance at the shoji screen and see Haruko's silhouette lit by the yellow glow of a small lamp. She is naked, squatting over something.

Quickly, I let myself into the room, positioning myself between my mistress and the door. "Haruko, what do you think your husband will say when he finds that anyone can see your body through the screen? What if Lady Tama sees this immodesty?"

"Do you think I care?" she replies. In the dim light of the room her eyes gleam bright gold.

She has taken her husband's kimono and piled them into a mound on the floor. Blue, grey, and black silk form a soft island in the center of the room. A dark stain washes over them as she empties her bladder onto the mound.

For once I have no words. All I can think of is

what Ikeda will do to us both when he finds his kimono ruined this way. My hands are shaking so hard that I drop the bowl of plums.

Haruko regards me with golden eyes. "Stop shaking, O-Shima," she says. "I'm relieving myself. Is that so awful?"

"You are asking for your death. And mine."

She stands up, grabs one of the sashes from the ground, and wipes herself dry. "Put the plums back in the bowl," she says calmly. "I'm going out. Do you want to come with me?"

"Yes," I answer, for I know I can't stay.

"Good." Swiftly she dons a black kimono, not bothering with the inner robes. "Follow me," she says, and slides open the screen.

I stop to take a lantern and as I do she whirls. "No," she says. "Carry that and they'll find us. Don't worry, I can find my way in the dark."

"To *where*?" I ask.

Again she makes her way across the gardens, heading north. The main gate to the compound is on the south; there are smaller strategic entrances east and west; to the north is only a high stone wall, the mountains rising steeply behind it.

At night the garden paths are lit by candles set in stone lanterns. But as we move farther from the house the lanterns become fewer. Once we cross the third footbridge, the grounds are no longer lit. The thin crescent moon is little help; it keeps slipping behind a wide blanket of clouds. Ahead of me Haruko's black robe and black hair disappear into the darkness. Sometime quite recently she mastered the art of walking silently; though she wears wooden *geta*, I can't hear her at all.

"Haruko!" I call as loudly as I dare.

"O-Shima, you're slow!" she replies impatiently.

I hurry, following her voice, stumbling over rocks

and roots. I've never been able to see well at night.

"Here O-Shima." She reaches for my hand and the night becomes even darker, so dense and black that I can't see even the wall in front of me. I can only feel Haruko tugging on my hand.

"I-I can't see at all," I tell her.

"This way," she repeats softly.

Blind with darkness, I let her lead me.

"Quickly now," she says. And then, "There. There's more light now. Is that better?"

I realize I can see again. Not well, but enough to make out trees and a nearby boulder. Enough to see that we are now on the other side of the wall.

For a moment I can't move. I don't even know what's holding me—fear of Ikeda or of Haruko, who is no longer Haruko, not the girl I raised from an infant.

The moon slips out from beneath the clouds, and her eyes glow like an animal's, as if there were fire inside them.

"What's happened to you?" I ask.

She stands up briskly. "This isn't the time to talk. Not unless you want my husband to catch us." She tilts her head to the side. "Do you hear it?"

"I hear the sound of the stream running."

"Not that. The vixen, she's calling us."

I listen as hard as I can, but there's no vixen. Only the sound of the stream. She's deluded. Some sort of illness came into her with the fever and never left. Some spell entered the house with Baron Nakamura's gift and works on us yet.

Without meaning to, I reach out and stroke her face as I used to when she was a child. "Haruko, let's go back to the house. I'll tell your husband that I'm the one who soiled his robes. He'll send me away, but he'll get help for you. You need a doctor."

"No," she says. "I have what I need." Then she

turns and begins to make her way through the trees.

I try to follow her. But the mountain rises steeply and is thick with small thorny bushes, roots, jagged rocks. The thorns pull at my robe, I trip over endless roots and rocks, and at one point I stumble and slide down the slope into a stream, where ice water soaks me up to my knees.

For a long while I continue to walk, even though I know it's senseless. I'm simply going farther up the mountain, deeper into the tangle of trees. There's no sign of Haruko. She's gone from me, swallowed by the night. I have lost her and lost my home.

At last I sink to the ground, too weary to go farther. I lie on my back, watching the branches of a eucalyptus rise and fall with the wind. The night air is cold and I pray that it will take me because I don't think I can stand to see another dawn. Then I hear them. The vixen calls and Haruko answers. Her voice is so familiar, I want to run to it. Yet I stay where I am, for wound through my mistress's voice is the shrill high bark of the fox.

Ogawa wakes me, shaking me roughly. It is mid-morning and sunlight pours through the trees. The weather, as fickle as Haruko's moods, has changed again. Already a damp summer heat rises from the forest floor.

"What are you doing here?" Ogawa demands. "Your mistress waits for you to attend her."

I say nothing but follow him back to the compound. Indeed, Haruko waits in her chamber, the quilt gathered around her, her hair undone. "O-Shima, help me dress," she says, as if I'd been summoned from the kitchen and not lost on the mountain.

"First tell me what happened last night."

"I'm sorry you became lost," she says stiffly. "I couldn't wait. I-I had to run. I can't explain it."

"And how did you explain his soiled robes to your husband?"

"I told him that one of the dogs must have gotten inside, though I couldn't imagine how. I don't think it occurred to him that his wife could be responsible for such a thing."

"And what did he say when his wife was not in his bed last night?"

She stands then and the quilt drops from her. Her body is covered with long, thin red welts. They cross her breasts, line her stomach, wind round her back and buttocks, make hatchwork of her arms and legs.

"He did this to you?"

"He didn't even know I was missing," she says with a smile. "My husband sees what he wants to see."

"Then why is your body scored with welts?"

Her voice becomes uncertain. "On the mountain last night, I—I thought I was covered, but I wasn't. I didn't even feel the thorns when I ran."

She's only making sense in bits. "What do you mean, you thought you were covered? By your robe?"

In the broad light of morning her eyes shine like topaz, and summer's warmth flees the room. The bedchamber is suddenly as cold as the mountain was the night before, and I'm shivering, backing away from her. "You've changed," I say.

"Yes," she agrees. "A bride always changes when she comes to her husband's house."

"That's not what I mean."

"That's what happened."

"Tell me how we got through the wall."

"There was an opening," she replies matter-of-factly. "Don't look so frightened, O-Shima. She has no desire to hurt you."

"*She?*"

Haruko glances around, as if to be certain no one

else is in the room. "You mustn't tell anyone," she says in a whisper, "but there's a vixen inside me now. She's 120 years old and very wise. You know a fox must be at least a hundred years old before it can possess a human."

"Don't," I plead, "please don't talk this way."

"Wait until you see her, O-Shima. She has golden eyes and a glistening black coat. You see, it covered me last night. When I was running on the mountain I could feel the wind lifting the hairs on my pelt. I never felt the thorns. I—"

"I-I must get you help, my lady."

She nods. "You must continue to help me, O-Shima, for though the fox is inside me, she's not strong enough yet. That's why I had to come back last night. I am not yet completely hers." Haruko touches her scratched arm. "This is the proof. I wore her pelt, yet it did not protect me from the briars."

"You wore a kimono," I say. "A black silk kimono."

Haruko takes my hand, holds it against her breastbone. "Can you feel her inside me? Her strength is growing but her power is still uncertain, so for now you and I must do everything we can to help her."

"Haruko, I can't—"

"Dress me, O-Shima," she says. "Soon you will have no need to do so."

The old woman takes out the lacquer box where she keeps her *kanzashi*, her hairpins. Her hair is her one vanity—as grey as iron shavings but still long and thick. She never was a beauty, that anyone can see, but she tells us all that when she was young her hair was so black and lustrous that handsome samurai composed poems about it. She says that if she were still young and Haruko stood beside her, Haruko would seem as plain as a nun.

"Dress my hair," she orders Haruko. "And use the ivory hairpins." But the ivory displease her and she asks for the onyx. The onyx make her hair look dim. Why did Haruko not suggest the coral? And is her son's wife blind as well as stupid? The coral do not go well with her kimono. Even a maidservant would have had sense enough to choose the jade. And where are the pearl? What do you mean they are missing? Has her lazy, dishonest daughter-in-law stolen the most valuable *kanzashi* of all?

It goes on for hours. Haruko trying to please. Lady Tama refusing to be pleased. She owns at least fifty different hairpins and before the afternoon is out, Haruko must try them all. She does not argue. She does exactly as she is bid, and though I hate Lady Tama's bullying, I'm relieved to see Haruko once again being the proper wife. But the gold is in her eyes all that afternoon, and later when I finally accompany her to her own room, she gazes at me and says: "It would be easy to drive the pins into her eyes. I think I should choose the onyx."

Just after dawn the next morning as I'm dressing Haruko I hear a woman's voice, ragged and keening. For a moment I can't even identify the sound, it seems so out of place. It's inconceivable that anyone would break the peace of Lord Ikeda's household by wailing aloud. Even the dogs here observe formal discipline.

I stare at the obi, not wanting to meet Haruko's eyes. "What do you think has happened?" I ask her. I can already feel a sense of dread roiling in my stomach. Haruko has not mentioned the fox since yesterday morning. I've been trying to tell myself that she's fine, that our life with Lord Ikeda will return to normal.

Now she looks down at her body, frowning. "O-Shima, do you think my breasts are heavier?"

The question takes me by surprise, and the answer gives me pleasure. "Indeed," I say. "Your husband has cause to rejoice. The child is growing within you—" The keening sounds again, a long drawn-out note of anguish. "Haruko, do you think there's been a death?"

"Of course not," she replies. "I'm sure everything is fine."

"No, someone is weeping or mourning."

"Go see if you must," she says, completely disinterested.

In the hallway I find O-Yuki and two of the other women servants huddled against the wall. They are watching Lady Tama with alarm, for it is she who is petitioning the heavens to hear her grief.

"What's happened?" I ask O-Yuki. "Is the lord all right?"

"He's fine," O-Yuki answers. "He's out hunting. It's her. She won't be comforted."

The old woman is cursing now, her voice hoarse, nearly breaking. And then I realize why—the long hair that she was so proud of is no more. It's been shorn. Now her hair sticks out in jagged grey tufts, none of them long enough to brush together, much less hold a hairpin. If there were ever any doubt, it's gone now: she's as ugly as her temper.

Women must shave their heads when they give up this world and enter a nunnery. For a moment I entertain a wild hope that Ikeda has ordered his mother to take just such an action. But nuns make a neater job of shaving.

Lady Tama stops screaming long enough to notice me. "You!" she says, jabbing a clawlike finger into my face. "Your mistress did this to me!"

"My mistress just woke up!" I protest.

"She's got a fox inside her!" the old woman shrieks. "Everyone knows that foxes cut women's hair!" She points at O-Yuki. "You'll be next, and then you.

You'll all look like half-plucked chickens and it will be Haruko you can thank."

"My lady—" I begin.

"She's got a fox inside her!" the old woman repeats. "I knew it from the day of the wedding. They say that when the sun shines during a rainstorm, a fox wife is going to her bridegroom. My poor son. He won't let anyone speak a word against her. But she'll steal his life, destroy his household . . . ."

Moving swiftly for one so old, she pulls a small dagger from her sash and rushes to the lord's bedchamber. We all run after her, afraid of what she'll do.

"Take it!" Lady Tama shrieks, holding out the dagger. "Do it now while it's still your choice!"

But she offers the dagger to an empty room, and her cries are mocked by the silence that greets them. Haruko is gone. The screen that leads to the veranda is slid open, and the bedchamber is peaceful, filled with the scent of wisteria.

"Open the cabinets," the old woman orders.

I do, and then she has me pull apart the quilts and kimono that are folded there. Finally, she has me take apart the bedding.

"Lady Haruko is not here," O-Yuki says in a soothing tone. "There's nothing to be found here, Lady Tama. Come, I will make you a fine silk headdress that will be the envy of all."

"She's tricked him," the old woman says. "My son has been tricked by her beauty. He no longer sees what is real."

I am left alone in the bedchamber to put away the kimono and bedding and wonder just what it is that is actually going on in this house. I find it strange that for once Haruko and Lady Tama are in agreement. Perhaps Ikeda *is* caught in the illusions of the fox and doesn't see what's happening to his wife. To my eyes, though, it's Haruko and not Ikeda who seems deluded. As for Lady Tama, who can take her seriously?—she's been skewed by her own bitterness for years. I wish I could trust my own eyes, my own heart, but my own stubbornness makes it hard to see clearly: I can't bear to believe that something evil lives inside Haruko.

I put away the last of the quilts and slide the cabinet shut. At least this much I can do, straighten a room. The space is light and orderly, everything in its proper place. O-Yuki was *almost* right. There is nothing to be found here—except that the quilt that was used last night is covered with short, glistening black fur.

Neither Haruko nor her husband return that day. I spend my day wondering where she is, hoping she's not roaming the forest, especially when her husband is out with a hunting party.

I want to look for her but Lady Tama has me scrubbing the veranda floors. So I tell myself that later, as soon as I can slip away unnoticed, I will search for her and find her. The lord will never even know she was missing. No sooner do I think these thoughts than I know them for a lie. Wherever it is Haruko has gone, I can't follow. Still, I take comfort from my plans. I can't bear to think of what will happen if she's truly gone.

At dusk when Lady Tama is eating her evening meal, I take one of the paper lanterns and go into the garden. The wind is moving through the trees, sweeping flowers from their stems, carrying them up and over the walls. Maybe it's the wind, I think. It steals from us whatever it can for the mountain.

I head toward the northern wall, wondering if I'll be able to find the opening that Haruko found, curious as to whether it even exists. I'm at the second footbridge when I see Lord Ikeda. He's holding Haruko by the arm, speaking to her in a low voice. She walks calmly, but her hair is loose and disheveled and I'm certain he caught her as she tried to run with the fox. His attention is diverted for just a moment as he hears my footsteps. It's all the time she needs. She sinks her teeth into his forearm and tries to wrench herself from his grasp.

He reacts instantly, instinctively. Without looking at her, he grabs her hair, yanks her head from his arm, then hurls her to the ground. She lands hard and lays there stunned, but when I go to her side she opens her eyes, calm and unsurprised. He watches as she gets to her feet. "I will not have you endanger my child," he says quietly. "Tomorrow you'll go to the hospital in the village."

"Let me see the lady to her chamber," I ask.

He leaves us and Haruko gets to her feet. "I found a fox's lair today," she tells me in a whisper. "High on the ridge, beneath the roots of a maple tree."

She runs her hand through her hair and pulls free a bit of earth. "Smell it," she says, holding it toward me. "It's sweet with the musk of the one who was there before me. You can even smell the milk she fed her little ones."

I do as she asks. "It smells like damp earth."

"Inside, beneath the maple tree, it was dark and warm," she tells me. "It was safe, O-Shima. I finally found a place that is safe."

We set off at dawn. Haruko is again carried in the palanquin. Ikeda rides on one side of it, Ogawa the other. I follow behind, a necessity if Lord Ikeda's wife is not to starve herself. Lately, Haruko has not only refused to eat anything that I do not feed her, but she's refused anything except *adzuki-meshi*, rice boiled together with beans which, Lady Tama informs the entire household, is the favorite food of *kitsuné*.

By midmorning we are following the dusty road from the mountain ridge down into the village of Nanshu. We've been isolated in the summerhouse for so long that the village astounds me. Bean and rice fields, wide and flat and unenclosed by walls; shops whose open windows reveal fish and straw hats and iron pots; laundry soaking in vats of boiling water; children and dogs running between the houses—I take it all in as eagerly as I once took in the colors of Lord Ikeda's gardens. Here there's none of the beauty of the samurai estate, and yet there's comfort in the ordinary things I thought we'd left so far behind.

The hospital is actually two houses joined together by a covered wooden walkway. In the smaller of the two is the doctor's office and the examining room. The larger house is where the patients stay. Between the two buildings and surrounding the walkway is a small garden.

A young man with a mild expression and long, delicate hands greets us at the hospital door. He wears a black kimono and Western spectacles. He introduces himself as Dr. Yorita and assures Lord Ikeda that he has been schooled in the traditions of his ancestors as well as in modern Western medicine.

Dr. Yorita helps Haruko from the palanquin, and his eyes go at once to the bruise on her cheek where she hit the ground.

"What's the matter?" he asks. "Did you fall?"

"*Kitsuné-tsuki*," Ikeda answers. "She is possessed by a fox."

The young doctor's eyebrows rise. "I have found," he says carefully, "that what is called *kitsuné-tsuki* is, in fact, often something else—apoplexy, epilepsy, alcoholism, mania, insomnia, hysteria, typhus, depression. . . ."

"It is a fox," Ikeda says, his tone forbidding argument. "You will get it out of her."

"She must stay so I can observe her."

Ikeda nods. "She may stay for three weeks. But see that she does not leave her room unescorted."

Ikeda returns to the summerhouse, leaving Ogawa to guard his wife and me to see that she eats.

Dr. Yorita leads Haruko into the examining room. Ogawa and I accompany her, as it would not be proper for her to be seen by another man without servants present.

Haruko sits stiffly in a straight-backed Western chair next to a tall apothecary's chest. The chest, made of cherry wood with iron fittings, is a marvel. I have never seen so many tiny drawers. Each one is labeled with the name of an herb, a root, a fungus, a powder, a bone. Surely, I tell myself, there's something in there that will take the sickness from my mistress.

The doctor peers into Haruko's eyes, ears, and mouth. He takes her pulse. Then he says, "I want you to tell me what's wrong."

"There's a fox inside me," she explains. "A vixen with golden eyes and a glossy black coat. She's 120 years old and very wise, and she does not like my husband."

"Why not?" the doctor asks. He is taking notes, using a fountain pen.

"He smells of pine soap."

"Surely she must have another reason."

"He snores. In fact, both he *and* his mother snore, and she doesn't like either one of them."

"Anything else?"

Haruko shrugs. "He is a man, like all others."

"Tell the doctor that you fear your husband," I interrupt. "That he—"

"I asked Lady Haruko, not a maidservant," Yorita cuts me off.

"The black fox isn't afraid of any man," Haruko

assures him. "What can my husband do in the face of the vixen's magic?"

"Has he hurt you?" Yorita asks.

Haruko pats her stomach. "He's given me his seed." She's still slim and flat, barely showing. "But the fox is taking care of that."

"How?"

Haruko looks perplexed. "I don't know. She hasn't told me. But she has assured me that his seed will not be a problem."

Yorita takes off his spectacles, rubs his brow, then puts them on again. "It's a great honor when a wife carries her husband's child," he says gently.

"Do you think so?" Haruko replies in a pleasant, conversational tone. "He's had two wives before me and both of them are dead."

"What did they die of?" the doctor wants to know.

"Have you ever eaten raw sparrow?" she asks in return. "It takes getting used to. I choked on the feathers the first time, but the taste of blood, you come to need it."

Dr. Yorita is beginning to look exasperated. "How is your health, lady?"

"Much better when I run at night," she answers. "If you want to heal me, doctor, you must let me run."

The doctor gives her acupuncture and herbs, which she loves, and Western medicines to make her sleep, which she spits out when he's not looking. He does not let her run or even leave the hospital. When he is not questioning her he spends long stretches of time watching her, as if he cannot quite believe what he sees.

As of the second day, he assigns her activities. To keep the fox at bay, Ogawa assures me, Haruko is given paper and brushes and is visited by an old man in the village who works with her on her calligraphy.

She's given flowers to arrange, a bonsai tree whose branches need pruning. She completes these tasks obediently, efficiently, listlessly, as she completes Lady Tama's.

And yet although Haruko seems relieved to be away from the summerhouse, she's sickening. She eats less and less. Despite the baby, she's losing weight. She's restless, often complaining of cold though we are in the midst of an August heat wave. And the gold is almost always in her eyes now. I have to remind myself that once it was there so rarely, I thought it a trick of the light.

Her visits with Dr. Yorita are much the same as the first. She can deflect any question with nonsense, though I've come to see that for her the nonsense holds truth.

On the third day he begins by asking how she is.

"As you see me, doctor. Do I look healthy to you?"

"And your fox?"

"She misses the mountain," Haruko answers. "I told you, if you want to heal me, you must let her run."

"Tell me," Yorita counters, "how did the fox get inside you?"

"There was an opening," she replies.

"Did your husband make this opening?"

"Oh no," she assures him. "He just made it wider."

Afternoons Haruko is allowed to sit in the garden with the other patients. But after our fifth day at the hospital the other patients leave whenever she enters the garden. Perhaps this is because Ogawa is striding around with his sword, as though he expects ninja to drop from the hospital roof.

No matter, those first afternoons in the garden are so warm and peaceful that I tell myself that we are entering a friendly rhythm, Haruko, Ogawa, and I. And then Haruko goes after him.

The first time it happens, Haruko is sitting on the stone bench by the lily pond, rocking back and forth and watching her reflection shimmer on the water's surface. I sit beside her, mending one of her robes. Ogawa stands over us, his hand on the hilt of his sword, his face set in its perpetual frown.

Haruko looks up at him with an unsettling curiosity, unsettling because I know she considers him beneath notice.

"Are you bored, Ogawa?" she asks.

"I'm doing as my lord asks," he replies.

"Tell me, Ogawa, how is your health?" Haruko's tone is identical to the doctor's when he inquires about her health.

"I'm well," Ogawa answers.

"I don't think so." She studies his reflection in the pond. "You look sour and constipated. Would you like to hump me?" she goes on in a solicitous tone. "That always makes my husband feel better."

"Haruko!" I all but drop the sewing in the pond.

"Don't worry, O-Shima, I'm perfectly safe. The honorable and loyal Ogawa would never hump his lord's mistress, though he thinks about it every day. Don't you, Ogawa?"

"My lady, you may not speak to him this way!"

"Why not? I want to know why Ogawa did not strip and swim for me that day. From the day he first saw me, he's wanted me to admire his body. You're very proud of those strong muscles, aren't you, Ogawa? You might as well admit it. You know you can't keep a secret from a fox."

A nurse walks past the garden and Ogawa summons her at once. "Lady Haruko is feeling ill," he tells her. "Take her to her room and give her medication now."

*   *   *

We're in Dr. Yorita's office for more of his questions.
By now he has pages of notes on Haruko, and as far
as I can tell that's his only accomplishment; she's gotten worse, not better.

"Can you remember ever having a head injury?"
he asks.

"I'll show you my injuries," Haruko offers. The
heat that morning is sweltering, so she's dressed only
in a *yukata*, a light cotton robe. Before I can stop her,
she's opened it, displaying her body to the doctor and
Ogawa.

"Cover yourself!" Ogawa orders her angrily. "You
shame your husband with such behavior!"

"Look carefully," she tells him, her voice soft and
fierce. "You've wanted to see this for a long time."
She turns toward the window. "Is anyone else curious
to see the lord's wife?"

Yorita steps forward and draws the robe closed.
"My lady, this is not seemly," he says gently.

For the first time since arriving at the hospital she
looks distressed. "It's confusing," she says in a small
voice. "My body belonged first to my father. He sold
it to my husband. Now the vixen claims it. Why was
it never mine?"

Haruko stays only two weeks at the hospital because
by the second week things are disappearing from the
village: a comb, a wooden bucket, a rice bowl, a quilt,
five baby chicks. Somewhere in Nanshu there's a
thief. No one dares suggest that it might be Lord Ikeda's disturbed young wife. I myself do not understand how it is possible—Haruko is always watched
by me, the nurses, Yorita, and, of course, Ogawa. And
yet one morning I open the chest where she keeps her
robes and find the comb, the bucket and rice bowl,
even the quilt. I do not find the chicks, but the quilt

is smeared with blood and bits of yellow down.

It's not possible, I tell myself. How could she have left the hospital without any of us noticing?

The answer is whispered throughout the village: *They say a fox can walk through walls.*

There's another possibility: Ogawa, who now regards her with the hatred of one who has been deliberately humiliated, let her out.

Ikeda does not come for us but sends four retainers. The reason is clear: the great samurai lord can no longer show his face in the village where his wife has behaved so badly.

As we prepare to leave Dr. Yorita hands Ogawa a scroll tied with a black cord and asks that he give it to Lord Ikeda. The doctor bows to Haruko and his eyes search her face. "My lady, I'm sorry."

"I'm sorry you have no talent for rutting in the moonlight," she replies lightly.

"No," he says, refusing to be shocked by her, "I meant that I'm truly sorry I could not help you."

"*Would* not help me," she corrects him. "You could have let me run on the mountain."

Halfway to the summerhouse we stop by a stream so that the men carrying the palanquin may cool themselves in the water. They drink, douse themselves, then stand talking with Ogawa. I go to see to Haruko who remains curled up in the litter.

"Don't you want to stretch your legs?" I ask.

"I have to read something first," she replies. She's holding the scroll that Yorita gave to Ogawa.

"How did you get this?"

"It came to me." She slips the cord from the scroll, unrolls it, and studies the writing. "Yorita has a fine hand, does he not?"

"Haruko, tell me how you got the scroll."

She looks at me as if I were simple. "Do you truly

think there's anything a vixen can't steal? Especially when it concerns her." She reads the doctor's words aloud, mimicking his intonation perfectly. *"My lord, please accept my apologies for failing to help your wife. As I told you, in the past I've encountered several cases of supposed* kitsuné-tsuki. *Always, they've proven to be other medical conditions and I've treated them accordingly. Your wife's case is different. The lady Haruko suffers from a sort of mania I've never seen before. There's no prescription that I know of to cure her. Therefore, I suggest you guard your lady and the child she bears carefully, my lord. I'm afraid your wife is quite mad."*

No sooner do we return to the compound than Ogawa leads us to the upper hall, where Lord Ikeda sits at the head of the room. The lord motions us to sit on the side and then we all wait in silence. Ikeda's eyes study Haruko. Haruko's eyes, pale amber, are lost somewhere in the painted seascape on the screen opposite us, the fogbound coast she claims to dislike. As usual, Ikeda's face betrays no emotion. I wonder if he's angry with her for the thefts in the village, if he'll ever see the doctor's letter, if it would soften or harden his heart. For now she's protected, I tell myself, safe from all harm at least until the child comes.

Another retainer enters the hall, escorting a man clad in the plain brown robes of a priest. He's an elderly man, thin with his vows, his face kindly. And it's clear from his robes that he's a devotee of Shinto, the Way of the Gods. I would lay odds that this is a first in this household. Like his ancestors, Lord Ikeda follows the austere precepts of Zen. He has little use for the animism of Shinto, with its gods and ghosts, spirits and nature worship. Furthermore, he carries the old shoguns' animosity toward Shinto, still resenting it for having displaced Buddhism. For him to sum-

mon a Shinto priest is the closest I've seen him come
to admitting fear.

The priest bows low to Ikeda. "How may I serve
you, my lord?"

"You can cure fox possession." The words come out
as a statement rather than a question.

"Who is possessed?" the priest inquires.

"My wife." Ikeda indicates Haruko with a nod. Haruko continues to gaze at the painting with trancelike
fascination. She seems unaware that she is the object
of discussion, or even that the priest has entered the
room.

The priest studies her only a second before answering, "I can pray to the god Inari. And if he's merciful,
his foxes will offer her their Divine protection and
cure the *kitsuné-tsuki*." Inari is the rice god, a god of
fertility in our land. It's believed that he's often accompanied by two silver-white foxes who are his mes-
sengers and invisible to human eyes. "If Inari grants
our prayers," the priest goes on, "his foxes will drive
out the *nogitsuné*, the wild fox, who possesses your
wife. We may also call on the thunder god to help us
purge the fox."

Though Haruko does not look at him, she begins to
tremble at these words; she's always been terrified of
thunder.

"You will pray for my wife," Ikeda says, "and I will
give a generous gift to the Inari shrine."

"May I speak with her?" the priest asks.

Ikeda nods and the priest bows before Haruko. He
waits until her eyes focus on him. "Lady," he begins,
"do you have a fox inside you?"

"Yes," Haruko answers.

"And what does that feel like?" the priest asks curiously.

"My fox"—Haruko hesitates perhaps because she
sees that the priest believes her as the doctor never

did—"she can see in the dark, smell the autumn before it's in the leaves. She knows the night and the sounds of the forest."

"Is she a danger to you?"

"She's the best of me," Haruko replies. "Everything in me that's quick and clever and alive—that's the fox."

"What about the others?" the priest asks. "Is she a danger to the members of this household?"

"She's an animal," Haruko says. "She would only attack those who threaten her survival."

"Or yours, lady," the priest adds.

He turns back to Ikeda. "Your wife seems content. However, she does not look well. I believe the *kitsuné* is a danger to her and to you."

"To me?" Ikeda asks with the arrogance of the bear who does not believe it can be stung by the bee.

"A fox will drain your *ki*, your life force," the priest explains. "Soon you will begin to tire more quickly, to chill in the heat of the day, to forget the simplest things. You will die before your time, lord. Also there is danger that she will immerse your household in illusion, that soon none of you will know kitchen from stable, garden from privy. And where there is a fox, there is often theft."

It occurs to me to be grateful that Lady Tama is not part of this audience.

"How soon can you rid her of the fox?" Ikeda asks.

"It would be best if you bring her to the shrine," the priest replies. "We'll make offerings to Inari's foxes, and perhaps they will listen to our prayers."

"If they do not," Ikeda says, "I will order a hunt and every fox in this part of the country will be destroyed."

"Come at midnight tomorrow," the priest says. "All will be ready."

*   *   *

We leave the compound at noon on the following day. It's a small party that travels to the Inari shrine: Haruko and her husband, myself and Ogawa. Ikeda does not even want the palanquin carriers, and so Haruko rides before him on his horse and I sit on the back of Ogawa's, holding to his waist. A third horse walks behind us, laden with hampers that contain food for the journey and offerings for the gods.

The horses have been uneasy from the start. Rather, from the moment Haruko approached them. All three reacted as one—they pawed the ground, their nostrils flared, and the whites of their eyes shone with fear. Yet they are horses trained by Ikeda for archery and battle. They would not dare shy or disobey him. His stallion allowed her to mount, its flanks quivering, and now it moves with a tense, jerking walk. This is the same horse whom Ikeda prizes for running as smoothly as flowing water.

We travel north through the mountains along winding trails that are barely wide enough for the horses to plant their feet. At times I hold too tightly to Ogawa, terrified that if I lean to the side, the horse will go over the side of the cliff. Ogawa rides as if I'm not there at all. Since the hospital he has not spoken to me, and he refuses to look at Haruko. I know he fears her, believes that she truly can read minds.

That's not what frightens me. I worry that we're already hopelessly lost and none of us even knows it. I think of the stories I've heard, the one O-Yuki told just this morning of a party of samurai warriors who wandered the entire night in a single rice field, convinced they'd journeyed miles. It wouldn't surprise any of us if the fox inside Haruko saw to it that we never reached the shrine.

There, I've said it, admitted what I've fought from the start. I barely know the girl I raised from an infant. I know only that she sickens, that there is some sort

of madness inside her. I have come to believe that
Haruko harbors a fox.

Darkness falls and we stop for the evening meal.
Haruko eats her few bites of rice and beans. She's
been silent since morning, accepting this journey
without protest or interest. It's as if she's barely noticed that she's just spent six hours on a horse in
search of an exorcism.

The moon rises, golden and full. We ride by its
light, following the scantest of trails, always climbing.
We leave the oak trees, the eucalyptus and maple far
below, and with them summer's heat. It's all ever-
green here, a cool fragrant forest that belongs to another season. As far as I can tell, there's nothing here
but trees—no homes, no people. If there are animals,
they must be hiding. The birds are still. Even the
crickets are silent. The rhythm of the horses' footfalls
seems to be the only sound on the mountain.

What finally breaks the stillness is the sound of a
fox calling, a high lone sound that cuts through the
trees like a battle cry. In the darkness I can't actually
see Haruko, but I see Ikeda's horse stiffen and come
to an abrupt halt as she returns the call. No human
ought to be able to make a sound like that—so wild
and piercing, so full of yearning and grief.

Haruko's cry is cut off suddenly, probably by her
husband's hand across her mouth. We ride in silence
again but only a short distance. Ahead of us torches
blaze orange and yellow against the night. Ikeda and
Ogawa urge the horses on and then finally rein them
in front of a tall, vermilion *torii*. We have reached the
shrine.

Like many of the shrines and temples in our land,
this one seems to be built in the most inaccessible
place possible. Through the *torii*, I can see the beginning of what are undoubtedly endless flights of stairs
cut into the side of the mountain. Who comes to a

place so remote to worship? Who, besides a desperate lord and his mad wife?

Ogawa ties and feeds the horses, then shoulders the hamper. Haruko stands silent, turned away from the shrine, her golden eyes searching the dark forest.

We pass beneath the *torii* and begin the climb. A few scattered torches light the stairway, casting just enough light to see that flanking every step is a pair of white stone foxes. They're only carvings, yet they are more. There's something eerie about them, as if within the stone the foxes are alive, their sightless eyes watching us pass through their domain. Even Ikeda and Ogawa feel it—they dart nervous glances at the statues, as though waiting for them to move, daring them to attack.

Haruko is fascinated. She walks with eyes locked on the statues, searching each one. Occasionally, she stops, tentatively reaches out a hand and rests it on a white stone shoulder or muzzle.

Ahead of us Ikeda comes to an impatient halt, obviously waiting for us to catch up. Instead Haruko grabs my sleeve and pulls me toward one of the carvings. For a moment I could swear that the animal's side moves in the subtlest of motions, a gentle rise and fall of breath.

"So you see it, too," Haruko whispers. "My kin."

We climb the stairs for what feels like hours. One flight leads only to the next, and each is steeper than the one before. Naturally, Ikeda and Ogawa show no sign of tiring. The night becomes colder as we climb, the air sharp with the scent of pines.

It is just after I decide that my knees have given out and I will have to tell Ikeda that I simply cannot climb another step that the stairs end and the ground actually levels into a small plateau, enclosed on three sides by the steep walls of the mountain.

We pass through another *torii*, this one made of

stone, and enter a small wooden pavilion that covers a well. Moonlight filters in through the open sides as we rinse our hands and mouths with cold mountain water. I watch Haruko as she runs the water over her hands, pours it into her mouth, seemingly unconcerned with the ritual purification. She looks fragile, exhausted by the climb and the ride before it. For weeks now she has refused to wear makeup. Tonight her skin is as pale as if it were covered with white face powder, paler even than the white kimono she wears. It's as if the moon were drawing all the color and life from her. What's going to happen to her if the fox inside her is actually cast out? What will be left?

Beyond the pavilion is a weathered wooden building with a curved and gabled roof. A row of bronze lanterns illuminates a porch that runs the width of the building. It's a modest shrine, and its simplicity makes me aware of other things: the shadow of the gables growing sharper as a thin cloud cover slides past the moon; the sound of running water; the wind tugging at my robes; a chipmunk scurrying close to the base of the building.

At a nod from Ikeda, Ogawa sets the hamper down, steps onto the porch, and pulls on a thick bell cord that hangs from the rafters. The deep tones of the bell are still echoing as Ikeda slips a crimson envelope into the wooden money box and the door to the main hall slides open. The elderly priest who was summoned to the estate stands before us, bowing.

We remove our shoes, Ogawa shoulders the hamper again, and then we follow the priest inside, through a dim center hall smelling of sandalwood incense. As we pass an inner room other priests appear and fall into line behind us, so that there are at least a dozen of us who pass from the main hall into a large courtyard.

When we lived in Kyoto I visited many shrines and their courtyards, but never have I seen or felt anything quite like this. This is more woods than courtyard, as if here in the middle of their sacred buildings the priests left the mountain intact. And here the mountain is somehow more wild than the forest we just rode through; it's easy to believe that wolves and foxes and even bears live here despite the presence of man. Lichen-covered boulders are scattered among the trees, and each has been engraved with the name of one of the gods; each is lit by a candle with offerings of flowers and water and tiny boiled rice sticks set before it. I recognize, among them, Amaterasu, the goddess of the sun and Susano-o, the god of storms.

Lights from another wooden building shine through cypress and spruce trees. "That's the *honden*, where the spirit of the shrine resides," the old priest explains. "But our prayers tonight will be offered up here."

He leads us through the trees, among the gods. The sound of running water becomes stronger as we go, and finally we reach its source—a narrow waterfall cascading into a small pool that perfectly catches the reflection of the moon. On either side of the pool sits a white stone fox, twice the size of a man.

The elderly priest nods at Ogawa who sets the hamper down for the last time. I unpack it, handing each item to a priest, who arranges the offerings before the foxes: smoked salmon and rice cakes, pickled ginger, and a large bowl of *adzuki-meshi*, the fox's favorite mixture of rice and red beans. After the food come candles; an earthenware pitcher; brass and celadon incense burners and bundles of incense rods.

The elderly priest, who is clearly chief among them, leads Haruko to kneel before the statues. Lord Ikeda kneels a short distance behind her, and the rest of us form two rows behind him.

Haruko gazes up at the statues and then speaks aloud for the first time that day. "I have a question," she says to the priest. "Do you believe that the good foxes cast out the bad?"

"By Inari's Divine will, I do," he answers her.

"It's not that simple," she tells him. "Believe me, priest, it never has been."

"Haruko!" Ikeda's voice is a low growl.

"It's all right," the priest assures him. "That's just the fox inside her speaking. Pay it no mind. Let us begin."

For a long while we sit in silence. As before, I'm aware of the wind and water, of the moon and clouds, trees and rocks. Shinto teaches that *kami*, the spirits, can live anywhere. And now I see why this shrine was built here. It is not, as the more elaborate shrines often are, a flamboyant tribute to a dead warlord. Rather this shrine was built on this site because here the mountain spirits are alive. They are in the foxes that line the stairs, in the water that pools beneath the moon, in the boulders among the trees, in the trees themselves. There is nothing here that does not breathe with life, including the two great white foxes who belong to Inari.

As other priests light the incense and candles, the chief priest fills the earthenware vessel with water from the pool and sprinkles it on the offerings. Then he waves a thin wand bearing strips of white paper over Haruko, and the ceremony begins. There are chants to the sun goddess and storm lord, to those who were there in the beginning of the world, First Mud Lord and First Sand Lady, to those in the Land of Reed Plains in the Place of the Issuing of Clouds, to the thousands of gods dwelling among us, and to the Eight Hundred Myriads who dwell in the blue Plain of High Heaven. After invoking the *kami* silence falls again.

The chief priest approaches Haruko and says, "I would like to speak with your fox."

"She will not speak with you," Haruko replies.

"Then you, lady, must join your prayers to ours."

"I can't," Haruko tells him. "Your words aren't mine."

"Pray with the truth in your heart," the priest advises. "All that matters is you ask the god Inari and his foxes for their help. You must open yourself to them. Will you try?"

"Yes," Haruko answers, her voice a whisper.

Another round of chants begins. This time the priests summon Inari, welcome him, and invite him and his foxes to partake of the offerings. The chants rise and fall with the sound of wind and water. Finally they cease and only the chief priest speaks. He asks Inari to purify Lord Ikeda's wife. He asks that he send his foxes to chastise the *nogitsuné* that possesses her. He asks that they purge the wild fox from her body and spirit. He asks that they show compassion and cast out the illness, leaving only health; cast out the evil, leaving only goodness.

I wish I were sitting next to Haruko. She looks so small and lonely, kneeling there between the two huge statues while the priest talks of the evil inside her.

The prayers go on for hours while above us the clouds mass and thicken until they cover the moon. And yet the full moon is so bright that even the clouds can't darken the sky. Rather they are lit from behind, a luminous silver-blue, and the silver-blue light makes the white stone of the foxes appear to glow.

I send up my own prayers, asking that Haruko be healed of whatever ails her. And I say a selfish prayer, asking that life be as it never quite was—a maidservant and her lady, living honorably and harmoniously in the house of their lord.

A bell rings and one of the younger priests announces that we have entered the Hour of the Bull. It's two hours past midnight, an hour when evil is known to be strong. The priests then start to drum and pray to the thunder god, petitioning him to drive out the *nogitsuné.*

I don't even notice it at first with the noise of the drums. Haruko is the first to notice—the skies and trees are shuddering. She cries out and falls to the ground as the clouds open, the thunder crashes, and the rains beat down. I start for her side, but one of the priests stops me. "Leave her," he says. "The gods are answering our prayers. We must let them work."

The downpour doesn't last long, but whether it rains or snows is no matter to the priests. We all continue to sit as it rains, as the rains taper off, as a cold wind comes in on the heels of the storm. No one moves except the old priest who covers Haruko's unmoving form with a robe. We sit till the dawn breaks and the prayers to welcome the Lady of Fire are said.

It's only after the dawn prayers that the chief priest goes to Haruko's side and shakes her gently. For a long while she doesn't move and I fear she's dead, but gradually she stirs and sits up. And turns and gazes at us all from cool amber eyes.

I have no memory of the ride from the shrine back to the estate, except of Ogawa, occasionally pulling at me when I would have slipped off the horse, nearly unconscious with exhaustion. I don't even remember riding through the gate or getting off the horse and escorting Haruko back to her chamber. But now I stand behind her, untying the white obi, and I feel her body stiffen.

"What is it?" I ask.

"That." She's staring at a two-panel screen beside the clothing chest. The frame is of polished magnolia wood, the panels of white rice paper. Across the first panel and edging onto the second are a crane and a turtle painted in spare, flowing lines. The painting is simple and lovely, clearly the work of a master.

"Where did that come from?" she asks in a shrill voice.

"I don't know. It wasn't here when we left for the shrine. It must be a gift, the auspicious animals to welcome your child."

"I know what it's for. Get it out of here," Haruko says in a low, deliberate voice. "Get it out of my sight. Burn it if you have to."

"You *are* mad," I say. "I can't burn this. Whoever sent it wishes good fortune for your child, and I won't—"

"Get it out!" she screams. "I don't care what you do with it, just make sure that I never see—"

Her tirade stops as Lady Tama sweeps into the room and slaps her hard. Haruko reels from the blow but remains upright, her eyes blazing with fury.

"I see the shrine did you no good at all," the old woman snaps. "You're as evil as ever. You think you're better than the ones who came before, don't you? The most beautiful woman in Kyoto! But you'll end just as they did, child or no child."

The fury goes out of Haruko at that and is replaced by curiosity. "What do you mean, end as they did?"

"The two wives before you. They—" She'd go on, gladly, viciously, but Ikeda enters the room. "Most honored mother," he says with scathing courtesy, "I suggest you retire to your chamber now."

"Of course, my son," she replies with a bow. She hesitates at the doorway to the room. "I would request," she says, "that your wife no longer serve me or come near me."

"We'll discuss this later," Ikeda says. He watches her go, then turns to the new screen. "It came out well, then," he says, sounding pleased. "I had it specially made for you, Haruko, to bring luck to our child."

"Get it out of here," she repeats. "Get it out of my sight!"

Something new comes into Lord Ikeda's eyes then, a cool, assessing look that identifies his wife as the enemy.

"O-Shima, leave us now," he commands.

I do as I'm told, and again hear the sounds of the wooden doors being lowered.

For the next few days an odd tranquility fills the house, odd because it is silence humming with tension, danger delayed but not averted, the proverbial calm before the storm. Haruko is once more playing the role of the proper, obedient wife. It can only be playing, though, for a chill air follows her when she goes from room to room and her eyes burn with golden fire. Clearly, neither doctor nor priest took the fox from her, and it's only a matter of time until the vixen roams among us again.

Five days after our return from the shrine Haruko approaches me as I'm in the lower hall, setting candles in the lamps. She's moving with the slightly swaybacked walk of a woman carrying a child. Finally, there's a slight swelling in her belly, though I notice her face has become thinner.

"I found it!" she says, sounding triumphant.

"Found what?"

"The place where he buried the others," she answers matter-of-factly. "There's a tiny cemetery on a hillside halfway between here and Nanshu. I found it the other night when I ran."

"You were out again? Haruko, you know you can't—"

"Listen to me, O-Shima, I found their graves. There

are two markers for Ikeda. The first wife was named Yoriko, 'the Trustful'; the second Kazuko, 'the Obedient.'" She picks up one of the candles, cradles it in her hand. "Now," she continues in an idle tone, "he has Haruko, 'the Tranquil.' I wonder if they were as trusting and obedient as I am tranquil."

"Haruko—"

"The markers tell only their names and the dates of death," she goes on. "They died four years apart— Yoriko eight years ago, Kazuko four years later. And now the fourth year has come round again." Her eyes glitter with accusation. "You once told me that the first was sickly and the second died in childbirth. Is it true, O-Shima?"

"I-I don't know," I confess. "Perhaps."

"Perhaps?"

"I-I didn't want you to be afraid of your new husband," I explain. "I was trying to protect you."

"You lied to me." She says it without emotion, a simple statement of fact that shames me, makes me heartsick.

"Forgive me, Haruko."

"Of course, I forgive you." She runs her thumb along my cheekbone, as she used to when she was a child, then quotes a common proverb, "To tell a lie is the beginning of a thief."

She hands me back the candle that she held. It's lit now, burning with the unmistakable white light of fox fire.

The vixen waits another week to surface. Or perhaps more accurately, it takes a week before we discover her handiwork. On a grey humid morning Lord Ikeda bids farewell to the musicians from Kyoto who have spent the last three nights entertaining us.

As they make ready to leave, O-Yuki and I bring them rice cakes and smoked fish, pears and *saké*, provisions for the road. Lord Ikeda, who has been well pleased by their performances, stands talking to their leader, a young man who plays lute and drum. Then he tells Ogawa to bring his money chest.

Ogawa soon returns with the heavy cherry wood box and its black-lacquered stand. He sets the chest on the stand, and Lord Ikeda opens the locked safe inside the chest. I see his eyes register confusion, and I can guess what's happened. Ikeda then gives low-voiced orders to Ogawa and lavish apologies to the musicians, asking their indulgence—will they be good enough to wait just a short while longer?

Ogawa returns with a second money chest. The safe inside this one, too, is found to be empty.

Embarrassed and furious, Ikeda charges the musicians to stay where they are. Can he possibly think the visitors are to blame?

Lord Ikeda disappears inside the house where he remains for quite some time. O-Yuki and I return to our work. A good deal later I see Ikeda return to the musicians and hand their leader an envelope. They depart at once and Lord Ikeda watches them go, a sickly look on his normally impassive face.

I find Haruko in one of the antechambers, sitting before a low cypress writing table, practicing her calligraphy. Since Lady Tama has forbidden her to attend her, Haruko has seemed more content though she still eats far too little.

"Where is it?" I ask, surprised at the anger in my own voice.

"Where is what?"

"Don't do this, Haruko. Your husband just lost face, not once, but twice in front of the musicians. By the end of the week the tale will be told all over Kyoto. Is that what you want?"

"It's not a matter of what I want or don't want," Haruko answers. "My husband's karma is his own."

"Did you steal the money from the chests?"

She drops water onto the ink stone and wets her brush. "How would I get into locked safes?"

"How did we get through the wall? How did all of the stolen articles in Nanshu wind up in your clothes trunk? How did you get the doctor's letter from Ogawa? Haruko, this can't go on."

"You can't stop it," she points out.

I kneel beside her. "What's happened to you? I've known you since you were a baby. You were never a thief. How can you steal from your own husband?"

"My husband is a very arrogant man," she says patiently, as if explaining the sunrise to a child. "He's had his way since he came of age. It's good for him to be shaken up. Like the rest of us, he must learn not to presume that he is safe. Really, it's much healthier for him this way."

"All right, we won't discuss your husband What occurs between you is private," I concede. "But we must talk about the thefts. Stealing from people, Haruko, going into their homes, their safe places, and taking what is most valuable from them is a violation. What do you think that will do to *your* karma?"

"O-Shima, you mean well," she says with a sigh, "but you don't understand. To see what everyone else refuses to see, to let the vixen run through me and take what she pleases, *that is my karma.*"

I try one last time. "Give the money back, Haruko. Just return it to the money chests, as though it were never missing. Save your husband that much face."

She dips the brush in the ink again and begins the characters for a well-known poem:

> They spoke highly of Munéchika
> When possessed by a fox . . .

It's an odd poem, but the story of Munéchika is an odd case of *kitsuné-tsuki*. Munéchika, who lived in the tenth century, is one of our most famous sword-smiths. They say he was possessed not by *nogitsuné*, but by one of Inari's foxes, and it was with the help of the sacred fox that he tempered his incomparable blades.

"Haruko?"

She doesn't look up from her painting. "I know. You want me to return the money," she says in a bored tone. "Tell me, why are you so concerned with my husband and his finances? He has more money than he knows how to spend. Why does this upset you so? Nothing's been stolen from you, O-Shima."

I take the brush from her, take her face in my hands. "You're wrong. The fox has taken what I hold most precious in all the world—you, Haruko. The vixen stole you from me as surely as you stole your husband's money, and I hate her for it."

Haruko gazes at me so calmly, I wonder if she's heard anything I've said. "You must try to understand," she says at last. "There is no longer a *her* and *me*, O-Shima. If you hate the vixen, then you hate me."

"I could never hate you." I let her go, get to my feet.

Her voice stops me as I slide open the screen to the antechamber. "Then you must pray for me, O-Shima. Pray as I prayed to the foxes at the shrine."

I turn, curious. "As far as I can see, nothing happened at the shrine except that we all got soaked. What did you pray for?"

"I asked the Inari foxes to strengthen the fox inside me and allow me to honor her. I asked Inari's foxes for help. And you will see, O-Shima, every day now, they are granting my prayers."

* * *

Summer is reaching its end. The nights are cool and you can feel autumn in the mornings, see its immanent arrival in the chrysanthemums flowering in the garden. The afternoons, though, are still hot and damp, and the mosquitoes have become twice as fierce, as if they know they don't have much time left. During the days Lord Ikeda's household moves sluggishly through the heat. We've begun cleaning and packing, preparing to shut down the house. In two weeks time we'll move to the winter house in Tokyo; a group of servants has already been sent ahead to prepare it for the lord's homecoming. All I can think of is that maybe in the city, away from the lure of the mountain, Haruko will let go of the fox and become herself again.

Haruko seems to take no notice of the preparations to move. She spends more and more time with her inks. She's abandoned calligraphy almost entirely in favor of painting. Fortunately, Lord Ikeda has been busy with more emissaries from Tokyo and has no idea of what it is she paints. She paints foxes. In less than a month, she's become adept at drawing the animal. She draws them sleeping, standing, sitting, running, crying at the moon, suckling their young, even licking their privates.

Today she paints a simple line portrait, a side view of a fox sitting on its haunches, one that resembles the two great foxes at the shrine. Beneath it she writes:

SEPTEMBER, THE DOG YEAR, 1886.
DEDICATED TO THE GREAT INARI GOD

She finishes the last brushstroke and sets the rice paper on the floor to dry; then she doubles over with a moan. "I don't feel well, O-Shima," she says in a strained voice. Her arms are wrapped around her belly, her eyes clenched tight against pain. "Help me to my room."

The pain is so bad she can barely walk. She leans into my side and we move through the halls at the pace of a child learning to crawl.

"You should be carried," I say as the pain makes her cry out. "Stay here. I'll find some of the other servants to help."

"No!" she says. "Just get me to my room, O-Shima. Please."

At last we reach the bedchamber. I slide open the screen and stop, momentarily stunned by the change in the room. The damp, green scent of the woods rises from the tatami mats, and the sound of running water is so clear I would swear that a stream flows through the center of the room. It's the first time that the mountain has entered the house while it is yet day.

Haruko doesn't even notice the change. She stumbles into the room, still clutching her stomach. Quickly, I unfold the bedding and lay out the quilts. "You can lie down in a moment," I tell her. "Let me undress you."

She stands quietly as I untie the obi but I see tears running down her cheeks. Carefully, I remove the obi and kimono and outer robes. I open the white under robe as Lord Ikeda enters the room and so we both see it at the same moment—the dark red blood that streaks her thighs.

"Haruko, what's wrong?" Ikeda asks.

She holds opens the robe, displaying herself to her husband. "You see, my lord, the prayers worked. I prayed to the Inari foxes to help rid me of your seed."

Lord Ikeda gazes at her in disbelief. "You're not well," he murmurs. "Don't make it worse by saying such evil things."

She starts to laugh but the laugh becomes a cry of pain. "It hurts," she gasps.

"Lie down, my lady," I urge her.

"No. My husband must see this." She straightens up and takes a deep breath, as if to control the pain. Then she spreads her legs so he can see the chunks of red tissue sliding down her legs, the pools of blood soaking into the mat at her feet.

"Don't you know what this is?" she taunts him, her eyes burning topaz. "The vixen inside me is eating the child. She's tearing it apart with her teeth as easily as she would a rabbit. See—this is *your child's* blood running from my body, a gift to you from my fox."

He backs away from her, his voice a rasping whisper. "You have evil inside you. You disgrace yourself and dishonor this house."

"Are you afraid of a fox?" Haruko asks. "Is the great samurai lord afraid?"

"One of us must end this, Haruko."

"I see," she says. "The child is gone and so I'm to be disposed of."

"Do you want me to do it or will you do it yourself?" he asks, his voice breaking. "You can still have an honorable death."

She presses her forearms against her stomach, her eyes wide and her face stark white with pain. "As your other wives had?"

Outside a vixen howls, high and shrill and inexplicably near.

He takes the small dagger used for *seppuku* from the sash at his waist. When men commit suicide, they disembowel themselves. A woman is expected to slit her throat.

"What will it be?" he demands. "Will you take your own life or shall I do it for you?"

She takes the dagger from him and turns to me, her eyes serene despite the pain. "O-Shima, I'm going to leave now," she says. "I can't stay here anymore."

Ikeda crosses the room to a low cabinet, on top of

which is the wooden frame that holds his swords. He lifts the *katana* from the holder, bows, and then unsheathes it in one quick motion. The blade gleams like a river of dark silver.

Haruko is still doubled over with pain, but she stares at the sword with unconcealed fascination. "Did you do this for your other wives?" she asks him. "Did you offer them the same honorable death?"

He steps behind her and raises the blade high, standing ready to be her second, to slice her head from her neck so that the suicide will be quick and merciful. But she turns to face him. "Tell me and I'll do as you ask," she bargains. "Did you kill your other wives?"

Ikeda does not answer at once. His face is contorted, whether by rage or grief I can't tell. Slowly, he lowers the sword and says, "Yes. I did for them what I now do for you."

"Why?"

"My first wife could not give me a child. The second lay with another."

Haruko nods, as if the answer was what she expected. "Thank you, my husband," she says. "That's what I wanted to know." She turns and kneels before him and gazes at the dagger in her hand.

"Don't!" I scream. "Please, my lord!"

Neither one of them is aware of me at all.

Haruko raises the dagger to her throat. Ikeda once again lifts the sword overhead.

And then, slipping through the screens as easily as ghosts, the foxes enter the room. Grey, white, red, brown, some the size of cats, others large as wolves, they fill the bedchamber, staring at the lord and his lady with golden, glittering eyes.

"My thanks, Inari," I hear Haruko whisper.

Ikeda stands stunned, the sword hanging loosely in one hand, his eyes darting from one animal to the next, as if he can't believe that they are real.

They're as real as he or I or the sword he holds. The room is filled with the overpowering smell of their musk, the heat of their breath. They mill around us silently. A red vixen lifts a delicate leg and makes water on the lord's ankle, and when he tries to move away he finds himself ringed by foxes, all of them baring gleaming white teeth.

"Haruko?" His voice is a plea.

Haruko does not bother to respond. Still on her knees, she lets the dagger drop to the ground and laughs with delight as the foxes sniff her, rub against her, lick her face.

She shrugs out of the white robe she still wears, takes the combs and pins from her hair, and looses the gleaming mass. She drops to all fours and her hair cascades over her back and thighs like glossy black silk.

She looks at me one last time. "I've left you a gift, O-Shima. Use it well."

Then as her husband and I watch she changes. The long hair becomes fur. Short, glistening black fur that covers her face and body, even concealing the blood on her legs. Her face, which has become so thin lately, grows thinner; her nose and mouth elongate into a muzzle. Her body becomes smaller, more compact, and from her tailbone a thick brush of a tail waves. Before us is one more fox, the black vixen. Her mouth hangs open, revealing pointed white teeth, and I swear she is grinning at the man who was once her husband.

The room becomes still, the other foxes watching the black one. She makes a high-pitched noise in her throat, and as one they turn from Ikeda. The black vixen among them, the foxes slip silently through the screens. I have no doubt they'll pass as easily through the compound walls and out to the mountain beyond.

* * *

Lord Ikeda has given me until sundown to gather my things and leave. "Where will I go?" I asked him when he gave the order.

"That's no longer my concern," he replied.

Where will I go? For the first time in seventeen years Haruko is not the center of my life. She's gone and I cannot imagine what I'll do without her. I can't go back to the village—surely they would not welcome the maid of a fox. Back to Koyata? I can't return to his house; he'd be disgraced to learn of his daughter's fate. I'm an aging maidservant with no mistress to serve. I have no money, no family, no home.

In the servants' quarters I pack my belongings, amazed by how little I actually own. Living in Lord Ikeda's house always made me feel wealthy, but I have three kimono, one obi, two pairs of shoes, and a tortoiseshell comb that Haruko once gave me.

And there is something else in the bedding. I reach under the quilt and pull out a narrow oblong box covered in sea green silk. I open it and my heart leaps to my throat. Inside are Lady Tama's pearl hairpins. Each is a long, tapered rod of gold with a delicate strand of pearls hanging from its end. I begin to shake as I realize they are Haruko's parting gift—a gift that may well end my life. If I return them to Lady Tama, she'll accuse me of being the thief. She would never believe I found them. I will be disgraced and worse. I think of Tadashi, the man who lost a hand for a salmon.

"Haruko, how could you do this to me?" I ask the empty room.

For long moments I stand unable to move. An idea, a very dishonorable idea, finally breaks my paralysis. I have no money, and the hairpins are easily worth enough to feed me for a year. Perhaps I can make my way to Kyoto or Tokyo and sell the *kanzashi*. I roll the pearls through my fingers, bright and glistening, as if they were just drawn from the sea; and the pearl at the end of the strand breaks off from the knotted string. My decision has been made for me. After all, there's no way I can return a broken hairpin.

I slip the green silk box inside my robe and gather my things. Ogawa waits for me outside the women's quarters. He gives me no chance to say good-bye to O-Yuki or the others. For the last time I am escorted through the gardens and footbridges, across the moat, past the gate house. He doesn't even bid me good-bye.

I start in the direction of Nanshu. Darkness is falling fast, and it's hard to find the narrow trails, especially since a dense fog is settling over the mountain. Soon I can barely see ahead of me. I'm stumbling into hollows in the ground, tripping over roots and rocks, as helpless as ever in the forest.

I'll stop, I decide. I'll wait 'til morning and travel when it's light. I sit at the base of a pine tree to wait out the night, and my mind circles back to my uncertain future. It will be all right, I tell myself. I have the *kanzashi*; they'll provide food and shelter until I find work and a place to live.

To reassure myself, I open the green silk box and take out the loose pearl. I rub it between my palms, loving the feel of its smooth, uneven surface. Before today I never knew what it felt like to hold a pearl. Perhaps it will prove a talisman of sorts, an amulet for luck.

I cup the pearl in one hand. To my surprise I can actually see it despite the fog that cloaks the mountain. It's glowing, white spun through with color, a tiny perfect moon nestled in my palm.

I can almost hear Haruko's voice whispering from the trees. *I followed the fox fire. It will lead you if you let it.*

Her final gift to me.

The pearl burns in my palm, a cool white fire. And I follow it up into the trees toward the sound of the vixen's cry.

The White Road

Neil Gaiman

Neil Gaiman is a transplanted Briton who now lives in the American Midwest. He is the author of the award-winning Sandman series of graphic novels and coauthor (with Terry Pratchett) of the novel Good Omens. Gaiman is also a talented poet and short story writer. Several of his stories have been reprinted in The Year's Best Fantasy and Horror. His collection Angels and Visitations reprints much of his short work.

"The White Road" is a poem based on the fairy tale "Mr. Fox." In the original, Mr. Fox gets his just deserts. In the Gaiman version this may not be the case. . . .

The White Road

"... I wish that you would visit me one day, in
   my house.
There are such sights I would show you."

My intended lowers her eyes, and, yes, she
   shivers.
Her father and his friends all hoot and cheer.

"*That's* never a story, Mister Fox," chides a pale
   woman
in the corner of the room, her hair corn-fair,
her eyes the grey of cloud, meat on her bones,
she curves, and smiles crooked and amused.

"Madam, I am no storyteller," and I bow, and ask,
"Perhaps, you have a story for us?" I raise an
   eyebrow.
Her smile remains.

She nods, then stands, her lips move:

"A girl from the town, a plain girl, was betrayed
   by her lover,

a scholar. So when her blood stopped flowing,
and her belly swole beyond disguising,
she went to him, and wept hot tears. He stroked
   her hair,
swore that they would marry, that they would
   run,
in the night,
together,
to his aunt. She believed him;
even though she had seen the glances in the hall
he gave to his master's daughter,
who was fair, and rich, she believed him.
Or she believed that she believed.

"There was something sly about his smile,
his eyes so black and sharp, his rufous hair. Something
that sent her early to their trysting place,
beneath the oak, beside the thornbush,
something that made her climb the tree and wait.
Climb a tree, and in her condition.
Her love arrived at dusk, skulking by owl-light,
carrying a bag,
from which he took a mattock, shovel, knife.
He worked with a will, beside the thornbush,
beneath the oaken tree,
he whistled gently, and he sang, as he dug her grave,
that old song . . .
shall I sing it for you, now, good folk?"

She pauses, and as a one we clap and we holloa
—or almost as a one:
My intended, her hair so dark, her cheeks so pink,
her lips so red,
seems distracted.

The fair girl (who is she? A guest of the inn, I
   hazard) sings:

"A fox went out on a shiny night
And he begged for the moon to give him light
For he'd many miles to go that night
Before he'd reach his den-O!
Den-O! Den-O!
He'd many miles to go that night, before he'd reach his
    den-O."

Her voice is sweet and fine, but the voice of my
    intended is finer.

"And when her grave was dug—
A small hole it was, for she was a little thing,
even big with child she was a little thing—
he walked below her, back and a forth,
rehearsing her hearsing, thus:
—*Good evening, my pigsnie, my love,*
my, but you look a treat in the moon's light,
mother of my child-to-be. Come, let me hold you.
And he'd embrace the midnight air with one hand,
and with the other, holding his short but wicked
    knife,
he'd stab and stab the dark.

"She trembled in her oak above him. Breathed so
    softly,
but still she shook. And once he looked up, and
    said,
—*Owls, I'll wager*, and another time, *fie! is that a cat*
up there? Here puss . . . But she was still,
bethought herself a branch, a leaf, a twig. At dawn
he took his mattock, spade and knife, and left
all grumbling and gudgeoned of his prey.

"They found her later wandering, her wits
had left her. There were oak leaves in her hair,
and she sang,

'The bough did bend
The bough did break
I saw the hole
The fox did make

'We swore to love
We swore to marry
I saw the blade
The fox did carry'

"They say that her babe, when it was born,
had a fox's paw on her and not a hand.
Fear is the sculptress, midwives claim. The scholar
  fled."

And she sits down, to general applause.
The smile twitches, hides about her lips: I know
  it's there,
it waits in her grey eyes. She stares at me, amused.

"I read that in the Orient foxes follow priests and
  scholars,
in disguise as women, houses, mountains, gods,
  processions,
always discovered by their tails—" so I begin,
but my intended's father intercedes.
"Speaking of tales—my dear, you said you had a
  tale?"

My intended flushes. There are no rose petals,
save for her cheeks. She nods, and says:

"My story, father? My story is the story of a
  dream I dreamed."

Her voice is so quiet and soft, we hush ourselves
  to hear,
outside the inn just the night sounds: an owl
  hoots,

but, as the old folk say, I live too near the wood
to be frightened by an owl.

She looks at me.

"You, sir. In my dream you rode to me, and
    called,
—*Come to my house, my sweet, away down the white
    road.*
There are such sights I would show you.
I asked how I would find your house, down the
    white chalk road,
for it's a long road, and a dark one, under trees
that make the light all green and gold when the
    sun is high,
but shade the road at other times. At night
it's pitch-black; there is no moonlight on the white
    road . . .

"And you said, Mister Fox—and this is most
    curious, but dreams
are treacherous and curious and dark—
that you would cut the throat of a sow-pig,
and you would walk her home behind your fine
    black stallion.
You smiled,
smiled, Mister Fox, with your red lips and your
    green eyes,
eyes that could snare a maiden's soul, and your
    yellow teeth,
which could eat her heart—"

"God forbid," I smiled. All eyes were on me, then,
    not her,
though hers was the story. Eyes, such eyes.

"So, in my dream, it became my fancy to visit
    your great house,
as you had so often entreated me to do,

to walk its glades and paths, to see the pools,
the statues you had brought from Greece, the
   yews,
the poplar-walk, the grotto, and the bower.
And, as this was but a dream, I did not wish
to take a chaperone
—some withered, juiceless prune
who would not appreciate your house, Mister Fox;
   who
would not appreciate your pale skin,
nor your green eyes,
nor your engaging ways.

"So I rode the white chalk road, following the red
   blood path,
on Betsy, my filly. The trees above were green.
A dozen miles straight, and then the blood
led me off across meadows, over ditches, down a
   gravel path,
(but now I needed sharp eyes to catch the blood—
a drip, a drop: the pig must have been dead as
   anything)
and I reined my filly in in front of a house.
And such a house. A Palladian delight, immense,
a landscape of its own, windows, columns,
a white stone monument to verticality, expansive.

"There was a sculpture in the garden, before the house,
a Spartan child, stolen fox half-concealed in its robe,
the fox biting the child's stomach, gnawing the
vitals away,
the stoic child bravely saying nothing—
what could it say, cold marble that it was?
There was pain in its eyes, and it stood,
upon a plinth upon which were carved eight words.
I walked around it and I read:
Be bold,

Be bold,
but not too bold.

"I tethered little Betsy in the stables,
between a dozen night black stallions
each with blood and madness in his eyes.
I saw no one.
I walked to the front of the house, and up the great
    steps.
The huge doors were locked fast,
no servants came to greet me, when I knocked.
In my dream (for do not forget, Mister Fox, that
    this was my dream.
You look so pale) the house fascinated
    me, the kind of curiosity (you know this,
Mister Fox, I see it in your eyes) that kills cats.

"I found a door, a small door, off the latch,
and pushed my way inside.
Walked corridors, lined with oak, with shelves,
with busts, with trinkets,
I walked, my feet silent on the scarlet carpet,
until I reached the great hall.
It was there again, in red stones that glittered,
set into the white marble of the floor,
it said:
Be bold,
be bold,
but not too bold
Or else your life's blood
shall run cold.

"There were stairs, wide, carpeted in scarlet,
off the great hall,
and I walked up them, silently, silently.
Oak doors: and now
I was in the dining room, or so I am convinced,

for the remnants of a grisly supper
were abandoned, cold and fly-buzzed.
Here was a half-chewed hand, there, crisped and
    picked,
a face, a woman's face, who must in life, I fear,
have looked like me."

"Heavens defend us all from such dark dreams,"
    her father cried.
"Can such things be?"

"It is not so," I assured him. The fair woman's
    smile
glittered behind her grey eyes. People
need assurances.

"Beyond the supper room was a room,
a huge room, this inn would fit in that room,
piled promiscuously with rings and bracelets,
necklaces, pearl drops, ball gowns, fur wraps,
lace petticoats, silks and satins. Ladies' boots,
and muffs, and bonnets: a treasure cave and
    dressing room—
diamonds and rubies underneath my feet.

"Beyond that room I knew myself in Hell.
In my dream . . .
I saw many heads. The heads of young women. I
    saw a wall
on which dismembered limbs were nailed.
A heap of breasts. The piles of guts, of livers, lights,
the eyes, the . . .
No. I cannot say. And all around the flies were
    buzzing,
one low droning buzz.
—*Bëelzebubzebubzebub* they buzzed. I could not
    breathe,
I ran from there and sobbed against a wall."

"A fox's lair indeed," says the fair woman.
("It was not so," I mutter.)

"They are untidy creatures, so to litter,
about their dens the bones and skins and feathers
of their prey. The French call him *Renard*,
the Scottish, *Tod*."

"One cannot help one's name," says my intended's
    father.
He is almost panting now, they all are:
in the firelight, the fire's heat, lapping their ale.
The wall of the inn was hung with sporting prints.

She continues:
"From outside I heard a crash and a commotion.
I ran back the way I had come, along the red carpet,
down the wide staircase—too late!—the main door
    was opening!
I threw myself down the stairs—rolling, tumbling—
fetched up hopelessly beneath a table,
where I waited, shivered, prayed."

She points at me. "Yes, you, sir. You came in,
crashed open the door, staggered in, you sir,
dragging a young woman
by her red hair and by her throat.
Her hair was long and unconfined, she screamed
    and strove
to free herself. You laughed, deep in your throat,
were all a-sweat, and grinned from ear to ear."

She glares at me. The color's in her cheeks.
"You pulled a short old broadsword, Mister Fox,
    and as she screamed,
you slit her throat, again from ear to ear,
I listened to her bubbling, sighing, shriek
and closed my eyes and prayed until she stopped.
And after much, much, much too long, she
    stopped.

"And I looked out. You smiled, held up your sword,
your hands agore-blood—"

"In your dream," I tell her.

"In my dream.
She lay there on the marble, as you sliced
you hacked, you wrenched, you panted, and you
    stabbed.
You took her head from her shoulders,
thrust your tongue between her red wet lips.
You cut off her hands. Her pale white hands.
You sliced open her bodice, you removed each
    breast.
Then you began to sob and howl.
Of a sudden,
clutching her head, which you carried by the hair,
the flame red hair,
you ran up the stairs.

"As soon as you were out of sight,
I fled through the open door.
I rode my Betsy home, down the white road."

All eyes upon me now. I put down my ale,
on the old wood of the table.
"It is not so,"
I told her,
told all of them.
"It was not so, and
God forbid
it should be so. It was
an evil dream. I wish such dreams
on no one."

"Before I fled the charnel house,
before I rode poor Betsy into a lather,

before we fled down the White Road,
the blood still red
(and was it a pig whose throat you slit, Mister
   Fox?)
before I came to my father's inn,
before I fell before them speechless,
my father, brothers, friends—"

All honest farmers, fox-hunting men.
They are stamping their boots, their black boots.

"—before that, Mister Fox,
I seized, from the floor, from the bloody floor,
her hand, Mister Fox. The hand of the woman
you hacked apart before my eyes."

"It is not so—"

"It was no dream. You Landru. You Bluebeard."

"It was not so—"

"You Gilles de Rais. You monster."

"And God Forbid it should be so!"

She smiles now, lacking mirth or warmth.
The brown hair curls around her face,
roses twining about a bower.
Two spots of red are burning on her cheeks.

"Behold, Mister Fox! Her hand! Her poor pale
   hand!"
She pulls it from her breasts (gently freckled,
I had dreamed of those breasts)
tosses it down upon the table.
It lies in front of me.
Her father, brothers, friends,

they stare at me hungrily,
and I pick up the small thing.

The hair was red indeed, and rank. The pads and
  claws
were rough. One end was bloody
but the blood had dried.

"This is no hand," I tell them. But the first
fist knocks the wind from out of me,
an oaken cudgel hits my shoulder,
as I stagger,
the first black boot kicks me down onto the floor.
And then a rain of blows beats down on me,
I curl and mewl and pray and grip the paw
so tightly.

Perhaps I weep.

I see her then,
the pale, fair girl, the smile has reached her lips,
her skirts so long as she slips, grey-eyed,
amused beyond all bearing, from the room.
She'd many a mile to go, that night.
And as she leaves,
from my vantage place upon the floor,
I see the brush, the tail between her legs;
I would have called,
but I could speak no more. Tonight she'll be running
four-footed, surefooted, down the White Road.

What if the hunters come?
What if they come?

Be bold, I whisper once, before I die. *But not too bold . . .*

And then my tale is done.

The Traveler and the Tale

Jane Yolen

Jane Yolen has well over one hundred and fifty books out, most of them for children and young adults. Her most recent publications include the illustrated fairy tales Good Griselle *and* The Girl in the Golden Bower, *as well as the young adult fantasy novels* The Wild Hunt *and* Passager. *The anthology* Xanadu 3, *edited by Yolen, has also recently been published. Yolen has twice been in* The Year's Best Horror *anthology and in seven out of the eight* The Year's Best Fantasy and Horror *anthologies.*

"The Traveler and the Tale," is, unusually for Yolen, a science fiction story. But within it is a version of the traditional changeling tale.

The Traveler and the Tale

TRAVELING SOUTH FROM AMBERT YOU MUST PASS THE old stone abbey of La Chaise-Dieu. It was near that abbey in 1536 that a young woman fell asleep on a dolmen and dreamed of the virgin.

There are some who said such dreams come as a consequence of lying out in the night air. Others that it was the cold stone beneath her that prompted such haverings. A few bitter souls said that she was, alas, no better than she should have been and women like that cannot dream of the Queen of Heaven and it was perforce a lie.

But the dreamer was a simple peasant woman caught out between Ambert and Le Puy, having turned her ankle on the rough road. She did not realize how close she was to the abbey or she would have gone there for the night. The dolmen, raised up as it was, kept her free of the damp and safe from vipers. Such safety was the extent of her imagination. She did not dream of the virgin; she was waking and she saw me.

I was caught in the Aura of a time change, when the centuries lie side by side for the moment of Pass-Through. The woman saw what she thought was a crown of stars on my head, which was nothing more than the Helmet. Aura and Helmet and an untutored sixteenth century mind. What else could she believe than that I was either an angel or the Mother of God?

When I saw her and realized that I had been caught out, I swore under my breath. "Merde!"

If the expletive startled her, she did not show it. I believe she must have mistaken it for a name.

"Marie," she whispered, crossing herself three or four times in rapid succession before passing out in an excess of ecstasy and oxygen.

I knew enough to leave her alone and hurry along my way. My destination was a small town in Auvergne where a cottage awaited me. I was well versed in the local dialect—Occitan. It sat comfortable on my tongue. The stories in Henri Pourrat's vast collection of regional tales I had memorized, my memory only sightly enhanced by Oxipol. I was always a good and quick study. As my teaching machine chose to jest with me in the same dialect: "Qu'aucu t'aye liceno." ("Someone has been teaching you a lesson!" No one has ever said machines have good senses of humor. It has to do with a lack of the funny bone.)

It was my duty to infiltrate the community and interpolate several stories artfully prepared by our Revolutionary Council some three thousand years in France's future. Odd, isn't it, that with all the time traveling we have done since the invention of the Module, it has become abundantly clear that no shot fired, no knife thrown, no spear in the gut has the power to change the world of the future. Le Bon Dieu knows we have tried. Hitler blown up. The Khan poisoned. Marie Antoinette throttled in her cradle. And all to no avail. History, like a scab, calcifies over each wound and beneath it the skin of human atrocity heals. Only through stories, it seems, can we really influence the history that is to come. Told to a ready ear, repeated by a willing mouth, by that process of mouth-to-ear resuscitation we change the world.

Stories are not just recordings. They are prophecies. They are dreams. And—so it seems—we humans build the future on such dreams.

If I am successful in my storytelling, the Auvergne of the future will be a garden of earthly splendor. Gone will be the long lines of the impoverished children walking dull-eyed toward Paris under the lash of the Alien Horde. Gone will be the ravaged fields, the razed houses, the villages' streets strewn with bones.

But when I stepped into the past, ready to play my part for the future, wrapped in the ocreous glow of transfer, a peasant woman lying uneasily on a dolmen with a bad ankle added a new story, one we had not planned: how the Mother of God visited Ambert that spring. The peasant circles would soon be abuzz with it and it would in its own way change the future of the Auvergne. Would it bring a resurgence of piety to the land whose practical approach to religion had led to an easy accommodation with the socialism of the twentieth century, the apostacy of the twenty-first, the capitulation to Alien rites of the twenty-second? Without the Council's Modular Computes I could not know.

"Merde!" I cursed, stepping back.

She crossed herself and fainted.

Smoothing my skirts down, I glanced toward the road. I had planned to add two stories to Pourrat's collection. One was a Beast fabliau, about two mice and a cricket who throw off the yoke of slavery put on them by a race of cats, the other a tale we call Dinner-in-an-Eggshell which is about discovering the alien that lives in your house. We hope that one or the other or both will have the effect of warning our people. The odds have been calculated carefully but I will never know if they will succeed. The traveler cannot return from the trip. I expect to live my thirty years as a weaver in the cottage hard by the mill, telling my stories that will pass from my mouth to my neighbors' ears at night when we work at our several tasks, one perhaps scutching hemp, another spinning, the servants tidying their threshing flails. Oh, we will have a lovely time of it, for what else is there to do on a cold harvest eve but tell stories before the fire before bundling off to our straw beds.

Dinner-in-an-Eggshell

A woman was nursing her baby and it was the sweetest child you can imagine, with bright blue eyes and a mouth like a primrose.

One March day, the mother took her child and put him in his crib by the fire and went out to get water for the stone sink. When she returned, she heard a strange, horrible snuffling sound from the baby's crib.

She almost dropped the jug in alarm, and ran over to see what was wrong. And what did she see? Instead of her sweet baby lying in his crib, there was a *something* on the pillow as ugly and misshapen as a toad. It had bulging eyes and a green tongue and when it breathed, it made an awful snuffling sound.

The mother screamed, but then she knew what she had to do because this was a fairy's changeling child. She would have to compel him to speak and it would be no easy task, because she would have to surprise him.

So for three days she pretended to the changeling that she thought it her own child. She petted it and praised it though its very looks made her ill.

On the third day, she said to herself aloud, "I have ten strong laborers coming over for dinner." And she rushed about the house getting ready for them, filling six milk pails with milk and four basins with cream, carving away a side of lard and taking down an entire rope of onions.

"Oh me, oh my," she sighed, "what a job to cook dinner for ten in an eggshell."

The changeling sat up in its crib, a startled look on its ugly toad face.

> *Three hundred years I have lived well,*
> *But never seen dinner in a white eggshell.*

At that, the mother took out a whip and she whipped and whipped the baby, crying:

> *Ugly toad in baby's cot,*
> *My sweet baby you are not.*
> *Who are you?*

And because the ugly changeling had already spoken, it had to speak again. It cried out because the whip hurt it. "I am a fairy child. Ow. Ow. Ow."

At that the fairies had to come and take their ugly baby home, bringing the mother's own child in exchange.

She picked him up and hugged him to her and she never let him out of her sight again.

To The Armies of the Revolution:

We greet you.

The enemy is gone. No more do we suffer under their whip. No more do we offer them our sons and daughters as slaves.

Now we must rebuild our nation, our world. Now we must tell the story of our travails and recall our heroes home.

—the Marian Council

My good Robin is as fine a husband as a woman could want. And a fine storyteller, too. His stories are of the land—when Fox stole fish from the fishmongers, when Crow lost his cheese. He expects me to tell only women's stories, the stork tales, the tales of *ma mère l'Oye*. This I know. This I do. I tell the tales my Maman told me. But—oh—I wish in this one thing Robin could know my heart. When Maman was dying, she often rambled about a world ruled by frogs and toads. A world in which humans were able to travel along the great river of time, but backward, only backward.

"I am a traveler," she would cry out, and weep. And Papa could not help her then, nor Jouanne or me. We would hold her hands and only when we said, "Maman, tell us a story," would she be comforted.

"A story," she would say, the mist going from her eyes. "I can tell you many stories. I *must* tell you many stories." She called them *pourrats*, these tales, and they were such strange stories. Hard to understand. Hard to forget.

I tell them to my own children, as Jouanne does, I am sure, to hers. But stories do not feed a mouth, they do not salve a wound, they do not fill the soul. Only God does that. And the Mother of God. We know that surely here in our village, for did not two women just thirty years past see Mary, Mother of God, on a dolmen? Her head was crowned with stars and she named herself.

"I am Marie," she said. "Believe in me and you will be saved."

One of the women who saw her was Maman.

The Printer's Daughter

Delia Sherman

Born in Japan at Tokyo Army Hospital, Delia Sherman was raised mostly in Manhattan, which makes her a Yankee city girl. She spent many of her summers with her mother's familiy in the wilds of central Texas and western Louisiana, which makes her a Southern country girl. She lived for many years in Newton, Massachusetts, which makes her a suburban girl. Recently, she moved to the urban environment of Somerville, Massachusetts, which makes her very happy.

Much of her life has been spent at one end or another of a classroom. She received her B.A. in English from Vassar College and her M.A. and Ph.D. in Renaissance Studies from Brown Uni-

versity. She has taught expository writing and fantasy at Boston University and Northeastern University. She also is a reviewer.

Her first novel, Through A Brazen Mirror, based on a British folk ballad, was published in 1989 by Ace Books as one of their distinguished Fantasy Specials. Her short fiction has appeared in The Magazine of Fantasy and Science Fiction *and in the anthology* Xanadu 2, *and four of her stories have been anthologized in* The Year's Best Fantasy and Horror. *Her second novel,* The Porcelain Dove, *was recently published.*

About "The Printer's Daughter," Sherman says, "when I was a child, someone gave me a large, romantically illustrated book called Fairy Tales From Many Lands, *which I read so often that my mother had to reinforce the spine with flowered contact paper. One of the stories in it was "The Snow Child," a sentimental Russian tale about a middle-aged couple's desire for a child. It was not my favorite story, at least not the way it was retold by H. Herda, but it is the one that has stuck with me, in part, I think, because I am an adopted child."*

Sherman's knowledge of the historical period in "The Printer's Daughter" is used beautifully in her version of this tale, and she creates something funny and moving yet not sentimental.

The Printer's Daughter

ON THE MORNING OF ALL HALLOW'S EVE, HAL Spurtle sat at the window of his shop and watched the children play. They were ragged children, as it was a ragged street, their faces and caps smudged with dirt and their petticoats and breeches tattered as old paper. Grave as judges, they linked hands and danced sunwise, chanting the while in their bird-shrill voices.

> *Thread the needle, thread the needle,*
> *Eye, eye, eye.*
> *Thread the needle, thread the needle,*
> *Eye, eye, eye.*
> *The tailor's blind and he can't see,*
> *So we must thread the needle.*

Hal remembered singing that rhyme himself. He'd taught it to his young sisters as they played on a Shoreditch street that differed from this not so much as milk from cream. As he watched little Rose and Ned Ashcroft, Anne and Katty and Jane Dunne winding up and down the cobbles, he told the rhyme over to himself, very soft.

The children laughed as they played. Hal sighed and turned his eyes back to the trays of type, the compositor's stick, and the manuscript pages stacked before them. The collected sermons of the good Dr. Beswick, passed by the Queen's censor and writ down in the Register of the Company of Stationers. Dull as an old knife, but legal to print and to sell, making a change from the bawdy broadsides, the saucy quartos, the unblushingly filthy octavos that made up the greater part of his stock-in-trade. The great pornographer Arentino himself might have turned color at *The Cuckold's Mery Iest* and expired altogether of shame at *In Praise of Pudding-Pricks*. But it had been a matter of Pride the son riding before Caution the father, for on being made free of the Company of Stationers, Hal must needs set up shop for himself, though he could scarce afford a press and its furniture. And so Hal had learned to converse with scarcity and rogues, until, by chance, a country clergyman approached him with a manuscript of sermons and a purse to pay for their printing.

Hal's old master, John Day, would have done the job in a week, but John Day had two 'prentices to ink, cut pages, and distribute type, as well as compositors, pressmen, gatherers, folders, and binders to do the work. Hal, working man-alone, had been at the business two weeks already, with Dr. Beswick threatening to take his sermons and his ten pounds elsewhere, God take the thought from him; for his ten pounds were scattered like grain among Hal's creditors.

Furthermore, Hal himself was weak and weary with poor feeding, and as like to drop a line of type as bring it whole to the imposing-table. On All Hallow's Eve, he did that once or twice, and then he transposed two lines of type, the which cost him fifty sheets of best French Imperial, and overinked a plate with so free a hand that he must pour the piss-pot over it to clean it. Not three impressions later, he did it again, whereupon Hal consigned Dr. Beswick and his sermons to the most noisesome deep of Hell; viz., Satan's arsehole. For overinking was such a monkey's trick as he'd not been guilty of for fifteen years or more.

An apprentice would serve the present need, he thought; a likely, lively lad who was content to live upon pulp and printer's ink, a lad who never reversed lines nor set them arsy-versy. But Hal well knew that were there such a 'prentice in London, he'd never bind himself to a press where half the texts were unlicensed and the other half unlicensable. He looked mournfully at twists of paper from *In Praise of Pudding-Pricks* and Dr. Beswick's sermons, equally damned by their ill-printing, piled in the corner where an apprentice might sleep. Seized by a sudden fancy, Hal gathered up sheets of piety and bawdry and twisted them into skinny arms and legs, wrapped scraps and wads into a lumpy head and carcass, and bound the whole with thread into a human shape. When it was done, he shook his head over the poor, blind face, and taking up ink and pen, carefully limned features: a button nose, doe's eyes, and a Cupid's mouth. He thought it favored his small sister Kate.

The wind, having risen with the moon, came hunting down the narrow street for mischief, the which it found in the shape of Hal's window shutter. Howling, it pounced upon the latch, tore it open, and slapped the wood to and fro against the glass. Hal laid his poppet upon a nest of paper and ran out-a-doors to catch it. He had put the shutter up and was going in again when a small, straddling fellow clawed him by the elbow and would not be put by.

"I seek Hal Spurtle the printer's," he said.

"I am Hal Spurtle," said Hal. "What would you with me?"

"To go within," said the man. "My business is not for the common street."

Loathe was Hal to oblige him, the hour being late and none save rogues likely to be abroad. Yet rogues were the chiefest part of his custom; and so he brought the stranger into the shop. In the lamplight, the man proved a veritable Methuselah, with a face like a shelled walnut and a back like the hoop of a cart. His hands and stump-trimmed beard were vilely stained, and there hung a stink about him of sulphur and brimstone. By which signs Hal understood the stranger to be an alchemist, the which he further understood to be a filthy trade and unlawful. So it was with faint courtesy that he demanded of the old man once again why he sought Hal Spurtle the printer?

"To give him a job of work," answered the alchemist, and poked and patted in his gown until he found a thick sheaf of vellum tied with tape, the which he handed to Hal, who took it as gingerly as may be.

"Untie it. 'Twill not eat thee," said the old man.

Slowly, Hal did so, uncovering a page writ margin to margin in secretary hand, damnably crabbed. Forty pages in quarto, or perhaps fifty, say two weeks to set and print if the edition were not large. He squinted at the tiny, curling letters.

> *Liquour conioynyth male with female*
>   *wyfe,*
> *And causith dede thingis to resorte to*
>   *lyfe.*

Hal dropped the manuscript hastily. "Your job of work would bring me to my neck verse, grandad."

"*In Praise of Pudding-Pricks* could lose thee thy right

hand, or any of the bawdry thou dost use to print
here. This goose is only a little more spiced, and lays
golden eggs besides. An edition of thirteen copies,
printed as accurate as may be, sewn for binding. Shall
we say twenty crowns?"

Hal's teeth watered at the sum. Twenty crowns
would rid him of his debts and buy him a new font
of type, an apprentice, even a pressman who knew a
platen from a frisket. Before he could gather his wits
to say yea or nay, the old man said, "It must be done
by Sunday moonrise, mind, or 'tis no good."

"Sunday moonrise! Why did you not come to me
earlier, pray? I cannot set, proof, print, and sew thirteen copies in two days, not if I worked without stop
or let from dawn to dawn. The thing's impossible. As
well ask a cat to pull a cart."

"You have no apprentice?"

"I have not, sir. And had I the two apprentices the
law allows, yea, and twenty journeymen, too, still the
job would take a week or more. And I've another
book promised and owing must take precedence."

The old man peered shortsightedly into the shadows. "Yet I thought I saw an apprentice as I came
in—a lad sleeping on a pallet, there in the corner."

Hal followed the goodman's gaze to the poppet. It
did look uncommonly like a sleeping child. " 'Tis
naught," he said shortly. "A pile of paper."

The old man heaved himself upright, took up the
lamp, and hobbled over to see for himself. "An ho-
munculus, as I am a man! You'd not said you dabbled
in the Art, Master Spurtle."

Hal crossed himself. "God forbid, sir."

The old man fixed him with a crow-bright eye that
pierced Hal's skull from brow to bald spot. "Art
lonely, lad?"

"Aye," said Hal, surprised into honesty.

"And no sister or wife to keep thy house or warm thy bed?"

"My sisters will not forgive me my learning, an it go not hand-in-hand with wealth. And as for a wife, I've no stomach for the wooing, nor coin for the keeping when she's won."

"No matter," said the old man. "See here, Hal Spurtle. Should I find thee a 'prentice fit for the work, wilt undertake to print my book by Sunday moonrise?"

"He needs must be a prodigy of nature."

"As prodigious as thou wilt. 'Tis a bargain, then. Thy hand on it, Hal Spurtle. This purse will stay thy present need."

The purse contained five pounds in silver: a goodly earnest. Hal weighed it in his palm. "Why, if I'm a madman, you're another, and there's a pair on us. My hand on it, then."

They shook hands solemnly, and then the old gentleman took up his carven stick, hobbled to the door, and, without another word, was gone like the devil in the old play.

St. Martin's tolled midnight. Hal rubbed his cheeks wearily and picked up the lamp to light him to bed. Catching a movement in the corner of his eye—*a rat*, he thought, and had turned him away when a voice arrested him: a small, dry voice, like the rustling of pages.

"Sinner," it said. "Look thou to thine end."

The hair crept upon Hal's skin like lice. What had the old rogue left behind him?

"To each thing must thou pay heed," said the voice. "To thy comings-in and thy goings-out, to thy pleasures and thy pains, that they be pleasing unto the Lord."

Hal considered. Surely a demon would not speak as from a pulpit; though 'twas said the devil could quote scripture to the soul's confusion. "Back to Hell with thee, demon," said Hal peevishly. "I've no wish to look upon thy hideous countenance."

There was a faint rustling from the corner. "The kingdom of God is of a fairness beyond the measure of man, and the tidings thereof are comfortable," said the voice at last, sad and something fearful, like Hal's sister Kate begging grace for some roguery. The memory softening his heart, he turned and beheld no horned devil, but a girl-child of six years' growth, sitting mother-naked in a nest of paper.

"Hallelujah, saith the angel, and the sons of man rejoice," she said firmly.

Hal squatted down before her and reached out one hand to touch her head. It was not bald, but covered with an uneven pelt, white mottled with black, like blurred print. Her face was likewise piebald and soft as old rags, her cheeks round as peaches, like Kate's or Ann's or any of the small sisters whom Hal had fed and dandled. Like them, she was as bony as a cur-pup, and as hollow-eyed. Only her mouth was fair, a pure and innocent bow.

The fair mouth opened, and she spoke. "A groat will buy my hand, good sir, and a penny my cunt. But 'tis three pennies for my mouth, for washing the taste out after."

"Out upon thee for a froward wench," cried Hal, and struck her with his open hand so that she wailed aloud with the pain of it. As shocked as he'd been by her bawdry, still more was Hal grieved by her piteous cries. So he caught up a clout from a chair, bundled it around her naked, flailing arms and legs, and gathered her, howling, to his breast.

"There, now," he crooned over the piebald hair. "Hush thee, do. Thou'rt not so hurt as astonished, the which may be said of me as well."

The child quietened at his voice, and sniffled, and settled against him. "His yoke is easy and his burden is light," she said tearfully. "Wherefore dost thou grieve him with thy sinning?"

Hal rocked her silently for a moment, then asked, "Art hungered, sweeting? Shall I fetch thee a sop of milk and bread?"

"Flesh and ale's good meat to my belly, and swiving thereafter."

Hal looked stonily upon the lass; she showed small, crooked teeth in an imp's smile. "Thou shalt cry, 'Pardon, Pardon,' and it will avail thee naught. For sin is stamped upon thy soul from thy mother's womb; thou art cast and molded of it."

" 'As prodigious as thou wilt,' " murmured Hal. "I begin to apprehend." He loosed his arms, and the girl-child stood upright on paper-twist limbs and made her ways to the composing-table, and began to distribute the scattered type into the cases, her arms spinning like flywheels. The clout dropped from her shoulders and she stood naked on the floor.

Hal slipped into the inner room, where he hunted out hose and a shirt only a little torn, and a rope to belt it with. These he carried into the shop and tossed upon the table where she could not choose but to see them.

She fetched up the clothing and held it this way and that against her body until Hal began to laugh, whereat she cocked her head, aggrieved. "So ask not, saying, how shall we eat, or how shall we drink, or wherewithal shall we be clothed; for after all these things do the Gentiles seek."

"Do them on nonetheless; the wind will not temper itself to a shorn lamb, and thou'rt prodigy enough in a clothed state. And thou'lt need a name. Textura? Roman? Bastarda?" The child blew a fart with her lips. Hal grinned. "Not Bastarda. Demy. Broadside." Gazing here and there in search of inspiration, his eye chanced to light upon the press, the frisket unfolded, the tympan empty. "Frisket," he said decidedly.

The child smiled at that, and uttered not a word, neither of bawdry nor of scripture, by which Hal understood that she was much moved, as, in truth, was Hal himself.

" 'Gie thee good den, Frisket," said Hal. "Now to bed, under the press, as snug as a mouse. We'll up betimes and begin work."

When he entered his shop at cock-crow next morning, Hal half thought he'd wandered in his sleep to his master's printing-shop at Alder's Gate. The composing and imposing tables were scrubbed clean of ink stains, the floor swept and garnished, the ink-balls washed and hung to dry, and the piebald girl was bent over the press, industriously greasing the tracks. She'd shot up in the night, mushroom-like, to a gawky girl of twelve or thereabouts, with her hair grown to rat's tails strewn across the back of Hal's shirt, and her bony arms black to the elbow with ink.

"Frisket," said Hal. "Is't thou in very sooth, lass?"

"When I was a child, I understood as a child; now I am become a man, I put away childish things."

"Thou'rt nigher heaven than thou wast, and something stouter." He glanced suspiciously at the cupboard. "Hast left me a sup?"

"Man doth not live by bread alone," said Frisket smugly. "Come kiss me, sweet chuck, and clip me close." And she gestured to the hearth, where ale was warming, and a half-loaf of bread and a crust of cheese laid ready on a plate, to which Hal applied himself right heartily.

"There is a wanton will not want one, if place and person were agreeable to his desires."

Hal swallowed hard and said, "List thee, poppet. Before we make a start, I would say a word. Sermonizing I can bear. Bawdry ill befits thy tender years.

Cleave to Dr. Beswick, an it pleaseth thee, and let *In Praise of Pudding-Pricks* be."

Frisket looked dumpish. "As the goose is sauced, so is the gander," she said.

"I'd think shame to read the knavery my poverty beds me withal," Hal said.

"Out upon thee, old juggler! Thy sparrow is dead 'i the nest, and will not rise up and sing, squeeze and kiss I never so cleverly."

Hal yielded the field, blushing, nor sought to engage again; but as they worked that day composing and printing the sheets, he made note that Frisket's tongue wagged less, and more upon a pedantical breeze than a bawdy. So the morning flowed into day and the evening into night like streams into a river, quiet and unmarked. But when St. Anthony's bell came tolling midnight, there were only three sheets made perfect, twenty-four pages out of fifty-two. Despairing, Hal sat him down for a brace of minutes to rest his aching back.

He woke to broad daylight and Frisket mixing ink.

"Wake thee, wake thee, sinner, for the bridegroom cometh," she caroled.

Hal started to his feet. Ten stacks of perfect sheets stood ranged upon the composing-table. He took one up and checked it, back and front. The inking was dark and even, the lines prettily justified, the text as sensible and correct as such a text might be.

"So thou shalt ask thyself; am I a sinner, or am I a righteous man?" said Frisket anxiously.

Hal looked up at her ink-blotched face in wonder. "A righteous man, beyond all doubt. In fact," he continued, "there's a question here, which of us is master and which 'prentice."

Frisket smiled to show her teeth—piebald as her skin and hair—and then he and she turned to collating the sheets, to folding and cutting them into books and sewing the signatures together. They worked in quiet amity, with the ease of long use and custom, the one giving the other a knife or thread at need, without a word exchanged. Now and again he'd glance from the sewing-frame to see her ink-drop eyes upon him, whereat they'd smile at one another and bend to their tasks again. Joy became a friend, who long had been a stranger to Hal's heart, and his mind began to wander in uncharted seas of poems and plays and philosophical tracts that might be registered and put for public sale in St. Paul's churchyard, and a little house in St. Martin's Lane, with a shop at the back and two journeymen to run the press, and Frisket, of course, properly bound and entered in the Rolls of the apprentices. She'd need a better name than Frisket, too. Mary, he thought—the mother of Our Lord. Mary Spurtle, his elder brother's child, if anyone were to ask. But he and she would know she was Hal's own, the daughter of his heart.

Come moonrise, Hal and Frisket were grinning at one another across the hearth, with thirteen quarto alchemical ordinals stacked neatly on the composing-table behind them. The door-latch rattled, and Frisket ran to open it.

"Behold, the bridegroom cometh, and upon his brow is righteousness," she said, flourishing a bow.

The alchemist beetled his brows at her, and at Hal, who sat laughing by the fire. "Thou art pleased to take thine ease," he said testily. "The silver I gave thee cost me something in the making. I trust thou hast not squandered it in liquor."

"Nay, nay, good Master Alchemist, I have not, nor so much as a moment in sleep or sup. There is your book as you required it, printed as fine, though I say it, as Caxton in his prime."

The alchemist took up the topmost book and leafed

through its pages, hemming here and hawing there, looking up at last and nodding to Hal almost with courtesy. "Excellent," he said. "Excellent good, in very sooth. Thou hast labored mightily, thou and thy 'prentice, in bringing forth this text. And so I will ask thee, Hal Spurtle, whether thou wouldst take a copy in payment, that is the only true receipt for the making of gold and silver, or content thee with twenty crowns."

Hal laughed aloud. "I cry thee pardon, grandad, but I'd leifer have ink upon my hands than quicksilver. Twenty crowns, wisely spent, will bring me to twenty more as well as thy receipt, and with more surety. We'll do well enough, my 'prentice and I."

The alchemist shrugged his shoulders, and having dealt the books here and there about his person, took out a purse and gave it over to Hal's hand and prepared to go his ways. Upon reaching the door, a thought stopped him. "Thy apprentice," he said. "How dost thou like him?"

Hal, feeling Frisket shadowy at his side, drew her forward into his arm. "I like her very well," he said.

"Her," said the old man. "Curious."

When he was gone, Hal tossed the heavy purse aloft, jingling. "Here's a weighty matter, poppet, must be lightened ere it burst. We've need of meat, and ale, and bread, and women's weeds to clothe thee withal."

"Smock climb apace, that I may see my joys."

"Aye, a smock, and petticoats and a woolen skirt and a shawl against the winter wind, and leathern shoes." He kissed her lightly upon the head. "I'll warrant thee to make a bonny wench. We'll to market at daylight."

Overwatched, Hal slept almost until noon, by which time Frisket had finished printing Dr. Beswick's sermons, aye, and cut and sewn them, too. Hal crowed with joy, swung her under the arms, bundled the books with binding thread, and carried them to Dr. Beswick's lodgings, where he gave them into the gentleman's hand, full of apologies for the delay and thanks for his patience.

"Patience," piped Frisket, "is of the Virtues the most cardinal; for all things come to him who waiteth upon the word of God."

Hal looked sharp to see whether the reverend gentleman be offended or no. "My new apprentice, sir, my brother's child. Touched by the finger of God, sir, but quick and good-hearted as may be."

"So I perceive," said Dr. Beswick. "My own words upon patience, pat as I writ 'em. 'Tis pity he's so ill-marked. Stay, now, here's another sovereign. I'd not thought to see my books this sennight."

Hal took the sovereign and thanked the reverend gentleman, and bore Frisket off to the old-clothes market at Cornhill. He bought a woolen gown and a shawl, two smocks, and after some hesitation, a petticoat of fine scarlet, lifted, no doubt, from some merchant's drying-yard, and a linen cap. Home again, he pinned and laced her into her new array as tenderly as a mother, even to braiding her magpie hair down her back and tying her cap over it.

"Thou'rt a proper lass now," he told her, "and the apple of mine eye. I'm off now to St. Paul's to hear the news, see perhaps may I come by a pamphlet or a book of ABC to print and sell. No more Merry Jests, my Frisket, or Valentines or Harlot's Tricks for us. From this moment, the bishop of London himself will have no cause to blush for our work."

"Here lieth an alehouse, with chambers above, and beds in the chambers. Pray you, love, walk in with me."

"Nay, child, I'll take thee another time. Take thou thine ease at home or abroad, but see thou stay within call and stray not, and, as thou lovest me, temper thy tongue as thou mayst; for not all have the trick of thy speech. If any ask, thou art my brother's child, called Mary, Mary Spurtle, come to keep my house and learn my trade." He took his purse then, and finding therein some coppers and a silver piece, wrapped them in a clout and bade her tie them underneath her petticoat.

She looked at the little bundle with bemusement. "I swive for love, and not for base coin," she said doubtfully.

"The daughter of the house must have coin when she ventures abroad. And thou art the only daughter I am like to have. So take thy purse. Thou hast earned it."

So Hal went whistling towards St. Paul's and Frisket watched him down the street, her eyes bright and shy as a mouse's.

"Hey there, wench." A boy's sharp treble hailed her from Mistress Dunne's front window. "What makest thou at Hal Printer's?"

Frisket stepped out into the street and smiled, which brought Jane and Ann and Katty forth across the cobbled street to sniff about her skirts in the manner of pet dogs: cautious, but more apt to fawn than to bite.

"What's thy name?" inquired Ann, who was the eldest.

Frisket opened her mouth and closed it again. "Frisket" was nowhere printed on her body. Yet Hal had given her another name, a name found in both sermon and bawdry, so, "Mary," she said. "Come, play with me."

"What wouldst thou play?" asked Katty, ever generous. "Wildflowers and Old Roger and Thread the Needle's our favorites, but we'll play a new if thou'lt learn it us."

Frisket had knowledge of many plays, all of them

new to Katty, and all of them from that part of her mind Hal disapproved of her speaking. Accordingly, she hoisted one skinny shoulder as one who defers to her hosts, and Jane said, "Let it be Lazy Mary, then. Dost know it?"

Frisket shook her head.

"Hast the cat a-hold of thy tongue, Mary?" taunted Jane; in response to which Frisket exhibited hers, catless, but mottled pink and black, whereat she laughed 'till Ann cuffed her ear and bade her mend her manners. Jane subsiding, Ann told her the words to the game, that were *Lazy Mary, will you get up, will you get up, will you get up? Lazy Mary, will you get up, will you get up today?*

"And then thou shalt answer," interrupted Jane, "that thou wilt not, whatever dainties we offer, until that we offer thee a nice young man."

So they laid Frisket down among them, with her apron over her face, and turned about her, singing. And when it was time for her to answer, Frisket frowned under her apron, opened her mouth, and sang.

> *My mistress is a cunny fine*
> *And of the finest skin.*
> *And if you care to open her,*
> *The best part lies within.*
> *Yet in her cunny burrow may*
> *Two tumblers and a ferret play.*

Jane giggled; Ann blushed rose, then white, then rose again.

"Nay, now, Mary, prithee do not mock us," said Katty.

"The devils of Hell mock the blessed," said Frisket, "for those very joys they are blessed withal."

"Art mad?" asked Ann. "We are not to play with mad folk."

"Sing again," said Jane, and Frisket sang again, by bad fortune just when Mistress Dunne was out at her door to see her children play. Now, Mistress Dunne was a God-fearing woman, a great enemy to oaths and tobacco and all manner of loose living; so that hearing Frisket's song, she screeched like unto a scalded cat, and pounced upon the girl, and boxed her ears until they rang like St. Paul's at noon.

Frisket put her hands to her ears wonderingly, as though she hardly understood the smart. "Well mayst thou look sullen," said Mistress Dunne. "Thou'rt overripe for a beating. Filthy girl. Dost not know so much as wash thy face?"

Frisket spat upon her hand and rubbed her cheek, then held her hand to Mistress Dunne to show it neither more black nor more white, but mottled as before, like the coat of a spotted dog. Mistress Dunne looked at the hand, and the face, and the thick, pie-bald plait lying over Frisket's shoulder, and made the sign of the Cross in the air between them. "Devil's mark," she cried, and spat, and gathering her children to her, chivvyed them within, Frisket trailing after, saying:

"May not a sinner, being penitent, enter into the Kingdom of Heaven?"

"God save us, the child is mad," cried Mistress Dunne, and clapped to the door against Frisket's nose, whereat Frisket, showing a perfect devil's countenance of red and black, cast a flood of Billingsgate upon the unyielding wood, drenching it with such verbs, nouns, and adverbs that would have stunk, had they been incarnate, as three-days' fish do stink. And then she turned and ran heedless among the lanes and alleys of East Cheape.

The force that drove her no man could tell, nor

could Frisket neither. She did not think as men thought, did nor feel or know or hope as a child be-gotten of man and born of woman. The highest and most base exhalations of man's soul had gone into her making, and the words they gave her were all she knew. Neither piety or bawdry taught her to say, "There is no place for me here; I must return to that I was." Yet such was in her heart. And so she sought the alchemist where he lay, that he who had made her flesh might unflesh her again and return her to her former state of ink and pulp and fiber.

Hal came again unto his house when the bells of St. Martin's were ringing for Evensong. His feet spurned the mud, and his eyes dwelt on the wonders of being able to command a font of print, and to buy the right of a pamphlet upon the making of cheese and enter it upon the Register, and still have money and enough in his purse to do the same again.

"Frisket," he sang as he lifted the latch. "Frisket, heart of my heart, come hither, and thou shalt partake of roast fowl and sack at the Doublet and Hose as 'twere any lady. Frisket? Frisket, I say! Beshrew me, where is the wench?" And receiving no answer, Hal peered and pried through his two small chambers where a mouse could not lie hid, searching in rising panic for his paper 'prentice, who in two days' time was grown to him the very daughter of his heart.

Presently did Hal go out into the streets around, calling for Frisket up and down, and then, weary and sick with worry, to Mistress Dunne to entreat her whether she had seen his niece or no.

"His niece, quotha!" she exclaimed. "His trull, more like, and a good riddance to her and her slattern's tongue."

Hal, hoping for news, kept firm hold upon his tem-per. "She knows no better, God forgive my brother that it should be so," he said humbly. "I've hopes of teaching her better ways in time. She's a good lass at heart."

"A good lass would disdain to know such oaths, nor profane the purity of her lips with bawdry."

"She is as innocent of offense as of the true meaning of what she says."

Mistress Dunne patted Hal on the shoulder. "Thou'rt a kind man, Hal Spurtle, and simple as a newborn lamb. Never doubt thy self-called niece hath cozened thee finely. She's off with thy purse or thy linen, or some costly matter of thy trade, depend on't." And from this opinion she could not be turned.

So Hal took him home again to his empty shop, emptier now of one piebald, cheeky wench, and soon came out again, determined as Jason to find that moth-eaten golden fleece the ancient alchemist, to beg of him news of Frisket.

The while Hal was seeking her up and down, Frisket had won through the alleys of Cheape Ward to Fish Street, that was a broad street of fair houses, very busy with horses, and men in furred gowns and velvet caps, and women in farthingales and hooded cloaks. They jostled her as she stood, heeding her no more than the lean dogs nosing at the fish heads in the road, save for one young girl with a feathered hat perched on her bright hair, who pressed a penny in Frisket's hand and smiled pityingly upon her. For want of a better direction, Frisket followed her, losing her almost at once in the bustle that bore Frisket with it across a bridge cobbled like a street and lined with rich houses. On the further bank, Frisket turned aside from the high way to walk along the river, flowing grey and brown as porridge between slick, pewter banks. The sky was pewter too, tarnished and pitted with clouds, and the houses along the wharf leaned between them like beggars at an almshouse board.

One in three of those houses were marked like taverns, with signs painted bright above their doors, as the Cardinal's Cap, the Bird in the Bush, the Silent Woman, the Snake and Apple. Outside this last, a weaseling, minching fellow accosted Frisket, who gazed thoughtfully at the one-eyed snake of the blazon, that curled from Adam's loins toward the Apple held between Eve's plump thighs.

"Hey, thou ninny," he said. "What maketh thou here, walking so bold in Southwark?"

Frisket's ado with Mistress Dunne had taught her to stick to scripture. So she bethought her a moment and said, "The ways of the Lord are surpassing strange and beyond the wit of man to tell them."

The man drew closer, darted out his hand like Adam's snake and, clipping her by the wrist, held her fast. "A prating Puritan maid, by Cock," he snarled. "Marked like the Devil's own, and comely as a succubus withal. What are thy parents?"

"We have no father or mother, save that Heavenly Parent is Father and Mother to us all."

The man's eyes gleamed in his sharp face. "Art meat for my feeding, then."

Frisket, finding no apt response recorded in the tablets of her mind, met his eyes gravely, then at his fingers about her wrist, and back into his eyes, whereupon he dropped her arm to shield him with his hand from her gaze. "Go thy ways," he said. "Thou'rt safe from me. Yet the Southwark bawdy-houses are an ill place for a maid to wander, even a maid touched by God."

Frisket nodded. "The way of righteousness is the way of truth, and much beset with thorns." Then she turned her about and made away from the river, leaving the bawd muttering and scratching his head.

Some things she did, that afternoon and evening of her flight, who can say why or wherefore: she bought

a loaf with the young girl's penny and divided it
among a man in the stocks, three beggars, and a
starve-boned dog; she slipped into the Bear Garden
to watch the baiting with ink-drop eyes, and when
'twas done, crept back to where the bears were kept
tied in the straw, undid their muzzles with quick fingers, picked apart the heavy knots about their feet,
and slipped away again, leaving the gate a little ajar
behind her. Just at dusk, she passed a tall wooden
building with cressets burning by the door, and a
noise within like a giant's roaring, and bills without
proclaiming that Mr. William Shak-spere, his *Tragedie
of Cymbaline* was this day to be played. The bills were
hastily run-up, and the inking over-heavy, so that the
letters were spread and blurred; Frisket frowned ere
she turned away.

Some little time later, she came to a tavern, and
passed it not, but entered under its sign of The Swan
and Cygnet. Within was noise and heat enough for a
liberty of Hell, from trollops and cony-catchers and
'prentices and clerks and wharfmen, all calling for ale
while tavernmaids and potboys scurried among them
with tankards and trays and wooden bowls.

Frisket made like a hunting dog for the back of
the house, where sat a young man drinking all
among the kegs and barrels. He, like the man in the
stocks, the bears, and the beggar, was in difficulties.
The host stood glaring while he expostulated, pale
as a ghost, showing a pair of strings across his palm
that might have borne a purse, before they'd been
cut.

"I'll leave the jewel from my ear in surety," he was
saying. "An I come not again to pay you, it will bring
you twenty times the price of the ale and meat."

"For all I know, 'tis base metal overlaid with brass,
and worth no more than thy word. I'm minded to take
thy two shillings out of thy hide, and set thee up for

an exemplum of a liar and a thieving knave."

He raised one hand like a haunch of beef, and the young man sprang to his feet, caught between pride and fear whether he would flee the host or close with him. And at such a pass things stood when Frisket slipped between them and laid her hand upon the host's uplifted arm, and said, "I'll pay thy price, though it be an hundred pound."

The host shaking her away, she took her pocket and jingled it in his ear that would hear no other plea, and it spoke to him, and calmed him, and by and by he took the monies owed him, and a little over to buy a pottle of wine to soothe the young man's nerves, and left them there together amongst the kegs and barrels in the quiet back of the tavern.

The young man smoothed his doublet that was worn and frayed at the cuffs, and then his beard, and having set himself to rights, handed Frisket onto a joint-stool as it had been a chair of state and she the Queen's own Grace.

"Robert Blanke the poet thanks thee, fair maid," said he. "Without thy silver physic, I had been as dead as Lazarus, without hope of resurrection. How may I call thee?"

"Mary, sir, and withal the merriest Mary thou hast melled withal."

The young man eyed her in the uncertain light. "A harlot? Sure, I grow old, that jades look like fillies to me, and trollops like young maids."

"For I am thy savior, saith the Lord, and a present help in all thy trouble."

"Now the Lord help me indeed, for I bandy words with a madwoman. Yet the mad are touched by God, they say, and own a wisdom beyond the understanding of the wise." He reached out long fingers and, taking her by the chin, tilted her head gently to catch the light. What he saw was a girl on womanhood's threshold, her brow serene, her nose straight and fine, her eyes large and smooth-lidded, her lips clear-carved in a perfect Cupid's bow, her expression open and grave. Thus might an angel look, he thought, or a spirit of antiquity dressed in flesh and a patched woollen gown, were an angel's skin marred and mottled everywhere with flecks of black like blurred print. He released her chin and caressed his beard. "What are you?" he asked.

"I am," said Frisket, "none of your plain or garden whores; I can read and play the virginals. We are children of God, each one, and His angels have the keeping of the least of us no less than of the greatest."

"Sweet Jesu preserve us. A very sensible nonsense, as I live. I well can believe that you, like the phoenix, are alone of your kind, and I accept that you mean no harm. I am your debtor for your mere acquaintance, the more for your saving of me. And therefore I ask of you what you would of me?"

Blanke was a quick-witted man, and eager to unriddle her cypher. Still it took Frisket long and long to make him understand what she was and what she wanted, by which time the tavern was empty and the host hovering by with a broom and a scowl.

"Hark ye," said the poet. " 'Tis dawn, or very nigh, and my head is a tennis ball betwixt your sermons and your bawdries. Company me to my lodging and rest you there, and we'll take counsel of a new day."

So went they their ways through the waking streets, and when they reached the tenement where the poet lodged, he bowed her reverently through the door, saying, "I serve you in all honor, Mistress Mary; in token of which I will leave you my bed to rest upon, and sleep myself upon the floor."

For the first time Frisket smiled at him, showing even teeth as mottled as the rest of her. "For the eye of God sleepeth not," she said, "but watcheth ever over thy slumbers and wakings."

So Robert Blanke slept and Frisket watched, and Hal Spurtle came at last to the goal he had pursued throughout the long, sad night: the shop of the old alchemist, on Pardoner's Lane in Cripplegate, outside London wall.

When the old man opened the door, he knit his brows. "Too late," he said. "The offer once refused will not be made again. Thou hast thy twenty crowns. Go thy ways."

Hal stuck his foot betwixt door and jamb. "And right content I am with them, I assure you. 'Tis my 'prentice, sir, the child you made from my poppet of paper."

"Hist," said the alchemist, and bundled Hal into the shop as quick as he'd been minded to bundle him out. "Hast no sense, man, to quack hidden things abroad in the public street? Thou'lt be the death of us both."

"And she's less sense than I, poor unbegotten mite, three days old, knows printing and naught else, not even her name, nor the skill to ask her way home again. Here are ten crowns, the half of thy fee, to inquire of thy demons where she may be and how she may be faring." And Hal pressed his purse into the alchemist's greasy hand.

"Put up, man. I'll help thee for kindness' sake, or not at all. Now," he said when Hal had put the purse into his bosom again, "now. The tale of the paper 'prentice. Calmly and simply as may be." He listened, his sharp eyes hooded and his stained hands laced before his long nose, while Hal told him of Frisket's cleverness and her goodness and her speaking in phrases either from Dr. Beswick's sermons or from one of the bawdy pamphlets whose spoiled sheets he'd used in her making. And when Hal was done, the alchemist lipped at his fingers and hemmed once or twice, and nosed out a great clasped book, and found a page in it, and ran his finger down the page, and hemmed again, and peered out another that was small and black and powdery with age, and consulted that, and shut it, and closed his eyes, and munched his jaws. And just as Hal decided that the old gentleman had fallen asleep, he sat himself upright and said:

"Thine apprentice, called by thee Frisket, was lent thee for a space, to answer thy present need. Give thanks for the loan, and grieve not the loss. For she is not of this earth, nor is there a place for her therein."

The tears started to Hal's eyes, nor was he too proud to let them fall, but wept for the daughter of his heart. And the alchemist rose from his chair, and laid his hand upon his shoulder, and pressed it. "Be of good cheer, man. The joy thou hadst of her is real. And consider that all children grow and leave their father's house, and 'prentices become journeymen at last."

"Yea," said Hal. "And yet may their fathers mourn them."

"Even so," said the alchemist.

And Hal went from him to St. Paul's church, and knelt within, and prayed a space, and from thence among the bookstalls, inquiring for a journeyman to hire.

And it came to pass that Robert Blanke the poet woke to the sun's golden fingers laid upon his face and Frisket seated in the peaked window of his chamber, that was small and damp and high in the house.

Blanke sat up, scrubbed his hands in his eyes, and raked his hair seemly with his fingers. "Art up, old snorter?" Frisket inquired. "Or shall I lend a hand to raise thee?"

"Peace, good Mistress Mary, I prithee, peace. I am up, as you see, but in no wise awake. Give me an hour to learn to believe in you again, and to think what I may do with you."

So Frisket accompanied Blanke to a cookshop, where she bought him a mutton pie, and to a tavern, where she bought him a tankard of small ale, and watched him eat and drink the same, and then into St. George's church, where she sat in a bench while he took to his knees, and so back to his lodging again as the dusk drew her mantle across the sky.

" 'Twas less magic than desire birthed thee," Blanke said to her, "the printer's desire for company; the alchemist's desire for his grimoire. So logic would argue 'tis desire must send thee back to thy papery womb. And there, dear Mistress Mary, is the rub. For my desire is rather to keep thee whole and sensible than to see thee senseless rubbish."

"Beware the Last Days, when all men are come to Judgement, and the inmost secret thoughts of their hearts laid bare."

And each in his own manner pled his case, to and fro like lawyers, until Blanke threw up his hands and declared himself desirous, at least, of pleasing her who desired no other thing than to put off her dress of flesh, that chafed her as it had been a dress of fire.

"I have considered, and I have prayed, and I have invented a rite seems to answer your purpose." And he opened his mind and said what he purposed, whereat Frisket nodded and did off her clothes and laid her down upon his table, that he had cleared of his writing and his candle and his pens. The which persuaded him above all else that she was not of mankind.

"The Lord giveth," he said solemnly, "and the Lord taketh away. Even as it pleaseth the Lord, so cometh things to pass: blessed be the name of the Lord." And he took his quill pen into his hand, and pressed the inky tip of it to her breastbone, that fanned apart as he touched it into leaves of paper, close-woven and white as snow, printed small and even, the margins wide and straight. Thus he unfolded Frisket and sorted her, praying over her all the while the Service for the Burial of the Dead, and when he'd made an end, he folded the great bundle of pages into her scarlet petticoat, that became a binding of scarlet leather stamped with gold on the cover and on the spine. And he lit a candle, for it had grown full dark, and turned the book to the light, and opened it.

The title page was plain and bare of ornament, bearing only the name of the book—*The Philosophy of the Senses: A Novel in Five Parts*—and the name of the author—Mary Spurtle. Blanke turned the page, crisp and white as a communion host, and read there, printed sharp and clear beyond all common type: "This book is dedicated to my father, Henry Spurtle, printer of East Cheape, and to Robert Blanke, poet and friend."

On the instant, Blanke started up from his chair and hied him to East Cheape, where he inquired high and low of one Henry Spurtle, printer, where his shop lay. And by and by he came to the lane behind St. Martin's church, and a low house that leaked out light and the heavy, wooden clacking of a printing press. Blanke knocked at the door, which was opened by a tall, sad-eyed man with a grandfather's lined cheeks under his nut-brown hair.

"I deal no more in curiosities," he said, and made to close the door.

"Stay, Hal Spurtle, an you would hear news of your daughter Mary."

A light came into Hal's dull eye, and he drew Blanke into his shop, that was all a-bustle with activity. A man sat at the composing-table, selecting and sliding type into a composing stick with the steady rhythm of a new-wound clock. A boy stood at the press, an inking-ball in each hand, ready to apply them to the form when his master should be pleased to return to the press. Hal wiped inky hands on his leathern apron. "A pamphlet on cheese-making," he said, and bidding his new apprentice and his journeyman make all tidy 'gainst the morning's work, he gestured Blanke into the inner chamber, where the poet told him of Mistress Mary and all that had befallen her that he knew or guessed. And when he had done, he give Hal the book bound in red leather and said, "This is the book. I read the title and the letter dedicatory, and not one word more. For the book is yours, and no man else hath the right to read it."

Hal wiped his hands clean upon a clout, and took the book, and ran his thumb along the spine and along the gilded edges, and opened it, and gazed long and long upon the dedication to the author's father, Henry Spurtle, printer of East Cheape. As one who leaves a mourner to his grief, Blanke crept to the door; but when he lifted the latch, Hal raised his eyes and said, "I thank thee, Robert Blanke, poet and friend. I'd repay thee, an I could."

"Thy thanks suffice, and Mistress Mary's tale, more wonderful than Master Boccaccio's. And yet am I bold to beg the boon of thee to read the book and learn what she became."

"Beyond question thou shalt read her, aye, and dine with me before, if thou wilt. So much would any father do for the man who returned his daughter to him. Further, I had in mind to print an edition of thy poems, had thou enough to make two perfect sheets or three, cut into octavo and bound in boards, the profit to be split between us."

Blanke laughed aloud and clasped Hal's hand and pumped it as he'd pump water from his mouth.

"Now am I fallen deeply in thy debt," he cried. "Yet why speak of debt betwixt close kin? For if thou art her father, then am I her god-father, and we two bound together by love of her who has no like on earth. Now, thou hast a great work here in hand, must be pursued i' the heat. Come Sunday next, I'll be your man, and we'll drink to Mistress Mary in good sack. In the meantime, I'll look out my poems and copy them fair."

Hal pressed his hand and took him to the door and latched it behind him and smiled at his journeyman, who was making his bed under the press, and at his new 'prentice, asleep already in the shadowed corner by the fire, and at the sheets of the pamphlet on cheese-making, all hung out neat to dry. And he went into his inner chamber and closed the door, and took *The Philosophy of the Senses* in his hands, and opened it, and began to read.

Recommended Reading

Fiction and Poetry

The Robber Bridegroom and Bluebeard's Egg, by Margaret Atwood
    This Canadian writer often uses fairy-tale themes in her excellent contemporary mainstream fiction.

Snow White, by Donald Barthelme
    This is an early postmodern short novel that would be politically incorrect by today's standards.

Katie Crackernuts, by Katherine Briggs
    A charming short novel retelling the Katie Crackernuts tale, by one of the world's foremost folklore authorities.

Beginning with O, by Olga Broumas
    Broumas' poetry makes use of many fairy-tale motifs in this collection.

The Sun, the Moon and the Stars, by Steven Brust
    A contemporary novel mixing ruminations on art and creation with a lively Hungarian fairy tale.

Possession, by A. S. Byatt
    A Booker Prize–winning novel that makes wonderful use of the Fairy Melusine legend.

Nine Fairy Tales and One More Thrown in for Good Measure, by Karel Capek
  Charming stories inspired by the Czech folk tradition.

Sleeping in Flame, by Jonathan Carroll
  Excellent, quirky dark fantasy using the Rumplestiltskin tale.

The Bloody Chamber, by Angela Carter
  A stunning collection of dark, sensual fairy-tale retellings.

The Sleeping Beauty, by Hayden Carruth
  A poetry sequence using the Sleeping Beauty legend.

Pinocchio in Venice, by Robert Coover
  Coover often parodies traditional fairy tales in his fiction. His reworking of the Pinocchio tale is particularly recommended.

Beyond the Looking Glass, edited by Jonathan Cott
  A collection of Victorian fairy-tale prose and poetry.

The Nightingale, by Kara Dalkey
  An evocative Oriental historical novel based on the Hans Christian Andersen story.

The Painted Alphabet, by Diana Darling
  This novel is a rich fantasia inspired by Balinese myth and folk lore.

The Girl Who Trod on a Loaf, by Kathryn Davis
  Uses the fairy tale of the title as the basis for a story of two women, and the opera, at the beginning of the twentieth century. A lovely little book.

Blue Bamboo, by Osamu Dazia
  This volume of fantasy stories by a Japanese writer of the early twentieth century contains lovely fairy-tale work.

Provencal Tales, by Michael de Larrabeiti
  An absolutely gorgeous collection containing tales drawn from the Provencal region of France.

Jack the Giant-Killer and *Drink Down the Moon*, by Charles de Lint
Wonderful urban fantasy novels bringing "Jack" and magic to the streets of modern Canada.
Tam Lin, by Pamela Dean
A lyrical novel setting the old Scottish fairy story (and folk ballad) Tam Lin among theater majors on a Midwestern college campus.
Like Water for Chocolate, by Laura Esquivel
Esquivel's book (and the wonderful film of the same title) wraps Mexican folklore and tales into a turn-of-the-century story about love and food on the Mexico/Texas border. Complete with recipes.
The King's Indian, by John Gardner
A collection of peculiar and entertaining stories using fairy-tale motifs.
Crucifax Autumn, by Ray Garton
One of the first splatterpunk horror novels; Garton makes use of the Pied Piper theme in very nasty ways. Violent and visceral.
Blood Pressure, by Sandra M. Gilbert
A number of the poems in this powerful collection make use of fairy-tale motifs.
Strange Devices of the Sun and Moon, by Lisa Goldstein
A lyrical little novel mixing English fairy tales with English history in Christopher Marlowe's London.
The Seventh Swan, by Nicholas Stuart Gray
An engaging Scottish novel that starts off where the "Seven Swans" fairy tale ends.
Daughters of the Moon: Witch Tales From Around the World, edited by Shahrukh Husain
A folklorist collects over fifty tales of witches and witchcraft from more than thirty cultures worldwide.
Fire and Hemlock, by Diana Wynne Jones
A beautifully written, haunting novel that brings the Thomas the Rhymer and Tam Lin tales into modern day England.

Green Grass Running Water, by Thomas King

This delightful Magical Realist novel uses Native American myths and folk tales to hilarious effect.

Thomas the Rhymer, by Ellen Kushner

A sensuous and musical rendition of this old Scottish story and folk ballad.

The Wandering Unicorn, by Manuel Mujica Lainez

A fairy-tale novel based on the "Fairy Melusine" legend by an award-winning Argentinean writer. Translated from the Spanish.

Red as Blood, Or Tales from the Sisters Grimmer, by Tanith Lee

A striking and versatile collection of adult fairy-tale retellings.

The Tricksters, by Margaret Mahey

This beautifully told, contemporary New Zealand story draws upon pancultural Trickster legends.

Beauty, by Robin McKinley

Masterfully written, gentle and magical, this novel retells the story of "Beauty and the Beast."

Deerskin, by Robin McKinley

A retelling of Charles Perrault's "Donkeyskin," a dark fairy tale with incest themes.

The Door in the Hedge, by Robin McKinley

"The Twelve Dancing Princesses" and "The Frog Prince" retold in McKinley's gorgeous, clear prose, along with two original tales.

Disenchantments, edited by Wolfgang Mieder

An excellent compilation of adult fairy-tale poetry.

The Book of Laughter and Forgetting, by Kundera Milan

This literate and cosmopolitan work makes use of Moravian folk music, rituals, and stories.

Sleeping Beauty, by Susanna Moore

An eloquent, entertaining contemporary novel that uses the "Sleeping Beauty" legend mixed with native Hawaiian folklore.

The Private Life and *Waving from the Shore*, by Lisel Mueller
Terrific poetry collections with many fairy-tale themes.

Haroun and the Sea of Stories, by Salman Rushdie
A delightful Eastern fantasia by this Booker Prize–winning author.

Kindergarten, by Peter Rushford
A contemporary British story beautifully wrapped around the "Hansel and Gretel" tale, highly recommended.

Transformations, by Anne Sexton
Sexton's brilliant collection of modern fairy-tale poetry.

The Porcelain Dove, by Delia Sherman
This gorgeous fantasy set during the French Revolution makes excellent use of French fairy tales.

The Flight of Michael McBride, by Midori Snyder
A lovely, deftly written fantasy set in the old American West, this magical novel mixes the folklore traditions of immigrant and indigenous American cultures.

Trail of Stones, by Gwenn Strauss
Evocative fairy-tale poems, beautifully illustrated by Anthony Browne.

Swan's Wing, by Ursula Synge.
A lovely, magical fantasy novel using the "Seven Swans" fairy tale.

Beauty, by Sheri S. Tepper
Dark fantasy incorporating several fairy tales from an original and iconoclastic writer.

Kingdoms of Elfin, by Sylvia Townsend Warner
These stories drawn from British folklore are arch, elegant, and enchanting. Many were first published in *The New Yorker*.

The Coachman Rat, by David Henry Wilson
Excellent dark fantasy retelling the story of "Cin-

derella'' from the coachman's point of view.

Snow White and Rose Red, by Patricia C. Wrede

A charming Elizabethan historical novel retelling this romantic Grimm's fairy tale.

Briar Rose, by Jane Yolen

An unforgettable short novel setting the Briar Rose/ Sleeping Beauty story against the background of World War II.

Don't Bet on the Prince, edited by Jack Zipes

A collection of contemporary feminist fairy tales compiled by a leading fairy-tale scholar, containing prose and poetry by Angela Carter, Joanna Russ, Jane Yolen, Tanith Lee, Margaret Atwood, Olga Broumas, and others.

The Outspoken Princess and the Gentle Knight: A Treasury of Modern Fairy Tales, edited by Jack Zipes

Presents fifteen modern fairy tales from England and the United States including works by Ernest Hemingway, A. S. Byatt, John Gardner, Jane Yolen, and Tanith Lee.

Modern Day Fairy-tale Creators

The Faber Book of Modern Fairy Tales, edited by Sara and Stephen Corrin

Gudgekin the Thistle Girl and Other Tales, by John Gardner

Mainly by Moonlight, by Nicholas Stuart Gray

Collected Stories, by Richard Kennedy

Dark Hills, Hollow Clocks, by Garry Kilworth

Heart of Wood, by William Kotzwinkle

Five Men and a Swan, by Naomi Mitchison

The White Deer and The Thirteen Clocks, by James Thurber

Fairy Tales, by Alison Uttley

Tales of Wonder, by Jane Yolen

Nonfiction

The Power of Myth, by Joseph Campbell
The Erotic World of Fairy, by Maureen Duffy
"Womenfolk and Fairy Tales," by Susan Cooper
   Essay in the *New York Times Book Review*, April 13, 1975
Tales from Eternity: The World of Fairy Tales and the Spiritual Search, by Rosemary Haughton
Beauty and the Beast: Visions and Revisions of an Old Tale, by Betsy Hearne
Woman, Earth and Spirit, by Helen M. Luke
Once Upon a Time, collected essays by Alison Lurie
The Classic Fairy Tales, by Iona and Peter Opie
What the Bee Knows, collected essays by P. L. Travers
Problems of the Feminine in Fairy Tales, by Marie-Louise von Franz
   Collected lectures originally presented at the C.G. Jung Institute
From the Beast to the Blonde: On Fairy Tales and their Tellers, by Marina Warner (Highly recommended)
Touch Magic, collected essays by Jane Yolen
Fantasists on Fantasy, edited by Robert H. Boyer and Kenneth J. Zahorski
   Includes Tolkien's "On Fairy Stories," G. K. Chesterton's "Fairy Tales," and other essays

Fairy-tale Source Collections

Old Wives' Fairy Tale Book, edited by Angela Carter
The Tales of Charles Perrault, translated by Angela Carter
Italian Folktales, translated by Italo Calvino
The Complete Hans Christian Andersen, edited by Lily Owens
The Maid of the North: Feminist Folk Tales from Around

the World, edited by Ethel Johnston Phelps

Favorite Folk Tales from Around the World, edited by Jane Yolen

The Complete Brothers Grimm, edited by Jack Zipes

Spells of Enchantment: The Wondrous Fairy Tales of Western Culture, edited by Jack Zipes (Highly recommended)

(For volumes of fairy tales from individual countries—Russian fairy tales, French, African, Japanese, etc.—see the excellent Pantheon Books Fairy Tale and Folklore Library.)